Holy City

ALSO BY GUILLERMO ORSI
IN ENGLISH TRANSLATION
No-one Loves a Policeman (2010)

Guillermo Orsi

HOLY CITY

Translated from the Spanish by
Nick Caistor

MACLEHOSE PRESS
QUERCUS · LONDON

First published in Great Britain in 2012 by

MacLehose Press
an imprint of Quercus
55 Baker Street
7th Floor, South Block
London W1U 8EW

First published in Spanish as *Ciudad Santa*
by Editorial Almuzara, Madrid, 2009

Copyright © Guillermo Orsi, 2009
English translation copyright © 2012 by Nick Caistor

This work is published within the framework of the SUR Translation
Support Program of the Ministry of Foreign Affairs, International
Trade and Worship of the Argentine Republic

ISBN (HB) 978 0 85705 062 5
ISBN (TPB) 978 0 85705 063 2

This book is a work of fiction. Names, characters,
businesses, organizations, places and events are either the
product of the author's imagination or are used fictitiously.
Any resemblance to actual persons, living or dead, events
or locales is entirely coincidental.

2 4 6 8 10 9 7 5 3 1

Designed and typeset in Minion by Patty Rennie
Printed and bound in Great Britain by Clays Ltd, St Ives plc

To Raúl Argemí, Carlos Balcameda,
Juan Ramón Biedma and Alejandro Gallo
– in alphabetical order, as in film credits.
To Eduardo, my brother.
To Estela, my partner.

You were the messenger of my death,
Of my metamorphosis.

ROBERT BROWNING

The spider you saved has bitten you.
What can you do about it?
When God is far away!
Don't even trust your brothers,
They hang you from the Cross . . .

"DESENCUENTRO", A TANGO BY
ANÍBAL TROILO AND
CÁTULO CASTILLO

PROLOGUE

TOURIST GUIDE:

JESUS CHRIST HAS HIS OWN THEME PARK IN BUENOS AIRES

Buenos Aires (A.F.P.). – *The crowd cannot contain its wonder at the sight of Christ crucified on Golgotha. Some of them cross themselves. Not far away, Roman soldiers keep watch, ignoring the peasant women in garish costumes who are selling Oriental sweets . . . this is the* Holy Land *theme park.*

Although only the heat is reminiscent of the banks of the River Jordan, here every weekend on the shores of the Río de la Plata in Buenos Aires the founders of the Holy Land religious park are recreating the real atmosphere for a cardboard Jerusalem.

Next to the airport for domestic flights, this park, which according to its owners is "unique in the entire world", is entirely dedicated to religion, above all the Christian beliefs. Although its seven hectares also contain a "mosque" and a "synagogue", the park concentrates on the Christian religion and the life of Christ.

From the first moment, visitors are invited to witness the birth of Christ in the kind of staging that is repeated throughout all the "attractions" in the park.

Deep inside a cave, a life-sized polyester crib takes the visitor back to Christmas Eve alongside an ox, an ass and articulated Three Kings.

The Catholic Church has given the park its blessing. The archbishop of Buenos Aires has called it a "place of cultural and spiritual enrichment".

WATERFALLS, TANGO, STEAKS, GLACIERS AND WHALES
AT KNOCKDOWN PRICES

Buenos Aires (United Press). – *Savage devaluations are the means by which the economic powers in Argentina regularly carry out their "profit-taking". The one that took place in 2002 – which tripled the value of the U.S. dollar – made fortunes overnight for the country's grain exporters and brought in foreign tourists like flies to honey.*

A country which has glaciers that crumble on cue, which shares with Brazil the biggest waterfalls in the world, which has leaping whales and a capital city with echoes of Europe where you can dance the tango and eat the best grass-fed beef in the open air is, without a doubt, a wonderful bargain for visitors.

PART ONE

The Queen of the Río de la Plata

1

The cop leaning on the door of his patrol car smoking a cigarette under the Avenida Mosconi bridge is dimly aware of a car zigzagging along Avenida General Paz at 140 k.p.h. He ought to put out a call for the driver to be pulled in for speeding and reckless driving. Instead, he prefers to take another lungful of his ghastly blond tobacco. Some day he's going to give up smoking, he tells himself, but when? Not as long as he's a policeman, that's for sure.

In the boot of the car veering from one side to the other as it careers down the highway, its driver skilfully dodging all the traffic, is Matías Zamorano. His hands are tied; he is gagged and blindfolded. He is not suffering from being tied up or because he can hardly breathe, but because he knows this journey is his last. The car racing along like an emergency ambulance is his hearse. The two gunmen should have killed him where they found him, in the toilets of the Central Market, but preferred not to run the risk of being recognized. They are in the pay of Councillor Pox, a.k.a. Alberto Cozumel Banegas, a man always known by his nickname. Everyone calls him the Pox, even though he has inherited one of the many empires built on the squalid outskirts of Buenos Aires: the absolute ruler of an area twenty blocks square in the district of Matanza.

The idea to doublecross the Pox was not his, Matías Zamorano thinks with relief. It was Ana's: just twenty-two, with the face of a cherub floating on a cloud, but guts enough to manage the gambling dens and whorehouses run by Zamorano, who in turn is run by Councillor Pox – as the Pox is by the governor of the province. Everything was going smoothly, but women, especially if they are young and beautiful, are ambitious. And if they are ambitious, nothing satisfies them. They think they are the centre of the universe, absolute suns of a planetary system that had its Big Bang when they were born, not a second before. And the rest of the world are nothing more than limp and decrepit pricks, stupid dummies with acrylic dentures who swallow half a packet of Viagra and think they have got a hard-on because the women they rent scream, close their eyes, shake like piggy banks while waiting for the old men to finish or be finished off, exhausted or paralysed by a heart attack.

The car leaves Avenida General Paz and speeds into Buenos Aires Province along the extension of Avenida de los Corrales, heading for the rubbish dumps at Tablada, where executioners can despatch the condemned without any problems. Zamorano knows the way: he has done it often enough behind the wheels of other cars, with stool-pigeons and hired guns squashed into the boot, people born of the garbage who return to it with grateful thanks because they can no longer bear being called "sir", or having some poor woman fall in love with them and demanding fidelity.

Zamorano is not afraid. Above all he is sad: a feeling of tremendous misery and self-loathing. Given the chance, he would have speeded things up, but the Pox does not give anyone a chance. That is why he rules with an iron fist his twenty blocks in the south of Matanza, an open sewer inhabited by the rejects of the system, zombies who steal and kill for food, ragged foot-soldiers in an army whose only discipline is the certainty that if they disobey orders they will starve to death.

Zamorano thinks of Ana as the car slows down and pulls into the street the Pox has chosen. "I want him to be an example and a lesson," he must have said, because that is a favourite phrase of his. "I want the whole neighbourhood to see how anyone who crosses Councillor Pox ends up."

The boot is flung open and the two thugs haul Zamorano to his feet. They take off his gag and blindfold. It's a bad, terrible sign, or perhaps merely inevitable, thinks Zamorano; a routine procedure, the tiniest drop of dignity allowed to the condemned man. There is a third man, probably the one who drove the car here, who taps him gently on the back to straighten him up, then pats his crumpled clothes so he does not die looking like a scarecrow. He wants the locals from the cardboard and corrugated iron shacks, honest Bolivian or Peruvian families, to see the prisoner's face, the look of terror – or in Zamorano's case, resignation – that is his last farewell. They need to realize that they at least (the Pox's men) do not kill just anyone, do not get their hands dirty with tramps or two-bit killers. The cops can take care of the riff-raff, says Councillor Pox, who boasts that his men are elite troops, the marines of these outer suburbs of the Holy City.

"You know who this is," the driver shouts to the gathered locals, putting an almost affectionate arm round Zamorano's shoulder. He was comrade Pox's right-hand man. "You've all bought stuff from him . . ."

He gazes round at the cowed faces of the crowd. A feudal baron condemning the disloyalty of one of his subjects, the black sheep who has to be sacrificed at once.

"We're going to amputate this right hand so that the infection does not reach comrade Pox. But tomorrow someone else you can trust will take his place. Comrade Pox is like a snake or an iguana: the corrupt limbs we chop off always grow back again."

He pushes Zamorano forward. Zamorano stumbles but stays on his feet in the centre of the empty space that has opened up between his executioners and the locals around this makeshift scaffold of beaten earth and stagnant water from the last downpour. They have untied him. He could make a run for it and get shot in the back, but he would rather stare at this pair of thugs he has so often given orders to, at the driver who is as accurate with his gun as he was at avoiding the traffic with his foot pressed to the floor.

Zamorano does not say a word, merely stares at them. He could say to them: what I did doesn't merit being put to death; there are people higher up than us who do far worse, who back-stab all the time and yet win cups and medals, people who double their fortunes with a single shady deal, then get their photos taken with Councillor Pox.

But Zamorano is already dead and the dead do not speak. He closes his eyes to see the cherub more clearly. Blinded by the car headlights, Ana's face shines in front of his eyelids. She smiles as she recognizes him, as she tells him yet again: yes, I'm with you, I like being with you.

That is why (the image of Ana beneath his eyelids), an instant before the shots ring out, Matías Zamorano raises his arms and wraps them round his own body.

As he slumps to the ground he is not alone: he is with Ana.

2

The legal profession is a lonely one. It is looked down on by all those respectable people who bathe their consciences in cologne and perfume, thinking they can disguise the stink. As lonely as a private eye in an American film, as scorned as any cop in any rotten city in the world.

In Buenos Aires, lawyers who defend clients already considered guilty are hissed and booed when they leave court. They are pursued by swarms of cameramen and reporters, who attack them for defending clients that the supreme court of public opinion has sentenced to be hanged from the very first day. It does not matter if there is any evidence to convict the accused thief or criminal, if the body or the stolen goods, the weapon used to kill the wife, the tools they are said to have used to break into a bank vault, have been found: there is a suspect who has been found guilty by the editors of newspapers and television news programmes, and a bonfire waiting for them which burns the twenty-four hours a day that the news channels are on air.

It was two in the morning when someone knocked on the lawyer Verónica Berutti's door. Verónica had just got rid of a lover who had come to ask her for money before they had even fucked and was watching the repeat on television of a crowd on the outskirts of Buenos Aires trying to lynch a paedophile rapist who the cops were pushing into their patrol car. She was not watching because it interested her, but simply because it was on, as people usually do, especially at that time of night and after the unpleasant scene when she had thrown her lover out. He could be a good lover, but lacked the braincells to tell his muscles to get moving and look for work. "You're a whore," her ex-lover shouted as she slammed the door in his face. "Whores don't pay, they charge people," she had replied under her breath, then waited until the lift had arrived and the landing light had gone off to add "bastard".

The peaceful inhabitants of Villa Diamante surround the police car the cops have managed to smuggle the paedophile into. They throw stones and beat on the roof with sticks. They even toss rotten tomatoes at the cop who is trying to ward them off so that the car can get out of there. The knocking on Verónica's door synchronizes with the beating on the police car roof, which finally succeeds in pulling off down the muddy street. The camera shows it skidding in the mud, and Verónica wonders how many of those wanting to lynch the paedophile are themselves paedophiles or wife-and-children beaters, drunkards on cheap wine, occasional rapists.

A shame she cannot turn down the sound of the hammering at her door, press "mute" on her remote control, and leave the world silent and far away for a while longer.

Although the lens of the spyhole distorts her face, Verónica recognizes the round, pink cherub's face with its marrow-green eyes, the golden curls, the beauty as polished as in a reliquary.

Why bother to say good evening when it is already nearly dawn and nobody turns up at this time on a social visit. Better simply to heave a sigh and head for the blue corduroy armchair she has sat in before, ask for a glass of water and, pausing for breath, apologize for how late it is.

"But I can see you were still awake, *doctora*," says Ana perceptively, so Verónica prefers to go into the kitchen, turn on the tap and let the water run for a while before returning with a full glass.

"You're not the first. It's been a busy night."

"Men," Ana guesses.

"They've all gone," says Verónica. "Who's chasing you?"

"Nobody for the moment. But I'm in a mess, I think, or I wouldn't have bothered you like this."

The lawyer thinks that around now – at this very instant, why not? – she should be climaxing, feeling in her vagina all the virility of the son of a bitch who had come and ruined her night. Exhausted, she collapses into the armchair next to her desk. She prefers the silent television to clients like Ana Torrente, involved in conflicts that last longer than the Middle East War, and with little or no inclination to pay or even reduce the debt she has run up with every appeal, every request for proceedings to be quashed, every postponed hearing, and all the other legal niceties that wear out so much energy, expenses and shoe leather.

"My varicose veins really ache," Verónica announces. "If I don't have them operated on this year, I'll have to employ someone to carry me round the corridors of the court on their shoulders."

Ana Torrente does not take the hint that she should at least open her purse. She is far too busy trying to protect herself from the violence exploding around her because of her business deals. She gulps the water down in one, then leaves the glass on a magazine.

"I don't want to spoil the surface of your table," she says, hoping Verónica will repay her consideration with a friendly gesture.

"As I asked before: who's after you this time?"

Another sigh. Ana searches for a painting, a mirror, a lamp, a file on the lawyer's desk she can gaze at like someone leaning on their elbows before they speak.

"Nobody as yet. But I'm scared." Ana explains she had agreed to see Matías: they were to meet at 10 p.m. in the Los Pinches café on the corner of Avenida del Trabajo and Pola. "When I got there they were already stacking the chairs on the tables and the owner was closing up. 'Someone called on Matías Zamorano's behalf,' he said. 'Don't bother waiting for him.'"

"It's two in the morning, so that was four hours ago." Verónica seems to understand how serious things are. "Why didn't you come straight here? We won't find any magistrate awake now."

Ana Torrente buries her face in her hands. It is obvious she is making an effort to burst into tears, because melodrama is not her thing, at least not in front of women, especially someone like Verónica Berruti, this qualified lawyer aged forty-five, who has twice been widowed. Once after her policeman husband was killed in a shootout; the second time when someone took revenge on her by shooting her partner (she had decided never to get married again), an ombudsman, a man of the law who begged her on his knees not to try so hard to get people out of jail and still less to put them there in the first place. "Why put them in jail if you're only going to get them out again?" he would ask, genuinely anxious and uncomprehending. One cool September morning his car was intercepted only three blocks from their home in the middle of the Villa Devtoto residential neighbourhood and he was shot to pieces before he even had the time to ask why.

"Don't try to fool me, Ana. I won't lift a finger for you. In fact

I'll throw you out right now if you don't tell me the truth." Ana squirms on the blue corduroy armchair as if she has sat on an anthill. She starts to blink as though suffering an allergy attack so strong not even corticoids can calm it. She is suddenly if fleetingly aware of the seriousness of what she has done. "The truth or the street," says Verónica, hurrying her up because she still has not lost all hope that the son of a bitch will come back, ring the bell, plead for forgiveness on the entry phone.

Slowly but surely, she hears the truth. She has to disentangle it from all the unconvincing pouts her witness puts on, all her half-truths, her unwillingness to tell her everything. But the truth arrives.

So Verónica concludes, without fear of being mistaken, that Matías Zamorano has already been dropped from Councillor Pox's team and by his own men. It was not a good idea of Ana's to try to double-cross him: could not have been worse, in fact, given these first results. "You can't mess with those who run the game," Verónica tells her; if they have reached that position, it is because they have learnt a thing or two, because they have people to guard their backs, their asses, the whole caboodle.

Veronica does not tell Ana this last part. She does not want to make her cry for real. She bites her tongue. You're a racist Bolivian bitch, she would tell her if she really wanted to make her cry. But it is the truth she wants, not tears.

"I've had it up to my ovaries with all the crap you Bolivians get up to. You should have stayed in Santa Cruz de la Sierra."

"Bolivia doesn't exist. Tomorrow or the next day, Bolivia is going to be more in the news than Iraq or Palestine. A dark night is coming, so don't talk to me about my home country: they're nothing more than a bunch of indians on the warpath, the lost tribe of the *puna*. They think Viracocha is going to come and save them – they're worse than the Arabs."

Now Verónica understands what is keeping Ana from seriously

crying: her hatred. She hates the place she has escaped from, that prosperous city on the Bolivian flatlands inhabited by cattle ranchers, corrupt bureaucrats and drugs barons. That was where only a year earlier she had been crowned Miss Bolivia: the blonde, slender Ana Torrente, one metre seventy-two centimetres tall, as shapely as high mountains, light-green eyes, a cherub with tropical lips and tits. She signed a contract to take her round the world, "the ambassadress of Bolivian culture and beauty", as the presenter said in the Santa Cruz amphitheatre to applause, ovations, camera flashes, microphones and a contract she signed while still blinded by all the floodlights, deafened by the shouting and the fireworks set off to celebrate her coronation.

Poor pale-faced Cinderella. The next morning, although her hang-over made it hard to focus, she managed to read the small print of her contract. The world promised to her was not the whole planet – it was a tour of Ecuador, Peru and the Bolivian interior, a night in every miserable village of its jungles and high plateaux. She was the bait for the campaign trails of unknown politicians, ambitious subalterns of a power installed to help the affairs of the rich and powerful who do travel in the real world.

Hatred, not tears, lends Ana that look of a fallen angel which so bedazzled Matías Zamorano he completely lost his head and thought he could double-cross the Pox.

"There's a lot of money in it for you if you help me out. It's a good deal, if I can get it off the ground."

Stony-faced, Verónica. "I disconnect my emotional hemisphere," she says of herself when she listens to possible clients before deciding whether or not to rescue them from hell. She settles in her chair by the desk and listens. She is only briefly distracted when she hears the lift coming up. She cannot help it: once a fool, always a fool, as her faithful friend Laucha the Mouse Giménez tells her. Apart from that she listens closely, notes down some phrases, does the sums, draws little diagrams that help her follow the thread of Miss Bolivia's confession. Slowly but surely she begins to understand why Ana reacted, tore up the sequinned buffoon's contract and abandoned her kingdom.

3

The *Queen of Storms* is a cruise ship that can carry 1,340 passengers, all of whom, in this misty August morning, are crowding to the rails on the port side of the ship in response to a call from the captain, a what you might call phlegmatic Englishman who has faced the raging seas of Asia, the stormy, cold North and South Atlantic, including Cape Horn, but is now seeing the enormous ship under his command run aground for the very first time in the brown soup of the Río de la Plata.

The tourists' pirouettes have no effect. They find the situation quite funny, especially since as soon as the mist rises they can see the reassuring outline of the city of Buenos Aires before their eyes. No-one is going to die, except of laughter; some of them even start to try out tango steps on the tilting deck. Eventually six tugboats appear in single file, sent by the harbourmaster. The English captain is no longer so phlegmatic. He was only expecting two of these shabby craft which, like the ticks of underdevelopment, will cling on and take with them a high percentage of the profits made by any luxury liner that ventures into this treacherous river.

Still sleepy, Verónica sits up in bed with her phone to her ear, listening to the story of the complicated disembarkation as told by Francisco Goya (who has the same name as the painter but does not paint): he seduces tourists with his guidebook knowledge of the cities they visit and gets paid in dollars for it. He always gives her a call when he lands for a couple of days in Buenos Aires. He offers Verónica a bit of time out – during those two days she can go to restaurants normally reserved for foreigners, dance in exclusive nightclubs and make love twice a day, so four times altogether.

She laughs, by now fully awake, when Pacogoya (as she calls him) tells him that the first dancers on the listing deck were a gay couple – "and you should have seen how the one who must be the woman in bed crossed her legs," says Pacogoya with that Paraguayan accent of his that women find so irresistible and which Verónica adopts for the couple of days they spend together. "I'll be there tonight," Pacogoya adds, from the huge ship stuck in the silt. "If they don't free us I'll swim to shore, but there's no way you're going to escape me, princess."

Verónica cannot help comparing her kingdom to that of Miss Bolivia, who slept on the sofa after keeping her up with the details of her betrayals and with whom she watched Crónica Television when it announced in a screaming red banner strapline that a body riddled with bullets had been found on a rubbish tip near the Matanza shanty town. "The victim is apparently a male linked to a prostitution ring, who was shot in a settling of accounts," said a provincial police officer to the cameraman and reporter on duty from the sensationalist news channel.

That was the outcome, the foreseeable climax to Miss Bolivia's declarations before she stretched out on the living-room sofa without shedding a tear. All she did was close her eyes and ask Verónica to wake her up so they could go down to the law courts together.

"You're in a good mood, *doctora*. Or something's aroused you."

"How would you know?" snaps Verónica. She has just had a shower and is examining her breasts when she sees Miss Bolivia standing in the bathroom doorway.

"I can see it in your face. And from your hard nipples: that's not because of me, is it?"

Embarrassed, Verónica gathers up the bath-towel and covers herself. In her mid-forties and with two dead partners on her conscience, she still feels a sense of shame that, despite being only just twenty, Ana Torrente seems to have shed completely.

"Get dressed or we'll be late," says Verónica. "The magistrate isn't going to wait for you just because you're the Queen of Santa Cruz de la Sierra."

"All magistrates are skirtchasers," Ana replies, pushing Verónica gently out of her way in front of the mirror with a swing of her hips. "The scent of woman is the only code they really respect."

"Get a move on," Verónica repeats as she leaves the bathroom. She is resigned to the fact she is going to have to spend the morning with Ana at the law courts. She cannot think of any other way to get her some protection and is sure that if she abandons her it will not be more than a few hours before the discovery of another body is reported with the same screaming headlines on Crónica Television.

The magistrate does not receive them, but his secretary does.

"His honour has taken a short vacation," he tells them, his eyes fixed on Miss Bolivia's chest as if it were a teleprinter he was reading the words off. "But you needn't worry," says this individual, a fat, balding man in his forties, with thick lips and the slanted eyes of a lecherous pig, as Miss Bolivia describes him when they have left his office. They needn't worry, because his honour has taken every measure to ensure that the days of Councillor Cozumel Banegas are numbered: "There is far too much evidence against him for the provincial government to go on protecting him; he will be judged and stripped of his position any day now," he promises in a reedy voice, thrusting his snout and dribbling lips up against Miss Bolivia's face. She leaves the court wiping off the microscopic spots of saliva.

"Stay at my place for a couple of days, at least until that skirtchasing magistrate gets back and puts some protective measures in place and gets you a police bodyguard."

"I don't want a bodyguard. I don't trust your country's police, *doctora*, I don't trust any cops. And I don't want to be in your bed when you turn up with one of your men; I don't like threesomes and tourist guides aren't exactly to my taste, particularly if they're Paraguayan."

"So you were listening behind the door. But who said I was going to bring him home? Pacogoya's got a fabulous apartment in Recoleta, with a balcony that looks out on our illustrious dead, and in an area with the best restaurants in town, or at least the most expensive."

With the air of a lodger who pays her rent and after extracting a promise she will not have to witness someone else's sex, Ana Torrente agrees to stay in Verónica's apartment. She won't sleep in the living room, won't leave even to go shopping, won't open the door even if she hears Leonardo di Caprio's voice on the entry phone and under her pillow she'll keep warm the Bersa .38 that Verónica's first husband left her.

"You take off the safety catch, raise the gun, keep your arm steady and bang!"

"What happens if it really is Leonardo di Caprio?"

"I've heard he doesn't do visits – they take women to his hotel suite."

Pacogoya is waiting for her at La Biela, a café packed with foreign tourists and local clients who fill the interior and spill out onto the broad pavement outside. It is mid-winter, but the weather is like a humid summer evening; costly furs are dangling over chair-backs, and bags stuffed with Buenos Aires souvenirs catch the greedy eyes of pickpockets who come and go, watched by their old acquaintances from the nearby police station. La Biela's owner pays the cops to put in an appearance every now and then.

"Wow, it's hot for August," says Pacogoya. "Hotter even than in Asunción."

He gives her a brotherly peck on the cheek and then in response to a gesture Verónica only just catches out of the corner of her eye, the florist from the flower stall on the nearby avenue enters, bearing two dozen freshly cut roses. He attracts everyone's attention and the envy of all the women. Pacogoya is good at these touches of an opulent lover, or a soap-opera star who can no longer tell fiction from reality and really believes that women love him for the dreadful scripts the writers pen for him.

"What am I supposed to do with this enormous bouquet?"

"We'll take it up to my place straightaway, put the flowers in water, then make love twice. Afterwards we can end the night at *Ci Lontano*, a delightful pasta restaurant recommended by some old landowning biddies who are travelling on the *Queen of Storms* with me."

A tourist night, as befits a guide like Pacogoya: roses in water, sex twice over and the *à la carte menu*, trout raviolis for him and *fetucini aglie bóngole mediterrani* for her, expensive ersatz food washed down with a Malbec 2001 from the La Caverna estate, fifty dollars a *boteglia* that they double like their lovemaking. "From my apartment to *Ci Lontano*, then why not back to my place?" he says.

"Because," she tells him sharply, "twice makes a night of love, three times is indigestion."

She leaps into a taxi before Pacogoya can react. She knows it is best this way, that if she gives in to temptation there will be no second night, which is usually the more satisfying, more relaxed one, the one that leads her now and then to believe she is not with some shyster from the tourist industry who is trying to impress her with expense-account luxuries or going to ask her for money, so that she can sleep peacefully in his arms without waking with a start when she hears the lift stopping at her floor and footsteps along the corridor which carry on past her apartment.

Her mobile rings while she is still in the taxi. Pacogoya tells her he loves her, that he had a great time, "but by nightfall we'll be on our way to Rio", says the guide, who is the favourite of the old landowning biddies and the gay tango-dancing couple. He is getting his cheap revenge in the hope that she will change her mind, beg him to see her again.

And perhaps she would, were it not that she sees she has a missed call on her phone, a call from heaven knows where – not from her apartment, that is obvious, because when she arrives there she finds no sign of her, no note, no dress and woollen jacket she lent her, nor the Bersa .38 which she hopes against hope that Miss Bolivia has not been forced to use.

4

That night the only companion in Verónica's anxious vigil is the television, on in the background as she comes and goes in her apartment, searching for something or other, a letter, a perfumed handkerchief, or the photograph of a lover that Miss Bolivia might have mislaid.

The television, which in the early hours endlessly repeats items as if they were still breaking news, is showing a reporter, microphone in hand, pursuing rich tourists as they disembark from the *Queen of Storms* that afternoon. Since none of them speaks Spanish, the reporter tries out his rudimentary English, which the American, Japanese, German or French passengers accept with a smile without even trying to decipher it: "How do you feel about being on board a ship that travelled thousands of kilometres to run aground in a polluted river close to the last civilized city on the continent?" Far too long and complicated a question – "very tired, very tired", respond the alien beings from the old continent, the Far East, and the most powerful nation on earth, which the struggling reporter translates for his audience.

Verónica pauses for a moment in her fruitless search when she recognizes Pacogoya's soft Paraguayan lilt: he is the only one who comes to a halt for the roving reporter. He tells him that although regrettably the liner needs some repairs, this will give the passengers the time really to get to know a city like Buenos Aires, the Paris of South America, a magnificent opportunity to learn to dance the tango and eat lots of steaks.

"Son of a bitch," says Verónica, remembering the excuse Pacogoya used to get his revenge for her standing him up. "Our nightly son of a bitch."

She says this out loud, as she often does when she is coughing up her resentment. She talks to herself the way lots of people who live alone do, detesting the male half of humanity. She is sorry now that she ignored Miss Bolivia's advances: so young and beautiful, and with such soft skin. She could have kept her near for a while and so perhaps saved her from the slaughter she was probably heading straight towards, even though she thought she was escaping it. Verónica could have embraced her as she brushed past her on the way out of the bathroom, let the rough bath towel drop to the floor. Pushed her towards the bed like the male sons of bitches did to her every night – well, perhaps not every night, only some of them. Caress her slowly like the men do, then let herself drift away with a desire she imagines must be all the crazier, more intense, for being unknown, unexplored: something so fashionable these days among single women, so that she could boast of her conquest, or perhaps even fall in love – why not? – with a body she would have liked to have had when she was Miss Bolivia's age.

But there is no sign of Ana – no name, no telephone number. She has left not a single trace, apart from the smell of her cheap perfume on the towel and the missed call which plays the flat, neutral voice of the answering message. She could be dead, but the telephone company would go on charging for her calls and messages. The companies have performed a miracle: no-one, not even the deceased, can be released until their inaccessible bureaucracies give permission.

But someone had called from somewhere. If it wasn't Miss Bolivia, who was it? Why wouldn't it be her? Verónica asks herself in an attempt to calm down, playing her personal game of chess with the board on her lap: no bishops or rooks can stay upright on their squares, no kings or queens are safe.

What kind of queen is Miss Bolivia anyway? Her Anglo-Saxon beauty hardly fits with what is expected of your average Bolivian girl; but then again Santa Cruz de la Sierra is not exactly the kind of city where they bow down in praise of the presidents installed on the roof of the Latin-American world. They hate La Paz and the filthy *colla* indians living there. They would like to get them off their backs as much as the Basques want to be free of Madrid.

"That's why they chose me," Miss Bolivia told Verónica when they first met. "Because I'm not a *colla*. When I went up to La Paz they booed me; it was horrible. I don't want to go back to Bolivia, *doctora*."

And in order not to have to go back there, Miss Bolivia made Matías Zamorano fall in love with her. She thought he really did have the power he was always boasting of, but in the end he turned out to be nothing more than a messenger boy, the muddy emissary of the river shark Alberto Cozumel Banegas, Councillor Pox, the governor's man who was lord and master of twenty blocks in the province of Buenos Aires. Miss Bolivia was dazzled by Zamorano's displays of authority: "The policemen stand to attention when they see him," she said. "He's got a direct line to the councillor and sometimes the governor even calls him personally."

"You don't say," was Verónica's first response. "So why do you need to see me?"

"I need help, *doctora*, and you're a lawyer. Not that I trust lawyers, but you're a woman." Miss Bolivia had no idea until then that women could be lawyers. She had discovered Verónica one night as she walked among the stalls of the Bolivian market on the banks of the Río Riachuelo in Buenos Aires. "I thought you were a customer, but Zamorano told me: 'No, she's the inspector. She's been appointed by the legal authorities.'"

"And who are you? What would I have to defend you from? I've got enough problems with this jungle here."

She owed her post as inspector to the magistrate in Lomas de Zamora. Contacts, mutual friends, colleagues of her first husband, the dead cop. The magistrate called her to his office and said:

"I need people who are honest and have balls. We have to plunge the knife in a pile of shit and come out clean."

"I'm honest, but I've got guts rather than balls," Verónica retorted. "What's in it for me?"

"The standard rate, all above board."

"Who'll be paying me?"

His honour smiled uncomfortably. A macho man, he had not expected this woman to get down to brass tacks so quickly.

"It's a career opportunity. You can't afford to let it pass you by."

"What career? In body bags? I've already had two of my men killed. Where else do you think you get if you try to make a career in Argentina?"

The Riachuelo market is an open-air emporium of smuggled and stolen goods. Asphalt pirates steer their commandeered trucks straight for the west bank of the river, where the market has been growing like a delta – the Mekong in Vietnam or the Paraná on the outskirts of Buenos Aires: tiny islands of thieves with permission to steal granted by the provincial police the way Harvard hands out *honoris causa* diplomas.

At midnight four times a week this tiny portion of the rotten geography of the filthy stream separating the snooty Argentine capital from the provincial no-man's-land dresses up like some latter-day Cinderella and all kinds of traffickers have a ball. The customers come from all over the country: who wants to miss out on the bargains when haggling is the order of the day, as if this were some oriental bazaar?

"Who is paying, your honour?" insisted Verónica, fed up to the back teeth of impossible missions where everything ends badly and the good guys are always the losers.

"There are honest tradesmen."

It was hot both outside and inside the court building. The air conditioning had broken down two years ago, the photocopiers did not work, the computer was on the floor because someone had stolen all the memory chips. All that was left was an empty shell. The hard drive had been installed in the computer of a chief inspector who needed the information for his shady deals and no-one had the will or the desire to raid his office for it. But the magistrate, his *machista* honour, was talking of honest tradesmen who would pay legal money for an inspector.

Verónica hoisted herself out of the padded chair she had warily dropped into a few minutes before.

"Help me," the magistrate surprised her by saying, sitting behind his desk and stretching his hand out towards her as if he wanted her to pull him out of a well. "Please."

The guy was on his own. He was on one bank of the river, with justice on the other and in between them nothing, a putrefying mess, the Río Riachuelo. He was in charge of a jurisdiction as empty as his computer, as useless as the air conditioning or the employees who stacked case files on shelves already bowing under the weight of them.

Verónica will never know, she never has known, why she obeys her instinct, intuition, gut feeling or whatever you might call the crazy compass needle pointing due south when all the rest of the flock is heading north as fast as it can, but she accepted.

"Who are you?" she asked the young woman who had stepped forward in front of her in the early hours, during her second visit to the market.

"I'm a beauty queen. Ana Torrente. Everybody here knows me as Miss Bolivia," the cherub explained.

5

She became a lawyer to fight the good fight. It has to be said that was another era: a ferocious dictatorship was on its way out, defeated in the military adventure of the Malvinas. Verónica truly believed her university degree could be of some use.

"But power isn't changing hands," she was warned by a man who shared her classes and her bed. A latterday Marxist, as he described himself, someone who never once tried to make her happy in a relationship that lasted several months, but simply to make her more aware. "The struggle of the people came to an end in the '60s," he would tell her, between bouts of lovemaking, like a voiceover for the adverts in the middle of a television programme. "The revolutions were defeated by revolutionaries who had turned into bureaucrats. The Soviet Union was the gravedigger."

Another fuck; another round of adverts. "Then came the Pope, the Internet, Bill Gates. Who reads Marx's *Das Kapital* today, or at the very least *What Is to be Done?* by that old baldy Lenin?"

He left her after three months, but by then she was already pregnant with disillusion. Yet during Easter week in 1986 she went to the Plaza de Mayo to condemn the military rebellion trying to oust the democratic government. She shouted with the rest of the crowd that the coup-mongers should be shot. Nobody listened. Three years later, the same president who had decorated the military rebels was forced out on his knees, not by the military this time but by the real power-brokers, the ones who never let it go. Verónica sought out her Marxist former lover to tell him at least he had been right. She was passed from one telephone number to another, until at the third try she found him: working as a personal assistant to a consultant for multinationals.

"It's not that I'm against democracy," he insisted when they met in the Las Artes bar opposite the law faculty. "But this system is a bourgeois farce. I prefer dictatorship." Nowadays he combed his hair across his head to hide his bald patch and had dark circles under his eyes. "I've got some good stuff," he said. "Let's find a quiet spot."

She said fine. "I'll be back in a minute." As she stood up, she ruffled his gelled hair to reveal his bald pate. She walked towards the toilets, but then skipped into the kitchen. She raised her finger to her mouth to keep the dishwasher quiet and he led her to the service entrance. She ran out.

"That was fifteen years ago," she says. "And I'm still running." She is talking to Damián Bértola, the psychoanalyst she shares her office with on calle Tucumán, two blocks from the law courts.

"You ought to stop, sweetheart. Sometimes it pays to call a halt and look at yourself. Today for example. Who did you sleep with last night to end up with a face like that?"

"No-one. I spent the night waiting for news from a blonde princess. First on the phone and then, towards dawn, on the radio or T.V."

Bértola listens. It is part of their agreement, although it is not in the contract: they listen to each other when they need to share their concerns or their expenses. One day a heartache, the next an inheritance.

The original idea had come from the blonde, Miss Bolivia, Verónica explains. A group of her fellow countrymen – petty smugglers, peasants selling their produce outside supermarkets – wanted to create a co-operative somewhere in the Buenos Aires area. They could not work in the city centre anymore: the police there made life impossible. The police chiefs had gone crazy. They all wanted to live the high life, drive imported limousines, buy houses in the gated communities where the jet set live.

"Cozumel Banegas offered them protection. All they had to do was set up in the zone he controlled. The tax they paid him would be reasonable, he told them – 'it's not for me, it's for the cause'."

"What cause?" asks Bértola. Used to listening to his clients in silence, he gets his own back when it is Verónica who is talking.

"The Party," she replies, scarcely able to believe the fantasy world the shrink lives in: the Freudian ivory tower where everything is solved by discovering at what stage in childhood their client was raped by the bachelor uncle, the mother's brother, who when he was alone at home dressed as a woman.

"The Peronist Party?"

"What other party is there in Argentina?"

"I dunno . . . the Radicals, the Socialists . . ."

"Let's be serious, Damián. I'm telling you a real-life story, not a clinical case like the ones you and your colleagues collect as if they were rare postage stamps."

Bértola smiles, unconcerned. The bullets whistling past Verónica's head make no sound in his ivory tower.

"'Cozumel Banegas'," he writes in his notebook, as if he was a client. "Why do they call him 'the Pox'?"

"Because . . . he's earned the nickname, don't try to find any Lacanian interpretation to it. I guess it's because he leaves indelible marks, scars, on those who don't end up dead."

"Bolivian, is he?"

"As Bolivian as Miss Bolivia. They did him the favour of granting him Argentine nationality. Payback time. For years he supplied many of the bigwigs in the province. He's earned his fame. Someone at the top of the tree decided it was time to keep him close. It's useful to have a general in the rearguard, far from the battle."

"San Martín always led his troops," Bértola reminds her.

"And look where it got him. Him and Bolívar. And look what became of the America they fought for."

"So where does the blonde fit into this bi-national chess game?"

Telling all this to Bértola allows Verónica to recap on the missing lady's biography. She had been brought from Santa Cruz de la Sierra to Salta in Argentina by an agent who wanted to sell her on the cheap. "Salta is horrible," Miss Bolivia told Verónica. "There are almost as many filthy indians there as in La Paz."

So she climbed onto a bus and eighteen hours later disembarked at the terminus at Retiro in the centre of Buenos Aires. Within a few days, as her money began to run out, she discovered that the capital was a jungle with no Tarzans to rescue her, an artificial garden where the roses and jasmine are fake, where the rich live in neighbourhoods built on rubble or the bones of the dead.

Nobody would come to save her. She realized as much by the time she had signed up for several model agencies and found herself employed, with other girls from the "book", to bring a bit of life to a private party being held in a Ramos Mejía mansion one January night. But Ana Torrente had not been crowned Miss Bolivia to end up in some lackey's bed; her stomach churned as she entered the house and her blue eyes surveyed this court of pretentious no-hopers dressed in clothes where the brand names stood out like those of the sponsors on football players' shirts. Fat slobs with massive bellies, and teeth and hair implanted at a thousand dollars a time. Flabby bodies and heads perfumed and cosseted on the outside, but with braincells inside devastated by coke and booze. The only thing left standing in this Hiroshima of the human condition was the desire for power, the need to elbow or shoot their way to the top, until they could reach somewhere that offered protection: become a mayor, win a seat in parliament or on the city council, become a union boss.

With a pout here, a purr there, Miss Bolivia crossed several of them off her list, until finally she found someone who was not quite as revolting as the rest. She danced on the table, like they do in Chicago gangster movies, drank all the five-hundred-dollar champagne she could take and more, then bedded Matías Zamorano.

Composers of tangos and boleros know it well: there is only a step between love and betrayal. Out of love for Miss Bolivia, the Pox's right-hand man was willing to stab him in the back. He handed the Bolivians and their market over to a Lomas de Zamora crook. "A nice little deal," he explained to the cherub in their dimly lit rented suite – king-size bed, with a water-fountain at the foot that was a replica of the Iguazú Falls – "20 per cent of all they make for us and the rest for the Lomas council boys."

When she learned just how much that 20 per cent was, Miss Bolivia let him fuck her like never before, as the waters of the artificial Iguazú splashed all over her. The Lomas de Zamora boys controlled territory ten times the size of the Pox's fiefdom: they had an army of professionals who made sure it was kept neat and tidy, and dealt with any trouble. When the Bolivians refused to leave their benefactor in the lurch, the boys from Lomas went to fetch them in trucks. They carted the families and their goods to the far bank of the Riachuelo and told them: "It's this or you can be repatriated first thing tomorrow. The documents are just waiting for the president's signature: one call from us and welcome back to Bolivia."

"I can't see the president getting mixed up in stuff like that," Bértola protests in disbelief.

"Not personally," says Verónica, happy to explain things for him. "His puppets, the puppets of his puppets. Everything is linked: there's a clever spider spinning away. It never stops making and spreading its web; if one part gets damaged, it patches it up somewhere else. To govern is to bring in money."

"'To govern is to bring in people,' is what President Sarmiento used to say. That's why he filled Argentina with immigrants. So that they would work. And he filled the country with schools too, to convince them it was better to be Argentine than wops, dagos or russkies."

"Bravo, doctor. Do you want to go on with your patriotic rant or should I finish telling you about Miss Bolivia?"

A few nights before the boys from Lomas de Zamora trespassed into the Pox's territory, there was another party, in another mansion. This time the lottery at the gangsters' ball was won by the councillor himself. Miss Bolivia allowed herself to be embraced, caressed, drooled over. She imagined she was being possessed by the Marlon Brando she had seen in old films on television, in the days when Brando was young and not this cheap Don Corleone she had to shout encouragement to, like the punter urging on the old nag he has bet on out of nostalgia, the nag who of course trails in last.

The plan was to stay close to the Pox while he was being fleeced, so that she and Zamorano would be the last people he suspected. The idea was to get rich without ending up dead in a ditch.

But anyone who does deals with power runs the risk of becoming part of the deal himself.

"The crooks in Lomas didn't want a fight with the people in La Matanza. Not because of the Pox, who's a nobody, but because of the politicians and the police chiefs there, who between them control all the drugs and prostitution in the province. You have to take care of your image when it comes to peddling influence. After they took the Bolivians to the other side of the Riachuelo, the two bosses did a deal."

"And the loose change from the deal was the names of the traitors," says Bértola, hazarding a guess.

"Wow! That's a record time for a psychoanalyst. I thought it took them years to arrive at the truth."

"That was before the digital revolution. Now we have to give instant replies on line, or the gurus of this third millennium steal our clients. I understand now why Miss Bolivia was in such a hurry to vanish into thin air."

The entry phone buzzes. Bértola's first patient. His clients arrive on time; they are predictable. There are answers for everything that happens to them in the textbooks. Verónica's clients on the other hand come and go at all hours, or get stuck in the revolving doors of violence.

And if they are killed, they do not pay.

6

Occasionally, very occasionally, Verónica wishes she had been in jail. In order to understand why thieves and murderers steal and kill again when they come out after so many years inside; why they cry out for someone to rescue them from a world they cannot bear any more.

She knows she is not living in a kindergarten. Two men buried below ground constitute a graduation diploma that bears much more weight than her law degree from Buenos Aires University. It is not fate, or chance, or karma, or any of the other excuses people invent when they mess things up, dream of their future, buy life insurance, abandon their partner or trade in their car for a brand-new one. It is something else, a monster as confused as she is, a hunchback begging for love who is rewarded only with a few coins when he is not given a kick in the pants or has the door slammed in his face. Loose change given out of astonishment, barely enough to pay the fare on a bus that leaves you in some corner of an alien city.

The lawyer lady does not ask much. All she wants is to understand. And she suspects that freedom is a hindrance, that roaming around aimlessly is bound to lead her nowhere.

Yet she has to keep going. She has to shield herself against all the frustrations and fight back when pain lies in ambush, attack first if the opportunity arises, go on in the absurd belief that from here on in she will not allow anything to surprise her, react to every death she meets by clambering to her feet, creating a new skeleton out of her own ashes.

"Where are you calling from?"

The voice on the other end sounds impersonal, laboured. It takes her a while to realise it is Ana on the line, the very same Miss Bolivia who disappeared the day before with the Bersa .38 that had belonged to the first man she lost.

"Don't come looking for me, *doctora*. I'm fine, but don't look for me."

"I didn't come looking for you. If you remember, it was you who came to me. All I ask is that you don't kill anyone."

Now that it is too late, she regrets having given Ana the gun. The call is from a public telephone; she could not trace it even if she had her own satellite. But the dethroned queen does not sound frightened, only agitated, perhaps from excitement. Perhaps she's in the arms of a man who's caressing her breasts at that very moment, Verónica imagines wildly.

"I'll contact you tomorrow or the day after, *doctora*, to see if that skirt-chasing magistrate is back from his holidays yet."

With that she hangs up. Veronica curses the fact that she is a lawyer for thieves and their women, that she has to splash around in the polluted mud of this city periphery, is clawing her way through garbage the whole time. She envies Bértola: the refuse he deals with doesn't stink to high heaven. It is an abstract filth in which client and therapist can roll around without getting dirty and it only lasts fifty minutes a session. Like someone watching a talk show about their own life, knowing they can switch it off if it gets boring or too intense.

The no-longer young man's arm does in fact stretch out towards Ana Torrente's young body. His hands play with her breasts, stroke them. He brings his mouth up to drink their sweet milk, imagining it is a nectar that will help him regain his youth, fountain in the midst of a garden of sugar and honey. She lets him come close, fondle, caress and suck her breasts. She is enjoying the older man's urgent desire. She looks on with amusement at first, then wraps her fingers round his erect penis, giving little taps at the base as if it were the Bersa the lawyer had lent her. When he tires of sucking her, she slides down and starts slowly licking him. She has learned by now not to close her eyes to hide her repulsion, to imagine she is in the arms of Di Caprio, in his room at a five-star hotel and not in this gangster hovel on the outskirts of San Pedro, where she has come to stay, following her instructions.

"Keep going, my love, keep going," groans the older man, worried he may lose his erection if she becomes distracted, if she stops sucking him so deliciously, stops plunging beneath the flurry of bedcovers that swallow her like quicksands, searching until she finds the survivor that he tries to keep in her mouth, his penis that is stiff but rough on Ana's tongue and mouth, like the mummified prick of a pharaoh who died two thousand years ago. Miss Bolivia feels as though she has reached the forbidden interior of an Egyptian pyramid. If she manages to get out alive, she will never again do what she is doing now, sucking him with the expertise she learned in the first model school she went to soon after arriving in Buenos Aires, with an agent who had a young, enthusiastic dick who told her yes! that's how she had to move her ass on the cat-walks if she wanted to take over from Naomi Campbell.

The older man shrieks as if someone were cutting his throat. When there is not much of life left to run, pleasure is this senile yelp from someone who has nothing but his money, if he has any, and the scant, fleeting power allowed him by some boss or other, some gang leader who has left him in charge after making him promise he won't fuck the blonde he is now busy fucking.

Ana spits the semen into his face. He throws her off, revolted by the watery, bitter juice this crazy girl has insulted him with. She wipes her mouth clean, then runs laughing into the bathroom. She locks the door behind her and studies herself in the mirror. The older man's curses reach her like the sound of a distant pack of dogs, something she got used to hearing in the desolate towns she visited as queen. It is the music – as bitter as the man's semen – that accompanied those winter nights when she shivered with cold and hunger at the start of her lengthy flight from Santa Cruz de la Sierra. Back in those days she dreamt of reaching Argentina and its capital, Buenos Aires, the Paris of South America, the city without indians where, if you are not careful – or so they told her – even the taxi drivers speak French.

They lied to you, Ana tells Miss Bolivia in the mirror, which is like a visitors' room in a prison where she is the prisoner and Miss Bolivia has come to visit her, to bring her news of the outside world. They had no idea what they were talking about, she tells her, Buenos Aires is as overrun by indians as any ruined city in Bolivia or Peru.

The man starts beating on the bathroom door, at first with gentle taps, a crescendo with the palm of his hand, then his fists, finally vibrato, kicking like a horse who has eaten too much oats and marihuana salad. "Open up you bitch" – bang! bang! like someone being stoned alive, bang! thump! bang! – "you asshole bitch, open this door or else!" The same blows, the same fury she had met when she was locked in the dairy of the German farmer who had taken her in only to force her to grow up shutting her eyes in the darkness. "Open up, I'm shitting myself," she hears from the other side of the bathroom door. It is as though oral sex has acted on him like a laxative, but Ana still does not open the door. Instead, she shrinks back to the corner of the bathroom behind the toilet, presses herself against the tiles and waits for the man's desperation to give him the strength to break open the door, which just at that moment gives way with a sharp crack.

As sharp as the cracking sound from the Bersa that Ana, this time accompanied by Miss Bolivia on her side of the mirror, uses to shoot him and watch him collapse in his own pile of shit.

7

"Foreign millionaires aground in Buenos Aires" is the headline of the evening newspaper that has survived the takeovers of the media groups in Argentina. It is a sensationalist rag bought by those workers who still have a job.

"Five-star hotel on the rocks" is how the news is put by the free paper handed out to the middle-class employees, secretaries and the unemployed who cram into trains and buses as they travel home after another exhausting day looking for work, or keeping it by pushing and shoving others out of the way.

The rest of the front pages of both papers are full of photographs of weary tourists and on-the-spot interviews with some of the 3,340 passengers from the *Queen of Storms*, who tonight should be sailing south to spot whales off Puerto Madryn, poor creatures who, like monkeys in a zoo, only come close to the coast so they can be seen by tourists.

The Río de la Plata is an estuary where the average depth of the water fluctuates between one metre and one metre ninety centimetres, depending on the winds. All vessels calling at the port of Buenos Aires have to follow narrow channels that are constantly being dredged – unless the crews of the dredgers are working to rule because they have not been paid the bonuses they were promised. This was what happened a couple of days earlier, although no-one was told about it; neither the travel agencies nor the officers on board the *Queen of Storms*, men trained to grapple with the wild seas of the Magellan Strait or to avoid the Antarctic icebergs that global warming increasingly places in their path, but helpless when faced with a measure decreed by the powerful unions that control the port, the tugboats and dredgers.

The reporter in the middle-class free sheet speculates that no-one said a word because the invasion of tourists stuffed with euros and dollars is a bonanza for Buenos Aires hotel owners. They claim to be unable to cope, but they have already divvied up the spoils they are likely to enjoy, if as expected it takes a week to repair the liner's hull. Two hundred dollars for the privilege of spending the night in a corridor, however well appointed, is a price the passengers pay only under protest, but it is immediately salted away in the hoteliers' black books, minus the percentage slipped to the tax inspectors whose frowns suddenly disappear as they count the notes in the equally well-appointed hotel toilets.

Pacogoya is not worried about the delay. His apartment looking out on the illustrious dead is far more comfortable than the bunk the travel agency allots him when they take him on as a guide. He is not complaining; the pay is good and he does not spend much time in his bunk: he comes and goes between cabins every night, and often strikes it lucky if the person succumbing to his charms is a young, uninhibited tourist. Swedish and German girls are his favourites; he does not understand a word they speak and they do not understand him. The entire cultural exchange is restricted to laughter and sighs, or gestures the other person interprets as they see fit. Sometimes the results are surprising; usually they are pleasant, except for the night when a German man in his fifties, one metre ninety tall and with a body honed in the gyms of the former East Germany, mistook his intentions and threw him face down on the bed with a quick judo move. Pacogoya had seen something similar with the cattlehands at San Antonio de Arecho, a "for-export" town on the edge of the pampas where tourists are taken to eat barbecued beef and gawp at the gauchos with their daggers and baggy trousers. The gauchos, though, do it with young steers. They upend them with a single flip, but that is where their prowess ends: they soon let the animal go, then stand up to receive the applause of their grateful audience.

But the German never understood that Pacogoya was not shrieking with pleasure. His own eloquent gestures were meant to convey how pleased he was, because normally he suffered from premature ejaculation, yet this time had managed to contain himself for another couple of minutes. In fact he was so delighted he gave Pacogoya the gold wristwatch he had bought for the ungrateful girl who had left him high and dry in Piraeus.

Pacogoya spent the next seven nights flat on his stomach in his narrow cabin, until the German did not re-embark at Rio de Janeiro. He got lost in the city, probably enamoured of some young *garoto* whom he doubtless rewarded, if he broke the record established by the tourist guide, with the necklace or earrings he had also bought for Miss Ungrateful of Greece.

Whenever river silt, Antarctic icebergs or a strike lead to a cruise ship being delayed in port, Pacogoya takes it easy. He tries to be his own tourist guide. He looks for amorous adventures outside the routine and for the business opportunities that all cities offer to those who know how to take advantage of them.

In Buenos Aires he is helped by the fact that he knows his way around. In recent years, as well as places to dance tango and restaurants where the tourists can stuff themselves with beef, the so-called Queen of the Río de la Plata has seen the growth of an activity that calls for speedy reflexes and a well-developed network of contacts. Selling drugs to foreign tourists is not the same as supplying the local pimply adolescents in their discos, schools or universities. The foreigners have no problem paying, but they insist on top-class stuff. They might spend silly money on a set of gaucho *boleadores* from some tourist trap on calle Florida, but when it comes to coke, they are experts. And not every dealer can get them what they want.

Pacogoya took their orders the night before. News of the delay in

Buenos Aires meant they were doubled. Anything unexpected creates anxiety among those who think they have bought every single minute of the rest of their lives, only to discover that the world, "external reality" as airheads and new-age psychologists call it, obeys its own laws. In the end, Pacogoya was scared by how much they wanted: he usually only made fifty- or sixty-gramme deals; this time he was expected to come up with almost half a kilo of topnotch cocaine. In addition, absolutely all of them had paid up front and in Argentine pesos, banknotes adorned with portraits of national heroes completely unknown to them, looking on sternly as if they had helped found a real nation.

His usual dealer meets him in his virtual office in the Florida Garden, a bar on the corner of Florida and Paraguay. Like liners in port, celebrities call in here for a while: local politicians and artists, intellectuals who write for newspapers that the middle class (although fewer and fewer of them) buy so as to know what to think, or more often to line the floors of their apartments with when they are going to paint the walls.

"That's a lot, I can only supply half."

"Where can I get the rest, Uncle?"

He does not say so, but the dealer knows Pacogoya has got all the money on him. He can tell it from his hands, his eyes: even the way his lip trembles makes him an open book.

"I'll give you an address," he says, writing on a scrap of paper. "Memorize it, then tear it up."

Glancing down at the piece of paper, Pacogoya immediately protests.

"But that's not in Buenos Aires! Where on earth is San Pedro anyway?"

"It's close by, *che*. A hundred and seventy kilometres away, no more than an hour on the motorway." With that he takes the bit of paper from Pacogoya and tears it up himself. "Give me the dough now and call me when you get back from San Pedro."

Pacogoya is carrying a student rucksack. His thin face disguises the fact that he is already forty-eight years old. A sparse beard gives him that Che Guevara look which often leads tourists to think he must be a left-wing guerrilla. In reward for his services they thrust books about Che written in French or Italian on him.

He unzips his rucksack and hands the dealer a wad of notes.

"Twenty per cent now. The rest tonight, when I've picked up the stuff and returned from San Pedro."

Despite sixty years of hard living, Uncle's face rejuvenates as soon as he sees the money. The skin around his eyes gets a botox injection when he handles the notes, counts them under the table, then like a conjuror makes them disappear into his jacket pocket.

Although everyone knows him as Uncle, it is only with Pacogoya that he has a real nephew relationship. Pacogoya has known him for fifteen years, since the days when the dealer was private secretary to the vice-president of the Chamber of Deputies, and Pacogoya's own position in the Foreign Ministry allowed him to use the invaluable diplomatic bag to bring shipments in directly from Colombia.

"Those were the days," says Pacogoya, while the two of them are smoking a cigarette outside the bar, now that the municipal authorities have banned smoking in enclosed spaces. "I should have stayed on. I'd be an ambassador by now."

"The foreign service is full of queers," says the dealer, taking a lungful of smoke, then breathing out a dark, polluted cloud that the east wind whirls around the walls of the bar, then off up calle Paraguay. "I'll see you tonight."

*

Anyone determined to believe God exists will find him on any corner, in the lift, or while he is walking along a lonely road. Any woman equally keen to find love will end up convinced that a noise in the corridor must be her lover coming back at any hour, at 3.30 a.m., for example. To beg her to forgive him for having stormed off the other night when she refused to give him what he had come to ask her for. For having been so stupid as not to make love to her first, to leave her well satisfied so that, still caught up in the dreamy haze of their second fuck, she would find it impossible to refuse him such a tiny favour, nothing more than three thousand pesos.

But neither God nor love exist, Verónica groans when she hears Pacogoya's voice on the entry phone. Or at least, this is not the way to find them, groping around in the dark, holding back as she gives herself in exchange for a meal and real French champagne in an expensive restaurant, followed by a lovemaking session in a room with a view of the noble dead.

"I thought you were back on your ship. What happened: did they throw you overboard?" she asks when he comes in.

Instead of replying, Pacogoya tries to embrace her, but she slips away like a cat who will not allow itself to be stroked. He lets his arms drop and sinks onto the sofa. He is exhausted.

"You know what happened. The ship ran aground, and . . ."

"I'm not talking about the cruise ship: what happened to you?"

Pacogoya looks at her in dismay. As though it were possible not to tell her, to say he saw her light was on and came up, to have a drink of the Argentine whisky which is all she has in the little bar she keeps under a table loaded with plants, then make love to her or take her to eat in an all-night restaurant run by fake Italians.

"I have to get up at seven," Verónica says impatiently. "Give me a quick summary of what happened, then you can go back and sleep in your cemetery." Pacogoya was always pallid; now his skin is transparent. All he wants is somewhere to spend the night: any corner, the dog kennel if necessary. "I don't have a dog."

"Wuff, wuff," he says, managing to bring a smile to her face, smothered with creams to make her look young. "I'll tell you in the morning. Go to bed now."

"You could be dead by morning. The refugees who come here seem to have a tendency to disappear."

Curiosity to find out what Verónica means has the effect of loosening Pacogoya's tongue.

"Until now everything had been fine. Fifteen years living off it and not a drop of blood."

"Living off it" meant the tourist guide was a low-level dealer practising low-intensity corruption, the only explosions coming with sex.

"So who's spattered you with it now?"

He has no idea. All he can do is tell her what happened and curse the dealer, the Uncle who loves him like a nephew, for sending him into that bloody lions' den – to the armpit of the world, a place called San Pedro.

"San Pedro is Saint Peter, so you must have been close to paradise. I know the town, it's a pretty place, surrounded by olive groves and with a beautiful view of the river."

"Well then, paradise must be next door to hell."

*

He has a hard time finding the address.

He has driven there at 180 k.p.h., dodging lorries and buses, forcing his way past other drivers, as if he was already aware that someone in the place he is aiming for is bleeding to death.

He finally turns into the street. A dirt track. Its name is on a hand-painted sign, although in reality the road is little more than a line crossing a grid of bare lots, scarcely half a dozen small, poor-looking, unfinished houses. Stray dogs watch Pacogoya's red Porsche go past – slowly, bouncing over the potholes. He tells himself he ought to have left it in his garage and rented something less ostentatious, but a nagging voice told him he had to get there as quickly as possible, without even pausing to think: after all, he could have got the drugs somewhere else. No, he had been with the Uncle so many years now, he trusted him.

"Trust makes you relax. It can be deadly," he says to a Verónica whose indulgent gaze for some reason reminds him of the dogs in San Pedro.

It is the fifth house along the dirt track called the Limes. A house every hundred metres; five hundred metres and nothing more than that hand-painted sign at the start. Groves of fruit trees at the far end. An intense perfume of oranges seeps into the Porsche, reminding Pacogoya he must have the bodywork looked at. Maybe rust was getting into it, and he cannot allow such an expensive car to go to rack and ruin.

There is a number, also painted on a piece of wood from a fruit crate: 59. Alongside the nondescript house stands a Ford Falcon, which must already have been ancient by the time they were used to "disappear" people during the dictatorship. From its design and the shape of the bonnet, Pacogoya calculates it is from the 1960s. It probably does not even work and has been left there for time or tramps to strip the carcass.

He claps his hands: there is no bell for him to ring. Better to pass for a Bible seller than shout who he is when he has no idea who might be inside. It is a fine winter morning; the sun is as hot as in January, but the air is cool. The kind of day it would be nice to be greeted by a friendly face, to be asked in for a cocktail beneath the climbing vine in the garden, to leave with the gift of a bag of oranges.

"San Pedro oranges are really sweet and juicy," Verónica chips in.

No-one comes out of the house; not even a dog. The ones in the street have lost all interest in him and gone back to their fleas. No neighbours either. Or children. And too late, Pacogoya realizes there aren't even any birds.

He takes a couple of steps back, still facing the shut door and windows, but he knows he cannot leave empty-handed. If he does not get the goods, no-one will buy from him again: in this business, reputation is everything. And once you have lost it, there is no way to get it back. And it is good money, always bulging in his pockets. No, he won't give that up just because of a moment's weakness. Besides, Uncle would not deliberately send him to the slaughter. "Fifteen years, nephew," he tells himself, hearing the dealer's affectionate voice in his ear, encouraging him to open the door.

"So he does telepathy as well as drugs," Verónica scoffs.

"I swear I could hear his voice. But he should have been telling me: get out of there, don't go in, don't get your hands dirty, go back to being a cruise-ship Romeo – you may earn less but as long as there are no shipwrecks, you'll live to a ripe old age."

"You will live to a ripe old age, Paco. Anyway, you're already old, it's just that you can't accept it."

The delivery faun stares at her. He really does seem to have aged after the race to San Pedro, then the terror in that rundown house by the orange groves.

He finally goes in. The door is not locked. It opens noiselessly as though the hinges have recently been oiled. It is dark inside; there is no electricity, only a shaft of sunlight halfway down the corridor. It falls vertically and is as round as the hole in the roof that lets it in, as round as the face of the man lying there, eyes wide open, staring up at this miserly midday zenith.

"You should have left the way you came."

"But trust makes you relax. And curiosity killed the cat, Verónica."

He had gone there to get what was his, on Uncle's recommendation. Never so much as a drop of blood before then. You get used to the world appearing to be something it's not.

He opens the door wide behind him to let in more light, but the corridor is still in darkness. It is obvious the man is not sleeping, but he could have had a heart attack. If anyone killed him, they must be far away by now. The best thing would be to leave straightaway without touching anything. Pacogoya does not follow his own advice, because he still wants to believe that if he goes further along the passage he might find what he came for.

He trips over something and comes to a halt, terrified. It is the feet of the dead man. He reaches down and pulls, to drag the body towards the light from the open door. It is only a couple of metres. The body is not heavy; it slides along easily.

He should never have taken money for orders he could not fulfil; he should not have driven to San Pedro; he should not have gone into the house. But you venture into the unknown thinking you are only going into the next room.

"I bent over the body looking for something; a piece of paper, a key, some clue, something."

It is then that horror tears at his guts and takes his breath away, as if he had brushed against a high-voltage cable. Far from the body, at the spot he had dragged the corpse from, the sun is still plunging like a knife into the dead man's open eyes.

8

By 6 a.m. next day Verónica is already in her office at the Riachuelo market. It is a circus caravan furnished with a notebook, printer, telephone, coffee machine and a whale calf, her bodyguard, two metres tall and weighing 120 kilos. He would find swimming difficult, but on dry land he can kill without turning a hair.

The smell of freshly brewed coffee cannot disguise the stench from the Río Riachuelo. Day has only just dawned, but the stallholders have already begun to pack up. They tell her it was not such a good night. There were bomb threats. One of the stallholders was kidnapped on the Camino Negro: he was taken to Lomas cemetery, made to dig his own grave, then brought back to the market.

It is not yet 7.00 a.m. when she calls the magistrate at home in Lomas de Zamora. The maid who answers reminds her rudely that it is Saturday, that his honour went to bed late the previous night because he had a social engagement, that if she phones him on Monday she is sure she will find him in.

"If his honour doesn't come to the phone at once, I swear on oath as a lawyer that tonight he'll be in the headlines of Crónica," says Verónica, without raising her voice a single decibel.

The whale calf gives a half-smile of approval. It is obvious the lawyer's methods coincide with his idea of how conflicts are meant to be resolved outside his marine world.

"I've only just got to bed," the magistrate tells her, as if anyone were interested in his carousing. Verónica responds in kind, informing him that she didn't sleep at all, that in the early hours the cable channels repeat every programme, including the news. "So why didn't you sleep? I never told you to go to the market at night. Going there a while in the morning is more than enough."

"I can assure your honour that if you were told one of these nights that someone had been decapitated, that there had been a bomb threat and a Bolivian had almost been buried alive, you wouldn't sleep either."

She takes a deep breath to replenish the oxygen she used up in giving her little speech. Silence at the far end of the line. The sound of someone clearing their throat, then more silence. He must be writing it all down, Verónica guesses. Magistrates note everything they hear down on a bit of paper, just in case.

"Where was this decapitated body?"

"In San Pedro, Buenos Aires Province."

"My jurisdiction is Lomas de Zamora. Tell me about the bomb alert and the abduction of the Bolivian." It is Verónica's turn to fall silent. She finds it hard to focus on what the magistrate wants to hear, to forget about the headless body in the orange groves. There is no apparent connection, so the magistrate dismisses it: he is keen to return to bed. "Don't let it affect you," he advises her, after Verónica has told him what she was told. "Is Chucho there with you?"

"Chucho?"

The whale calf flaps his flipper and blinks as though he is having his passport photo taken. His way of showing his delight at being included. Verónica hands him the phone and Chucho listens to his instructions. He nods several times in rapid succession and waves his flippers again – as if he was in the pool catching fish thrown to him, thinks Verónica.

When Chucho hands her back the phone, the magistrate has already hung up.

"He's gone off to sleep, the bastard!"

If Verónica quits now she will lose a lot of money and will return in a bad mood to her apartment, where she will find Pacogoya sleeping like a fallen angel on her sofa, after trying to force her down onto the living-room carpet like the second-rate porno movie actor he imagines he is. A knee to the balls from Verónica finally convinced him of one thing: that violence had become part of what until then had been a comfortable existence as a cheap seducer.

"You've got nothing to fear, *doctora*," says Chucho. He seems to have grown even bigger – probably due, thinks Verónica, to the words of encouragement from the magistrate.

Verónica smiles, pretending to be flattered. She feels slightly sorry for this hulk with his Magnum .44 and the Uzi in the boot of his grey car with tinted windows that he uses to fetch and carry her to and from the market. He seems like a nice kid, a baby whale, no pretensions to know everything like her, but not someone who takes advantage of the fact that he is armed and two metres tall to extort money from taxi drivers or shopkeepers, like so many youngsters of his age do. Youngsters Verónica springs from police stations so they can be shot from any passing patrol car without even leaving the neighbourhood.

Fed up with waiting for the accountant who promised to meet her at the market but who is probably off fishing in the lake at Chascomús, Verónica leaves the caravan to walk round the market.

The stallholders are loading their goods onto trucks worth two hundred thousand dollars or onto broken-down jalopies. There is even one horse-drawn cart. Nothing is left of what until a couple of hours before had been a busy market: no underwear from Taiwan, no two-dollar Swiss watches, no brand-name clothes, no M.P.3s or thousand-dollar notebooks selling here for three hundred. Everything disappears onto trucks, jalopies or carts, off on the provincial merry-go-round until Tuesday night's market brings them all back here once again.

Birds' guano is starting to fry on the tin roofs of the shanty town barely a hundred metres from the open-air market. Barefoot kids are already diving into the trash left by the stallholders, searching for what might have been thrown away: radios not even a deaf person would have bought, perfumes that stank as badly as the waters of the Riachuelo, leftover goods that could find no home. There is always something, and the kids are rats with sharp teeth and claws. If any of them happens to stay asleep when the market is being packed up, there will always be a stepfather or some other man to get them going with a couple of slaps.

There is not much for Verónica to do in her office at the market this Saturday morning: her accountant has gone fishing and the magistrate has put her life in the hands of the whale calf. She asks him – the whale calf, that is – to take her to Liniers. There she gets out of the car and takes a number 28 bus, despite protests from Chucho, who insists his job is to pick her up from her apartment, leave her at the market, then take her home again. Veronica explains she wants to go home alone and that nobody is going to do anything to her. She boards the bus and sits in the back row. She opens the window so that the breeze can ruffle her hair and make her feel more alive, not enveloped in some air-conditioned fishtank, hooked up to telephones that only ring to cause problems.

She is not surprised when she sees Chucho's car following the bus, then drawing up alongside in the middle of Avenida Paz. Chucho sounds his horn at her. He was not going to abandon her just because she asked him to, it is the magistrate he answers to, not a female lawyer who is not even from Lomas de Zamora. "Whose idea was it to send her to that den of thieves as inspector?" Chucho must be thinking, if his cetaceous brain is capable of thought.

*

While Verónica is travelling on her bus with the whale calf alongside to make sure she comes to no harm, a Colombian couple – a fifty-five-year-old man, a twenty-two-year-old woman – are being led from their room in a five-star hotel in the city centre by men armed with revolvers and sub-machine-guns. To reach the room the men – four who go up, two at reception and another two outside the hotel – have had to step over the tourists sleeping in the corridors. "Be careful, they're coughing up two hundred dollars a night," the hotel manager told them, after all eight identified themselves as federal-police officers.

They burst into the room using the magnetic card the manager has given them, after insisting they are not to let on to anyone he made things so easy for them and did not even ask to see a search warrant.

The fifty-five-year-old Colombian man and the twenty-two-year-old Colombian girl are sleeping in each other's arms. They look more like a honeymoon couple than the drugs baron Osmar Arredri, boss of the Carrera Cuarta neighbourhood in Medellín, and his girlfriend. They are in Buenos Aires because they were on board the *Queen of Storms* on a pleasure cruise. The blonde girl is called (or says her name is) Sirena Mondragón. She is the pleasure in the fifty-five-year-old's cruise. When she jumps from the bed, naked and with her hands above her head, her tits dazzle the four feds training their guns on her.

"Poppa's out for the count. We drank a lot last night because the ship didn't leave," Sirena explains, pouting and looking so sad the leader of the group gives her a handkerchief to wipe away her tears.

They shake Poppa roughly, then throw the fresh orange juice that room service brought up with the rest of his breakfast a few minutes earlier in his face. Poppa sits up, cursing them; when he makes to reach for his 9 m.m. gun sleeping like a cat on the bedside table, a karate-expert federal cop smashes his hand, then with the same imperceptible movement sends him crashing against the mini-bar.

Down below in reception the manager is sweating like a boxer working at the punchbag. Half a dozen employees are nowhere near enough to look after the dozens of tourists complaining about the night they spent in the hotel corridors. They have mutinied, or something close to it, and are refusing to pay a single dollar or euro unless they are offered somewhere decent to spend the nights until their cruise liner is repaired.

"We came here to dance tango and eat your famous steaks, and we get treated like immigrants, for God's sake," one of them protests in an unidentifiable Spanish accent. He explains to his partner, who has an equally unidentifiable Spanish accent, that Argentines are more Italian than Spanish and that's why you can't trust them. They promise you one thing and do something completely different, for God's sake.

The manager watches as the posse of feds leaves without so much as a thank-you. The Colombian couple are only half-dressed; he stumbles along, but she is as upright as if she were on the catwalk at a Cacharel fashion parade.

"I've got one free room," the manager shouts to the line of first-world refugees. There is uproar, shouts of "I was here first", while he looks meaningfully at one of his minions for him to go upstairs and see what damage the feds have caused.

*

It is four hours later, towards midday (by which time the stranded, mutinying tourists have formed a gypsy encampment in the lobby) and the classic red headlines of Crónica Television announce two breaking stories to the world: "Ghastly beheading on outskirts of San Pedro," screams the first. Then, after the weather forecast – "30° in the shade: no let-up to the summer!" – the second news item: "Kidnapping in central hotel: fake feds rifle minibar and abduct Colombian couple."

9

"Urgent service needed for oil levels in my noddle," says Verónica when she recognizes Damián Bértola's voice on the phone.

"It's Saturday night and I have a private life too."

"What does a psychoanalyst do with his private life on Saturday nights?"

"If he's a Lacanian, he reads Freud. If he's Freudian, he examines the interpretation of Jung's dreams. If he's a vegetarian, he could invite a criminal lawyer to come and eat a decent barbecue on his roof terrace."

"What about your children?"

"Fine, thanks. The boy's in Spain, the girl in Mexico."

"You're on your own? You were going to make a barbecue just for yourself?"

"My dog's with me. He's the only patriot who hasn't left Argentina. And that's only because they won't give him a European passport."

In less than half an hour the lawyer and the psychoanalyst are standing side-by-side in front of the glowing barbecue, the spicy smoke from grilled sausage fat swirling round them.

Bértola lives alone in a large house he kept after his divorce. The children left seven years ago. Villa del Parque is a quiet neighbourhood; the burglars walk on tiptoe, the serial killers go about their business quietly, the streets are lined by chinaberry and jacaranda trees, there are no noisy avenues near the house and the barbecue smells delicious.

"Just look at that moon." Bértola points up through the leaves of the chinaberry that is putting on its nightly display above the terrace, creating tiny shadow figures. The moon he is talking about is sitting on the highest branch. "It's like living in the country," he says enthusiastically. "But what brings you here? I know, an oil check. I can check the level alright, but changing it takes years. And remember, it's Saturday."

"You talk like a supreme-court judge," protests Verónica. "You said you lived with a dog, so where is he?"

From a corner of the roof terrace it is the enormous dog that replies rather than his master. He has been so focused on the barbecue he has hardly even wagged his tail since Verónica appeared.

"Living on your own is complicated," says Bértola. "Most people in cities live alone. They say that's fine, that it's their choice. Crap." He turns the meat over and carefully pricks the intestines, adding, "People say that to protect themselves. First came fire, then the wheel and then muuuuch later, in the twentieth century and above all in the well-off parts of Buenos Aires, the word."

"The paid-for word, you mean."

"That's how I make my living, Verónica. But at least when I write a

48

report or a clinical record I don't end them with bombastic stuff like 'in accordance with the law'. The meat's going to dry out if I leave it much longer. Do you like it juicy?"

He stabs a piece of spare rib, lifts it and holds it under the light so that she can decide if it is juicy enough for her. Verónica suggests they start with the sausages and intestines; she is a lawyer and so follows written legal advice that does not leave much room for improvisation. Although strictly speaking there is no law to cover this eventuality, precedents suggest it is offal first.

"After that, the meat and salads," she concludes her speech.

Bértola again laments the fact that he lives on his own. He does not know how to make a salad. He always ruins them by smothering them in oil and vinegar, he does not know how to wash a lettuce. Hygiene is a female thing, he says: it's woman's work. That's why he's sorry his wife left him: because of the salads.

They sit down to eat, still a little uncomfortable but beginning to get used to each other. A roof terrace in Villa del Parque is not the kind of place where foreign tourists eat their barbecued meat. They get taken to cattle ranches or restaurants where steak is paid for in hard currency. There are cattle and gauchos (as plastic as their credit cards), sometimes even "traditional" *malambo* dances and "typical" *boleadores* whirled round the gauchos' heads. A roof terrace in Villa del Parque can offer none of that. It is, though, a good place for a psychoanalyst and a lawyer who hardly know each other, who are work associates more than friends, to begin to glimpse each other's concerns, to wait patiently for the secrets to be revealed.

"His name is Mauser," says Bértola, when Verónica jumps as the dog's tail tickles her shins under the table. "He's happy. He's always happy when there is a barbecue. He dreams of the bones before he starts to chew them."

Once she has explained what Pacogoya means in her life (little more than nothing: a good dinner once in a while, love making that is not always so good), Verónica tells him what happened the previous night.

"I live waiting for a skunk I happen to be in love with to reappear," she says, "but the only people knocking on my door are ghouls like Pacogoya and Miss Bolivia."

"Then don't open your door. The early hours are no time to go visiting. Nobody who's in love with you is going to come and ruin your night's sleep."

Just to contradict his arrogant psychoanalyst's tone, she points out that the last time she saw the skunk was in the early hours.

"The guy's a swine, I'm sure he didn't come to make love, did he?" A sad smile from Verónica. She pushes the intestines to the side of her plate: too greasy for her. "Give them to Mauser. He can eat anything." The dog snaffles them, but then does not seem too happy to eat them under the table. He prefers meat too. Bértola tells her he does not know what breed he is. "He looks like a cocker spaniel, but he's the size of a sheepdog and has their eyes. He's probably one of those fashionable genetic experiments. Alright, don't talk to me about your love life: I expect it's the ghouls who brought you here, isn't it?"

Verónica explains she senses that something is about to explode. The same feeling she had shortly before the death of Romano, her first real man, the cop.

"Who killed him?"

"The police."

Bértola's moon has climbed down from the top branch of the chinaberry tree. Now it is creeping furtively across the neighbouring flat roofs, skirting the water tanks.

"I always knew it wasn't a good idea to be a cop."

"It's a simple story," Verónica says. "I didn't tell it to you before, because there's nothing to tell."

"Nothing fits, nothing can really be explained when it's too simple," says Bértola, with the look of a Socrates.

They both laugh. The laughter comes from a long way off, from the need (as simple as the story of her cop) to laugh at all that is impossible to explain, all that is dark and gloomy.

PART TWO

Pichuco Opens his Eyes

1

Pacogoya drove back slowly from his trip to San Pedro, Verónica tells the psychoanalyst on his night off.

He chugs along steadily at ninety in the slow lane. Other cars zoom past, almost brushing against his car, as if rebuking him for driving like a human being rather than a madman. This does not mean his road manners have suddenly improved: it is just that he cannot concentrate on his driving the way he had when he left Buenos Aires. He needs to think about what happened, although he cannot get that clear in his mind either. All he sees are images and the feeling that nothing is real, that he dreamt the house by the orange groves and in a moment he will wake up in his Recoleta apartment, his wretched bunk on the *Queen of Storms*, or in the cabin of some Swedish or German woman who, recovering from their alcoholic haze in the wan early morning light, will peer at him suspiciously, then tell him to get out, in languages only they can follow.

But deep down he knows he is awake and that there is no way out. To make matters worse, he is returning to Buenos Aires empty-handed: he will have to try to explain, to give all the money back. Because when he arrived and went to look for Uncle in the Florida Garden late that night, there was no sign of him. Not at his usual table, or at the bar, or anywhere around. There is no reply when he telephones his mobile.

Pacogoya does not leave a message, then curses himself for phoning: now his number will be registered somewhere that it probably should not be.

As night progresses, the corner of Florida and Paraguay becomes another planet. Unlike its daytime earthly inhabitants, the nocturnal aliens are stealthy figures on the prowl. They glide along silently, or sit in bars that are about to shut like the Florida Garden, where the waiters gradually close in around them as they pile chairs on tables and finally tell them they have to leave, they're just closing. The waiters' union is as homophobic as the rest of the trade unions in Argentina. The only exception is the Queers' Association, but that is not a real union; they do not sit down round a table with the other labour bosses to decide whether they are going to support the government or plot against it.

Pacogoya stares back at all the queers he meets in the night world. Sometimes one of them follows him and accosts him; it is only then that he puts the record straight. Although not always: when he feels very alone, as he is tonight, and very lost, like a new-born babe in a world devastated by a nuclear catastrophe, he accepts their invitation. And then in some charming apartment nearby, he fucks or is fucked and earns himself a few pesos or dollars. A reward for taking it up the ass or leaving his manhood to one side, like an umbrella in its stand on a rainy day.

Tonight he is about to agree to one of these deals with a man who like him is around forty, although he looks over fifty. He is bald and paunchy, wearing a suit but no tie, his shirt collar unbuttoned to show a scrawny neck. Two days' growth of stubble at least. He makes it clear he is not a pansy, what he is looking for is a warm, inviting ass. Pacogoya's ringtone interrupts their bargaining: "It's Uncle, you stinking faggot, get away from me." He pushes off the decrepit forty-year old, who spits at his feet like a guanaco in the Atacama desert, then waddles off, his bulk heavy as a cow that's already too old for slaughter.

Uncle is calling, but it is not Uncle. A murderer's voice always sounds muffled because of the hood he is wearing. To a killer, a head separated from a body is nothing more than an anatomical curiosity, a subject without its predicate, a flower plucked from its bunch. "We were following you," the voice says. "In the end we had to overtake because you were fast asleep. What happened, did your Porsche get stuck in second?"

Whoever it is using Uncle's phone does not expect him to answer. The caller knows that at the far end of the line there is someone who is about to wet himself with fear, but who wants to do the deal, to keep his promise to his cruise-liner customers. "You can come and get your stuff," he hears. "It's on the bed. Leave the dough on the bedside table, on top of the *Playboy* magazine Uncle jerks off over every night. Don't touch anything or go looking for Uncle. We're in charge now."

Pacogoya's first reaction is to get out, run away as he did from San Pedro. But it will not wash to present himself to his customers like a popcorn seller who has had his cart stolen. He has to be able to offer them at least half of what they ordered. He could even up the cost. "The market's difficult," he could tell them. "Lots of cops on the lookout." The other option, which he dismisses as moral cowardice, would be to end up in the arms of the pansy for a couple of pesos.

He has never been to Uncle's place. He has the card with his address – "but don't ever even think of coming here unless I invite you", Uncle warned him the first day they met. It is only three blocks away, on Viamonte. The tenth floor of an old building with windows you can see the river from.

He has known him fifteen years but never got the invitation. He knows nothing about Uncle's way of life. They have always talked about business, women, football occasionally – although Uncle prefers polo: "A sport for gentlemen," he says, "with no riffraff, where it's the horse that is in control." He has no children; perhaps that is why he is called Uncle. He does have nephews and according to what little Pacogoya has heard of them – from Uncle himself – they are all up to no good. "They're like you," he would tell him. "Nobodies, lightweights, nothing solid, chancers."

At first Pacogoya bridled at this. He would get up and leave the Florida Garden. Uncle would sit there watching him walk off, with a wave to him in the distance, mouthing "you'll be back". And of course he always did come back: there was no-one like Uncle when it came to deals.

Besides being old, the building is ugly. And dark, almost as soon as he gets beyond the unlocked heavy oak door – perhaps because they are expecting him. While he waits for the lift – as old as the building, a cage with black bars, cracked mirror, feeble light – Pacogoya tries to assess the possible consequences of going up to recover the drugs. What most worries him is that if he does not do it, he will end the night kissing a guy who forces him to suck his dick.

Tenth floor, the last the lift reaches. Beyond that there is only a narrow staircase which probably leads to the concierge's quarters and to the roof terrace, if there is one. Pacogoya imagines it covered in soot and pigeon shit. He rings the doorbell, like an errand boy come to collect a package. No-one opens the door.

He has left the lift door open, although if he has to get away he will use the stairs. If he runs down, at least he won't offer them a fixed target. He rings again and waits.

*

"This meat's good," says Verónica, interrupting her account. She chews slowly, enjoying the mouthful of rump steak. "It's a bit dry, though; I'm not sure Mauser is going to like it."

"I wouldn't have gone in there," says Bértola. "Two corpses is too much for one day."

In the end, he grasps the door handle.

Pacogoya wasn't too happy about it either, he tells Verónica. He knew it was a bad idea to step into the trap. Why had they called him when they had the drugs? They could sell the coke to anyone and for more money. They did not need him.

Yet he steps inside. After all, in fifteen years he has not been allowed in. And curiosity killed the cat, Verónica.

The apartment is neat and tidy. It is full of ceramic pieces, exotic statues, oriental monsters from Indonesia, Malaysia, Laos: of late, Uncle had acquired a taste for distant climes. "You can even go on excursions in Vietnam," he told his favourite nephew. "It has museums, good hotels. The Vietnamese who were not killed by the Yanks are all very polite. And before them the French were there. If you close your eyes, Ho Chi Minh City, which used to be Saigon, is like Paris, only cheaper." Uncle always came back from these trips with fresh statues and new contacts. "We have to open up markets," he used to say. "The world is globalized, and so are prostitution and drugs."

It was true, Pacogoya discovers as he reaches the living-room window: you can see the river. And there's a shadow on the horizon that must be Colonia del Sacramento in Uruguay.

"Don't move." The gun barrel pressed against the back of his neck does not give him time to be surprised. If the man telling him not to move had shot first, Pacogoya would not even have realized he was dead. "Don't turn round. Just look at the river."

The river is clearly visible, as if it were daytime. The full moon cannot be the same one which a few hours later comes and sits on Bértola's chinaberry tree. This moon seems bigger, rounder, more airy, like a Chinese lantern hanging above the estuary.

The voice is that of the man who called him on his mobile. It sounds clearer now – he must have taken off his hood. That is why he warned Pacogoya not to turn round.

"Don't be scared. Nothing will happen to you if you do as you're told. We're businessmen, just like you. We like to keep our word with clients." He talks in the plural, so he is not on his own. He probably never is. In the same chilly, polite tone he tells Pacogoya to put his hands on the pane of glass and to spread his legs. "We want to see all of you, like an X-ray, while we're talking to you. The coke's on Uncle's bed, as promised. Did you bring the dough?"

Of course he did. He has had the money on him since yesterday. He is the richest dead man walking in Buenos Aires.

While the voice of the man holding the gun to his head still sounds quite distant, another pair of hands searches him and strips him of banknotes showing the stern faces of San Martín, Rivadavia, Belgrano, all the nation's heroes.

"Why the fuck are those gringos carrying Argentine money?" the man searching him complains. "Or did you change it all?"

Pacogoya shakes his head vigorously. He explains:

"I pay with what they give me. I don't go near money exchanges. Too dangerous. And banks want identity documents, so you're trapped."

The man finishes his task. He counts the banknotes more quickly than a mechanical sorter.

"All here," he reports.

Pacogoya freezes in his uncomfortable stance at the window. "Now for the bullet," he tells himself. "You're going to die for being so stupid."

Yet the voice of the one with the gun has not changed. He seems to be following a pre-established script.

"When we leave, count slowly to a thousand. Then pick up the coke on Uncle's bed and get out of here. But before that there's something you have to do if you don't want to end up in the river." He knew it. Nothing is free in this world, not even cocaine, he tells Verónica he told himself, although the truth is that he is not thinking, he is praying while the man explains what he wants. Still behind his back, the one who took his money hands him some sheets of paper and a red marker pen. He tells Pacogoya to sit down, still facing the river, in a small armchair. He brings a standard lamp over to it.

It is the passenger list for the *Queen of Storms*.

"We know you've been a tourist guide for as many years as you've been a dealer and a cocksucker. We know you have the memory of an elephant, and that on each voyage you make sure you find out the females who are gagging for it and the males who are rolling in it. It's a good idea, that's how you manage to put a bit aside. We grow old before we know it, so it's best to be prepared."

"What do you want me to do?" asks Pacogoya. Hearing the story of his life at what could well be his final hour makes him realize how easy it is to be disgusted with yourself.

"Where it says 'Osmar Arredri and wife', write down the name of the hotel they're in and what room number. And if you want to be alive tomorrow, don't get it wrong."

"They're putting people up in corridors," says Pacogoya, not because he does not know what they are asking him, but because things might have changed and he does not want to die due to an administrative decision.

"People like him don't sleep in corridors. Make sure you write it so we can read it, nice and clearly. Then from that lot choose a dozen who are really wealthy, not show-offs. You know who they are."

It is true, he does know. A cruise liner is a luxury talking shop; everybody gossips about everybody else. By the third day the class war has produced its typical alignment: the rich on one side, the nobodies on the other.

"There are more than a dozen," Pacogoya says generously.

"Only the topnotch ones. Take your time, there's no hurry."

He looks down the long list. Starts to put crosses beside some of them. He knows each cross could be their tombstone, but instead of feeling bad about it he is calm, almost excited. Just this once, his choice is what matters. He is the one who decides. Somehow he does not feel he is betraying them: anyone would do the same in his position. This is what too much money in too few hands produces: people like him, like the ones with their guns trained on him, like Uncle. There is a full moon over the river and crosses on the paper.

Like a diligent pupil, he finishes his exam. The man who searched him picks up the sheets of paper.

"We're going now. But we're watching you. If you've got anything wrong, pow!" says the other man.

"He looks a bit like Che Guevara," the first one says.

"It's true, but Che was a revolutionary and this guy's a heap of shit. You know what to do – count to a thousand."

They leave. Pacogoya cannot believe they have gone, or that the drugs are there, intact, in their pretty little bags on Uncle's bed. Better not to think about what they made him do. He scoops up the bags, counts to five hundred and goes out into the corridor. They must have walked calmly down the staircase, because the lift is still there with its door open. He gets in and looks at himself, split in two in the cracked mirror.

"Ever onwards to victory," he says, pressing the ground-floor button.

2

When the moon left the stage and a moist south-westerly breeze sprang up, the two of them went down to Bértola's living room for a whisky. Only Mauser stayed on the terrace, gnawing bones that had become a reality.

Verónica was worried Bértola might try something after the whisky, but the guy (he was a psychologist, after all) must have made a mental note of how she had kneed Pacogoya and did not want to repeat the experience. Or perhaps he really was becoming her friend, as well as sharing the office costs.

Too much baggage, Verónica told herself later, trying to explain Bértola's good behaviour. She had called him on his night off, then turned up on his terrace with stories more suited to a pathologist than a psychoanalyst.

Occasionally, when she looked at herself in the mirror on one of her rare self-indulgent mornings – good figure, tits still firm, backside as perky as her nice nose, light-green eyes, thick jet-black hair that was all hers and was never dyed – Verónica forgot she was twice a widow and that men are superstitious about women who have buried their men.

Bértola was a saint. He had put up with her – for free – on his night off. He had fed her the steak and everything else he had bought to share with his dog. He must have taken pity on her when he saw how bowed down she was by the weight of all her worries.

"You were very young when you married your cop."

"I was twenty. At that age, you don't understand a thing. You talk about everything, but you don't get it. You're an open book – plus I was a student at the time. I have a good memory. I talked and talked, always quoting Greeks and Romans."

"So you hooked up with a Roman. You fell in love with his name."

Verónica smiles. Her hand grows cold on the whisky glass.

"Argentina was a mess. I wanted to get out. I had all my papers and a contract to work in an Argentine restaurant in Barcelona. I couldn't give a damn about graduating as a lawyer. Then Romano came on the scene."

Bértola bites his tongue to avoid the all too obvious associations: "Chaos looks for authority". He recalls yet again that it is Saturday night; she is not a client. But it turns out Verónica can read thoughts as well as case files.

"He was authority and I fell for it," she says. "I got pregnant before

I finished university. We used to screw in a cheap motel for cops where they played sirens instead of muzak. Romano had just finished his police training. He swore he'd never tortured anyone; I've even got a friend who's a communist, he told me."

"How touching. What happened with your pregnancy?"

"I lost the baby."

Romano reacted with a violence he had been careful not to display before. It was her fault, she tried to do too much, she wanted things that normal women did not aspire to. He demanded she stop studying; she refused. Then one night when she came home from the faculty she opened the apartment door and ran straight into his fist. She had not told him she would be back so late – "look what time it is, what motel have you come from, you whore?" The landing outside was filled with shouts and the faces of their neighbours, consortium hyenas roused by the smell of blood.

She left him, but he followed her across half the city before tracking her down to a room in a boarding house in Lanús Este, lent as an emergency measure by a fellow university student. He went down on his knees and begged forgiveness. He loved her, he never thought he could stoop so low: "But you have to understand, I'm under a lot of pressure, I work with the dregs of society," he said, trying to justify himself. "They're clearing everything out because democracy is on its way. They don't want to be sent to jail or lynched."

"Poor Romano, I could have saved his life. 'I'll resign tomorrow,' he told me, 'we'll go far away, into the interior if you want. We can live in peace there. You set up your lawyer's practice and I'll open a shop, a baker's for example. My old man was a baker, so I know the trade, it's great.'"

She almost agreed. She imagined herself in a typical small town. Just another local couple, the lawyer and her baker husband. Dawns with the smell of bread and freshly baked cakes, happiness with yeast.

"If I had said yes, maybe he wouldn't have done what he did."

But she was scared. She might not be a psychoanalyst like Bértola, but Verónica knew that men who turn to violence are almost always hopeless cases. And she had not studied the law all those years to end up as a punchbag for Kid Baker. She imagined the scandals there would be in that small town, the fingers pointed at her as she went by with her bruised face. She said no.

Out of spite, or because he was really convinced (she would never know which), the next day Romano went to see a magistrate and denounced what was happening in the federal police: files being burned, threats so that no-one said anything. The mafias thought democracy would not last long, so all they had to do was resist. Everyone was to stay quiet below ground until the triumphant crowing of the communists had died away again and the moustachioed Kerensky who had won the elections by reciting the preamble to the Constitution had been brought down a peg or two.

"Romano obeyed his conscience," says Bértola.

"He'd already fired the bullet that blew his brains out the day he went to see the magistrate a month later," Verónica concludes.

Still Bértola did not make a move, sitting primly opposite her, holding a glass of whisky (made in Argentina, to boot) that would be mostly water by the time the ice melted. All he could say was that she should stop collecting all these ghouls, should let go a little, try something different. He advised her to keep away from the scrounger she had taken in the previous night. She told him at least she had not given him a gun, as she had Miss Bolivia.

"You don't mean to say that . . ." She did mean to say that. The Bersa was the same one that Romano, "presumably and according to all the evidence", used to kill himself – as stated in the report she was sent, together with the few belongings he kept in his police locker.

"You should have got rid of that revolver."

Bértola's years of study cannot cope. He would need to be a guru, shaman, North-American psychiatrist and Middle-Eastern ayatollah all rolled into one even to begin to understand the beautiful woman sitting opposite him. He says goodbye to her with a kiss on the cheek. As soon as she has climbed into the taxi and he has shut his front door, he gulps down the whisky she left untouched.

Back in her apartment, Verónica finds Pacogoya sprawled on her living-room sofa, fast asleep in front of the television. On the screen there is a boxing match going on. Two overweight zombies are sporadically exchanging blows in the ring of a Las Vegas casino. The presenter is going on about how many millions of dollars the one who falls over last will make, and about a world-boxing federation that hands out and withdraws championship titles (Verónica has an image of them getting together in a smoke-filled room, gaunt Marlon Brando and Robert de Niro lookalikes, protected by baby-faced bodyguards, to decide who is to be crowned champion, who is to be dethroned).

Tempted by the fact that Pacogoya is fast asleep, Verónica slides her fingers into the pouch where he keeps his mobile. She would like to learn – she says, to justify her voyeurism to herself – who exactly this guy is who gets given books by Che Guevara in languages he does not understand and which he would not read even if they were in Spanish, because not reading is at the root of his ability to take the world as it comes and gain his feeble rewards from it.

The list of names on the mobile screen means nothing to her. Most of them are women, some companies, a few men's first names and then, as if daring her to take the next step, five glowing letters: "Uncle".

She suddenly thinks of *Call for the Dead*, the John Le Carré novel, one of the many good books her friends have never returned. She ought to ask Laucha the Mouse Giménez for it. Not only is she a voracious reader of borrowed novels, she is called "the Mouse" because she chews and digests everything she comes across: newsprint, the nocturnal terrors of her women friends recently turned forty, tales of lost happiness.

So this is not Verónica indulging in a spot of private phone tapping as she presses the mobile key. It is a homage to a great thriller writer that she performs while Pacogoya is out for the count, as though one of the blows the zombies are dishing out in Las Vegas had caught him squarely on the chin.

The phone rings somewhere or other.

"Don't ever call me again, you idiot."

She rings off immediately. In Las Vegas, the referee counts to ten and raises the winning arm of the zombie left standing. But Verónica is the one who has been knocked out.

It is scary to hear dead people talk when they are angry.

3

Like Jerusalem, Buenos Aires is a Holy City. Pacogoya wakes with this idea in his mind: he is being pursued by a mob of federal mercenaries, crucified – I didn't feel any pain, he tells Verónica – and then displayed in the middle of Plaza de Mayo.

"The Mothers were walking round as they have done every Thursday for the past thirty years. They were dying of old age before my eyes, Verónica. Collapsing like trees uprooted by drought, still demanding to know what had happened to their disappeared children. The people of Buenos Aires were looking on with their proverbial indifference: the middle classes who run from one bank to another and then at six in the evening choke all the entrances to the underground. And there I was, like a crucified Che Guevara no-one would ever shed a tear over, bleeding to death, giving up the ghost."

Pleasant conversation to spread on her toast, drink her lukewarm black coffee with and rush downstairs from as soon as the entry phone goes.

"It's my whale calf," says Verónica, pleased that for once someone has arrived in time to rescue her. "Don't move without telling me where you're going," she tells Pacogoya by way of goodbye. She has not told him about the call she made on his mobile to Uncle's apartment, the threatening voice.

*

Buenos Aires is a city of merchants and pilgrims, of monarchs free from control by any parliament who arrive at Aeroparque in their private jets and stare with genetic disdain at the grey line of the city's buildings to the West and the river like a brown sea to the East. They bound down the exclusive steps like thoroughbreds and ask their advisers who speak the native language of Argentina:

"Where is Patagonia?"

On the southern bank of this city as arrogant as the princes without principalities, the caravan Verónica uses as an office by the Riachuelo stands out from the metal skeletons of the stands, all of them dismantled because today is Monday and tonight there is no market.

The sun pours pure ultraviolet radiation over the caravan on this early August morning. There is no electricity. The batteries have run out and someone has cut the illegal connection to the supply network the magistrate had set up so that the inspector could use the sophisticated equipment inside: a computer almost as old as a pedal sewing machine, running a Windows 95 operating system that refuses to contemplate any less archaic diskette.

"Let's talk about it then, if that crappy machine won't work," says Verónica.

Back from his weekend fishing trip, the accountant says that is impossible. He cannot put into words what the black hole in the accounts signifies. Not a single transaction in order, not a single figure that adds up, no stamps or proof of origin that can be authenticated.

"This market is a joke, *doctora*." Fake and real goods have been cleverly mixed together, never sold on their own. "These people weren't born yesterday. They haven't come from Bolivia to improve themselves or save pennies for their vegetable plots."

"There are all kinds here," says Verónica. "The hard-working Bolivians who got here first are at the back of the queue now."

"So I'm right: this place is an open-air den of thieves. What I don't get is what happens to everything on days like today when there's no market. Where does it all go?"

"The merchandise circulates, crosses bridges, looking for other places to be sold. There are fourteen million souls in greater Buenos Aires. No-one is going to relax with so many potential customers."

The accountant almost understands. He is a man of numbers: even on his fishing trips he is not so worried if he catches huge *pejerreyes* or tiny *tariras*. What matters to him is how many there are and if they are fit to eat. He accepted the position – he explains to Verónica – because the money he was promised will come in handy.

"But I like a quiet life, I don't want my head to explode. Even the Ministry of the Economy is child's play compared to this."

"What the Lomas magistrate wants," Verónica explains, "is a façade of legality. He needs a file with figures he can bring out, even if it's only in the half-light, when the journalists or opposition politicians on the campaign trail start sniffing around for fresh scandals in this garbage."

"Who does the magistrate report to?"

"I suppose he has his own convictions."

The accountant spews out a guffaw and Verónica finally breathes more easily. His cynicism clears the air. In the end, what she wants is the same as the accountant: to live a quiet life, get paid what is owed her, then head off so that she can be a long way away when the shooting starts.

"Sort out all the figures on that," she says, pointing to a diskette which, even if there were electricity, the museum-piece computer would refuse to read. "Put them in a nice folder, like at secondary school, and make a neat cover with my name on it. I'll sign whatever you like, but let's get it done before the weekend so we can go home and wait for their call for us to come and collect our money."

The accountant's eyes clouded over as quickly as if he had taken an overdose of diazepan. A suicide on his window ledge would have been more reassuring, and would have had a less complicated immediate future, than having to face sitting at a working computer to draw up a financial report that did not blow up in the face of anyone daring to read it in public. Verónica knows as much and so she says: come on, Rosales.

"Come on, Rosales, you've done more complicated and less well-paid jobs than this. We're working for the state and the state doesn't really care about anything."

Touched by the magic wand of a witless fairy, Rosales confesses he had thought of visiting Disneyworld.

"To Disneylandia, as we used to call it. My two grandchildren asked me to go. I thought that with what I earn from this crap and with some of my savings, I could treat them. The kids are very excited about it: there are real Mickey Mouses, Red Indians who attack stagecoaches, giant hamburgers and roller coasters as high as our national debt."

If granddad Rosales gives up now, the whole precarious edifice created by the Lomas magistrate will come crashing down. The people across the river, the ones betrayed by Miss Bolivia and her bullet-ridden lover, are not going to stand around waiting with their arms folded. In fact, they are probably already enlisting their mercenaries. The slaughter could start at any moment.

"You can trust Rosales," the magistrate had told Verónica. "He's an honest sort. He's worried at already having reached pension age – 'I've managed to put a bit aside,' he told me, 'but they pay so little.' People like him move me, *doctora*. Their lives go by and yet they always respect the system. They don't make Argentines like that anymore."

"It's one week of hard work, Rosales. Possibly less. I promise I'll talk to his honour. You'll be able to go to Disneylandia without having to smash your piggy bank."

He gives a distant smile, a smile from the other side of a misted-over window. Rosales is no fool, but it is his grandchildren peering back at Verónica through his grey eyes, as well as Donald Duck, Daisy, Goofy and Walt Disney himself before he was cryogenically frozen.

"Nobody's going to kill us, are they?" he asks, still expressionless, his eyes lacking any spark.

"One week, Rosales. Then you can pack your bags for your trip with the kids. And don't forget to take an overcoat. It gets cold at night in Disneylandia."

4

The presenter announced the two runners-up before he opened the envelope with the name of Miss Bolivia in it. As he did so, Ana Torrente looked up into her still-adolescent sky, trying to find the stars that the stage spotlights prevented her from seeing. She closed her eyes to invent for a few seconds at least her own small firmament. She was just nineteen and had recently broken off her relationship with a fifty-year-old Colombian coffee grower whom she had fallen in love with when she saw his palace in Santa Cruz de la Sierra's most elegant neighbourhood. "I live here peacefully," he had told her, "but if I go back to Colombia I'm a dead man."

Even before she was crowned Miss Bolivia, Ana Torrente realized that the coffee her Colombian grower sold was the colour of milk. She imagined him shot dead by associates he had cheated or impatient rivals, with her lying beneath him on his bed, unable to force her way out as he stared at her through unseeing eyes and she had no idea why she was not dead too. This was no nightmare: it happened soon enough, but Ana was not in the bed at the time. Instead she was waiting, eyes tight shut, for the master of ceremonies to read her name out on the stage of the packed theatre in Santa Cruz.

The applause, lights and camera flashes snapping voraciously at her, a cheque in her name, a fake diamond crown and lots of bouquets of flowers led her to believe, for a few hours, that her life could change, that she was a real queen. The illusion faded when she was taken on tour through wretched villages in the Andes by a manager who promised her all the tinsel in Hollywood while they bucketed around in a clapped-out motorbike with sidecar. Time and again he presented her as the Queen of Bolivia to stony-faced indians packed into the villages squares, while scrofulous dogs and kids clung to her skirts, begging for toys, food, miracles.

Her manager, a shady *mestizo* who wore blue, yellow and red check shirts, a shiny formal waistcoat and black jacket with jeans, told her to be patient. They would soon reach the big capital cities and there she would be inundated with contracts for the catwalks of Europe. But they did not even reach Lima. A group of survivors from the Shining Path guerrillas intercepted their motorbike in the middle of the jungle, anxious to collect the debt the manager owed them for drugs from the tour he had made with the previous year's beauty queen. Once they had shot the manager and the leader of the gang had raped Miss Bolivia, the perpetually fleeing guerrillas melted away, pleased with their day's work. Rescued some hours later by a police patrol, Ana was returned in rags and bleeding to the place she had left by the wrong path.

Few people were surprised – and little was made of it, because it is well known that Shining Path are a bloodthirsty lot – that the body of the shot manager was missing its head when it was found.

*

Early Tuesday afternoon sees the arrival of the trucks, vans of all kinds and carts pulled by horses or pushed by squat, powerful Bolivians. Along with them come dozens of other Bolivians and indians from the north of Argentina. They carry huge bundles on their backs that often weigh more than they do. They are as laden down and blind as ants, and seem equally determined to reach their allotted destination. Each of them has their spot in the five hectares of the market on the banks of the Riachuelo. They have paid for the right to be in that exact place and will defend it, waving papers that have no legal validity. If anyone should question them, or try to take their pitch, they will pay with their blood.

"They're peaceful people," the Lomas de Zamora magistrate told Verónica, to convince her to accept the post of inspector at the market. "They only become violent if somebody tries to cheat them. Even then it's not individual violence: they organize as a group to defend themselves."

It is not violence from these miserable creatures struggling to survive that Verónica is afraid of. The judge is right: he spouts phrases and facts he has read and stored in his memory, although Verónica suspects that his only experience of the world beyond Lomas de Zamora is more related to Paris or New York, when someone powerful is set free in a case of faked bankruptcy or smuggling, in return for a new make of car, a nice house, or a trip abroad for his honour.

But the whale calf appointed by the magistrate to fetch and carry Verónica to and from the market does not agree with his honour's description of the market vendors.

"They're all filthy thieves," says Chucho as he drives along, more concerned to spy on his passenger's reaction in the rear-view mirror than to pay any attention to the vehicles that insist on crossing in front of him. He wrestles the wheel from side to side to avoid them and tells her: "Never trust a Bolivian, *doctora*. They shouldn't be allowed into Argentina. We should do what the Spaniards do with all those black Africans. They don't offer them land to plant their potatoes or hold their markets on. No, they drown them like kittens. Or send them back the next day, take them to the borders and let them loose in the desert."

"I see you don't have many Bolivian friends," says Verónica, more worried by Chucho's driving than his ecumenical racism.

"They aren't even friends with each other, *doctora*. They're treacherous. They're indians, so what can you expect? My little sister got the hots for one of them once. She even brought him home and wanted us to treat him like a proper boyfriend. He had money and he wasn't even Bolivian. He was from Jujuy in Argentina, but all indians are the same, aren't they? If you follow me."

"Yes, I follow you . . . mind out for that bus, it's almost on top of us!"

Chucho swung his arms and returned to more important matters.

"The *mestizo* did his best to ingratiate himself, but their dirty blood always gives them away. Those shifty eyes they have, they never look you in the face. When he had the nerve to ask me for Catalina's hand – I'm the eldest, you see, and with the old man pushing up the daisies I'm the one in charge in the family – I bust his nose with this fist here, see?" He shows Verónica his left hand, taking it off the steering wheel to do so. The car bounces off the avenue's central reservation. "I hit him with the jack I use for the car. He didn't cause any more trouble. He disappeared for good."

"What about Catalina?"

"She cried for a while, but now she's got a proper boyfriend, a skinny guy from a good family. They live out in San Isidro, but he's not one of those long-haired youths you often get there. He's a skinhead and knows what's what."

"I can imagine."

"You should see him! I think the kid's German, or ought to be. He knows the whole history of Germany. Those are proper countries, aren't they, *doctora*? No nonsense from Jews or Commies: look how they pulled down the wall they'd built. There may be democracy here now, but it won't last."

"So the boy's from a good family?"

"The best in San Isidro."

5

Not all the vehicles unload their contents at the market. One grey pick-up, with seats for carrying workmen, turns left a few metres before it reaches the stalls. It travels along a track for another five hundred metres, then makes its way into the Descamisados de América shanty town, a running sore on the wet ground close to the bank of Argentina's most polluted river; a tumour made up of hundreds of shacks, most of which are built out of cardboard, wood from fruit crates, planks stolen from construction sites and lots of bits of metal. Some of the roofs are corrugated iron, but the rest is scrap from the clandestine car yards which abound in the desolate realms of Buenos Aires Province.

The pick-up which turned left is a latest model Hiatsu 4×4. Air conditioning on so that the German couple inside reach their destination comfortably and without becoming dehydrated. Their carefree wandering round the newly laid-out streets of Puerto Madero in the centre of Buenos Aires was rudely interrupted by four armed men who abducted them in broad daylight, wearing no masks and only two hundred metres from a naval guardhouse.

The German couple had left their five-star hotel at 10 a.m., following the sort of abundant breakfast that only northern Europeans can stomach. They wanted to stretch their legs for a while before they sat down again in a restaurant where for a modest twenty dollars tourists can stuff themselves with the kind of juicy rump or sirloin steaks they could not get for three times as much in Europe.

The language of Goethe is not very popular in Argentina, despite the considerable number of German immigrants who settled in the northern suburbs of Buenos Aires and in the provinces of Córdoba and Rio Negro, drawn to Argentina by the fall of the Third Reich and guarantees from the government of the time that they would not be bothered by the fanatical Jews who after the war tried desperately to seek redress for some of the Nazi atrocities. The couple cried out for help in German, but before any polyglot could translate their pleas, they were beaten into silence and forced into the Hiatsu. Several passersby looked on indifferently, turning away from them just as their parents had done back during the dictatorship in the 1970s, even though the people being kidnapped then were shouting in Spanish.

With this couple – a man and a woman in their sixties who both have very blond hair – now being asked to get out of the car at gunpoint, that makes six passengers from the *Queen of Storms*, staying in three different hotels, who have been abducted. So far no reports, no official complaints have surfaced in the media. Nothing to disturb the tourists grounded in Buenos Aires. Not so much as a rumour. The three kidnappings were clean, lightning operations carried out by professionals. All of them took place almost simultaneously, in the street and far from their respective hotels, while the victims were walking along without a care in the world, but separated from the rest of the herd.

"The Babel of a city you see before you is best enjoyed if you walk around it without following any fixed route, wandering as you please," each couple was informed by one of the guides from the ship, the one who often gets given books written by his revolutionary lookalike, or T-shirts with his image printed on them. "You'll always come across a local who will be happy to help and direct you if you are lost," Pacogoya told them by way of encouragement. "We Argentines are very friendly towards all foreigners, provided they don't come from Bolivia."

Only the capture of the drugs baron Osmar Arredri and his beautiful girlfriend Sirena Mondragón appears to have aroused the interest of the charlatans in the press, if not the police. The latter are well aware that the Colombian drugs-mafia boss's kidnappers come from within their own ranks. The credentials they showed to get into the hotel were real. Worst of all, and what most infuriates Deputy Inspector Walter Carroza of the serious-crime squad in the federal police, is that he is sure several of those involved work in his own office at headquarters. Possibly they even sit very close to him and smoke his cigarettes while they are writing their reports.

"Let's meet and talk of old times," Walter Carroza tells Verónica. She called him when she saw his ungainly figure on television. As ever when facing the press, he made declarations he did not want to make and, like most of his colleagues, resorted to phrases such as "no comment while the investigations are ongoing", investigations which are always "about to be brought to a successful conclusion".

They meet in a bar on calle Alsina. At midday it is full of office workers having lunch, but by this time of evening it has taken on the charm of a refuge. Only a few of these secret hiding places are left in Buenos Aires and this one only stays open since its owner stubbornly refuses to close earlier because, he says, "I like watching couples kissing and cuddling at nightfall over a cup of coffee". The couples who give pleasure to this immigrant from Ourense in Galicia, who has been living in Argentina for forty years, are penniless adulterers, office workers and shop assistants whose only opportunity to meet, talk of love and play at being happy comes at this time of day, and in hidden corners like this one.

"You know I can't talk in the department. All our phones are tapped by the intelligence services, no matter what our rank is or what case we're on," says Walter, lighting up a cigarette that the bar owner lets him smoke so long as he keeps it hidden under the table. Verónica did not want to see him for old time's sake. She is more interested in passing on the information she received the previous night when she went round the market with Chucho. "You should never have accepted that job, Verónica, it's too dangerous."

"Yeah, I could be killed, I know. So what? Every time I open my front door I tell myself: here comes some animal who's going to beat me up or stab me so he can get his hands on fifty bucks to feed his habit."

"Thoughts like that can become premonitions. Try to think positively."

"Look who's talking!"

When he laughs, the teeth Deputy Inspector Carroza reveals are 90 per cent nicotine and 10 per cent tooth enamel. His sharp, angular features look even more gaunt. This is something he cannot or will not change – "my skull has the right to enjoy life too" is his motto.

Verónica's informer at the market is a smuggler from Jujuy, an indian who has made a pile but still likes to take a personal interest in his peripatetic business. From the first day, to win the inspector's favour he has offered to find her a digital camera or a latest model laptop, at a cost equivalent to half a dozen pairs of the knickers the Bolivian women sell.

"He lives on the quiet there in the Descamisados de América shanty town. He saw them when they were being taken out of a Japanese 4×4 in broad daylight. In twos: a French couple, then a Japanese pair, then two Germans. All of them elderly and all obviously rolling in it."

"If he saw them, others must have done so too."

Carroza's thought is both banal and pointless. Both he and Verónica know that nobody in shanty towns talks to the police. Every shack is a silent tomb.

"Why haven't there been any reports of the kidnappings?"

"There have been, but they've all been quietly filed away. The minister spoke in person to the police chief. He passed on the order. When people in power have us by the balls, we cops are even more silent than the shanty-town dwellers."

Carroza explains that the minister wants everything sorted out quickly before the news gets out. There are big cheeses in the hotel owners' associations and tourist agencies. In recent years tourism in Argentina has turned into a gold mine: investment funds have poured millions into the hotel business and so have important money launderers, the kind of people who do not take kindly to a bunch of gunmen spitting on their barbecue. Nor does the minister want the enticing prosperity that comes ever closer with each new hotel built (contravening all the city-planning regulations) to be put at risk by any untimely request for information from the opposition, egged on by members of his own party annoyed that the minister did not invite them to the trough.

Veronica and Carroza agree that the secret cannot be kept much longer. The money to be made from revealing the kidnappings is increasing with every passing hour. The dealers in leaks to the press (most of whom nest inside the Central Police Department) are simply holding their breath, testing the atmosphere, judging how best to do a deal with the media without getting caught out.

"Some colleague or loudmouth from the shanty is going to strike a match in the distillery in the next few hours," says Carroza.

"Talking of fires, you're filling this place with smoke. You'll get the poor Spaniard's bar closed down."

"The fire-brigade chief is a friend of mine," Carroza reassures her. "Now tell me the real reason you called."

"Romano," says Verónica, point blank. "I want to know who killed him."

Carroza crushes out the cigarette on the floor. The bones of his skull stand out as if it were Hallowe'en. He leans back in his chair, shaking his head slowly from side to side.

"What for, Verónica? Knowing who it was won't change anything."

"Do you know?"

She has been asking him this ever since he has known her. Almost from the time, soon after their marriage, that she and Romano invited him to dinner. Before turning up, Carroza went down to the port. Ignoring the tramps in the street, he called in at a bar on the corner of San Martín and Córdoba where the ladies of the night gather, and picked out the one who looked least like a professional whore. After speaking to her for a minute to make sure she did not swallow her "s"s, he told her to go to the bathroom, wipe off her make-up and come with him. "I'm not arresting you," he said. "We're going to have supper at a friend's place."

"It was a nice evening, really pleasant," says Verónica when Carroza mentions it now to ease the tension.

"That whore was a good sort, they don't make them like that anymore. Even Romano was fooled into thinking she was my girl." They both laugh, but laughter is not much protection in the middle of a storm. Ever since the recent evening with Bértola, Verónica cannot escape the memory of her ex-husband. As if he were coming out of the dark to look after her. Or to beat her again. "You know I have no idea who killed him. I suspect everyone on the roster, but they're very careful. There was some kind of plebiscite, Verónica, and Romano got the thumbs down."

"Did you vote too?" Carroza does not defend himself. He has never been one to pray for the fallen. He never sheds a tear when he goes to the funeral of a colleague gunned down on duty or shot by the kind of petty crook who boards buses to steal people's spare change. Romano's death did not move him any more than that of any other guinea pig used by the system to try out their medicines. It is true, he was his friend, but he could have kept his mouth shut. He does not like saying it, but Verónica is forcing him to. "You could have prevented him being killed. He would have asked to quit the force and nothing would have happened, if only you'd agreed to go into the interior with him."

"And probably today Kid Baker's little wife would be dead thanks to him and buried in the bucolic cemetery of Villa Dolores or Serrezuela. But you didn't tell me whether you voted as well . . ." Deputy Inspector Carroza stands up. He has no more cigarettes anyway and it is true the bar reeks of tobacco. If a health inspector came in now, the Spaniard would have to bribe him to avoid having the bar closed and Carroza would end up paying. Verónica is still sitting there, not looking at him. "I'll go and see what I can do with the information that grass gave you, before my colleagues start using it."

At that moment another couple comes in. They are young: she is short, he is on the lanky side, wearing a worn suit and shirt. The pair of them have obviously been at work for the past ten hours. The brides of Dracula at dawn would look healthier than they do, but they keep going in the knowledge that for the price of a couple of coffees they have half an hour to stroke each other's hands across the table and stare into one another's eyes as though they were someone and somewhere else.

Verónica does not turn round, either to look at the couple entering the bar, or to say goodbye to Carroza, who is paying the bill with the owner, parapeted behind the counter.

"You shouldn't smoke so much," the Spaniard tells him in a fatherly way.

"I promise to stop when I make inspector."

Carroza turns to leave the bar. He pats his empty pocket just in case a last cigarette has fallen down the lining. He is as on edge as he always is almost twenty-four hours a day, and fed up with cops' widows. He sees the car screech to a halt outside the plate glass window.

Verónica, who was expecting him to walk past her without a word, cannot understand why Deputy Inspector Carroza suddenly flies though the air from the counter and lands on top of her, knocking her to the floor and smashing the table, their empty cups and the two glasses of water as he does so.

Carroza's flying dive must have disconcerted the gunman in the car too. Bewildered, he fires and cuts down the lanky lovelorn clerk before he has even got properly settled and begun to whisper sweet nothings to his Cinderella. The car disappears long before she closes her eyes, feels the tears welling up and lets out the funereal howl common to all women who have lost their man.

6

It was not easy for Ana Torrente to reach Buenos Aires. It is not the same arriving at Ezeiza airport on an international flight, even if it is from Bulgaria with connections, as getting off a bus at the Retiro terminus following a journey of almost twenty-four hours from Salta. It is not the same kind of people and the smells are very different. At Retiro you disembark amidst the ruins of the city; it is not the atmosphere of the elegant neighbourhoods, it is another planet. Although the sun shines for everyone, it is the distance between Pluto and Mercury. The air is saturated with the smell of cheap fried food from the stalls, dark-skinned people are everywhere, street vendors and beggars, thieving youngsters out of their heads on glue who will never reach adolescence.

And Ana Torrente, like so many of the local immigrants, was scared.

"But I didn't stop to look at the Torre de los Ingleses or the Sheraton opposite Retiro square. I went straight to the post at the terminus and asked for you."

"You did the right thing." She has come back to him, just as she did the day she arrived. She likes to hear his voice. It does not matter what he is saying, it comforts her, satisfies her, calms and encourages her. It must be something to do with her hormones, because the man beside her is on his way to the scrapheap. In the gloomy, sordid room, stretched out on a bed they are not the first to use, he is like a fake Egyptian mummy, a papier-mâché android, a robot whose only practical use is to listen to her, hold her and, occasionally, to prevent her being killed. "You'll have to get out of here," he says.

"Where to, Bolivia?"

The noonday sun is glaring even through the slats in the shutters. He almost has to close his eyes when he goes over to look out at nothing, the filthy pavements, people walking past head down, caught up in worlds there is no point getting too close to, worlds that explode every so often, spattering him with blood, wounding him if he is not continually on his guard.

"I nearly got killed yesterday," he tells her. "Near here, only three blocks away, in a miserable bar on Alsina. The shots weren't meant for me, but I was close enough." Miss Bolivia is not impressed by his stories anymore. They are all he has to tell her, like a grandfather telling fairy tales. She dozes off, even manages to dream a little. "I've got a friend. Retired from Interpol. He lives in Spain now, in the Canaries."

"What does he do there, play horseshoes?"

"When he was in service in the mother country he helped organize a network of Latin-American girls. All from the Southern Cone, white women," he explains. "They're all so contented no-one can persuade them to come back. They're saving in euros."

"So your friend is an elderly pimp."

He feels so weary he starts to get dressed. She asks if they can stay a while longer. She feels sleepy and can never relax outside. It is only in here, with him, that she still feels her life could get better.

"So you're going to stay."

"There's a job to be done," she says. He smiles his nicotine smile; he is already desperate for a cigarette, but he has run out of them again. He rescues one of the butts from the floor and lights it. The flame from the lighter singes the bunch of hairs protruding from his nostrils. "You've got more hairs on your snout than on your nut." Ana ruffles the fuzz on the top of his head. "Of course I'm going to stay, to finish what we began," she adds. She pulls him towards her while he is taking a drag at his cigarette, laughing at his cough and the wheezing sound like an out-of-tune organ in some abandoned cathedral that comes from his chest. "Afterwards, if you like, I'll be a whore in Spain. But let's finish first."

*

Sometimes he enjoys being like this with women he hardly knows. Although the previous evening his pleasure had been spoiled: first of all by Verónica insisting on knowing who killed her husband, allowing the doubt to ruin her life in a way he cannot conceive, but which leaves him feeling uncomfortable for days.

What's dead is done with. Like the lanky guy who sat in the wrong place and, to top it all, suffered the indignity of the people who took his corpse home having to explain to his widow "in what circumstances the death took place". The widow, a truculent, obese woman – 140 kilos of fat in a ball a metre and a half round – refused to accept the dead body. "Throw him to the dogs," she said. "Let that little tart bury him. No, better still, let her dig a double grave, because tomorrow I'll find her and kill her."

Why make a moral judgment about someone who, one sunny morning or evening with the threat of rain in the air, like yesterday, is gunned down, stabbed to death, or killed in whatever way occurs to the hired killer, whether by accident or design? What's dead is done with.

He is no Clark Kent, to disappear into a phone booth and come out as Superman in Metropolis. It is true he did fly yesterday evening, but no more than a metre. He had not flown like that for years, not since he stopped playing scrum-half for the university team in Montevideo, back in the days when he still dreamed of defending the law some other way.

Yesterday evening's flight saved the skin of Verónica Berruti. The widow of his colleague Romano. An attractive woman with whom, in his nicotine way, he has always been in love.

He is proud of what he did; it is the best thing that has happened to him in a long while. He would not have liked her to be killed under his hairy nose, thanks to some obnoxious, complicated business involving contraband mafias, asphalt pirates. That was not why she had graduated as a lawyer, just as he would not have graduated, if he had gone on with his studies, to defend cheap thieves, rescue them from young offenders' institutions and let them roam the streets armed to the teeth, on their own or in gangs, raping and killing for pure pleasure, crack cocaine oozing from their pores.

Before the patrol cars arrived, while the Spaniard was shouting from the basement – "Don't shoot, I'll give you everything, I'm unarmed" – and the dumpy woman was trying to clasp her lanky lover to her although he was already a corpse, Deputy Inspector Carroza plucked Verónica from the floor like King Kong grasping the blonde from the Empire State building and got her out of the bar. He crunched his way over the shattered glass and threw her into the back seat of his car, parked in a no-parking zone thanks to an out-of-date police permit.

It was then that Verónica finally realized she was in way over her head, even if she had a massive, well-armed whale calf to fetch and carry her to and from the market. That son-of-a-bitch judge should have warned her what she was getting in to. And to top it all, his honour wanted a nice, tidy report, a novel with a happy ending so that his party boss did not write anything unkind on his file and spoil his chances of becoming a minister. He had gone to war with an army of cheap clowns, fake lions, who were defeated before they had opened fire. And as he held forth on his tapped telephone about the independence and majesty of justice, all the while he was receiving instructions and advice by text on his mobile.

Carroza wanted to take her somewhere safer, but Verónica insisted on going home.

"Have you got a gun at least?"

"I lent it to a friend."

"Great. And what happens if your friend kills someone: her husband, for example?"

"I don't think she has one."

"Her lover then, or anyone she runs into."

"I didn't lend it her so she could kill someone, but so she could defend herself. It's here, halfway down the block," said Verónica, pointing to the entrance to her building.

They said goodbye inside the car, with a friendly kiss on the cheek. Smooth skin against papyrus.

"You never answered my question," she said.

"Go straight up and ring me on my mobile," he said. "Confirm everything is O.K."

"Any further advice?"

"Don't go out alone. Call that miserable excuse for a magistrate and tell him to give you twenty-four-hour protection. At least until you've finished with the market."

He has been in love with Verónica for so long that now, seeing her walk off calmly swaying her hips, he is glad he abandoned his studies in Montevideo, that he is not a lawyer but occasionally an ageing Clark Kent zipping in and out of phone booths in Metropolis.

7

It is not a twin tower miraculously still standing in the far south of America and is no target for Al-Qaeda fundamentalists. It is an old forty-floor building near Retiro, a few blocks from Catalinas. That is where the modern office blocks are, glass-fronted to imitate the ones in Manhattan and crammed with hundreds of salaried bureaucrats.

This older building is called Alas. It stands out from the others and was built in the 1950s. The people who live here are Argentine air-force officers with their wives and children, those who have not managed to acquire a residence in Buenos Aires apart from these dilapidated, antiquated apartments. To reach them you have to travel in lifts that usually do not work, or get stuck between floors, causing panic among those who are claustrophobic and protests from the security guards, who have to come and rescue all those trapped several times a day.

On the fortieth floor, one step from paradise, there was once a big room for a radio-communications network. Nowadays, with the advances of mobile technology, the internet and other computer plagues, talking by radio has become a pastime for the nostalgic and the radio has been shut down.

This eyrie perched on top of a city that rarely bothers to look up, a place with a view over the Río de la Plata and Puerto Madero, and very close to Uncle's apartment, was where the federal police chose to house Osmar Arredri and his beautiful girlfriend Sirena Mondragón.

They guard them in pairs: two cops replace each other every six hours. They come in, mutter "hello" and sit down to read the newspapers, do the crosswords (only ever half-finishing them), scribble combinations for the winners at Palermo or San Isidro racetracks, drink their *maté* and let time go by (something all of them are expert at). The Colombian and his girl cannot respond to the greeting because they are both gagged. These gags are only removed so that they can eat the provisions brought up by Rosamonte. She is the maternal touch in the kindergarten, a junior officer in the police public-relations department. Her real name is Rosa Montes, but she is so skinny her colleagues always call her Rosamonte after a brand of *maté* leaves, because in that funny, clever way of theirs they reckon she is as thin as the metal straw used to drink the stuff.

A fourteen-inch television screen shows the programmes the guards are interested in watching. Only they can hear the sound because they are wearing earphones. Rosamonte listens in whenever there is a cookery show on. Their guests cannot see the screen. The idea is to keep them isolated from the world, to break their spirit without having to resort to physical violence. Someone used to living the high life on everything that easy money can buy is not going to take being tied up and gagged for long, unable to touch his beautiful mermaid or scratch his nose or arse, only allowed to go to the bathroom every eight hours and having to eat the junk Rosamonte buys from the local fast-food stores.

Rosamonte has been given special permission to do this job. She prefers her public-relations work at headquarters, where she attends people, visits businesses, does institutional promotion. On the side she also sells personal and property security services from the company run by Oso "the Bear" Berlusconi.

"There's going to be trouble," says one of the cops just coming on duty. He stabs at the television screen with the remote, trying to find a news programme. "They're taking tourists from the stranded ship."

"Who is?" asks Rosamonte.

"What's that sound?"

There is a sound from the ceiling like a trouser zip being pulled. "Rats."

"Don't give me that. How does a rat get up to the fortieth floor?"

"In the lifts I guess, when they're working. Who's snaffling the tourists?"

"Nobody knows," says the other newly arrived cop. "But everyone's in a state about it."

Rosamonte pours a *maté* for the first new cop.

"This is the port area. There are more rats than people." In order to sweeten his mood, she explains that there are rats even in Puerto Madero, where an apartment can cost a million dollars. "Pedigree rats come off the boats and mix with the native ones to create a new oligarchy. Buenos Aires, a melting pot for rats."

"She sure knows how to talk, doesn't she?" says the cop who spoke last. Even with his bulging eyes he cannot make out any breasts on her.

"How long is this going to last? I'm fed up with it," says the one who was looking up at the ceiling. He sits down: "I don't like being here." He gazes across at their captives. They are not moving and seem to have dozed off. "The Colombians could turn up at any moment to take them back. They'd shoot the crap out of us."

"They won't take on the air force," says Rosamonte. "That would be war. Besides, Oso is coming to take over tonight."

The male cops laugh. A war with Colombia, that's all we need, they say. The talk turns to football. They recall the time Colombia thrashed Argentina 5–1; what a disaster, a worse defeat than in the Malvinas. Football bores Rosamonte and there are no cookery programmes on television, so she turns to look at their prisoners. Oso has told her they are not to see her face, but she stares at them openly. What are they going to remember, if they do manage to get out of there alive? Rosamonte's face is thin and bony. There is hardly anything feminine about her – and she likes women. Her male colleagues had better not find that out, or she will be in for a hard time. Dykes are harassed in every police station until they cannot stand it any more and resign, or end up raped and beaten. Ordinary women, the ones who join thinking they are Charlie's Angels, also get treated badly, but in general they say not a word, they just put up with it: the benefits they enjoy on the force outweigh their disgust. And if any of them are crazy enough to report their tormentors to the courts or television, they can forget about a career in the police: their male colleagues will not rest until they are turfed out or shot to pieces in a gun battle.

Rosamonte passes the time surveying their captives. She does not feel any pity for them. They are foreigners and, not only that, Colombian. And all Colombians are drug traffickers. Wherever they go they are regarded with suspicion. Nobody wants them around: in Europe they ask them for visas and documents that do not even exist. They put them through an X-ray machine before they let any of them in. Argentina is not like that, say the immigration officials. They can all get in with no problem – diplomats with enough drugs to kill a horse, politicians loaded down like mules with saddlebags stuffed full of dollars. But if some poor fool tries to smuggle a Japanese camera in, he had better watch out, because it will be confiscated and he will end up in jail.

Osmar Arredri opens his eyes and Sirena Mondragón seems to have woken up too. They allow Rosa to gaze at them and stare back, gagged, tied up, not struggling or protesting. Rosa Montes thinks they would look with kinder eyes at the rat still scuttling above the ceiling.

8

Crunching their way over broken glass and warm blood come the newsmen, cameras on their shoulders and microphones at the ready. They arrived even before the ambulance and police. As soon as she saw them, the dumpy woman went even more pallid. The Spaniard went out to meet them.

"It was a robbery, but they didn't get anything," he said, following instructions from Carroza, who a couple of seconds earlier had recommended he not even mention him.

"Tell them the lanky guy and his bit on the side were here on their own."

"What if she says something?" asked the Spaniard.

"Yes, who else is going to say something, the lanky squirt isn't going to, is he?" Carroza asked, telling him: "Say another couple was here, you don't know who they were, but they ran out as soon as the shooting stopped. Perhaps they were part of the gang, tell them."

The Spaniard was not convinced by this version: "If I say that, they're going to take me in to make a statement. Perhaps I'd better tell them the truth."

But Carroza insisted: "None of that crap, don't give me away. If she says another couple was in here, tell the press the guy was tall, fair-haired and blue-eyed."

"I can't lie that far," the Spaniard muttered, just before the newsmen appeared and before Carroza could repeat that he was not to give the game away, that he would pay for the smashed windows and the lanky guy's work insurance would pay for his funeral, if he had kept up with the instalments.

That same night he went looking for Ana Torrente. They met the next day.

When she had come to see him as soon as she reached Buenos Aires, Carroza had not wanted to fuck her.

"She's only a girl," he told Scotty, "and she's scared stiff."

Scotty did not believe him.

"When did that ever stop you?" Scotty asked.

"I'm no paedophile," Carroza insisted. (At that point he still thought Ana Torrente was a minor.) "She can't be seventeen yet. It's priests who are the paedophiles. They have it off with the schoolgirls who go to them to do penance. They touch them up in the confessional. Either that or they get choirboys to go down on them. I'm a cop, Scotty."

Scotty stared at him in complete astonishment, as if he were a Siamese cat in a shanty town. How could he believe him? They had known each other since they both joined the federal police. Scotty is of Irish descent, but in Argentina they call him Scotty, just as they called all Spaniards Galicians and anyone from the Middle East a Turk. All these places are so far away, in the north of the planet. What recent graduate from police training school knows where Glasgow or Dublin are? They barely know the names of the streets of Buenos Aires.

"So why did you end up fucking her, if you're not a paedophile?"

"Because she turned twenty two months ago. And because Patrón sent her to me."

Patrón is chief of the federal police in the province of Salta. He was appointed for a year as a temporary replacement for someone who had died, but has stayed for twenty. "Not even the president can shift me from here" is Patrón's boast, as he goes through the list of all the presidents who have come and gone while he has remained untouchable in his northern fiefdom.

"This is my place in the world," he had told Carroza when a few glasses of gin loosened his tongue the time Carroza was following the trail of some asphalt pirates all over Argentina. "This province is a patriarchal society – what am I saying, it's pure feudalism, Yorugua." He calls him that because it is back slang for Uruguay, where Carroza was born. Nobody in the federal police ever forgets to remind him that he is an outsider, that despite the fact that he has sworn loyalty to the national anthem, flag and emblems of Argentina, he is still a foreigner. "Salta is a business paradise. And I don't even have to move from here," Patrón says, slapping the table in the bar opposite police head-quarters.

The members of the provincial police hated his guts. Every time there was a "fishing expedition", as they called raids on the coca-drying operations, Patrón would get there before them. "This is a liberated zone, only the federal police can enter," he would say, waving warrants from federal magistrates and secret orders from the central government that he pulled out of his magician's top hat. Since he had no federal force of his own in Salta, he recruited from among the *mestizos* in the provincial police, the ones worst hit by hunger or vices, a brutish army that followed him the way farm animals follow the first one to move.

"They picked her up on the streets in Salta, poor thing," Carroza says. "Miss Bolivia, just think. If you saw her on T.V. or in a magazine you'd fall on your knees. She's a virgin, Scotty. When they saw she was blonde, they took her to Patrón. They must have thought it was a federal offence."

The two cops laugh. The gin not only loosens their tongues, it encourages their flights of fancy. She is like a Botticelli painting or a De Quincey poem. They are inspired for a few moments, as far as a cop in this Holy City ever can be.

He did not want to fuck her, Deputy Inspector Walter Carroza, the Yorugua. The girl showed him her I.D. card.

"See? I'm an adult." She convinced him. He let her lead him on, slowly, it takes time to get him aroused.

"I'm too skinny," he warned her, "it'll be like embracing a skeleton, I don't think you'll like it."

There is no way that anything like love can be born in the sordid rented rooms near headquarters, but a calm sort of relationship did grow up between them, one they both needed and was useful to both of them. He protected her, she gave him a hand when he asked her to. Ana told Carroza that every bone, every cartilage of his was stuffed with wisdom and tenderness. That was all she needed, she said, begging him not to abandon her even if she was the one who asked him to. And Carroza told Ana that her beauty was a chemical weapon of mass destruction, an arsenal concealed in her perfect body, a dose of genocide in her blue eyes and gaze, and that if she helped him she would never be alone, at least as long as she was in Buenos Aires.

"You sent her to the stake. Now the bonfire's alight, you're trying to save her by throwing petrol on it," said Scotty when Carroza told him he had advised her to leave the country.

"All my women are getting shot at, Scotty!" Carroza protested. "I've been a confirmed bachelor for far too long to end up twice a widower."

Impossible for them not to mention Verónica, as they had done when Romano was killed and Carroza had told him he would let some time pass, then approach her and see what happened. But someone else got in before him, the ombudsman, a man twenty years older than her, the father she was looking for.

"The first time Verónica was left a widow by Romano, Yorugua. But the second time, when her ombudsman was killed, she was left an orphan," Irish Scotty tells him. "Try again, don't let anyone else get in before you this time. And don't wait for her to get shot."

9

She knows it is too late to get off; the carousel is spinning too fast. If her parents had been watching they would have found her funny, with her scared face and her fruitless lunges to grasp the prize. But this time on the merry-go-round there are no horses or Dumbos or planes, only murderers, and she is having no fun at all. Nor are her parents watching her, or her men: she is all alone, looking at herself like someone about to stick a knife in her own body.

She calls the magistrate, but he is not there. He is not in Lomas de Zamora. "He isn't even in Argentina," the court secretary tells her. "He's gone to Melbourne for a jurists' conference."

"A magistrate from Lomas at a jurists' conference?"

"Yes, interesting, isn't it? Comparative jurisprudence must mean as much to him as Jung's deep psychology does to a forensic scientist, but the Party is paying and the Party is paid by the taxpayers who support this rotten system; stupid men and women like you and me."

Laucha Giménez, who has offered to bolster her spirits for a few hours, says Verónica has become anti-democratic. Halfway to becoming a fascist, in fact.

"What do you want, another dictatorship?"

"They don't need one," Verónica tries to explain. "That's why it doesn't happen. Now they've got these unspeakable thieves. They don't cost as much as the military and they have one big advantage: they don't go round making speeches about the fatherland and it would never occur to them to go to war with Chile or England."

The day before a poor innocent bystander had been shot in the centre of the city, but today none of the media even mentioned it. Only her and the Spanish bar owner remembered it, for very different reasons. Too late to pull any punches. Even if the accountant drew up a report in which the Riachuelo market came out looking like the Disneylandia he had promised to take his grandchildren to, her appointment as inspector had lit a fuse. And if it was one big powder keg, the tiniest spark meant danger.

"We have to get to the bottom of it, now we've gone this far," she tells the accountant on the telephone, to the dismay of Laucha Giménez, who cannot understand where her friend's vocation for suicide comes from.

"I do my job, *doctora*," says the accountant. "You have to understand, I'm a professional, not a mercenary. I'm not going to throw my reputation to the dogs for the sake of a magistrate."

"A magistrate who's abandoned us," growls Verónica, then immediately wishes she hadn't said it. Laucha's warning grimaces are too late to stop her. At the far end of the line, the accountant is silent as the grave, until finally he blurts out:

"What do you mean, he's abandoned us?"

Verónica gestures back at Laucha who is waving her arms at her. It's as if the two of them were trying to work out how not to scare a coward with a tale that would make Poe or Lovecraft's hair stand on end.

"Nothing. He's out of the country for a couple of days at a conference for jurists. I called to discuss it with him."

"To discuss what, *doctora*?"

"Getting to the bottom of what's going on at the market."

She tries to wriggle free from the avalanche of questions and to reassure him, but the accountant is a grandfather who has principles. He has grandchildren he wants to take to Disneylandia, but not at the expense of his integrity. He is a professional, not a mercenary.

They laugh when he hangs up, after Verónica's efforts to reassure or confuse him.

"While you were at it, you should have told him that when you were having coffee with a policeman friend they sprayed you with bullets," says Laucha. "Then you'd see how quickly he forgets the idea of going with his grandchildren to the land of Mickey Mouse and Donald Duck."

"It's the magistrate who is in for a surprise," Verónica replies. "If he knew what's about to hit him he would hide in a kangaroo pouch and ask for asylum in Australia."

Laucha points out that Verónica is the one most in danger, not the magistrate or the accountant.

"You're the inspector. It's your face everyone has seen in those dark market alleys." Laucha is already nibbling at fifty with her tiny, sharp teeth. She stopped ovulating two years earlier and now when she is with a man has no idea if she is flushing because she is turned on or because it is the menopause. She is small, one metre sixty tall, still shapely, with a healthy sexual appetite, although that is causing her problems. She does not understand frigid women. "They don't know how to fuck," she says. "They're the victims of a lamentable *machista* education."

"They start with what should be the end," says Verónica knowingly. "They want to get married."

She says this out of bitter experience. She is forty-five and has an exultant body, a cup overflowing with life that has suddenly become target practice for dark, shadowy figures.

"You need a lover," Laucha declares. "One who isn't a cop, a magistrate, or a certified accountant. And not that useless guy you stay up all night waiting for. A man like a sports car with the hood down, so that you can see the stars even if you're flying along at a thousand k.p.h. Someone who's more interested in the beauties of Andromeda than the traffic lights on the street corner. An artist, a romantic, even if in his spare time he's a whore or a drug addict."

Verónica reminds her of the experience she had with the Tibetan, a rock musician.

"I gave up everything when I fell in love with him. I closed my office and joined him in the caravan he and the band went on tour in. Rehearsals, interviews, concerts with hallucinating, noisy adolescents shouting 'Do it! Do it!' all the time, as if it was a mass love-in."

"That's what they buy the tickets for, don't get jealous," the Tibetan would tell her between the screaming and the drum solos, concerts where they sweated on stage like miners digging in their mines, cursing a capitalist society destined for the holocaust in songs impossible to decipher, then between tours getting together with an accountant the spitting image of the grandfather Verónica has just been talking to. They wanted proper accounts and safe investments for their money. "There's no way we're going to leave any of it here in this country, it's bound to get stolen," the Tibetan used to insist. When he was not drugged, he dreamt of a white house with windows looking out on the Mediterranean.

"And when he was drugged?"

"Two white houses overlooking the Mediterranean. It's the same world, Laucha. There aren't two planets circling around one on top of the other, the unknown dimension is part of the system, the mysteries of having to pay taxes so that the powerful can continue to pull the strings and go on making money. When our bones ache, or our joints feel stiff, it's not due to our hormones, Laucha, it's the strings digging into our flesh where we've been pulled and pushed around so much at other people's whim. 'They climax,' the Tibetan used to boast to the others in his band, 'well, some of them do, I've never counted how many, but they touch themselves while we're playing. But it's not sex, just madness.'"

It lasted three months. That was as long as Verónica could hold out. The tours did not always bring in money, so what Verónica had saved went on emergencies and debts, concerts cancelled due to bad weather or because nobody turned up – the Tibetan was no Charly García. Also there were towns in the interior where the only tunes they ever heard were folkloric dances: when they saw "THE TIBETAN AND HIS BAND" on posters, the people in those godforsaken holes thought they could dance square dances and quadrilles to their music.

"I hit rock bottom and decided that was enough. Besides, I'm a lawyer. After three months his probationary period was up and I fired him."

She had opened her legal office again. As she did not have a cent, she put an advert in the paper and that was how Bértola turned up. From then on they shared expenses: traumas and inheritances, Oedipal complexes and habeas corpuses.

"And what happened between you and Bértola the other night when you went to his place?" Laucha wants to know, already savouring what she expects to hear from Verónica.

"He said goodnight with a peck on the cheek."

10

Fewer than ten blocks separate the Alas Building and the Buenos Aires Sheraton. In the Alas building, Osmar Arredri and Sirena Mondragón are still tied up and gagged, under the watchful eye of the guard who is the twin of the rat scampering along the rafters. In the Buenos Aires Sheraton, the manager is trying to convince the dozen journalists and as many cameramen who have gathered that nobody has called a press conference there.

The executives of the hotel owners' association are adamant: the abduction in broad daylight of three tourist couples from the *Queen of Storms* cruise liner has to be kept quiet until they reappear. Buenos Aires is not Bogotá or Lima; Argentina is not Chile or Peru. If the kidnapping for ransom of foreign tourists were to hit the front pages, the lucrative tourist industry could be badly hit. It is one thing to travel to the Third World because it is cheap and they copy what is on offer in Europe so well. It is quite another if travellers become goods to be bartered for. The government has called the tourism bosses to make sure the news does not get out. The *Queen of Storms* needs a few more days' repairs; meanwhile, according to the government "the law enforcement officers have begun a painstaking search of the whole city", starting of course with the usual dens where criminals hide, "the shanty towns or *favelas* where those scum live", as the government officials are shouting at local bureaucrats in places where the city is not quite as glossy as in the tourist pamphlets.

But the tourists from the liner are up in arms. Not so much over the fate of their kidnapped fellow passengers, but because many of them have still not found rooms and have had to spend a second night in hotel corridors.

What at first was only a rumour is now confirmed. No-one can locate the three couples, who just happen to be the richest of all the group, the ones who drink vintage wines at their tables and prefer to travel round the cities they visit in limousines rather than agency mini-buses.

The only abduction that has been officially recognized (because it took place in a hotel and in front of everyone) is that of someone who, they now find out, runs the drugs racket in a large part of Bogotá. Nobody knows or cares whether the drugs boss boarded the *Queen of Storms* for a rest or to carry on his deals on the ship. "It's high time that travel agencies took more care when they draw up their passenger lists," one English tourist protests, in English, during the curious press conference taking place in the central hall of Retiro railway station.

The old, refurbished Victorian station (built over a century ago by the English) is an opera house where baritone and tenor voices, sopranos and contraltos, respond discordantly to questions put to them by a group of very young journalists all trying to get a scoop. They are there because their editors have shouted at them to "come back with a big story, really big, or you can start looking for another job". They are pushing and shoving each other and shouting even louder than the bleating tourists. The office sheep on the way home from their daily slaughterhouses stare in astonishment at this impromptu performance, although most of them rush straight past without looking in order not to miss their daily commuter train. Both the foreign tourists and the office sheep are travellers. They share a desire to continue with their journey; the only thing that distinguishes them is how much they have paid to arrive at their destination.

On the television screen that the two captives cannot see on the fortieth floor of the Alas building, Rosamonte and Sergeant Ramón Capello watch the rowdy press conference that is being shown live from Retiro. Sergeant Capello is not from the federal police but the air force. He is a "redneck", as the air-force officers like to call their N.C.O.s. He is there under orders from Group Captain Castro, who is a close associate of Oso Berlusconi. Castro lives on the twenty-third floor of the same building with his no-longer young wife and spinster daughter. She is almost as unattractive as Rosamonte and he has already given up hope that one day someone will take her off his hands.

Oso personally asked Captain Castro to do him this favour. At night it is hard to find policemen to guard the prisoners; nearly all of them are trying to earn a bit on the side in private security firms, or as stewards at football games. So there is a gap of six hours before he, Oso, can come to interrogate the prisoners himself.

"I'll send my adjutant up," Captain Castro told Oso. "He's a trustworthy redneck from Chaco Province. He can deal with any emergency; he was brought up in the hills slitting pigs' throats."

Oso is wary of Castro's boasts. Castro is someone whom his comrades-in-arms would not have in their airports scam and who is trying to curry favour so that he is not kicked off what they call the "drugs jumbo", a virtual airline that comes and goes, passing with its cargo through all the controls without a problem, carrying more cocaine than passengers and never showing a profit. Oso does not trust Castro after he heard the story that he chickened out in 1987 when the rebel army officers were about to topple the constitutionally elected president Raúl Alfonsín. In those days, Castro was a flight lieutenant in charge of a helicopter gunship that was meant to strafe all those travelling in the presidential limousine. The mission failed when he asked over the radio if all the rebels were off their heads, landed his helicopter at the port of Olivos, then embarked on a yacht with his lover, the daughter of a big landowner. The attempted coup was a failure. Castro was saved from the purges that followed, but he never reached the rank of brigadier and was still living with his family in an apartment block where the rats ran the tenants' association.

An expert in survival techniques, Castro had managed to keep a mistress on the seventeenth floor of the same building. She was the widow of an air-force captain who had served with the United Nations in Afghanistan. He had died of fourteen stab wounds a year earlier while on patrol on the outskirts of Kabul – or more exactly, inside a whorehouse, where he was killed for the gold watch awarded him by the air force for his years of looping the loop.

At 10 p.m., bored with staring at the silent television and of having to listen to all Rosamonte's sentimental misadventures (and fearing that before midnight he might find himself obliged to reject her explicit invitation to have sex), Sergeant Capello calls Captain Castro's apartment to tell him there is no news and ask if he can leave. He hears the sleepy voice of the captain's wife answering, "Of course I'm asleep, it's night time, isn't it? But I don't know where that bastard is. Sometimes when he can't sleep he goes down to have a chat with the night guard."

The sergeant knows the captain well enough to suspect he does not go downstairs to talk to the guard at that time of night, but to climb into bed on the seventeenth floor.

"Captain Castro, sir? Sergeant Capello here."

"I told you not to phone me here unless it's important. What the fuck do you want?"

"To leave, Captain, sir. Police officer Montes is giving the little birds their supper. They're very quiet and no trouble. I'm bored up here."

"You'll be even more bored in the brig if you leave now. Wait for your replacement as per your instructions."

"How long will you be there, Captain, sir?"

"What the fuck is that to you?"

"Just in case I have to report anything, sir. I wouldn't want to wake your lady wife again."

"So she's already asleep is she, that witch? She takes pills, that's why she's out of it so early. You're right, call me here if there's anything to report. I'll be at this number until two or three in the morning, when I've cured my insomnia."

Captain Castro gives a squeaky laugh like a contented mouse that has found a cheese store in the cellar. The wife of the airman who died on a whorehouse mission in Afghanistan snickers alongside him.

Rosamonte has removed the two prisoners' handcuffs and gags. Silently, they eat the cold meats with Russian salad she has brought them from the nearby foodstore, together with a white wine she swigged half of before splashing the rest into plastic cups for them. She apologizes to Capello for not bringing him anything. She is not going to have anything either; she prefers to wait until their replacements arrive and then, if the sergeant goes with her, they can get a meal at a restaurant she knows where lots of actors go after their shows – it is open till 4 a.m.

Capello shudders to imagine how Rosamonte's breath will stink of raw onion and booze if, as he suspects, she gets heavy and wants to finish the night's entertainment in a cheap bed nearby. As he was told on his first day at N.C.O. training school, the armed forces do not mix with the security forces. Not even rednecks like him.

"What actors?"

Rosamonte finds the sergeant's question hilarious.

"Why, are you going to ask for their autographs?"

"Why not?" replies Capello, opening his briefcase as he does so. It is a plain black leather case, like those office juniors carry when they go to banks, or brokers use to carry their receipts and purchase orders in. Out of the corner of his eye he glances at the little birds eating their seed. They respond stealthily in the same way, as though exchanging a silent password.

A crash startles them. The door between the two rooms has slammed shut. The building starts to sway almost imperceptibly.

"We're experiencing turbulence, please fasten your seat belts," jokes Capello the aviator.

Rosamonte smiles. A philologist would be envious of her ability to interpret silences, to read from the lips all that has not been said. She imagines the late-night supper, or rather, the late night without the supper, the room in semi-darkness where the aeronautical redneck will undress her with all the urgency of someone putting on a parachute when his plane has gone into a nose dive. She will cling to him and whisper for him not to take off his uniform; the straps excite her, she loves to caress the military jacket and its gold buttons, then to zoom away with that feeling in the pit of the stomach that pilots get when their fighters lift off the flight deck of an aircraft carrier.

Rosamonte realizes too late that the slamming door means that the Colombian and his mermaid are shut in the next room with their hands untied and without gags. The colour drains from her face and she turns as white as the corpse she would be if the .38 that has suddenly appeared in the sergeant's hand were fired.

"Open the door."

"Be careful," she warns him, sounding maternal. "It's Oso Berlusconi who's in charge of them."

The first thing Rosamonte was told at her police training school was to beware of anyone from the armed forces. They are clumsy and stupid. They might be able to hit a fixed target, but they fire wildly and kill anyone and everyone if they have to shoot in the street. And besides – she was warned – they look down on the police.

"Open the door," insists Capello, stroking the gun in his right hand like a cat wanting some attention. Rosamonte feels for the butt of her regulation revolver, but the sergeant stops her in her tracks. "Don't try it," he says. "Keep that hand still. Now for the third time, open the door. If I have to ask again, I'll put a bullet between your eyes."

"What's going on?" Rosamonte asks indignantly. "Do you work for the drug traffickers? You're nothing but a traitor. You open it: who do you think you are?"

She is furious, not because she is afraid he might shoot, but because by now she is not so sure she would enjoy clinging to his jacket, exciting herself by stroking the straps crossing his chest, then lowering her hand until she finds what she is looking for. The wind rising from the wide, muddy brown river howls round the city like a pack of hounds. It whistles along the corridors of the Alas building, but the airman stands firm, used to storms in the sky.

Rosamonte decides to obey and opens the door.

11

Where does love come from?

Babies, in Spanish at least, come from Paris. Whingeing, opportunist exiles from Argentina. But where does love come from?

She should not have thrown him out the other night. Three

thousand pesos is not that much money; she has often transferred bigger sums to her expenses. She should have given him the money, or waited until the second fuck to be honest with him: "I cheated you," she could have said. "God will repay you."

Where was love when she married her ombudsman?

"Don't complain," Laucha Giménez told her. "You've had men. And if you lost them it wasn't your fault."

That was a white lie; it was her fault. Romano had never hit her until the night he punched her in the face. He had not even been aggressive towards her; he worked that off elsewhere, in his work, where he felt no compunction about taking out criminals, even killing those whom he knew were just dreaming of killing a cop and eyed him greedily.

Yet he always came home at peace with himself and without a single bloodstain on his hands. Like a general or a multinational company executive who cause massacres during their working day, then drive home to their families humming songs from their teenage years that are played on the car radio at that time of day.

What unleashed his fury that night? Could she have been stirring it up unwittingly by creating her own world behind his back, a world in which a policeman, an ordinary cop like him, a bandit with an official badge, could never even imagine being included? And if that is how it was, with no love, only speculation and disdain, why did she stay with him?

After his death there was no grieving. She was taken in again soon afterwards, this time by her ombudsman. She met him when she was representing one side in a very complex inheritance case. A big land-owner's estate had to be divided up and there were three carrion crows – two men and a woman, young graduates from private universities, members of exclusive clubs they would do anything to keep their membership cards for. Verónica was representing the woman, the sister, who thought she was some kind of princess.

In the end, none of them inherited a thing. Creditors started to appear like cockroaches on a sinking ship or in hospital wards at night time. There were more of them than the trio of crows could ever have imagined. The inheritance proceedings ran aground like the *Queen of Storms* and everyone, lawyers included, was left stranded. Verónica cried on the ombudsman's shoulder. She told him she had been planning to use the money finally to buy an apartment of her own. She had already paid the deposit: who would have thought that an inheritance for land out in the pampas could become so complicated? Every inch a gentleman, the ombudsman took her in his arms and consoled her.

"That wasn't love," Laucha objects, "it was a property transaction." Verónica had just turned forty. The menopause had ceased to be a topic in women's magazines and was tiptoeing round her like a spectre. She was getting sudden flushes and unexpected pains which meant the ombudsman often had to stay in another room, resigned, unfailingly polite. "A father figure – he was twenty years older than you."

"But I would have liked to have a child with him."

"With an old man?"

"He wasn't that old. Only fifty-nine."

"What kind of children can you have with an old man?" Laucha insisted. "Little old men."

She is certain he died because of her.

"There was no investigation. A guy is killed in the street – and not just anyone, a federal ombudsman – and he gets buried with no questions asked. There wasn't even an autopsy to remove the bullets."

"You're a lawyer; you could have done something."

"I was scared stiff. On the night he was killed, I got a threatening phone call. Whenever I went out, for a walk or in the car, I was followed. They were never near enough for me to shout at them, but sufficiently close for me to feel they were on my heels, that they could kill me and disappear whenever they felt like it."

She lived with him for fourteen months. Every morning when she woke up she found it impossible to understand what she was doing there, but felt reassured and comforted.

"As I said, he was your father."

A widow and an orphan, both deaths by shooting. An illness or an accident are shadows in a landscape of sharp contrasts. If they happen, it is possible to live on, make plans, think of something resembling a future.

"But I've lived a war's worth of devastating personal battles, Lauchita."

"And contemplating your navel instead of defending yourself."

She is referring to Bértola when she says this. Her theory is that it is no coincidence that Verónica chose an analyst to share her office expenses with. She cannot stand those charlatans: she prefers the people in her native province who offer a talking cure but do not pretend they are doctors.

Laucha Jiménez is not called Laucha "the Mouse". Her real name is Paloma, or "Dove". Verónica is in fact the only person to call her Laucha, but she has to admit that her face and her behaviour were mouse-like when they studied an introduction to law together. She was the only student with a permanent cough in the huge, silent faculty library. A dry, rasping little cough that got on everyone's nerves as she scratched at the pages of books in her haste to get on to the next one. She was reprimanded and even warned she would be barred from the library because of this mousy habit of hers. "I can't keep my hands still, I get cramp in my fingers. Sometimes I'm afraid I'm going to wake up one morning with little claws. It's all very Kafkaesque," she would say, laughing at this nervous habit gnawing away at her.

The Mouse was born in Tucumán Province, in a town called Monteros that was surrounded by sugar-cane plantations and lemon groves, although what she most remembers from her childhood is the army. She was ten years old when the guerrillas started their rural adventure there, an adventure inspired by Che Guevara and doomed to failure like his had been.

"I have to go." Verónica gathers papers and her coat when she hears Chucho sounding the horn, then seconds later the entry phone.

"You've changed your car at least, haven't you?" Laucha is worried. A single individual and a good shot, according to Verónica. Did she see him shoot? No, it's a joke. And she uses the same car every day.

"It's late. Why don't you stay the night?" asks Verónica, brushing aside her friend's advice. "I'll be back at dawn, like a vampire."

"What happens if one of your lovers turns up?"

"Switch the light off. All any of them want is a fuck. I don't think they could tell the difference between us."

12

The wind swirls round the wide, dirty pavements outside the Alas Building. Rain and cold squalls have ruined a night which only a short while before boasted a bright, round moon. Oso Berlusconi parks his grey Toyota with no licence plates on Viamonte, round the corner from the main entrance. On this side are big locked shutters that were once the entrance to the tiny studios of the state-run television channel. The channel moved and now the place is shut up.

Oso thinks they must be storing something there, but has no idea what: phantoms no doubt, and the skeletons of sets and bit-part actors who are either long since dead or confined to the actors' hospice. In the days when they made television programmes here, they were still in fuzzy black and white, the actors cried live on screen and singers did not mime to soundtracks, but sang out of tune or forgot the words. The television cameras had valves and were enormous, and often overheated.

"To think Pichuco once played here," Oso says, then explains to his extremely young companion that Pichuco was a famous tango musician.

"I've seen photos of him," she says. "A fat guy with jowls who looked like he was falling asleep over a tiny accordion."

"That wasn't a tiny accordion, Bolivia, it was a *bandoneón*. And he wasn't asleep, he was playing it. My God, could he play."

"Don't call me Bolivia," she protests.

"*Esquismii*, Miss Bolivia. Wait for me here. Lock the doors as soon as I leave. If there's any trouble, get out of here." He hands her the car keys. It is useless for her to protest yet again that she does not drive. The car is armour-plated, Oso explains. "If you hear shooting, stay where you are. Don't even think of getting out. Put the radio on, there's bound to be some good music."

The night guard at the front desk does not seem surprised when he sees Oso's imposing face filling the monitor screen. He has seen him somewhere before, or perhaps it is because he looks so much like a cop, he tells himself. Oso hardly needs show him his credentials and tell him he has come to see Group Captain Castro.

The guard knows that the birdcage up on the fortieth floor is occupied. And that the little birdies must be important, because there has been a stream of federal cops coming past, as well as others, like Oso, who are not ordinary policemen.

"How can any military officers live in this mess? The Albergue Warnes housing estate was like the Sheraton compared to this," says Oso when the guard opens the side door for him.

"They do complain about the rats," the guard admits. He cannot be more than twenty and is from Corrientes Province. A quarter of a century earlier his superiors would have sent him to die in the Malvinas.

"I think it's the other way round," Oso says. "I bet it's the lady rats who complain about the officers."

"Have you got an appointment with the group captain? It's midnight."

"You don't say! Does the group captain go to bed that early?" Oso is already turning his back on the guard and heading for the lift.

Oso detests the way they grovel to their superiors in the armed forces these days. Before, when he was young, Argentina had conscription. Civilians were obliged to enlist almost as soon as they were out of adolescence and were trained in the use of arms, combat practice, and keeping the officers' quarters spick and span. They always had to serve them fresh *yerba maté* tea and could only chew on their anger until they were released. Now that there was no more national service, those who enlisted were human doormats, shrunken men and women who, unlike policemen, did not even risk their lives picking up the garbage of society.

The lift climbs slowly, lurching upwards. "If this is what their planes are like, I pity the airmen," thinks Oso, "and I'm sure they are."

The lift door finally opens at the thirty-ninth floor. He wants to take the stairs up to the fortieth – because the lift does not go that far and just in case. If anyone is waiting for him, it is better to be able to move. His 9 m.m. Browning offers him fire power and there are some of his own people up there, so there should be no problem in getting in to greet the prisoners.

The rain is heavier up here and the wind howls more loudly. God must be just outside. Oso has never liked heights, he has always had his feet firmly on the ground. He is a prize-winning marksman. He went to Tokyo once to receive a cup, with all expenses paid. Geishas going down on him, smiling all the time. That's culture for you.

He climbs the stairs slowly, on his guard. The Browning sits snugly in his right hand. A light that is not from the corridor is spilling weakly out of the room. He does not like that one bit. The birdcage door is wide open.

He wonders whether Castro brought in some of his own men as backup, as he asked him to do. He does not trust that ingrate an inch. In fact, he does not trust anyone; that is why he is still alive.

Oso flattens himself against the corridor wall and slides along it to the open door.

"Sergeant . . . ?"

He cannot remember Rosa Montes' name. All he can recall is that she is a lesbian; she tried to hit on one of her female subordinates, but all she got was a slap and a complaint for misconduct, which Oso rejected. "She's a good cop. They've punished her by sending her to public relations, but in the street she never took pity on those young hoodlums, she would shoot first then draw up very convincing reports afterwards."

Oso does not like dykes, though, or queers. Nor the Pope, although he is a fervent Catholic.

He calls out her rank again. When there is no reply, he edges his way into the room, swivelling his gun round 180°. Nobody had better appear now, because he will fill them full of lead.

He searches the apartment, then uses his mobile to call Group Captain Castro's home number.

"What do you mean, he's not there? Doesn't that bastard son of a bitch sleep with you?"

Groggy from the pills she has taken, Castro's wife cannot get out the words properly. She has no idea who is calling, or why he is shouting at her like this.

"Wait, I'll go and look for him if it's so urgent," she manages to stammer, but Oso is already thundering his way down from the fortieth floor to the group captain's apartment. He hammers on the door, kicking it hard to stress the message. The whole building trembles, more from his boots than from the wind. If he had been Frankenstein's monster, his hair would have stood on end when he saw her, but Oso has seen uglier women: he has even slept with some. Nothing is going to stand in his way. He does not wait for her to ask him in, but pushes past her, then searches through every room, behind every bit of furniture. The wife is furious, but not with him. An onrush of hatred can clear the mind of any amount of drugs. Her central nervous system gleams like a warrior's sword. "I know where to find him. Follow me . . . that swine."

She lurches out of the apartment, pulling Oso with her in the slipstream of her anger. She stumbles, but immediately rights herself and plunges on. She is wearing an ankle-length nightgown, her face is covered in cream and she has a hairnet on. Add an oxygen mask and she could be an alien from a lost world, the kind of alien for whom marriages must continue at all costs and man must not separate what God (who is a little further off now, as they have descended twenty floors) has joined together.

"That bitch! As if she didn't have enough losing her husband in a whorehouse in the asshole of the world, the stinking cow!"

She starts pounding on the door of the apartment on the seventeenth floor, but Oso quickly pushes her aside and fires at the lock. Then he kicks the door open with his boot. He tries to get past the cuckolded wife and ends up shoving her onto a table, where she smashes a collection of small ivory statues the dead airman must have brought back from his heroic missions to the furthest east.

The apartment looks neat and tidy. The lights of Puerto Madero are reflected in the dining-room windows. It must look very picturesque in the daytime. "The rats have got a privileged view of the river," thinks Oso as he strides towards the bedroom, where catastrophe awaits him.

It is the scream from the woman behind him, who has managed to extricate herself from the ruins of Asian art, that horrifies him more than the massacre in front of him. The group captain is sitting up against the headboard of the bed as if he is about to be served breakfast – except that he would not be able to enjoy it much, because he has no head. The widow is lying prone across his body, face down on Castro's prick. Shot to death in full fellatio.

Oso Berlusconi is not having a good night. If only he had the murder weapon in his hands he would finish off the surviving widow, just to stop her screaming.

He leaves the apartment and leaps down the stairs four at a time. The exercise makes him feel twenty years younger. In the end, it is all a game and in his youth he was always a good sportsman.

The guard is surprised to see him coming out of the door to the stairs.

"Don't tell me the lift broke down again, at this time of night. Did you find the group captain?"

He does not seem to hear the screams of the recently bereaved widow seventeen floors up. When Oso points this out to him, he smiles briefly. "It's normal," he says. "There are married couples fighting every night in this slum."

"What happened?" asks Miss Bolivia, turning the radio down as he thumps back into the car.

"Nothing. A few problems."

Oso turns the radio up again. That *bandoneón*.

"It's been playing for quite a while," she says. "Ever since you left. It's nice music; a bit sad."

"It's tango, you idiot. And it's Pichuco playing."

He switches on the engine and pulls out slowly, glancing warily at the former studios of the state-run television station. He thinks he can see what looks like candlelight inside and before speeding off wonders once again what on earth they are storing in there.

Beyond the street corner, in some darkened back room of the Holy City, Pichuco, Fats Troilo, stops playing and opens his eyes.

PART THREE

God Exists, Man Only Sometimes

1

The taste of blood mingling with the sickly savour of lipstick. That is how her nights so often finish.

She should have stayed in Bolivia. Or at least in that lawyer woman's apartment. What's the use of the Bersa if she can't empty it into the body of the bastards who beat her up when something goes wrong? Or worse still, those who fondle her, ask her to kneel in front of them, "You know what you have to do, baby". Second-rate actors, dreadful scriptwriters, there is never a happy ending, an embrace, a fond farewell. Only corpses.

Oso brought the car screeching to a halt two blocks from headquarters. Instead of unlocking the doors, he sat behind the wheel staring into the distance, as if looking for something in the deserted street.

"You talked to someone." He had switched off the radio, the engine, the city. "Don't be frightened, Bolivia. I know you didn't give me away. I'm just asking a question."

Obviously it was not a question. He wanted her to give him a name. It did not even matter what they had talked about.

"I talked to my godfather, Deputy Inspector Carroza."

"I'm your godfather."

"You're my sugar daddy." The back of his hairy, hard hand, a warm hand she has kissed and licked in grateful thanks, split her lip. Another night of blood and lipstick. "I didn't betray you!" she groaned.

"Of course not. If anyone betrays me I don't slap them, I kill them." He unlocked the car doors. She wound down the window, desperate for some fresh air. "Get out of here. What are you waiting for?"

To Ana's surprise, he switched the police siren on.

"I didn't know you had a siren on your Toyota."

"We cops have sirens in our assholes. Get out, I don't want to see you."

She had difficulty climbing out of the car. Oso had parked some way from the kerb, in a puddle. She tottered on her high heels, then finally managed to straighten up and feel more sure of herself.

"Don't do anything to my godfather."

She slammed the car door shut, knowing that having his car door slammed made Oso more furious than any insult. She slipped her hand inside her bag and felt reassured at the cool touch of the Bersa. The Toyota pulled away, its siren howling like a dog that has had its tail trodden on.

Ana ran her tongue over her bloody lip and realized something. She had been right to come here from Bolivia.

*

But no-one can escape from hell. It accompanies us wherever we go: when we die there are no surprises, we are on familiar ground.

In his lair on Azara in the Boca district not far from the Río Riachuelo, Deputy Inspector Walter Carroza is looking at photos he has downloaded from the Internet. He bought a computer a couple of months earlier and is still learning how to use it, but it already has become indispensable. He threw out the last woman who dared leave a pair of knickers and a toothbrush behind, then reappeared the next day aiming to cook dinner for him. He gets more turned on by porn on the net than by the dregs of womankind who, because of his age, history and economic situation, are all he is able to pick up. The rotting hulks on the banks of the Riachuelo are closer to Atlantic liners than these conquests to any real woman.

Miss Bolivia is not love. Both of them are clear about that, yet it feels good to meet her now and then, to caress each other while there is still some warmth in their bodies, to console one another like shipwreck victims who drink a toast in salt water on their liferaft.

He dreams of Verónica. Even when he is with Miss Bolivia he closes his eyes and dreams of Verónica as a bride in white, with an orange-blossom bouquet. A choir of drug-addict angels is singing the Ave María while he whispers in her ear and she laughs softly, although he is not whispering words of love but telling her in great detail how Romano was shot and who did it, and how they celebrated afterwards, just as when Boca Juniors football team wins a championship. After all, if Romano beat her the way she claims he did, if he smashed her face like that, the world is not as unjust as preachers say it is.

It is 2 a.m. and Carroza has been staring at photos for three hours. He has printed out half a dozen of them, but he is not happy about the way they came out. They were better on screen, the depth behind their gazes, the splinters of hell glittering in their pupils.

He had downloaded the file that afternoon at headquarters and put it on his hard disk earlier that night. These are not ordinary murderers, people who simply kill to get rid of someone out of lust, passion, or greed. These are beasts that would make even Beelzebub cross himself if he saw them. Carroza too, although he is little more than a skeleton held together by memories and a certain sadness, finds them repulsive, finds it hard to look at them peering out so defiantly from the screen: powerful, invincible, even though some of them (he does not know how many or whom) are already dead.

It was Scotty's idea that he glance at this gallery of rapists, murderers and shit-eaters genetically programmed or sent by God, the hard core of the accursed seed from which the universe once germinated.

"There they are," Scotty said. "Nobody pays them any attention. Some are already stiffs, others are still cooking human flesh or eating it raw, but they make no noise about it, they go around silently, disguised as ordinary people. Every so often I see myself in them, it's better than looking into a mirror."

Somebody, on some occasion, arrested them, took them in for a misdemeanour that was more than just a parking ticket. Somebody knew what they were, even though most of them were never accused of anything and had to be released, lions with their appetites sated, part of the pack.

The computer programme lets Carroza group them together in an album. Just as when he was a kid and collected stickers with famous actors, football stars, heroes from history. They have all done something: they cannot hide it, unable to pretend they are innocent even if their faces were burned away with acid. Nor would they want to, it is obvious: they are proud of themselves, they are free forever of any torment of guilt.

"One of them looks familiar to me."

Scotty asks who the sweet Jesus is talking at 2.30 a.m.

"It's you, Yorugua, who else could it be? At this hour in the morning everyone's either asleep or fucking. Only you would think of doing overtime."

"More than familiar, he's someone from my close circle, Scotty. As if it was your own face but for the moment you can't remember your name."

"I'm not one of your close circle," Scotty defends himself. "What you've got is called Alzheimer's. I can recommend the pills my father-in-law takes. They'll at least stop you talking all this shit." With that he hangs up, but since the person who called is Carroza, the line stays open until Scotty picks it up again. He feels as though he is being watched by a pitbull in the middle of the night, its eyes fixed on his neck like a bone in an *osobuco*, just waiting for him to shut his eyes so he can leap on dinner. "What do you want?" he asks.

"You to tell me where you got those photos."

"I told you, off the Internet, from search engines, broadband genius. Once you've learned how to use your P.C. you won't be such a balls-breaker. What does your relative look like?"

"Big forehead, but it's intelligence, not baldness. The evil is concentrated in his eyes. Even if he was blind it would still shine. And he's not my relative."

Carroza hears the sound of springs from Scotty's bed, female protests – the woman sleeping beside him is being pushed aside so that he can sit up and read a notebook or consult his mental archive. Scotty stores a database of criminals where others have thoughts.

"Write this down. Then get off the line and let me sleep. I'm on duty tomorrow and besides, I'm not sleeping on my own like you are. Your relative is called Torrente. Ovidio Ladislao Torrente Morelos, to give him his full title. His surname comes from an army officer who they say took charge of him when he was newly born in the mountains. That officer was known for such heroic feats as being part of the personal bodyguard of General Banzer, the dictator who ousted Torres. You'd know who he was if you had the slightest idea about the recent history of Latin America."

"I couldn't give a flying fuck about the recent history of Latin America," says Carroza. "What has this Torrente got to do with Ana Torrente?"

"I thought Miss Bolivia would have told you her story, Yorugua. I like to know who I'm taking to bed."

"She doesn't say anything. She's an angel and angels don't have stories, Scotty, they come down from heaven and are at your side when you need them. You tell me. If you gave me his photo it's because you knew him and knew I would recognize something about him."

"All right, you've ruined my night now anyway. But put your light on, make sure the street door is locked and bolted. Believe me, it'll scare you rigid."

*

He hangs up on Scotty, but immediately calls Verónica directly on her mobile. He does not care if she is asleep or locked in the embrace of someone who has descended from the ships, he has to talk to her, to share the information with her at least. If he is going to be killed tonight he does not want to take all this hangover to the grave with him; his motto is to go to bed on an empty stomach so that he will not have nightmares.

Verónica is not in bed. She is at the Riachuelo market and she is wide awake.

"I never heard from her again," she says, referring to Miss Bolivia.

"I have, that's why I want to talk to you."

"Come to the market. You can find everything you want here, at the best prices. The market's crammed with people, Walter."

Verónica is the only one who remembers his name, which is another reason he loves her: she preserves his identity as if it were something valuable. "People come from all over to buy here. People with lots of money; some of them even bring their bodyguards. The market is like a convention of bankers, gypsies and gangsters."

"Talking of bodyguards, where's yours?"

"Right beside me, like my shadow," Verónica lies.

Chucho has fallen asleep in the caravan that serves as her office. Boredom and gin have left him curled up in a corner, watching the *doctora* working on her laptop. This was the opportunity Verónica was looking for to slip out and walk through the market without drawing any attention to herself, mingling with the crowd.

Carroza promises to be there in fifteen minutes. This is not exactly good news for Verónica: he is a bird of ill-omen, an owl with a police

I.D. She would not be surprised if he swivels his head round 180° when he prowls the dark streets of Buenos Aires. It is not that he is afraid of being shot in the back, more that he wants to see the face of whoever has fired at him. He has put so many people "to sleep" that he has lost count. But he has never received a reprimand or an official warning, although his bosses do not consider him a hero either. Romano liked him, but admitted in private that you had to be careful with him: he lives on his own in rented rooms, never in the city centre and never for longer than six months. His number is not in the phone book; he does not use credit cards; he does not leave any traces or befriend any shop-keepers. He turns his collar up or looks the other way when he meets a doorman.

Verónica heads down the central aisle of the market. She is still amazed at the brazenness with which smugglers and asphalt pirates display their wares. Even she is almost tempted to buy a twenty-dollar Christian Dior perfume that a circus dwarf who has run away from the circus is waving at the level of her knees and which, despite the difference in their heights, her sense of smell tells her is genuine.

*

It is the time and the day – 3 a.m. between Saturday and Sunday – when discos fill with dancers and A&E departments overflow with overdosed addicts and people who have been shot or stabbed. The medics cannot cope, and the police come and go sounding their sirens but always arriving too late to do anything: "Attention base, young male badly wounded; attention base, homicide in street brawl; attention base, female raped and thrown in ditch, no signs of life."

Deputy Inspector Carroza enjoys the police radio the way others do their favourite nightly music programme. Every call is a hit that his police imagination fills in until he has created an Impressionist canvas he would like to paint one day when he has retired – if he is still alive.

He studied art in his beloved Montevideo, back in the days when he never dreamt he would cross the widest muddy-brown river in the world, not to sing tangos like some of his school mates, but to shut himself away in cells, ruin his freedom, sink the wolf's fangs he could never admit to that rose like a nauseating wave of flesh and blood from his throat on that endless night when Carolina was killed.

*

From the depths of the Descamisados de América shanty town, the Riachuelo market looks the way New York does from the Statue of Liberty. Or, less spectacularly, the way Buenos Aires looked to Tito Lusiardo as he leaned with Carlos Gardel over the deck rail of the liner bringing them home from Europe. The lights of thieves and sultans glittering in the dark, the spectacular gleam of all that fake gold and all those costume diamonds shamelessly displayed like a Bible or *Don Quixote* on the bargain tables of the bookshops on Avenida Corrientes.

The three couples snatched near Puerto Madero as they were enjoying the European climate with which Buenos Aires sells itself in travel brochures have been split up in three separate but neighbouring shacks. They are resting, in a South-American way, bound hand and foot on earth floors, gagged to the point of suffocation.

They are kept awake by wafts of the warm, rotten stench from the Riachuelo, fouling what little air they manage to suck in through their gags. The guards take turns in the boring task of staring at them like insects. Every three hours a new man or woman appears (because female personnel are also being used in the operation). No-one has told any of them how much ransom is being demanded, if their prisoners are going to die or to be allowed to go home once the payments have been verified in accounts held in distant islands, accounts opened in the names of the typical frontmen who run all the illegal payments that contribute so much to the flow of capital around this globalized world.

It is probable that Oso Berlusconi forced Carroza out of the way as he raced down the Avenida General Paz at 140 k.p.h., on his way to the Riachuelo. During his long police career, Carroza has been more concerned not to use his siren than about the bullets that have whizzed past him or even buried themselves in his meagre flanks. Oso Berlusconi enjoys speed. He likes to push his way past unsuspecting motorists, siren blazing, forcing them to skid or to end up on the verges facing the wrong way. That is why he became a cop, as well as to sink an iron fist into the flabby stomachs of the Jews of Once or calle Libertad whenever he is searching for the fences of gold and precious stones after a jewellers' or bank security boxes have been raided.

Oso's grey Toyota turns silently into the main alleyway of the Decamisados de América, looking like just another of the old wrecks that litter the banks of the Riachuelo. Oso was careful to switch off the siren when he left headquarters on this unofficial mission, to enter the shanty town at walking pace, and then pull up next to a heap of bricks and sand that the local worker priest hopes to use to build his church for outcasts, to sell them the Christian illusion that it is possible to save their souls and to multiply the loaves and fishes.

Oso Berlusconi's heart is clouded by the same Catholicism that inspires the worker priest. That is why he calls his snub-nose 9 m.m. "Rerum Novarum", a homage to Pope Leo XIII's encyclical that proposed to save the poor from capitalist oppression without falling into the clutches of the totalitarian red devil. Oso remembers it in the same way he does the fairy tale of Snow White and the seven depraved dwarves, or Little Red Riding Hood and a transvestite, gluttonous wolf. He was forced to read the encyclical out loud in the church of San José in Almagro by a faceless nun stinking of old people's urine-soaked nappies, who insisted on hugging him while she gave him a gentle warning about the eternal punishment awaiting him if he did not study his catechism. The fans from the Los Penales bar applauded and fell about laughing in the church doorway, to the horror of the nuns and the parish priest, and the delight of his school mates and friends. That childhood humiliation branded the encyclical on his mind for ever more, so that like some black medieval monk he swore he would annihilate any poor person who crossed his path with any thought of expropriation: "Most true it is that by far the larger part of the workers prefer to better themselves by honest labour rather than by doing any wrong to others. But there are not a few who are imbued with evil principles and eager for revolutionary change, whose main purpose is to stir up disorder and incite their fellows to acts of violence," said the encyclical, and Oso, still in those days little Oso, swore he would employ his last bullet so that "the authority of the law should intervene to put restraint upon such firebrands, to save the working classes from being led astray by their manoeuvres and to protect lawful owners from spoliation".

This crusade of Oso Berlusconi's is a long, bloody and often exasperating one, although he has not come to the Descamisados de América shanty town following his ideals, but in search of finance. He strokes the butt of Rerum Novarum like a father caressing his young son's head, as if his weapon were in more danger than him.

Yet he smiles tenderly, with satisfaction. This is also why he became a cop.

2

When he knocks on the door of the caravan that Verónica uses as an office, Carroza still has Carolina on his mind. Strictly speaking, he is not thinking: it is more like an intense red image, the dark waters of death the uninitiated confuse with blood. He shakes his head like a dog refusing to be stroked. Deputy Inspector Carroza has the ability to push away his troubles without even having to scratch.

He leans his right hand against the door and heaves. It barely shifts, so instinctively his left hand closes round the handle of the .38 he has stuffed down his trousers.

He has seen films, documentaries and Greenpeace propaganda where whales are shown stranded on beaches or harpooned on the high seas, and then cut up on the deck of a Japanese factory ship. But he has never seen a whale calf so close, or stumbled over one, although he knows, even before he sees him, that this particular specimen was not butchered by the Japanese.

The barrel of the .38 is the first thing inside the caravan before Carroza manages to ease the door open enough to slide his bones in, then spin round like a top, expecting either an attack or to find Verónica's body as well. For one despicable moment he thinks it would be a relief to find her dead. That way there would be no room in his life for another disappointment: he could go out and kill without worrying that someone might be waiting for him with his dinner cooked, the bed warm, an armchair and soft lights, a fire for the winter that will soon arrive and never ever leave.

But Verónica is standing behind him, her splendid figure framed in the open doorway like an improvised, fleeting Modigliani canvas. Like her skin, the silence she adopts to avoid screaming and convulsing with rage and fear, perhaps bursting into tears, is smooth and fragile as porcelain.

"You said Chucho was with you," Carroza reproaches her, because that still comes easier than embracing her.

*

The hustle and bustle of the market continues uninterrupted by the arrival of two police cars and an ambulance. A moment before he is lifted into it, Verónica draws her finger round the hole in Chucho's forehead where the bullet penetrated his brain, already switched off by gin and boredom. All that firepower he had, all the energy he expended to fetch and carry her, even following her when she decided to get out and catch a bus, all that armour plating and the tinted windows in his car, which he boasted was like a tank, *doctora*, so that even if Serbs and Croats united and decided to attack they would not even make a scratch on it. "You get on with your work in peace, put all this gang of criminals behind bars where they belong, I'll take care of you."

"And I left him on his own."

"Yes, and drunk," Carroza reminds her. "I would have killed him myself if I had found him stretched out like that and you wandering alone around the market." It even seems easier to talk about Carolina than about what has just happened for this sentimental skull of a man, who has a vague idea scratching at the back of his mind and who is still clutching the butt of his .38 as he pours whisky into their plastic cups. It is no more than a feeling, a flash of light in the darkness, that he prefers to close his eyes to and go back to his cop routine. "Call that unscrupulous rat of a magistrate tomorrow morning and resign."

"I asked for whisky, not orders," says Verónica, picking up the beaker and downing the drink with a grimace as if it was medicine.

"They're going to kill you, Verónica. They're going to kill us all and no-one will even lift a phone to ask for any explanation."

"They could have done that before, while I was walking through the market."

"That's true, but they don't want any fuss, for now at least. Who the fuck is interested in a bodyguard? He didn't even have a name apart from 'Chucho'. I bet the magistrate doesn't know his name either. They could have shot us in the bar, they know how to shoot when they want to."

"You know something."

"That's why I came. I only took a quarter of an hour, driving carefully. And look what happened."

"You should have put your foot down, Walter. You let laws over-rule your instinct. You'd let your mother be killed rather than go against the regulations."

"And this is a lawyer speaking."

"I don't defend laws, I defend people."

"There aren't any people in this city, Verónica. Only monsters," Deputy Inspector Carroza says. He chews the end of a pencil and starts to draw oval shapes on a sheet of paper he has torn from the diary. "Murderers, the sort who ought to be dead and even when they are, you need to make sure they won't come back."

"That's what you lot are there for," she says. "What are you drawing?"

"Heads. Three up to now. The three heads missing from three bodies. I only just found out about them. That's why I called you and came to find you."

"Whose heads are they?" asks Verónica, her voice reflecting the ever-present fear that the end of the world is much closer than the Scriptures say.

Three isolated incidents, not even remarked on. In chronological order, the first headless body appeared in the Peruvian jungle. Shining Path was nothing more than a memory: Abimael Guzmán was behind bars in his striped pyjamas, but a few of his followers carried on robbing travellers, hunting birds, small-time drugs dealing, in order to survive.

"I went sniffing around in the Peruvian press when I learned how Ana Torrente's coronation as Miss Bolivia ended up." With a shudder, Verónica realizes that this thinking skull knows more about Ana than she does and that she might not like to hear what he knows, but that this is the reason for him being there, not to scrape up the corpse of a gin-soaked whale calf. "I told her to go and see you," Carroza admits, referring to Ana. "She needed a lawyer and didn't trust any of the police ones. Come to that, nor do I."

But even the remnants of Shining Path did not go in for beheading their counter-revolutionary enemies. Of course, habits can change: extremes of climate and hardships can alter the behaviour of even the most orthodox believers. If there had been only one case, it might have gone unnoticed, possibly attributed to a gourmet puma or a stray head-shrinker. Losing one's head is not news even for prominent politicians, the ones who are so keen on having others beheaded.

No, it was the second headless body that caught Deputy Inspector Carroza's attention.

"The body appeared in San Pedro, 170 kilometres from Buenos Aires. The local police say there was no head, but as far as I know heads don't get up and walk away." Carroza takes off his jacket and wraps it round Verónica's shoulders. She is shivering, affected by what has happened and by the ghoulish story Carroza is telling her. "Ana Torrente had been in San Pedro," he continues. Verónica draws the jacket closer around her. The air is an icy dagger at her throat. Carroza does not give her time to ask how he knows this. "I sent her," he says. "Miss Bolivia and I work together."

3

Sated by now with tango and the best steaks, the tourists from the *Queen of Storms* stranded in Buenos Aires are beginning to ask one another when they are going to leave this crazy port of call, this noisy, dirty city so full of ragged poverty once you step outside the circuits marked by the guides, the threatening sort of poverty that tourists find attractive in Bombay or Rio, but do not expect to find in Buenos Aires, so far away in the south, but so European. "And talking of guides, what can have become of that charming man, born somewhere down here, in Paraguay wasn't it?" says an old, jewel-bedecked woman in a restaurant in the smart Palermo Soho district, rummaging in her bag for the gold card that will allow her to pay for her barbecue and vintage wine in six installments.

"He's a Casanova, a babe-fucking machine," says the blonde woman in her forties sitting beside her. She has kept her legs closed since the night the charming guide fucked her in her cabin for a hundred dollars, including the hit of cocaine he sold her: a real bargain. The blonde asked Pacogoya for a kiss when he left before dawn the next morning: "That'll be another twenty dollars," was the charming reply from the fairytale Paraguayan Casanova, that miniature version of the mythical *guerrillero* who turned Fidel's hair white when he called for the revolutionary flame to ignite the whole of Latin America, until Fidel could breathe more easily again after Che's ordeal and crucifixion in Bolivia.

Pacogoya himself is facing another ordeal in the Descamisados de América, one that has nothing to do with the socialist revolution. Nobody told him he could not go home when it was all over. They simply asked him to stay in the fourth shack for now, to offer support for the changing guards. He knows the prisoners and their names; he can even speak their languages a little, so the captors need him. They do not seem at all concerned that the tourists from the *Queen of Storms* have begun to notice his absence. He may not be the only tourist guide – "but I'm the only one who supplies them with drugs," he says in his own defence. "Bunch of stinking junkies, they can put up with it for a couple of days, or commit suicide if the withdrawal symptoms are too much for them," Pacogoya is told. "We need you here, your job isn't finished yet."

It had all been too good to last. The drugs within reach, ready to be sold, on Uncle's bed. The delivery of the three couples to vehicles travelling with special permits along streets barred to traffic in the city centre. Pacogoya thought all he had to do then was to return to his apartment in Recoleta to sit and wait. Perhaps he could call Verónica, by now she must be sorry for kicking him in the balls like that and wanting to spend a satisfying night with him, lent added flavour by a visit to a Greek restaurant in Las Cañitas district where he had promised to take her.

That is what he did, or tried to do, after the third handover. Like the Pied Piper of Hamelin, he took the third couple to try out a pretty little restaurant between two side streets. "Only people from Buenos Aires go there, they serve tender meat, pizza with real cheese and a rough wine from the coast," he told them, as if promising the delights of the Garden of Eden. The Hiatsu cut them off at the cobblestoned corner in San Telmo and three men who spoke no German bundled them into it head first, without even telling them where they were going. The German pair (the third couple Pacogoya had handed over that day) did not at first understand that this little unprogrammed diversion was not part of the tour, because their guide sat up front with the driver and started talking animatedly with him in that tribal language Latinos have, while the other two gentlemen tied them up and gagged them with thick plastic tape, and then covered their eyes with masks like the ones they themselves used to get some sleep with on planes.

When they reached the Descamisados de América shanty town and unloaded the Germans, by now rigid with panic as well as manacled, Pacogoya clapped the driver on the back and said to them all, "Well, lads, it's been a pleasure working with you". The fourth man, who had not taken part in the abduction but remained sitting silently in the vehicle keeping an eye on the captives like a mastiff watching over a pair of cats, opened his mouth for the first time to say: "'Well, lads', my ass, you're staying with us – where do you think you're going?"

*

Fewer than two hundred metres separate Pacogoya's endless vigil and the whispered conversation between Verónica Berutti and Deputy Inspector Walter Carroza. If the guide who supplies cocaine and tourists knew that the woman with whom he imagined spending the night was so close by, he might have made a desperate attempt to escape. Nobody is guarding him and the darkness around the shacks is barely lit by the glow from the market.

Verónica does not know whether to confess to Carroza that Pacogoya is on the list of people who have been to San Pedro. She is even less inclined to do so when she learns that Ana sprayed the drugs dealer with bullets from her own beloved Bersa, the trophy from her first widowhood she should never have lent her. Especially because, although it is apparently a known fact that Ana executed the dealer, nobody has arrested her. And that nobody is of course Walter Carroza.

"Because I wasn't born yesterday. Your Bersa would be nothing without Ana Torrente. It would be safely hidden in the drawer you got it out of and that bastard in San Pedro, who besides selling drugs to eight-year-old kids on the way home from school wanted to fuck her up the ass without paying, would be alive and trafficking like so many others, licking the hand of the Lomas police chief."

So that was it. A bag of bones and cracker-barrel moralizing held together the skeleton that is Deputy Inspector Walter Carroza. His alliance with Miss Bolivia is nothing more than a cocktail, a brew created out of their common hatred of rapists. But how does he know, or imagine, that there was no kitchen knife after the Bersa? Isn't it too much of a coincidence that her manager, brought to justice by the remnants of the Maoist revolution in Peru, also appeared headless? Or is there a butcher following in the footsteps of Miss Bolivia, someone who tidies up the mess she leaves behind her, like someone switching off the light in a room that someone else has left on?

They leave the market. Veronica locks the door to her caravan as if she were leaving her cottage in the country. A man hired to protect her has just been killed and then removed from the scene like a drunk lying in the road.

"What do you mean, you're from the federal police, deputy inspector? This is a matter for the province," the officer in charge of the removal of the body told him coldly. "The stiff is one of his honour's men and his honour works for the mayor of Lomas. Let them take care of it. Tomorrow is another day. This isn't your jurisdiction, deputy inspector, go and get some sleep – if possible, with the young lady, ho ho."

Not a drop of blood remained on the caravan floor. Instead of chemicals to analyse it, a floor mop with bleach and then everyone home to bed. And the whale calf to the morgue.

"Now tell me the truth, Walter. What is there between you and Ana? What do you have in common, what did you discover tonight that was so urgent to tell me?"

They are travelling in Carroza's car, a battered old Renault with garish-coloured bodywork that makes it look like an old underground train or one of those provincial buses that clatter along colonial cobblestones always on the point of falling apart.

"I'm not in love with Ana."

"Why should I care about that?" Verónica laughs, astounded at how stupid Carroza can be. As if he could ever be in love with anyone.

"I guess I'm like a father to her," he says, determined to continue with the kitsch.

"A father who fucks her. But Ana is an adult. And Miss Bolivia."

"Why did you give her the Bersa? I didn't want her to be armed, Verónica. She would have made sure others did the shooting for her. Like in the Peruvian jungle. Who is going to keep her on the leash now?"

"Where is she? Who does the third head belong to?"

The Renault runs on natural gas. Carroza says it's safe, there's no risk it will explode.

"You can't imagine the money I save. I charge the federal police for ordinary unleaded petrol and keep the difference."

"If Miss Bolivia doesn't cut off the heads, who keeps the trophies – and whose is the third head?"

"It belongs to a woman," Carroza finally admits. "A policewoman, if you must know. She worked overtime babysitting for a Colombian drugs boss and his girlfriend. The federal cops arrested them three days ago."

"I saw it on T.V.," Verónica remembers. "It was a smart operation, it looked almost like a movie. But it wasn't all strictly legal then?"

"That was the first mistake." Carroza is driving increasingly slowly along the deserted avenue, as if he is about to pass out. He justifies himself by saying he cannot talk and press his foot down on the accelerator at the same time.

"They came to Argentina with the group of tourists on the cruise liner that ran aground on the river sandbanks. He didn't intend to stay here: he was travelling incognito, but somebody here was expecting him."

Carroza is driving close to the kerb. He has put his flashing light on to warn people he is going very slowly. Speed distracts him, he explains to Verónica. It is a drug and he has had enough of druggies. If one day he kills himself it will be by putting a bullet in his brain, not crashing into a truck. By now Verónica is convinced he really is a desperado, a skull and nothing more, someone who for a reason as yet unknown to her has crossed over to death and come back, and can still talk.

"Who was expecting him?"

"Not one but several people. A senator on the government side, a loyal judge, people very closely associated with our Argentine way of life, Verónica. Osmar Arredri, the drugs baron, had not come to go whale-watching in Puerto Madryn or to see the glaciers melting in Patagonia. People like him couldn't care less what tricks nature gets up to. He was coming to give his blessing to his network of distributors in the south of the continent, the ones he affectionately called his oil-slick penguins. A drugs baron is like the Pope, or perhaps the Pope is like a drugs baron: they only travel once the business has been set up and is functioning. They come to receive the applause of their subjects and to see their faces. They want to get a good look at all those who they are going to have killed tomorrow or the next day."

"Why was he arrested?"

"Abducted, you mean. They couldn't take him to court, because there are no charges against him. He's not wanted by Interpol and he's a great respecter of human rights. But he was declared persona non grata. He was coming to try to ruin things for the bosses in Neuquén, people born and bred in Patagonia. What is the Colombian mafia doing in Patagonia? We've got enough on our hands with the English, the Yankees and the Italians. They've bought up half of southern Argentina and fenced it off."

"So it's a question of sovereignty?"

"Sovereignty over drugs. The main dealer in the area happens to be in the provincial government house. But that of course is not and should never be known. Drugs are a very profitable business, Verónica, and competition is frowned upon."

Verónica tries to wind down her window, but it is stuck. Carroza shows her how to thump it from the side. She does so and the window drops like a guillotine. It does not let in any air, though. It is a damp, sticky early morning. The police radio forecasts a storm of murders: "Attention base, adult male with deep stab wound on calle Cuzco; attention base, female hacked to pieces on Sarmiento railway line near Liniers station; attention base, brawl involving followers of Saint Cayetano, stones thrown at saint by group of male troublemakers; attention base . . ."

Deputy Inspector Carroza hates music, the boleros and tangos the commercial stations play at this time of night, "sentimental pastiches" he calls them. He prefers the reports from patrol cars and the metallic voice of the operator back at headquarters announcing the discovery of dead bodies at different points in the city. In a place like Buenos Aires there is a certain harmony to the crimes; it is like a good, well-established orchestra that has no virtuosi, but where no-one plays out of tune either. Even the adolescents are veterans of a neighbourhood war who do not study military manuals, but who were brought up on the Holy City's human rubbish tips, received their first beatings before they could walk unaided and know they cannot avoid the betrayals that keep them alive. The only thing they feel sorry about is not having killed.

Verónica finds it impossible to listen to him and the police radio at the same time:

"Put some music on or I'm getting out, Walter. Here comes a taxi." Carroza gives a smug smile; he knows she will not carry out her threat. For two reasons – the first (and less important, he suspects) is that she might be killed. Then again, she wants to learn more about Ana Torrente. To keep her happy, he spins the dial. He finds the Los Panchos trio singing the tango, "The Day You Love Me", a golden oldie as clammy as the weather outside. Veronica is satisfied. "Where does Ana fit with the drugs baron your colleagues kidnapped?"

"He was taken to a hideout in the Alas building. It's in the military zone, on the fortieth floor. Not every prisoner gets to fly so high. The operation was co-ordinated by Oso Berlusconi."

"Who is this 'Oso Berlusconi'?"

"A professional, Verónica. Like you or me, someone who works for others who want to see results. Don't ask too much; the less you know, the better for you."

Verónica accepts that, in his twisted way, the skull is trying to protect her. He wants her to know only what he considers important: who Miss Bolivia is for example, or why she should give up the job the Lomas magistrate has asked her to do, or about himself, to a certain extent at least.

Above Oso Berlusconi there are a lot of people giving instructions from their comfortable armchairs in carpeted offices. People who keep accounts and only learn to use computers to make bank transfers. Patagonia is a windswept desert, home to more paleolithic fossils than human inhabitants. It costs twice as much to live there as in the rest of Argentina, so only the Tehuelches and Araucanians even think of staying: the foreigners only come to shoot deer and fence off what they consider to be their land. There are government officials who have become rich simply by looking the other way when the world's millionaires buy up national parks with deer included – but without Araucanians – they insist, to clinch the deal.

"But a Colombian drugs baron is a different matter. Imagine the scandal; no politician would survive it."

"Was he killed then?"

Carroza switches off the flashing light and starts to speed up. Glancing in his rear-view mirror, he changes up to fourth.

"The idea was to show him who is in control in Argentina. To keep him until a couple of hours before the cruise ship left and negotiate with him."

That was why Oso Berlusconi had gone to the Alas building. The Colombian already had his own people installed down in Patagonia – locals, of course, and opposition politicians in a good position to embarrass the governing party with requests for information if the governor tried to make things difficult for them. The only way to weaken them was by going to the source, to cut off the flow of white stuff: if they wanted drugs, they would have to go to Colombia to get them. They considered killing him and his mermaid, faking an assault in the street (it happens all the time in Buenos Aires) but in some government office or other they discovered the crock of gold and made their move before the two could be killed.

"So the federal cops saved their lives," Verónica concludes.

"You're learning; we're not such bad people."

But this was no humanitarian gesture; they were following orders.

The air force provided the logistics: a couple of group captains and a brigadier. There are always officers happy to supplement the meagre wages democracy concedes them. Oso Berlusconi had precise instructions: there were areas that they would allow the Colombian to control, tourist centres still being developed, small but prosperous towns. It was all a matter of negotiation and recalibrating, standard business practice. It would not be quite such a good deal for the Colombian, but it was still a fortune. And the clinching argument: if he did not agree, he would lose his hide.

But Oso Berlusconi arrived too late. Someone else had got there first.

"Someone betrayed him," spits Carroza, still peering into the rear mirror. "We're being followed," he says, moving up into fifth and accelerating.

Alarmed, Verónica turns to look behind them. There are lots of cars and headlights, any one could be tailing them. Carroza's instinct is working overtime.

*

A few hours earlier, two men in flight lieutenants' uniforms enter the Alas building. They respond to the ground-floor guard's salute by touching the visors of their peaked caps and head straight for the lifts before he has time to ask them where they are going or if they are from the building.

As it draws closer to the thirty-ninth floor, the lift judders like Carroza's Renault. "It's like a Douglas D.C.3 in the midst of a storm," says one of the lieutenants. "Don't tell me you've flown a D.C.3," the other lieutenant says admiringly. "I've never been in a plane in my fucking life," replies the first man. Their laughter adds to the cocktail-shaker effect of the lift.

They walk up the stairs to the fortieth floor. The door to the disused radio transmitter converted into a hideout opens, and Sergeant Capello greets them with all the formality of a court flunkey receiving the King and Queen of Spain. Sitting as if waiting to see their dentist, Osmar Arredri and Sirena Mondragón smile at the newcomers. On the floor next to them what looks like a rolled-up carpet is a rolled-up carpet, but with a filling. Although she is bound and gagged, Rosa Montes from police public relations looks relieved to see the newcomers: they are members of the armed forces and the armed forces are men of their word. They fight in wars and sacrifice their lives for the fatherland, but they do not touch women. To them, every woman is a mother, girlfriend or sister. All the same, she quickly decides to close her eyes again in case they think she might give them away.

One flight lieutenant takes the untied Colombian couple with him. When asked, they say they have been well treated and follow him down the corridor. The other lieutenant orders Capello to take care of Group Captain Castro. Of course he will and more than willingly, replies Capello. "What about her?"

"I'll see to her," says the air-force lieutenant who has never been in a plane.

No sooner has the sergeant left to carry out his orders than the lieutenant lifts the filled carpet at one end and drags it over to the window. He opens it and manoeuvres the carpet out onto its launching pad.

It is useless for Rosamonte to try to claw at the carpet to prevent the ejection of her poor, stick-thin body. The lieutenant shakes the carpet out of the window frame and Rosamonte falls through the air like a rocket that has run out of fuel, a stray bullet buffeted by the wind that is still blowing strongly. For a brief second it lifts her and pushes her towards calle Madero. She shuts her eyes more tightly than ever, just as she did when she was a little girl and Snow White's stepmother came to offer her an apple, or when the man with the sack came into her room to steal it from her. A sudden gust of wind, which high up among these buildings around Retiro has gathered enough strength to become almost an urban hurricane, lifts her once more and carries her across the railway lines of the port like a sheet of paper or an angel.

The Californian tourist who is coming out of a restaurant, singing the praises of juicy Argentine beef, suddenly feels the wallet where he has stashed his gold card snatched from his grasp. By the time he recovers from his surprise, his wife is still shrieking with terror at the sight of the body that has splattered against the pavement right in front of them.

The tourist's wallet was the last thing Rosamonte desperately tried to clutch at after freeing herself in mid-air from the ropes round her wrist. Perhaps she was trying to fly, or to soften the impact; perhaps she was trying finally to switch her bedroom light on and put an end to her nightmares.

*

A hundred and twenty. Now Carroza is having real difficulty speaking: reasoning while racing along at what for the battered Renault is breakneck speed is highly dangerous. Every now and then the car glides out of control across the soaked asphalt. "It's called aquaplaning," he manages to say to a female lawyer who is beginning to suspect this night could be her last. The car shudders as if they were going at two hundred k.p.h. Their pursuers must be having a high old time, splitting their sides laughing at the Yorugua's feeble attempts to get away from them. They flash their headlights for him to stop: what is the point, they must think, of putting off the final moment for a minute or two? But when Carroza does not see sense, they accelerate and pull up alongside.

"Hold on tight and get down!"

Verónica throws herself to the floor, but can find nothing to hold on to but Carroza's leg as he pushes his foot to the floor. The Renault starts to spin like a giant top round the vast illuminated expanse of the bridge over Avenida Cabildo. By some miracle, it ends up heading towards the exit – except that this is no exit, it is the entrance to the motorway, which Carroza speeds down the wrong way. The bored driver looking at the timetable on his bus cannot believe his eyes when he sees the Renault passing him by on the wrong side of the road. He looks into his rear mirror expecting to see it crash, to hear the smash of metal against the barrier, but all he glimpses for a fleeting moment are its red rear lights and the car disappearing round a bend. He curses a thousand times having to work on Saturdays – "It's a night for drunks, they ought to pay us double," he protests out loud to the passenger in the front seat who complains, "the police should do something to stop those idiots getting behind the wheel".

"Less than an hour went by between the forced landing of the public-relations policewoman and her arrival at the morgue," says Carroza. He is again dawdling along at twenty k.p.h., but this time in the leafy, quiet and empty streets of Saavedra. "Goyeneche used to live in this neighbourhood," he says nostalgically.

"So now you like tango, do you?"

"I used to like Goyeneche. And the neighbourhood he lived and died in. Saavedra, where the trees provide shade even at night, the birds sleep but sing in the dreams of the local kids. Even in their nests there is sadness." Verónica stares up at the trees, trying to imagine the birds, their nests, the sadness. "She arrived without a head."

This is what Deputy Inspector Walter Carroza says, as he crawls along at twenty or less per hour with the widow of the murdered cop who was his buddy.

"Who cut it off? Who could cut off the head of a body smashed to smithereens after falling forty floors? And in the middle of the street?"

"Or in the ambulance," speculates Carroza. "First aid."

"*The Last Binge*," Goyeneche would have sung if he had been there now, at 4 a.m., on the stoop of the house where he spent all his life, on calle Melián, in the shade of the shade, so deep in the night as always, drawing a curtain across the heart.

4

She finds Laucha asleep on the living-room sofa, with the television still on. It is showing a repeat of an interview programme with politicians. It is 5 a.m. on a Sunday, but there they are, smooth-tongued as ever, oozing hypocrisy, talking about democracy, about the disasters the government is committing and the action each of them would take – one of them to restore order, the other to bring in a revolution – when they come to power. "They're ridiculous at any time of day," Verónica tells herself, "but they're especially pathetic at this hour of the morning."

She does not switch the set off because that might wake Laucha. She prefers to sit in the armchair opposite and stare into space, zapping between channels until she too dozes off, knowing that if she goes to bed she will not get a moment's sleep. She should have said yes to Carroza's invitation and gone with him to his lair on calle Azara to look at his gallery of photos of serial killers as if they were holiday or wedding snapshots. But Verónica has had her fill of criminals: "That's enough for one day," she told the skeleton man. "Anyone can be a murderer, it doesn't matter what they look like," she added by way of a goodbye, demonstrating a wisdom Carroza acknowledged with a grunt.

One of those faces means Carroza joins the band of brothers who spend another sleepless Buenos Aires night. The face has seared itself into his memory not so much because of the mad intensity of the gaze, or the inevitable scar. No, it is something else, a similarity, a family likeness.

"It's number 347B in your gallery," he tells Scotty, who answers him at 7 a.m., sounding as if he has got up this early on Sunday to go and play tennis rather than to work his shift at headquarters.

"Let's see . . ." He flicks through the files, the cardboard indexes of the computer age, trying to find more information while he juggles with the black coffee he had just made himself when his extension rang. "Here it is. But it doesn't add much. There's just a photo; whoever stuck it on is an idiot. He must have put it there, then gone to the toilet for a wank and forgot all about it."

"Who is he, at least? He must have a name."

Scotty, a descendant of Irish immigrants born in Argentina, looks at the card as if it were a stamp from Bantusaland, an anonymous eccentricity from a non-existent country.

"It could be anyone's photo, Carroza. But they must have got the wrong department, this is the federal police, not the zoo. Underneath it says 'Jaguar'. Must be his nickname, his alias, the name the guy wants to be called to keep his spirits up, so that he can go on murdering people."

"Who started the file and when? Am I talking to a cop or the zoo?"

"To the zoo, head monkey here, you asshole. The man who started the file left the force three years ago."

"Who is he, where can I find him?"

"Dardo Julio Martínez, legal clerk. Transferred against his wishes to Lomas cemetery."

"Lomas!" Carroza shouts triumphantly, as if a lightbulb has just come on in his brain. "All the crap that's happened in the past few days has come from Lomas."

"But he's dead," Scotty reminds him. "Tuberculosis, complicated by pancreatitis, it says here. We've got full details of how he died: they keep tabs on us in the force, but say nothing about the criminals. Apparently it was A.I.D.S."

"Nobody dies forever, Scotty. Look at Jesus and what a surprise he gave the Jews in Galilee."

"But this is Buenos Aires, Carroza. Get some sleep. This isn't Jerusalem."

"Second mistake," says Carroza, as if he was still talking to Verónica. "Now more than ever, Buenos Aires is a Holy City."

*

A couple, a man and woman in their forties, with two children. A typical family entering a church in Buenos Aires looking solemn, searching for somewhere to sit in the back row of pews in Our Lady of Pompeya church. Nine o'clock Mass, a time for devout Catholics who go to church every week and take communion, regular donors to Caritas: charity is inseparable from doctrine and the Christian way of life, there are so many poor homeless people, so many single mothers, so much abortion.

The boy and girl go to confession first, then the mother. They return to their pews looking contrite, with their different penances: ten Ave Marías or twenty, depending on the sin. Finally it is the man's turn. He walks over head down, his sins weighing on him like Jesus's cross on the streets of Jerusalem.

The slow, gruff voice emerges from the darkness inside the confessional as if it is coming from hell itself:

"We've got Osmar Arredri. In twenty-four hours he's going to sing like a canary to the local and international press. You know what you have to do. Remember, two million dollars cash for the community. Ah, and fifty Ave Marías, you have sinned too often, my son."

Weighed down still further, genuinely saddened and almost as troubled as the Virgin on the altar who already knows what the future holds for her son conceived without sin, the man leaves the confessional and looks for a quiet corner where he can use his mobile.

"Those bastards have raised the price. And they've brought the deadline forward. What shall we do?"

He receives instructions, words that only half-reassure him. There is no absolution or condemnation, so he returns to his family and kneels beside his wife.

"What did the father tell you?" she asks, eyes tightly closed in holy devotion.

"To keep praying."

*

Oso Berlusconi does not seem surprised by the price hike his subordinate has just told him of.

The Argentine economy has always been plagued by inflation and then again the *Queen of Storms* is due to set sail at noon on Monday, so there is no time to tie up all the loose ends. Besides, when it comes to business, improvisation always benefits the speculators.

Nor are the negotiations over the three couples going smoothly. The people meant to be paying their ransoms are demanding proof they are still alive, guarantees they will be set free once the payments have been made. They want to know who they are dealing with, how reliable they are, if they are really in charge: they do not want to risk wasting the capital of their respective companies. The kidnap victims are not just anyone and Argentina (they insist) is not the Middle East. You can negotiate with the Arabs, they are serious about this kind of thing: if they say they are going to kill, they kill, if they say they are going to commit suicide, they blow their own guts out without a second thought. But Argentine gangsters are tarred with the same brush as their colleagues who operate supposedly on the right side of the law.

Oso Berlusconi visits the three shacks where the couples are being held. It is daytime now and Sunday – "Perhaps some of you would like to go to Mass?" But none of the kidnapped can understand Spanish. Nobody in the Anglo-Saxon world is really interested in a patois spoken only by Chicanos, Colombian drugs dealers, Argentine thugs and the new rich of the far west of Europe. Not in any truly civilized country.

Oso strolls among the living dead, concealed beneath his hood. Tall, massively built, his voice a rasping growl, muddy boots, he peers at them, assessing their worth. Each of the men is tied back to back with his female partner: the French couple are already sitting in their own shit. Oso gives orders for them to be moved and for the floor to be sluiced before the heat of the day and the smell attract flies. "We can't hand over damaged goods," he explains to the guards.

What pleasure, though, what memories it brings back. Far too many years since he has done this, walking round slowly, clicking his boot heels, gently prodding someone on the floor, or cuffing them round the head, then when they protest or complain, increasing the dose slowly: protest and a blow, complaint and a kick, if someone sobs that merits a boot to the kidneys, or a casual treading on their genitals, howls muffled by their gags, bodies trembling and shaking as if a stick of dynamite has exploded inside them, the cardboard walls of the shack reinforced by thick layers of polystyrene, until one of the guards, a shanty-town dweller he himself hired, timidly suggests he stop, the cries can be heard outside, he whips the butt of his gun across the man's face, his mouth is smeared with blood, only his eyes are glowing, still fixed on him, "shit-faced cunt, who asked your opinion, remind me to kill you", and Oso goes on punishing the prisoners until the violence gradually subsides, the kicks are no longer to the kidneys, the blows to the head are little more than his hand touching their matted hair and the sweating bald patches, it is as if Oso Berlusconi was stepping away from himself.

What pleasure, though, and what memories it brings back.

5

Nobody rings Verónica on her mobile with good news before midday on a Sunday. She does not have friends to invite her to come and eat ravioli, she is not a member of any club where she can go and play tennis, a game she gave up years ago when she was widowed for the first time.

"Verónica, I need to see a magistrate."

It is the strangulated voice of Pacogoya. He is so out of breath it sounds as if he has been running all night.

"There are none around. They're either on holiday or giving seminars abroad."

"This is no time for jokes. They're going to kill me."

"Me too, but I don't go disturbing people for such trivial matters. What trouble have you got yourself into this time?"

Pacogoya explains in a brief, confused way. As she listens, Verónica wonders how all these people – Miss Bolivia, Walter Carroza, Pacogoya – have become part of her life, what window she left open. Too late to throw them out now, they are so firmly installed that she herself is in the line of fire as well.

Laucha Giménez, who has finally woken up, shares a semi-cold coffee with her and departs. "I'll leave you on your own with your delivery faun," she says with a laugh, not even wanting to know what the faun has just told her friend.

"I escaped any way I could," Pacogoya tells her as soon as he arrives, still out of breath.

"My friend Laucha as well: she ran off when she heard you were on the way here."

"I met her on the ground floor," Pacogoya says. "She didn't even say hello; I don't know what you've been telling her about me."

"She's still half-asleep. You woke her up when you rang. Why do you think no woman can pass you by without ogling you?"

Between tremors, Pacogoya bestows her a brief smile. Although it has not rained during the night, he is soaking wet.

"Don't tell me you crossed the Riachuelo . . ."

"Swimming, yes. It's not that polluted. That river doesn't deserve the bad reputation it has. The ecologists have made it a scapegoat; where the painter Quinquela Martín saw beauty, they only find filth. Anyway, I prefer to die poisoned. That at least takes time, you've got a better chance than if you're shot to pieces."

"A better chance to do what, Paco?"

"To say goodbye to my friends, to be here with you now."

He reaches out for her, but Verónica pushes him away. The thought that he has been swimming in that sewer is enough to stifle any attempt at seduction.

Pacogoya does not tell her the full story. The kidnappers wanted to kill him because he had become an obtrusive witness; but he does not mention the part he played in the kidnappings. It does not take Verónica long to see through his subterfuge, though: what was he doing in the shanty town, why did they take him there if he had only been in touch with them when Uncle disappeared?

"They made me do it," Pacogoya says, trying to justify himself. "I had no choice if I wanted to stay alive."

"I defend self-confessed murderers, Paco. The dregs who write 'life sentence' with a 'v', who cut their girlfriends or their mothers to pieces. But what I really can't stomach are informers, grasses. Get out of here."

"Don't abandon me now."

"You abandoned me first. You said the ship was about to leave when you knew it wasn't and you were already choosing human beings to do a deal with. Get out and don't come back." The shudders running through Pacogoya's puny body become uncontrollable. This T-shirt revolutionary, this seducer whose batteries have run out: Verónica is not going to protect him, she is not going to call any magistrate or allow him to hide in her apartment. If she is about to be killed, she prefers it to be for something she herself has done, not for somebody else's misdemeanours. "If I had the Bersa, I'd shoot you myself, for being such a creep."

Pacogoya still looks at her incredulously, his grimace saying: you cannot be serious, this is a game, isn't it? You relented just now and let me in. "Let's have a rest together."

He stretches out his arm. His intention is to brush against her cheek with the warm hand Verónica has so often leaned her weary head on, breathing in the smell of imported perfume: lotions from France, oranges from Paraguay. This time, though, his hand stinks of the Riachuelo, of a watery grave, of someone resurrected who has stopped to ask the way when he has already come to the end of the road.

"Go to the bus terminus in Retiro. I've got friends in Tucumán, good people, friends I share with Laucha. They could help you if I tell them to."

"What does it depend on?" he asks, still shaking.

"You have to go to the police first."

Sore from exhaustion and having to swim across a filthy river, Pacogoya's eyes flash.

"A magistrate! That's why I want to see a magistrate, to get some legal protection."

"I'm not taking you, Paco. I don't believe in magistrates. Or in you anymore."

Bemused, Pacogoya adopts the pose of a fencer preparing to lunge in what he knows is an unequal fight. He protests:

"You're not going to tell me you believe in the cops, are you?"

"In one cop, just one," says Verónica.

*

Whenever a corpse gets too heavy for him, Deputy Inspector Carroza unloads his emotional baggage onto a psychoanalyst. Only occasionally: it is not therapy, nothing serious. Damián Bértola regards them as unofficial visits; he does not like thrillers, although he does admit to Carroza that perhaps one day he will sit down and write about some of the horrors he has described. Enough to make Chandler's hair stand on end.

"Give me time to die first," says Carroza. At that they laugh, and sometimes Carroza even pays the analyst for the session and the others for which he still owes him. Why some corpses and not others? What is the difference? What sort of death makes a professional pause and stare it in the face? "The death of a fifteen-year-old kid, for example."

Bértola listens to the story on the telephone. He writes one word, "patience", in his notebook. Carroza lights a fresh cigarette from the tip of the one he is smoking. He needs to smoke himself down to the bones, to disappear behind his nicotine cloud so that he can tell the story: he went into the poor-looking house in Floresta, one of the working-class districts built during the first Peronist government at the end of the 1940s, when Perón was still keeping his promises. The old couple were lying on the kitchen floor. The old man's throat had been slit, the old woman gasped her last breath in his arms.

Carroza leapt out into the yard, climbed onto the dividing wall and spotted the kid squatting in the next door yard, staring at him. He had not had time to escape and so sat there calmly, waiting for a moment's inattention or to be taken before a judge for minors. He was clean, no trace of blood on his clothes, crouching there like a goalkeeper preparing to save a penalty. The knife was in the kitchen and more than likely had no fingerprints on it: the boy had taken the precaution of wearing gloves, like a real goalkeeper, like someone he might be if he were given the chance to grow up and play in the youth team of a club like River Plate or Boca Juniors, if he was good enough.

But Deputy Inspector Carroza did not give him that chance. Perched up on the wall, he shot him twice, right between the eyes. He split his head in two like a fig, then dropped back down into the old couple's yard. A dog that must have been their pet, a mongrel that had been shut in until it was let out by the cops who followed Carroza into the house, suddenly started barking at him as if he was its owners' killer.

The same feeling, but for different reasons, takes hold of Carroza now, as he stares at the photo of the Jaguar. When he finds him, he will have to kill him. His instinct tells him he is still alive, that at some point their paths are bound to cross, that he will have to kill him. And for some reason or none, but due to something hidden like a marked card in the cardsharps' game he finds himself playing, he will once more feel the weight, the weary, choking sensation of a death like so many others.

The man in the photo, and what he has learned so far about the Jaguar, has something about him that disturbs Carroza. It is a family likeness that immediately put him on Carroza's most-wanted list, made him someone he takes mental note of, someone he is already on the lookout for all the time, even in his dreams.

Yet his criminal career is no different from that of other monsters who kill for pleasure rather than obvious gain. The only distinctive feature about the Jaguar's handiwork is that his victims arrive incomplete at the morgue. Sometimes the heads turn up two or three days later; at others, they never appear. Plus something else: the ones that do appear are empty, like those of so many people who go through life pretending to human beings. The brain, eyes and tongue have been scooped out, like pumpkins on display at Hallowe'en.

"Why do you tell me these things, Walter? They sicken me." This was Verónica's protest the night before, but that was why he had been to see her, to tell her the story. The dead bodies Ana Torrente had been leaving in her wake, like the prints from Cinderella's glass slippers, were all headless. The manager executed by the remnants of the Shining Path, the San Pedro dealer Miss Bolivia had gone to see thanks to Carroza and before him Matías Zamorano, the amputated right hand of Councillor Pox. Carroza has just found out that he too had been decapitated after his death. "It can't have been her," Verónica protests yet again. "She didn't have the tools or the strength. Although I'm no forensic expert, I suppose you can't cut a head off with a single blow."

"I'm not saying it was her," says Carroza, drawing tobacco smoke down as far as his soul, then expelling everything, soul included.

"Her manager was killed by the Shining Path; Zamorano by Pox's men. As far as we know, she was nowhere near Mary Poppins, the flying policewoman. The only death she could be accused of is that of the dealer. And with my Bersa."

"I checked yesterday and the gun isn't registered. It never was: it's a phantom gun, so don't worry on that score."

"I'm not losing any sleep over him. Scum like that deserve to be where they are," says Verónica. "How else can they be got rid of, except by exterminating them?"

"What about the law?" Carroza said, amused at the sudden outburst of violence that has turned Verónica's usually pale skin bright red.

"Law authorizes violence. Every law is a cross on a headstone."

"And in some of those tombs lie bodies who have something missing, Verónica. Corpses whose heads are somewhere else."

6

Now he is all alone.

He searches for a public telephone he can call Uncle from without giving away his identity. Perhaps Uncle has been resurrected and will answer, "Nephew, what a surprise"; perhaps he has come back from the dead and all this is no more than a nightmare he has just woken up from, which is why he has such a headache, is shaking so much and feels he is about to collapse, and is utterly alone in a way you can only be alone in cities like Buenos Aires.

There is no reply. He imagines Uncle's apartment stripped bare, with even the furniture gone. Someone who was always such a private person and would not even let his nephew come near. How things can change from one day to the next, thinks Pacogoya, in a tango moment.

Verónica for starters. Why has she got on to her moral high horse all of a sudden? Someone like her, with two dead husbands and many more (him included) queueing up to get into her bed.

The business world is always bloody, he tried to explain to her, as if she did not already know, nobody does a deal without putting pressure on, or trying to get rid of, any rivals. Armies do not go to war to free nations, but for business reasons, give and take, you are worth this much and no more. So what's the game this do-gooder lawyer is playing? It must be the menopause, hot flushes: the last few times she even complained that his Che Guevara pistol hurt her.

The cruise ship is leaving tomorrow. Tonight he ought to be back in the hotel, with the kidnap victims all set free, their ransoms paid and

154

him with a nice commission in his pocket. They had promised to pay him in cash at the very moment they were threatening to blow his brains out in Uncle's apartment unless he gave them the list of the richest among the rich, those who had spent the trip showing off clothes and jewels that had dazzled even the dolphins leaping alongside, conversations Pacogoya had heard on deck or in the dining rooms about investments all over the world, oil, computers, mergers and take-overs, all the financial chit-chat of people who will never know the joy of trying to scrape together enough small change for the bus.

Pacogoya kept his word: he identified the richest passengers and handed them over personally. With the promised commission he could retire straightaway, leave Argentina, even change his identity. He could shave off his beard, no longer be an imitation Che Guevara, the de-livery lover of women who were never satisfied, but spent their time masturbating as they criss-crossed the world, the tourist guide sleeping in a bunk while he serviced and comforted bloated lords and ladies who moaned endlessly about their suites as if they were being kept in cells, corrupted by so much wealth and power until they had nothing left to do but fill themselves with botox and silicone, fooled into thinking they could cheat death through plastic surgery.

He hangs up. No Uncle, no Verónica. He is not going to call that cop, hand himself over like an idiot. Who does that menopausal do-gooder take him for? In his hiker's backpack he has got enough stuff to be able to spend several months without having to worry, in some spot where nobody is looking for him. After all, he is not important enough for them to want to pursue him. They only kept him in that filthy shack in the Descamisados de América slum as a precaution. Then again, they did not know him well enough to be sure they could trust him and people like them had to be careful: perhaps they would have set him free in a few hours, along with the Europeans. Of course, then the victims would have identified him and goodbye Pacogoya, farewell to any more deals, he really would be joining Uncle or rotting in jail, where he would have been raped as soon as he got there, poor little, fragile little Che Guevara lookalike.

"Give him a call," said Verónica, meaning the skeleton who never stopped smoking. "Tell him where the kidnapped tourists are. Explain the exact location; he'll protect you, he never hangs his informers out to dry, as long as they can be of use to him. You don't have to hand yourself over. I'm not asking you to do that, just call him and tell him. Don't do it for the sake of your conscience, I know you haven't got one. Do it for your own safety. If the cops raid them, they'll be so busy shooting each other they'll forget to kill you."

But Pacogoya did not speak to Carroza. He did dial the number, but hung up as soon as he heard the smoke-filled skull's voice, echoing from another world.

He is near the Retiro bus station, but has no intention of going to Tucumán as Verónica suggested. Instead he buys a ticket south, to Esquel. He knows the region and there is a cabin by a river, with a Swedish woman who has discovered a tiny Sweden in the far south of Argentina where she does not have to pay taxes. She will always be waiting for him, she said the night he ended up in her bed during another cruise, in another ship, the *King of Madness*. This Swedish girl will open the door of her Nordic cabin to him, delighted to have someone to fuck so far from anywhere. Pacogoya might not even have to sell drugs to survive, if she includes him in her list of monthly outgoings. The Swedes – men and women – are fond of giving people asylum: they have that going for them, and Bergman.

An hour later, Pacogoya boards the bus that will take him non-stop to Esquel. It is a long journey, but what a relief to be able to sit comfortably and safely next to the window, to watch the city gradually losing density, dissolving into itself, into its suburbs, into increasingly open spaces, green pastures, flat green pampa, wheat, soya, green cows, *ciao* Buenos Aires, *ciao* Verónica menopausal Berutti, *ciao Queen of Storms. Adios*: the Che Guevara lookalike is heading for mountains where there are no malaria, Bolivians, or Rangers, only a rich Swede with whom he can fuck and fuck until the end of the world.

Scarcely half an hour has gone by when the bus pulls up at a toll booth. Pacogoya has already dozed off, but is woken up by the flashing red and blue lights of a police checkpoint by the roadside. A couple of Alsatians, held on a long leash by a cop with a gun in his right hand. Another two cops protecting him with shotguns. The dogs board the bus and before Pacogoya can even touch his backpack they are barking at him like hounds round a wild boar at bay. The cop with them orders him off the bus.

"Yes, you, sonny, the guy with the backpack. Get off the bus, you asshole!" If the other passengers had been a jury, they would already have found him guilty. A guy with a backpack and a straggly beard: he must be a drug addict. Under his jacket he is wearing a T-shirt with the image of the real Che on it. To the stake with him! Pacogoya is hustled off the bus. One of the dogs has its jaws clamped round his calf. A signal or whistle from its master and it would rip him to pieces. "What a weight he's carrying," the cop says, taking the backpack from him.

The bus speeds off, heading for Sweden.

Pacogoya promises himself he will call Verónica again as soon as they let him use a phone. She will curse him of course, but deep down she is not a bad sort and will end up being concerned about him, she will call a magistrate and get him legal protection, he will be alright. He would have been far worse off with the gang of kidnappers, waiting to be executed in that filthy shack by the Riachuelo.

"You must be Pacogoya." A rasping, distant voice, like that of someone who is already dead and buried but still has something to say. "Tourist guide, friend of Verónica Berutti, the lawyer who's such a good friend to criminals . . ." Somehow there is a friendly note to the voice. It has the sound of someone who never sleeps, the monotonous drone of a person reading a script without bothering too much about it. The guy is huge, the size of a mountain. The other cops slip away into the darkness and the dogs settle back meekly beside the patrol car, no doubt waiting for the next bus and the next asshole like him. "Where were you going?"

"To Esquel."

"Wow, a paradise on earth! Just a tourist visit?" Pacogoya knows this is the way cops ask questions. They never say anything straight out, like doctors do. Yes, just a visit, a few days, possibly a couple of weeks, someone is waiting for him. "You don't say! Who is waiting for you, so far from the rest of the world?"

"A young lady."

Pacogoya sketches a smile he hopes will get the cop on his side. He would have had more luck with the Alsatians.

"Poor woman, she's going to grow tired of waiting."

Still without raising his voice, the man twists Pacogoya's arm behind his back, handcuffs him, and drags him over to a grey vehicle parked a few metres from the federal and provincial patrol cars. A young woman is sitting in the front passenger seat. When Pacogoya is pushed into the back of the car, she turns towards him.

"Are you Paraguayan?"

The young woman is very pretty. She pronounces her "s"s like a Bolivian and seems friendly.

"I was born in the capital, Asunción," says Pacogoya, trying to recover, although he is still grimacing from the pain in his right arm. "But as a student I lived in Buenos Aires, then I travelled all over."

"I'm Ana Torrente."

She is blonde and blue-eyed, as friendly and beautiful as the death awaiting someone who has nothing left to lose.

"But she's known as Miss Bolivia."

This is not necessary, but the cop is enjoying himself as he clambers into the driving seat. He is glad he has annoyed her and looks into the rear-view mirror to see if there is any reaction from Pacogoya. Then he pulls out onto the motorway and starts to plunge back into the bowels of Buenos Aires, siren blaring on the grey Toyota.

He accelerates and, although he is not hungry, Oso Berlusconi licks his lips, imagining the feast.

7

He never goes to cemeteries, they are not his style. Not even for the funerals of colleagues killed in action, or to visit relatives whose faces and personal histories are buried along with them. But this rainy, grey Sunday afternoon he has made an exception. He can feel his body rejecting the idea: the sensation that if he leant over any grave it would be to vomit.

Class divisions do not end when life does: they go on discriminating against the dead. Some are buried in vaults with fine stained-glass windows and proud marble walls. Others are filed away in endless rows of niches, while the poorest are tipped straight into the ground, where profaning dogs dig up their bones at night.

This afternoon, Deputy Inspector Carroza is another of these dogs. The chief attendant warns him the cemetery is going to close in half an hour: why doesn't he leave his car outside in the street, because he has to lock the main gate at six on the dot? If he comes in on foot, he will be able to leave by the little side gate that, if he would like to contribute to the municipal pension fund, he would be happy to leave unlocked.

Carroza does not even bother to get out of his car. He asks where he can find Dardo Julio Martínez's grave.

"The register is closed today. It's Sunday."

"So what happens on Sundays? Do the dead come back to life, and go and watch football, or have picnics?"

The attendant's nervous giggle is silenced by a ten-peso note, but he waves an arm as if to suggest that is not enough to open the files. He does not have the key: with the transfer of another ten pesos it appears as if by magic. Well, Carroza thinks to console himself, he saves enough using gas for his car: he can allow himself the little luxury of bribing a poor wretch like this rather than smashing his teeth in.

"I'll wait for you to come out then," says the attendant, guessing he might receive a further contribution to the pension fund. The rain keeps beating down, it is only logical that skeleton man does not want to get wet.

How many of all those buried here might have crossed my path? thinks Carroza as he stares at the rows of graves. Lust, riches and that crazy impulse to finish the other off, to erase them from the map. Damián Bértola, the inspector of consciences with whom Verónica shares her office expenses and whom he himself turns to occasionally, has not got the faintest idea, although he does offer some relief. It is not a question of guilt, it is more like the weight on him. That sometimes becomes too much and then the psychoanalyst can help. It is as though he is choking on something and has to flush it out or bring it up. But Carroza pays him for that – or does so occasionally. Bértola does what all witchdoctors, shamans, or exorcists do – a little bit of the devil shared out between everyone, it is impossible to bear the weight of all of it alone.

"What if it wasn't the kid?" Bértola asked him when Carroza told him the story of the old couple slaughtered in their own home in the working-class neighbourhood of Floresta. All that was taken was some loose change, a few picture cards of the Virgin, a television set and a gold-plated locket. "And even if he did kill them," the analyst insisted, "didn't he deserve his day in court? Couldn't he be rehabilitated, offered

160

the affection he never knew, perhaps even just be fed him properly, so that he understands what he has done?"

Sometimes Carroza wonders if it would not be better to talk to a priest, make donations to Caritas, or help build a new parish church. He does not believe in Him and He does not believe in him, he is sure of that. But they could come to an agreement to collaborate, a pact between informers, with priests as intermediaries. If He really were all-knowing, it could save Carroza unpleasant trips such as this one to a cemetery, finally to locate the grave of Dardo Julio Martínez, the person who started the file on the Jaguar. A wooden cross lost among hundreds of other crosses. Carroza comes to a halt, levers himself out of the car. He immediately gets soaked, but opens the car boot, takes out a spade and starts to dig.

He is grateful for the rain. Alleluia! the earth gives way generously, soft as a whore's vagina or as obliging as a queer's arse. He digs with the same fury as the rain lashing down – alleluia! Perhaps the agreement is already working and the all-seeing He already knows what he is looking for, and he will not be soaked in vain. He reaches the coffin. He does not bother to scrape any more earth off, but instead beats at it with the spade. The rotten top soon splits open. Using the tip of the spade as a lever, he prises up the aluminium sheet nailed over the stiff when he was laid out, just in case he woke up and changed his mind.

It is all too easy. If this was a safe Carroza would be a millionaire by now; all he would have to do is bend down and scoop up the banknotes, the gold coins, the jewels. But there is no treasure trove, only a heap of bones, and alleluia! none of them from a head.

He tosses the spade into the boot and gets back into his car. He could back up twenty metres to the end of this section of graves in order to turn, but he has had enough. He does a U-turn across the graves, hearing some of them crack and knocking over at least half a dozen crosses. Back on the asphalt, he puts his foot down.

The attendant, who had been hoping for a further contribution to the pension fund, sees him racing in his direction like a Formula One driver. He rushes out to open the gate, but is too late. The crash as the bonnet of Carroza's Renault smashes open the locks causes great enthusiasm among the group of flower sellers and tardy relatives seeking cover from the rain on the pavement opposite.

"One of the dead is escaping!" someone shouts and they all cheer, just as they heard the fans cheer Boca's third goal against Chacarita on the florist's radio.

*

Something very serious has to happen for ambassadors to interrupt their Sunday leisure pursuits. Those of the rest of the week as well, but especially on Sundays, because then they are far away from their embassies, playing golf or sailing their yachts on the Delta.

At least the afternoon's heavy rain makes it less of a sacrifice to return to the city in such a hurry. The ambassadors of France and Italy have been summoned by their German colleague to his private apartment two blocks from the embassy, a mansion in Palermo Chico copied from a Parisian town house. Possibly due to nostalgic feelings inherited from a great uncle who was an officer in occupied France, Günther Weber feels at home in French-style surroundings, neighbourhoods or residences that retain or have restored the ruins of a civilization that had no need to respect human rights to come out on top. Almost everywhere in the world, German official buildings have fallen foul of a detestable modernist aesthetic that makes them look exactly the same as those of the North Americans, their victors.

André Villespierre and Giácomo Montegassa arrive on time, one coming from the north, the other from the south. The French diplomat was playing golf until he was floating in water like a poached egg at an estate in San Andres de Giles, about a hundred kilometres from Buenos Aires. The Italian was cantering along the windy beaches deserted at this time of year between Cariló and Pinamar, followed by a pair of body-guards who are veterans not of any colonial war but of trying to save their own lives and keep up with him.

The German Ambassador, who had not left Buenos Aires, received a call from a friend who worked as a Reuters correspondent. At a bar-becue for foreign journalists, his friend had just heard about the kidnapping of the three couples from the cruise ship. The bearer of the news was an Argentine from Córdoba, a friend of the owner of the house who turned up uninvited, downed a bottle of Vents du Bour-gogne and then called for silence so that he could tell everyone his story. No, he said, it was not a joke like the ones that made people from his province so famous, but something that his source, a government official who was usually very careful about what he said, had made him swear to keep secret until at least Monday afternoon.

If the devil were to turn up in a Carmelite convent, it is only logical that despite their vows of silence the nuns would run off screaming. But the man from Córdoba could not understand what happened to every-one, where they all got to, when the foreign journalists suddenly ran from the barbecue in search of their laptops and mobile phones in order to transmit the scoop to their respective employers.

"All Europe knows about it," the host Günther Weber tells his col-leagues. "The news is already on the Internet, but the bunch of *arrivistes* in this government are still calling for discretion."

"Precious hours have been lost," says André Villespierre.

"*Mascalzone, porca miseria,*" adds Giácomo Montegassa.

The German Ambassador pours brandy into goblets bearing the embassy crest. It's a vintage drink, he explains, that the communists used to make for several decades and kept well hidden in their East Berlin cellars.

"Those communists didn't do everything so badly: this brandy is excellent," the Italian enthuses.

"Almost French," André tops him.

They make a toast to the European Community of hedonists, laugh in their different languages, down the brandy and pour themselves another glass. Then they want to hear what else Günther has to tell them.

"While you were travelling back here," he says, "I got through to Jennifer González, the Interior Minister's private secretary." Two lustful glints appear in the German's eyes. He is not yet fifty, a metre ninety-five centimetres tall, blond and athletic, the superior race. It is obvious, at least to his community colleagues, that he is not happy sleeping with his wife who is ten years older than him, despite the fact that the companies she owns offer him a valuable safeguard against the always unpredictable fortunes of a political career like the one he is pursuing in his own country. "Thanks to Jennifer . . ."

The deliberately lengthy pause is so that his colleagues can imagine Jennifer, and her twenty-five delicious and obliging years romping over the vast surfaces of the only apparently resting Teuton.

Thanks to Jennifer, the minister called him not long ago to put himself at the disposal, not merely of Germany, France and Italy, but of the whole of Western Christendom in order to rescue the kidnapped tourists that very night.

"He's a practical, determined man, who I believe has some business in hand with a German company, whose major shareholder just happens to be one of the people abducted. He has immediately given orders to the federal police and an elite force of specialists in recovering kidnap victims has been assembled. They were all trained at the School of the Americas in Panama and will not stop or even sleep until they have found what they are looking for. I have their names here."

He shows them the fax he has just received on the direct line from the ministry. All ranking officers, no greenhorns, that is obvious from their position and their records. They have freed a number of executives from leading companies without a single one of them being hurt.

"They are commanded by a man who enjoys the minister's absolute confidence, someone Jennifer herself knows and admires, because she is the one who hands him the cheques the minister makes out in his name so that he can continue to defend the constitutional order with such enthusiasm."

He is implacable, Günther says that Jennifer says. Hard as a rock, rasping voice like a blues singer, one metre ninety tall, a hundred and ten kilos of muscles forged every day in the gym, and a prize-winning marksman. The Italian Ambassador seems delighted when he reads his name.

"Berlusconi, like our Prime Minister! *Forza Italia!*"

Italians and Germans, all that is missing is the Japanese Ambassador and they could form a new Fascist Axis. The French Ambassador twists his mouth in distaste. He feels outnumbered; he particularly mistrusts Italians and Third World policemen. He is not worried that the squad are hired assassins; he wants them to be serious about it. He points out to the Italian that Berlusconi is listed by his nickname, "Oso" the Bear, rather than his real name.

He willingly accepts a third glass, however. At least the brandy is communist.

8

Verónica knew nothing about Carolina until the rainy morning Romano was buried. She had returned distraught to her apartment from the funeral, not wishing to reach the following day, wondering what on earth came next, whether anything was worth it: all the usual stuff when your world crashes around you. When the phone rang she thought it must be someone unable to go to the funeral ringing to offer condolences, so she did not answer, until it rang again half an hour later.

It was Carroza, calling from some noisy place. Verónica could hear laughter and music in the background, and wondered if he had not heard about Romano: what was going through that guy's head? She said she was hanging up, because she could not understand what he was saying, he was either drugged or very drunk. And yes, he had called to offer his condolences, but almost as soon as she answered, Carolina made her appearance: "She's got her arms round me," said Carroza, "I can't bear it, I want to go with her right now."

In her mind's eye, Verónica saw a hostess, a pathetic forty-year-old in some bar down by the port, embracing Carroza with arms jangling with cheap bracelets, shamelessly stroking his groin, arousing him for the price of a couple of drinks and one of the always crumpled banknotes the cop carries in the back pocket of his trousers. She hung up, but a faint buzzing told her Carroza was still there, still on the line with his whore. Verónica could not understand it: was he phoning just to show off, or was he going to tell her what he knew about how Romano had died?

"Don't go," she heard Carroza's slurred, desolate voice. "I don't want Carolina to get her way."

He pronounced the word Carolina with a kind of shaky tenderness. Nobody spoke about a casual pickup that way, still less a prostitute. But it did not sound as if he was talking about a girlfriend or a lover either, there was no passion in his skull-like voice. Someone as desiccated as Carroza only stayed upright thanks to his obsessions and fears, and if he was in love, as Verónica thought he must be, he went about it like a sleepwalker. He was only aware of it as a headache, as the remote memory of something else he had done, Carroza crawling like an insect across his tiny, vast world.

Carolina, Verónica thinks at once when she picks the phone up late that Sunday evening. Again she hears laughter and background music from some low dive; alcohol, women and Carroza, although this time he is speaking clearly and urgently.

"I'll come and pick you up," he says. "Don't leave until I get there. Don't open the door for anyone."

He stifles Verónica's protest by reminding her of the night of broken windows in pre-war Nazi Germany, when gangs of S.S. rampaged through cities and towns beating up thousands of Jews, and killing many of them. "*Kristallnacht*," Carroza says in a harsh German that surprises Verónica. She asks him what on earth the things the Nazis did in 1938 have got to do with her life.

He promises to explain the moment he gets there. She is not to open the door, even to her friends – that could be a trick to get into her apartment. Verónica decides Carroza must have had an attack of paranoia. She calls Bértola.

"What did you give him? What drugs?"

"I don't prescribe drugs," says the analyst in self-defence. He is sprawled out on his sofa with his dog, Mauser. "I was reading Derrida. We cannot ignore melancholy, Verónica, or we will forget everything and that will be the end of us."

"What will be the end of us, or me at least, is something else entirely, Damián. What did you give that cop?"

"In the first place, 'that cop' is your friend. He was your deceased first husband's colleague, who was also a cop. Second, it's not usual for a cop to come and see me. They don't much like looking at themselves in the mirror, except to shave. What does his job consist of? Putting people in jail. And yours? Getting people out. What is there in between the two? Ordinary people, deserts, agonies."

"Don't play at being a philosopher on the brink of the abyss, Damián. Help me understand what I'm up against."

"That's my job, Verónica. But today is Sunday."

"I know, and yesterday was Saturday. Nobody commits suicide at the weekend."

"I never said that, don't exaggerate. That cop would deny his own shadow. That's why he never eats and smokes like a chimney. But he believes that something exists beyond his personal wasteland, some promised land. In his own way, he is a believer. And like all believers, he's mistaken."

Mauser, who had been asleep, suddenly pricks up his ears. He stares inquisitively at Bértola, then pushes his snout towards the receiver, sensing Verónica's voice, her anxiety.

"He managed to scare me. What they did not succeed in doing by killing my bodyguard, or following us last night, Carroza is doing right now. He says a night of broken glass is at hand."

An admiring whistle comes down the phone. The psychoanalyst is delighted by any revisiting of mankind's macabre history.

"And that's what scared you? Are you Jewish?"

"I don't know why your clients don't tell you to take a running jump, Bértola."

"They do, believe me. Not very often, but sometimes. That guy doesn't play games, Verónica, he kills for real. He's a born killer, it's a talent he has. The rest of us would have our consciences torn to pieces; he only needs to talk, to find someone who will listen, but he is the one who chooses what he wants to repent for. And from what he has told me so far, he doesn't see any reason to repent. In that sense he's a disciple of Spinoza."

"I don't read philosophy. It bores me."

"But God exists, Verónica. And philosophy helps you understand what his intentions are."

*

Oso Berlusconi's Sunday has been ruined. The sudden call from the minister has ruined the peace of his country retreat, which he reached transporting Pacogoya in the car boot as if he were a tent and equipment for enjoying a camping holiday.

Oso has a small cottage, a few metres from Route Eight, out beyond Pilar. It is an area with lots of weekend places, and gated communities where the rich dream of their paradises and hire people like him to defend them, if necessary by force. But Oso chose to build his refuge outside these bourgeois concentration camps. He loves nature and therefore danger, the fight to survive: it is part of his confused D.N.A.

"You have to find them, Oso," the minister told him. "You know how to. Set them free tonight and tomorrow you'll be police chief. I'll call the president right now to tell him what's going on and he can draw up the decree."

The minister did not give him time to object. Being made police chief is no reward, more like a sop for losers who never learned how to make serious money. A police chief is a moving target all politicians can open fire on when something goes wrong, when lefties stir up trouble by infiltrating the trade unions and the slumdwellers' associations, when they block roads and upset nearly everyone, then get themselves killed so they can call themselves martyrs, or scream that the police chief has to go, along with the minister, why not the entire government while we are at it?

Oso thought he would enjoy Sunday with Pacogoya, but now it is ruined. He carries him, bound and gagged, from the boot of his Toyota. The cops on duty at the road toll booth, on the lookout for drugs mules coming and going from the north of Argentina, breathed a sigh of relief when Oso told them, "I'll take care of him". It is Sunday and no-one likes to have to sit at a computer or an Olivetti to draw up reports or fill in forms. They might miss the best of the day, the results of the football matches, if they had to take statements from some poor wretch who knows nothing, who was only used because he is desperate to eat, or is an outcast.

Oso stands Pacogoya up and kicks him into the house. He shuts the shutters and switches on the lights. There is a smell of damp. One day he is going to have to settle accounts with the builder who robbed him blind, charging him for the most expensive materials and pocketing the difference. A bad apple; every line of business has them.

He lifts his forefinger to his lips for silence before he undoes the gag. Pacogoya is whiter than he has ever been. Even after death, his face would look healthier than it does now, confronted by this hired assassin on the state payroll.

"Where are we? What do you want from me?"

Pacogoya thinks Oso wants information about the kidnapped tourists, so he spills the beans at once, as if the gag were merely holding back the outpouring of details. Oso is highly amused at such willingness to collaborate. If every prisoner was like the Che Guevara lookalike, interrogations would be kids' birthday parties.

Oso does not think that this skinny little drug-addict queer has the information he wants. On top of that, there was the minister's call. He has to start phoning people to assemble the group in the next couple of hours. The most sensible thing would be to kill the little songbird, throw him into a ditch somewhere, then head back to the capital, getting in touch with his recruits along the way.

He decides against this. Perhaps it will all be over and done with quickly, and he can deal with Pacogoya in the early hours. Oso refuses to accept that Osmar Arredri has been snatched from under his nose. He has to find him, or vent his frustration on someone. Impossible to come up with the money they are demanding at such short notice; they were given until seven on Monday morning, not a moment later. The *Queen of Storms* sets sail at noon and all deals have to be done by then.

What if Pacogoya knows something? What if as well as handing over the tourists, he heard something, some information about where the Colombian and his girlfriend were being taken? It is unlikely, because it was the military who did it and they work on their own: they have their own planes and ships, they do not need tourist agencies.

Before leaving he switches the lights off. He has gagged Pacogoya once more and left him hanging upside down, in handcuffs, swinging from the wooden beam in the dining room.

What is Pacogoya thinking, lonely as a pendulum in the darkness, with all the blood rushing to his head? He is thinking that if he had agreed to spend that second night with Verónica, perhaps none of this would have happened to him.

9

"It's only for tonight," says Carroza as soon as he gets there, explaining what is going on. The operation is starting as he speaks, he himself has to report to someone called Oso the Bear Berlusconi, a retired cop, garbage left over from the dictatorship who for some reason all the politicians are protecting. No-one has ever accused him of anything, even though there were more than a few suspicions about him. He is an effective butcher, Carroza recognizes, especially when it comes to organizing clandestine operations. Which is what this one is.

"What risk am I running? I haven't kidnapped anyone and have no intention of doing so, unless they try to leave without paying."

Carroza does not know what she is talking about. Nor does Verónica herself; she is simply trying to take the drama out of the situation; she is so tired of emergencies, of pursuits. But perhaps the skeleton man is right: because of her role as inspector at the Riachuelo market she is in the line of fire in a battle nobody claims responsibility for, one of those habitual pretences of restoring law and order, a spectacle put on for the media to show how the authorities are fighting corruption, a firework display, smoke and mirrors no-one believes in but everyone applauds.

So she is going to spend the night in his spider's nest. Verónica finds the idea slightly repugnant, but it does not seem as if there is any more palatable alternative.

"I've been living there for two months. It's not the best neighbourhood, but that doesn't matter, because you're not going out, until tomorrow at least."

"Where is calle Azara?" Verónica asks, refusing to remember the names of streets. "I'm not a taxi driver, I have enough trouble trying to remember the numbers of our laws," she adds in self-defence.

Carroza pulls up outside his apartment and hands her the keys. It is true, the neighbourhood does not seem very welcoming: old houses, deserted streets of colonial cobblestones, high pavements for the days when the river rises, overflows the drains and floods everywhere; mist creeping up from the nearby Riachuelo.

"Don't open the door for anyone or answer the phone. Only your mobile and only then if I call you."

Verónica feels protected and defenceless in equal measure. Carroza is the one least at risk if blood really starts to flow, because he has already lost most of his. His skinny tissues feed more on memories than on red and white cells. She trusts him, but the immortality she attributes to him is not transferable.

It is too late to reconsider anything now: within the hour all the sharpshooters Oso Berlusconi has called are due to meet up. Fifteen men trained to kill and ready to carry out whatever orders they are given. Carroza still has no idea what it is all about and perhaps will not know until the minute before he has to swing into action. He thinks it must be a big raid, combing through an area where they can discover something to show the press next morning.

"We're to meet near here, that's why I thought it must have something to do with the Riachuelo market," he tells Verónica. "As far as I know, which isn't much, the place where they're hiding those tourists can't be far from that tribe of wandering delinquents."

Verónica is jolted upright.

"Are the kidnapped people from the *Queen of Storms*?"

Carroza is no expert in English, but thinks yes, the tourist liner that ran aground in the river. Verónica asks if anyone who was not a cop called him that afternoon. Carroza says no, although he was not at home, he was out digging up the dead, as per usual. He did not miss anything on his mobile – he checks it: no messages or missed calls.

"Stay here, I'll be back as soon as I can," Carroza repeats. He is not too concerned with her question, he is in a hurry to get to the meeting point. Verónica bites her bottom lip hard. "We'll talk later," she says. She does not know whether Pacogoya's partial confession that morning has anything to do with all this, but she intends to give him a call as soon as she is alone.

*

Far from the Swedish woman in Esquel – although he had not warned her he was coming – and too close to Buenos Aires – although he has no idea where he has been brought to – hanging upside down from the ceiling, Pacogoya starts to swing from side to side, like one of Hemingway's bells. He is encouraged by the increasingly loud creaking sounds from the wooden beam that the monster tied him to. If he does nothing, his head is going to explode like a blood-filled pomegranate, or the devil is going to come back and torture him to reveal what he does not know.

In extremes such as this, his weak physique is a positive advantage. He does not need iron muscles to overcome gravity and sway energetically to and fro. It is like being in a hammock, although not quite so comfortable, and he becomes as enthusiastic as he was in his childhood.

The beam creaks even more loudly. Now Pacogoya is worried that the whole ceiling might come down on top of him, but even so, to die buried like that could never be as fearful or painful as to be slowly finished off at the hands of an unscrupulous son of a bitch who has complete impunity on his side.

The sound of his mobile, which his captor left on the table, takes Pacogoya by surprise. At the first ring, the beam gives way and cracks into several pieces. The clapper drops out of the bell and falls heavily to the floor, although he quickly arches his back to avoid splitting his skull open. Even so, a sharp snap and a stab of pain between the shoulder blades tells him a bone must be broken. He clenches his teeth; he is gagged so tightly he can hardly breathe and the handcuffs are cutting into his flesh; only his feet are free now that the rope has come loose. He tries to stand up, but the pain is so bad he can only kneel: all this penance and not a single virgin in sight. And the mobile is still ringing.

Holed up in the Azara apartment, Verónica ends the call, although she promises herself to try again in a few minutes.

She searches in the kitchen for something to drink, even if it is only water, but the fridge is empty. So are the cupboards. This may be a spider's nest, but it is hard to see how its usual occupant manages to survive, what he has to eat, or how he amuses himself – there are no books in sight, the radio has no batteries and the black-and-white television only receives ten channels of the seventy or more available on cable. Pushed into a corner is a computer that runs on the kind of D.O.S. system that Viceroy Sobremonte must have used to compose his letter of resignation when he heard the English had landed on the shores of Quilmes in 1807.

Verónica makes do with what there is: tap water tasting of chlorine. She can put up with it for a night, she might even try to sleep a little, but at first light she is determined to get back to her own routine. She is not completely convinced that what Carroza calls the *Kristallnacht* is going to happen, or that she is part of it, or could be hit by some stray bullet. If as seems likely they want to get rid of her, they have already shown how good they are about letting her know it. Now they must be waiting for the report she gives the magistrate, based on her own observations in the field and the accountant's calculations. With Chucho out of the equation and after the chase the previous night, they probably feel they have made their point. The magistrate will thank Verónica for all she has done so that nothing will change and she will at last receive her well-earned fees.

The land line rings and Verónica freezes. She scuttles warily round the room like an insect, tempted to pick up the phone. The ringing stops, then starts again a few seconds later. She is touching the handset with her fingertips when it goes silent again. She realizes that although Carroza has no answerphone, he does have a call register. And the number on the dial looks familiar.

She rings it and waits. She is not surprised when a beauty queen answers.

"Where did you get my number, *doctora*?"

"I want my Bersa back."

Miss Bolivia laughs. She is so young that she plays with death the way she did until recently with other dolls.

"You gave it to me. I didn't ask for it."

"So that you could defend yourself. I didn't want you to take the initiative."

"Nobody has died, *doctora*," she laughs, then goes on calmly, sure of herself: "Nobody of any consequence. How did you get . . . ?" Verónica has no intention of telling her; that would be giving her position away. She does not have to, Miss Bolivia can think on her feet. "You're with him, aren't you? I knew you were friends, but not lovers."

Verónica does not bother to correct her. For years now she has let people believe what they see, even if that is only shadow puppets.

"He's not here. He's been called out on a mission tonight."

175

"So you stayed in charge of the home. Congratulations, *doctora*, on the cops you choose."

"I want my gun, Ana."

"OK, I'll come and bring it back straightaway."

*

Deputy Inspector Carroza does not have to go far to reach the meeting place. He parks in a desolate street in Barracas, parallel to the railway embankment, in front of an old rusty iron shutter with a red tin "For Sale" sign attached. During the dictatorship, this abandoned warehouse was probably a place where they tortured people. Better not to think about it.

He goes in without knocking through a small side door that has been left ajar. Inside it smells of oil and rat droppings.

"Well, look who's here!"

Oso Berlusconi celebrates his arrival. The others are already there, standing round him in the middle of the warehouse like cocks round a hen. Each of them has got his toy with him, automatic rifles distributed as and when they arrived. They are joking and hugging one another. "It's been a long time since the gang got together, just like the good old days, you've put on weight, haven't you? And you, where did you leave your toupée?"

Carroza is a good fifteen years younger than Oso, although if they were stripped and photographed together he could be taken for his undernourished grandfather. They have never worked together, but were always aware of what each other was up to. Neither of them is a cop of the sort who joins the force with one idea in mind: to be pensioned off as soon as possible and then grow old working for a security firm. Oso was very young during the dictatorship, but did his bit in the killings and is proud of it. Carroza joined later on and is sickened by torturers, although he has always suspected that if he ever came face to face with a *guerrillero* he would have shot first and asked questions later. But Carroza is a good marksman and he is proud of that: it saves the police ammunition.

Oso talks to the whole group, but is looking straight at Carroza. He does not trust him, but had to call him in because he is the best shot in all the federal police force. He explains what he calls "Operation Tourism". The military and the cops always call their day- or night-time raids, legal or illegal, "operations". He outlines the location and where each of them is to position himself. He will be out in front, that is why he is the leader, and besides, he wants to make sure none of the tourists is killed. All their necks are on the line, he warns them. "You can forget about your career in the police force if any gringo gets hurt."

Oso is calm and reasonably satisfied. The ransoms for the Italian and French couples have already been paid. The money has been transferred to Switzerland and Thailand, to solid banks and serious countries backed by reserves supplied by pension funds from all over the world. Only the Germans refused to pay up: the old Teuton arrogance. They still consider themselves superior, they still cannot accept that they lost the war. Oso was hoping to soften them up tonight, but the minister's phone call forced him to change his plans.

The orders are clear. Both the ones he gave to the people guarding the kidnap victims half an hour ago in the Descamisados de América shanty town: "When you hear the first shots, slip out at the back. As usual, we'll come in from the front and sides, firing into the air, just to make some noise. You run off as quickly as you can, then tomorrow when you've had a bath and changed, come for your money." And the ones he has just given to his squad: "Choose five of you. They are to get behind the shacks and as soon as the guards come out, shoot them. I don't want a single one to survive: we have to cut down on medical expenses, they're running out of bandages in our hospitals."

There is only one thing still sticking in Oso's throat, a bone that prevents him really enjoying the feast. Somebody betrayed him, tore the choicest morsel from his hands: Osmar Arredri and his lovely girlfriend Sirena Mondragón.

And he cannot even bring himself to imagine that it was the man or woman he is beginning to suspect.

*

They travel in five cars, three to a car, just as in the good old days some of them took part in and which the others have heard of. They are not in Ford Falcons anymore, "those really were armour-plated", chortles a bald fat man, 130 kilos without a weapon, a retired inspector, "three months in jail, at the mercy of those crooked lawyers and all those bleeding heart lefties in human rights", he shouts from the back seat of the Renault Carroza is driving, silent and concentrating hard.

"Who do you think you can catch in this old jalopy, Carroza?"

They go round the Río Riachuelo, through neighbourhoods with no people, only rubbish and rats. The rats' eyes shine through the mist, a dark blue mist like spilled ink, mingling with the smoke from the piles of garbage. Carroza's Renault is bringing up the rear. The others tried to convince him to get into another car, but he has not been anyone else's passenger for a long time now. He would not accept a ride even if he were dead. And he is not dead yet.

He feels a vibration in his kidneys: a call on his mobile. From Verónica.

"Don't open the door to her," he whispers curtly while the fat inspector goes on laughing at his own exploits when he weighed forty kilos less and was a member of the dictatorship's "task forces"; "it's dangerous, don't open the door."

With that he hangs up. He gives Verónica no time to tell him the door downstairs has already been buzzed open and she is on her way up, so young, so beautiful, so Miss Bolivia, to the spider's nest.

10

He has got it. Scotty has got it.

Shame that Carroza has switched his mobile off. He does that whenever he goes into action; he leaves it behind so that he does not confuse it with his 9 m.m. or whatever gun he has with him when the shooting starts. Answering the phone rather than pulling out his gun could cost him his life.

But Scotty has got it. It was so easy, right there within his grasp. Being on duty at headquarters meant he could watch the whole of the Boca–River match as well as have a look at what the blonde Miss Bolivia had been up to. Inspector Margaride (who has the same name and rank as another one in Argentina, notorious in his day for arresting long-haired youths and shaving their heads) dug the information up for him. This Margaride works for the police in Santa Cruz de la Sierra and has been a friend (or whatever the relationship between cops in different regions or countries is called) of Scotty's ever since they attended a Panamerican police convention where the North-American instructors explained that human rights were for middle-class suspects with good lawyers, not for the indigenous scum packed into the margins of the big cities of Latin America.

It took the Bolivian Margaride no more than an hour to find the files on the person who liked to be known as the Jaguar.

"His real name is Ovidio Ladislao Torrente Morelos." Scotty writes this down and whistles in admiration, while at the same time watching Sabiola advancing towards the Boca goal. "As far as I can tell, he shares parents with Ana Torrente, chosen as Miss Bolivia in September 2004."

"Hang on a second . . . what do you mean by 'shares parents with'? They are brother and sister . . ."

"Not necessarily," Margaride says, staring at the photo of the Jaguar, blue-eyed, staring into nothingness, dark-skinned, the face of a Nazi refugee burnt black by the Andean climate. "But they are twins: I'm not sure if they are identical, I don't have that information. They themselves are probably unaware of it."

A peal of rejoicing in Buenos Aires, because of Margaride's comments and because Sabiola has just scored a fabulous goal. River 1, Boca 0. Scotty can scarcely believe either piece of news.

"They were born the same day, but in different places." Scotty's laugh turns into a dry, incredulous cough, because Palermo has intercepted a ball that was heading safely into the hands of the River goalie. Margaride goes on: "The mother, whose personal details we do not appear to have, gave birth to the Jaguar in Yacuiba on 23 January, I suppose in the early hours. That same day, but twenty hours later, at almost midnight, she brought into the world a baby who grew up to become a beauty queen, the pride and joy of my beloved Santa Cruz de la Sierra."

Boca score, to make it a draw on the hour mark. Unbelievable, obviously unfair, the referee observing an eclipse of the third moon of Saturn and the linesman chewing a hangnail while Palermo broke every offside rule in the book and scored. The whole stadium erupts: an evil hour is coming, Scotty can sense it.

"Late that same night she had an emergency operation," the Bolivian Margaride, the soul of patience, explains. "The birth that morning had been up in the mountains, with no-one to help except perhaps a local midwife who helped her pull the Jaguar from her entrails. Then the indian, because that's what she must have been, a poor ignorant indian, continued on her way on the back of a truck, still bleeding and with a high fever. She didn't die on the way because God is Bolivian."

"I thought he was Argentine."

"That's another God; ours is called Viracocha and he protects indians, not the descendants of European imperialists. In Santa Cruz de la Sierra the woman gave birth to the remainder. We have a record of that, because she was dealt with in the Central Hospital, and before she died of septicemia she chose the name Ana for that remainder."

"And the father of the twins?"

"I've no record of that. Come on, Scotty, I've already done more than enough for you, seeing as it's Sunday."

It is only when Scotty has recovered from Palermo's goal that he takes a proper look at what he has scribbled while the Bolivian Margaride was talking to him. It is then that he tries without success to talk to Carroza.

*

She does not ring the bell, but scratches softly with her manicured red nails at the door to Carroza's apartment in calle Azara in Barracas. When she realizes she is being studied through the small circle of the spyhole, she explains quietly that she is on her own. The door opens.

She had been missing the fresh pink oval of Verónica's face.

"It's not what it seems."

"You don't say. And anyway, who cares?" scoffs Ana, amused at the attempt at an explanation that no-one has asked for, her least of all, because she never holds anyone to account. She has learned to recover her debts without the need for an invoice. She leaves the Bersa on the coffee table, the only piece of furniture in this spider's nest. This initial friendly gesture is a declaration of intent that reassures Verónica, who is still unsettled by Carroza's phone call.

Languid warmth outside and inside the apartment. The mist creeps through the slats in the closed shutters and seeps into the room, which has probably not been ventilated since Carroza first rented it two months earlier. The heat is swamp-like, the air is catacomb grey, barely enough for bats to breathe in.

"I don't know how that skeleton man can sleep in a place like this."

"I was wondering the same," Verónica agrees.

"Perhaps that's why it suits him: there is no air or light or hope in here." They laugh together, with that mimesis that has been theirs since the first meeting. It is as though they mirror each other and when they laugh at the slightest thing they are pulling faces at one another. "What are you doing here, *doctora*, what are you looking for?"

The direct question catches her out, leaving her no chance to make conversation. Verónica feels at a disadvantage, even though the Bersa is there on the table and Ana's voice sounds even more friendly, trying to win her over. She decides to respond equally directly, like someone who rides a punch and waits for his chance.

"I know Carroza, probably from before you do. He was Romano's colleague." Ana says nothing and again Verónica feels uneasy. Every so often she gets the feeling that this beautiful blonde woman is a mythical idol given human form for heaven knows what mission on earth. And as if she did not have enough problems already, she had to be a client of hers. Ana sits down on the coffee table and gestures for her to come closer. "Where do you know him from?" asks Verónica, refusing to budge.

Ana's ironic smile illuminates her face as if she were lighting a cigarette.

"The skull? I found him in an archaeological museum, liked the look of him and brought him home with me. Afterwards, I felt bad about it: perhaps I had stolen him from someone without meaning to."

She insists Verónica goes over to her, but now she has no need to gesture or pout. It's enough for her to be there, like a magnet, and for Verónica to realize too late that she has nothing to cling on to.

She is pulled towards the magnet – in this case, Miss Bolivia – like someone falling into an abyss.

*

He has been given his orders by Oso Berlusconi. These are always the same anyway: spread out and surround the house, do not go any closer than a hundred metres, at the command "fire at will" on the radio link, ratatatat, spray the windows with bullets, the walls too if they are made of tin as they usually are in the shanty towns. "The people kidnapped are not going to be sitting out enjoying the cool night air," says Oso. "They'll be tied to a bed, that's what always happens, or sitting cuffed together on the floor. The ones walking around are the mastiffs guarding them. You can shoot them without a problem, no-one is going to hold you responsible."

That was why Carroza was surprised when Oso stopped at the end of De La Noria Bridge and the five civilian cars, crowded with cops like landing craft off Normandy, pulled up on the beachhead in sight of the nearby provincial police post. Three minutes later, and the small caravan of headlights coming from the province turns out to be two armoured cars full of uniformed provincial police equipped with rifles and helmets, which halt on the other side of the road.

"Nobody warned us we were going to war with Iraq," says the bald guy who weighs 130 kilos without his weapon.

"I'm not getting out of this car," says the lantern-jawed cop sitting next to Carroza, his head shaven and wearing dark glasses typical of the service he provides, which is not exactly customer service. "They shoot you in the back."

"Let's wait and see what happens, if we want to be alive tomorrow," says Carroza, still staring into space as if not wanting to see what he already knows by heart, like a blind man who sets off walking down an avenue, his useless eyes wide open, only to find death avoiding him at every step.

The two men in charge get out of their vehicles: Oso and the commanding officer of the provincial troops. The glow from the cigarettes they smoke nervously in the middle of the beach-head are like two red fireflies. They agree on deployment and firing positions, knowing that if they are both there it means the medals will be shared out between them and wanting to make sure that if anyone is going to die it is not going to be either of them.

They clamber back into their vehicles and the two armoured cars pull slowly away, making their way around the Río Riachuelo. In the distance they can see the lights from the contraband market, where at this time of night the deals being done outside any tax or penal law are at their height. Verónica calculates that ten thousand people visit the market whenever it opens to the public and that nightly sales must come to around six million pesos: that is too much money exchanging hands only a few metres from the biggest hideout of traffickers in the region, the Descamisados de América shanty town.

If the struggle to control the market has cost the lives of first Matías Zamorano, Councillor Pox's right-hand man and Miss Bolivia's boyfriend, and shortly afterwards poor Chucho, the whale calf the Lomas magistrate had delegated to look after Verónica Berutti, it seems as though this Sunday night the fight to enjoy its profits is moving towards the final battle, even though Oso has presented their expedition as a simple rescue operation.

Despite this, the man in the front with Carroza is wary. He insists he is going to stay in the car until it is all over. Carroza has no opinion and the bald man weighing 130 kilos plus his gun has also fallen silent.

The three of them are veterans. Nobody likes to die, even if they grumble about needing false teeth, their aching joints and Viagra failing, leaving them alone and limp in a hotel bed while the young whore who cannot be more than twenty-five mocks them, "old fart with your droopy prick", instead of saying farewell with a tender "goodnight poppa". All that might make them feel like dying, but not really: instead, they want to be as far as possible from the scene of the uncommitted crime, as far as possible in time, looking back to days when they were good-looking, tough and aroused instincts other than pity when they showed off muscles as hard as the guns they kept at their waist or under their shoulder. Days when they were in charge and slammed the door on any romantic pretensions the woman of the moment might entertain, leaving her to choke on her own tears rather than finding themselves abandoned, sagging, existential mincemeat.

They hear instructions on their car radio. They all know what to do, but Oso Berlusconi is a perfectionist, he takes care of every last detail, knows his men by their Christian names and their blood groups. Then again, he cannot allow a single rabbit to escape tonight; that is why he is insisting that they shoot to kill at anyone running away – there cannot be more than three of them, he says, one for each couple of prisoners. Oso knows what he is talking about, because he recruited them. His only fear is that they come out shooting and one of them escapes, then calls a press conference. That is why he will personally make sure he is there in the waste ground behind the shacks, taking aim with the others, gunning down anyone he sees and finishing them off one by one.

"It'll all be over in five minutes, then we can go and eat a barbecue with red wine in the market restaurant," he encourages them over the police radio.

"That guy's a psychopath," says the bald man, by now covered in sweat.

"That's why he's the boss," says the other one.

"I'm hungry," says Carroza, leaving the car.

Crouching down and in indian file, the federal cops move into the shanty town. Oso signals for them to fan out to cover the three shacks where the kidnap victims and their guards are meant to be. The darkness in among the tin and cardboard shacks of the Descamisados de América shanty town is complete. It is as though night itself were lurking in the alleys where two people collide if they are going in opposite directions, where filthy water flows as if it were an open sewer and where from every hut come the sounds of shouted abuse, the cries of children, the words and the panting breath of love.

Nor is there any light inside the three shacks that Oso waves them to surround. He chooses Carroza as one of the three men who are to go with him to cover the rear where the guards are bound to try to escape if they have any hope of getting out alive. The provincial police have surrounded the outer perimeter of the slum. Oso has no worries about that squad's marksmanship. They have been trained with all the rigour of infantry marines: they are only brought out when the provincial authorities give them precise instructions to resolve a situation by shooting first and asking questions afterwards.

What Oso agreed with their commander has left no room for doubt: they are to shoot the kidnappers even if they come out with their hands in the air shouting that they want to surrender. They are to reach the morgue weighing twice as much as usual because of the amount of lead in them. As Oso knows from experience, wars, even private ones, are only really won when no prisoners are taken and all witnesses are disposed of.

Deputy Inspector Carroza spits on the palms of his hands and rubs them together, then carefully closes them round his Czech rifle, one of the fifteen that Oso handed out when they met in the empty warehouse in Barracas. When the mobile starts to vibrate in his back pocket, he hesitates over answering this call from an unknown number. This is no time to talk, although he can listen: he takes the call and says nothing, but pays close attention.

At the moment of going into battle, it is not good to discover that the enemy is within your own ranks and that you yourself are in his sights.

11

They have reached that moment when they stare at each other in silence, share a cigarette, start to laugh in a way which begins in either of their faces, then spreads to the other one. The moment for gentle kisses, lips caressing where they had previously been devouring, hands building castles, one on top of the other, "if men only knew", says Ana, stroking where she has previously penetrated, moving her first finger as if tracing the outline of that other pair of lips where she has just seen her passion ignite and then fade.

Verónica paints Ana's lips with a soft, shiny lipstick, then licks it off again.

"Some men want to be women, though," she says.

"But they have no idea where to start. They confuse the trappings with the essential." Ana, Miss Bolivia, allowing her to rub off the lipstick and lifting the hair from Verónica's perspiring forehead so that she can give it a kiss, laughs as she leaves her wet imprint on the wrinkles that the forty-something-year-old covers with make-up.

How long has Ana been there? She came in through not one but two open doors, in spite of Carroza's warnings. Who did that wreck of a cop think he was, with no more meat on him than a resentful skeleton?

She laid the Bersa on the coffee table as if she was about to sign some kind of armistice, then pulled Verónica towards her. Verónica allowed herself to be drawn in. Nothing like this had ever happened to her with any man, not even Romano, who arrested her without reading her rights. Their hands fluttering like falling leaves between their two bodies, so close to each other, pulled together as if by a magnet. They came together cell by cell, blended into one another unhurriedly, like paint settling in a bowl. They sought each other out because someone or something that is not them has already decided they should be together tonight, that they should meet without offering any explanation, two tightrope walkers balanced above the abyss of this strange night, an abyss of only a few hours that will not appear on any official register, ghostly hours they both wanted so much.

A mobile ring tone goes off in the distance, like one of the ambulance or police sirens crossing the city streets in the early hours. Neither Verónica nor Ana bothers to answer: "My phone sounds just like yours," says Ana. "We're the same even in that."

"It might be urgent," says Verónica, pretending to be worried, but Ana's warm palm is there, waiting for her wet lips and tongue.

"Gypsy tongue," says Ana, probing her mirror image, slowly substituting her lips for her hand, then tightening her arms around Verónica's waist as if she were going to lift her however heavy she was, to rescue her from wherever Verónica's life might be in danger.

But the only danger Verónica faces tonight is that of falling in love with another woman. Perhaps that is why she claws at Ana's body to try to break free, and reach out to grab the mobile that is still ringing and is hers. The ring tone dies – Beethoven filtered through cybernetic acid – before Verónica can light the dial. Ana's arms rescue her and again pull her irresistibly back to her, her lips close on Verónica's mouth, her tongue pushes in so deep she can hardly breathe. Verónica ought (whether or not she wanted to, she ought) to fight her off, to be able to see herself as they say those who are about to die float out of their bodies but remain nearby, up on the ceiling, tame spectres who brush against the world beyond simply to get a better view of the world down here.

Yet Verónica cannot, does not want, does not have the strength, has never had the strength to break free of desire when the fight is no-holds barred, outside the ring, outside the laws she has been brought up to respect. She gives herself again, opens up, feels how the hands that could be a man's hands tear her trembling body like a silk gown, strip her bare. She does not care that the voice says "it's so good to have you, *doctora*", when she has always demanded to hear "I love you".

There are many ways to fuck and be fucked, as many different ways as there have been men on her forty-year-old body, but this time it is different. This time it is an invasion, one body taking over another one cell by cell, replacing them entirely. Miss Bolivia's hand searches inside her, lights up Verónica like someone lighting candles in a temple that until now has been in darkness and without idols. Verónica is engulfed, pushed, lifted, held. Everything is bright and warm, fire has lips of cool water, the trap is laid like a last supper of the senses.

Too late – intensely, implacably too late – as Verónica turns so that Miss Bolivia can continue to open up her body with more hands than the goddess Kali and opens her eyes trying to find something to cling on to in order to delay a little longer reaching the bottom of her abyss, she sees that there is nothing on the coffee table.

The voracious cold now pushing her legs apart can be nothing other than the barrel of the Bersa.

12

Pacogoya, delivery faun, Che Guevara lookalike in full retreat, is running and running, clinging on to the only weapon he knows how to use with his eyes shut: his mobile phone. His hands are shackled, but his feet are free to fly over the grass like a bisexual spore once he has sent a message to the number of the cop Verónica recommended, the colleague of her first conjugal stiff. "I'm a friend of Verónica's, a cop in a grey Toyota abducted me," he texted, ending the message "Pacogoya". Then the reply that lit up his screen a few seconds later: "Run".

So Pacogoya runs across the fields. The thistles tear at him, draw tattoos on his translucent *guerrillero* skin that Sylvester Stallone would love to have on his ageing Rambo body. He runs with his hands behind his back, his feet stumbling on mounds of earth and stones. He falls, hits his head, but gets up again like a roe deer chased by a puma: the cop in the grey Toyota might return and come looking for him, shoot him down, and before or afterwards tear him apart with the razor-sharp teeth and claws of a corrupt, murdering policeman.

Why bother with all those trips to the sauna, all those massages, all that botox round his eyes, all those hours in the gym and all that waxing, if now he has to run through the night with thorns tearing at him, falling over, struggling back to his feet? Every step takes him still further from the ideal he has pursued for so long in gyms and massage parlours, turning him into a scarecrow, a bag of rubbish at the mercy of any stray dogs that might be around. He plunges on aimlessly; his telephone rings again and the screen lights up: "Run, run as fast as you can".

Who can this cop friend of Verónica's be? Why trust him when all cops are the same, why did she send him off to ask the cop for help, why did she push him away from her? Who has the right to cast the first stone, what is so wrong about pointing out millionaires who are only going to be held for a few hours? Why is the whole of the civilized world scandalized when one or two hairy guys are kidnapped, but nobody turns a hair when a thieving kid is shot down in cold blood? Or when they rob a workman of his seven hundred pesos pay as he gets off the train in Quilmes and kill him if he refuses? Things like that never appear in the papers; the president carries on sleeping, the ambassadors continue their game of golf, their wives a game of bridge; the Pope goes on scrawling encyclicals to comfort the poor in their eternal, celestial poverty.

*

Another cop, not the one who sent the text "Run" several times on his telephone, but who is so close to him he could almost touch him, is thinking of Pope Leo XIII as he lovingly strokes the butt of Rerum Novarum.

"With sword, pen, or word" says the hymn to Sarmiento. Any weapon will do in the fight for liberty and you can blow anyone's brains out: the indigenous savages and the unruly gauchos were the enemies of Argentina's founding father who way back in the nineteenth century admired the United States, and dreamt of erasing the original inhabitants of the barbarous pampas from the face of the earth. Sarmiento used words and the pen, General Roca the army, to spill the blood of gauchos, Tehuelches, Mapuches, Yagans and Comechingons. With sword, pen and word they reduced the proud first peoples to rubble. They wrote the history that even cops like Oso Berlusconi had to learn in primary school. What better name then than Rerum Novarum (a manifesto for the extermination of all undesirables) for the 9 m.m. toy Oso caresses at his waist while he cradles the Czech rifle he chose when he distributed them back in the warehouse? He checked them all, one by one, and kept the best for himself, the mortal Stradivarius which in the hands of a traitor like Walter Carroza could lead to the failure of tonight's concert, could ruin the night, send him to hell.

"What are we waiting for now, if it's not a rude question?" asks Carroza, who for the first time in his life is so close to the mythical, despised commander. The damp from the ground is penetrating his bones, bones once protected by flesh and even a layer of fat.

Oso growls and stirs uneasily. He does not like a subordinate asking him questions. He detests nosy people; he never gives press conferences.

If he had his way, all journalists would be lined up and shot so they could not interfere with his work anymore. They never have a good word to say about the police, they only encourage thieves and murderers until they have become victims of police brutality; then lawyers, sociologists and communists of every stripe still hiding under the ruins of the demolished Berlin Wall spring up like mushrooms to squawk that criminals are not responsible for their crimes, that it is society as a whole which creates them. Imbeciles.

Oso Berlusconi chews on the stem of a wild flower to avoid having to answer Carroza.

The pager he is wearing on his belt next to Rerum Novarum bleeps twice. That is the signal: everyone to their positions, the game is about to start. He points his Stradivarius at the roof of the first shack and pulls the trigger: a tin sheet two metres long and half a metre wide flies off like a bat.

"Fire at will," he shouts and the police orchestra launches into its version for Czech rifles of Tchaikovsky's 1812 Overture.

*

Scotty does not hear the shots. He is a long way from the gun battle in the Descamisados de América slum, just leaving his shift at the federal-police headquarters. He is even more convinced than when he started that morning of how useless it is to keep such an expensive mechanism as justice going.

A person, or whatever he might be called, a genetic throwback like the Jaguar, who has a long police record but has always been found not guilty, in and out of the courts' revolving doors, laughing fit to bust at the victims' relatives, killing as if he is playing billiards or bowls at his local club, out of boredom and with no sense of guilt, feeding on his perversion like someone slaking his thirst on his own urine.

"Ana Torrente Morelos," says the file sent by fax by the Bolivian

Margaride. "Born on 23 January 1982 in Santa Cruz de la Sierra, Bolivia. Mother unidentified, presumed dead after giving birth. Father unknown. Presumably given in adoption. No criminal record."

Scotty's passion – which his colleagues know nothing about because it is hardly macho enough for the police – is to restore paintings. He does not do it professionally; he has never studied or been to any workshops. A painter uncle who died in anonymity and was buried with his talent intact taught him the rudiments and passed on the pleasure of rescuing something in danger of being lost. Blurred figures, gazes that were once happy, ferocious, or vacuous, colours fading to nothingness. Removing the veil, driving away the phantoms of decay and oblivion – that is what Scotty devotes his leisure hours to.

He spent his Sunday shift at headquarters with little to do apart from sort out reports, file complaints about domestic violence and sexual abuse, watch a lot of football and sketch the angelic face of Ana Torrente, Miss Bolivia, and the demonic oval of Ovidio Ladislao Torrente Morelos, alias the Jaguar. When he got back to his minimal apartment that night, he pinned both drawings to the living-cum-bedroom wall, then coloured them in and stretched out on his sofabed work table to stare at them, like someone arriving home exhausted who collapses in front of the television.

Scotty has lived on his own for the past two years, ever since his wife swapped him for a criminal lawyer, a well-known legal eagle who spent his time preventing middle-class children who spurn an expensive, stressful university career in favour of the easy money to be made out of drug trafficking from ending up in jail and being raped by common criminals or being thrown into a ditch because they used someone else's capital to start up their own businesses.

Scotty's wife, a stranger to him after thirty years' marriage, took with her a mink coat (as in the tango) and the comfortable four-room apartment where they had lived together through three decades of arrests, shoot-outs, lost pregnancies and bitter arguments about the meaning of life. If Scotty has achieved anything it is to live now, aged fifty-five, as he did when he was an adolescent. It is no small thing, to keep going, find yourself again, only to end up being observed deep on a Sunday night by the sketches of a cherub and a devil who (Scotty suspects) have also started out on the road to meeting each other once more.

13

No-one is going to teach Oso Berlusconi how to rescue hostages. Let the toffs in the embassies play their golf and bridge – that's what they were trained to do, but we're the ones who pay for that bunch of pansies, Oso snarls to Carroza: the peace treaties they sign are drawn up on the bodies their armies have spread all around. We dig the trenches to defend the salons where those leeches dance the waltz.

"I don't think they dance the waltz any more," Carroza corrects him, intrigued by Oso's attitude. "That was in the nineteenth century."

A calm silence followed the first volley of shots. Oso ordered them to stop firing, although it took some time for everyone to react. As so often, some of the men have forgotten to switch on their radios, they are thinking more of their pensions than the details of the operation, wishing they were at home already, clutching their wives if they can still bear each other, then climbing into bed as soon as possible, happy to return home without a scratch. They have already made enough of a sacrifice, stretched out on the wet grass and taking orders from a madman.

The silence is so profound they can hear the music from the nearby Riachuelo market.

"I'd like to see them out here on the ground in their best sports clothes and four-hundred bucks running shoes." Oso is referring to the diplomats of course, in particular the Italian Ambassador who has just called him on his mobile, breaking all the rules of the damned protocol, shouting at him that he had to make sure he respected the lives of his fellow countrymen. "As if this was the Dubrovka Theatre in Moscow and not the Descamisados de América. Fuck that pedantic fascist." Oso Berlusconi suspects that some rat with a walkie-talkie is keeping the ambassador informed step by step about the rescue operation. "I bet it's one of those provincial boys. They'll kill people for a few bucks, but want paying in foreign currency to betray someone."

"They sell themselves dear," Carroza agrees, wondering what is going on elsewhere, where the fugitive that Verónica put on to him could be now, what Verónica herself is doing at that moment in his hideout on Azara. He ought to have answered the runaway cretin, to have found out from him which side the fatal shots might come at any moment. Although he already knows that well enough; that is why he lies on his left-hand side, so that he can keep a good eye on Oso.

"To hell with international pressure," growls Oso, giving the order for his men to open fire again.

This time he gets the result he wanted. Shouts come from the shacks, lights flick on as though the people inside were just waking up from a deep sleep, one of them screams, "Don't shoot, we surrender," but what matters most are the silhouettes, the dark mass pouring out of the back doors that gradually turns into identifiable shapes as the figures come leaping towards them, arms protecting their heads, others running as fast as they can, straight towards the guns, including those of Oso and Carroza, all of them more than ready to finish the fleeing figures off before they can even identify themselves.

Too late Oso discovers that behind the first three people fleeing the shacks – the guards, who should be the only ones – another group is emerging, running helter-skelter without even obeying the natural instinct to crouch as low as possible or to cover their heads, shouting out in incomprehensible foreign languages for them not to shoot, that it is them, the kidnap victims, the richest of all the tourists on board the *Queen of Storms*, the ones who a few minutes from now ought to be appearing safe and sound on television so that the ambassadors can praise the efficiency of the Argentine police, express their gratitude that they are representing their nations in a country that protects its visitors more than it does its own citizens.

Too late, Oso bawls for them to stop firing. His earlier instructions were so precise and emphatic that nobody believes him now. The only one who does not carry on shooting is Deputy Inspector Carroza, but that is because his Czech rifle jams, refuses to do anything. Seeing it is useless, he throws it aside and draws his 9 m.m. He points it straight at Oso's head.

*

Pacogoya can see lights at the far side of the seemingly endless field; what he cannot do is force any more air into his lungs. He falls exhausted, breathing in mud, several worms and filthy water. He moans like a wounded dog, struggles back to his feet, then slumps back to his knees again, only to get up once more until through his tears he sees the lights. Despite his bound hands, he is still clinging to his mobile as if that is his oxygen supply. Someone must come to help him, he cannot die like this, he does not want to die now, or ever, if possible. He curses his bad luck and the mistakes he has made to stay alive; he would even declare his love to Verónica and take her to live in the Recoleta apartment she likes so much. You have to give women what they like; there is no point digging into their hearts to find answers, there is nothing there. Pacogoya has been convinced for ages now that women are the opposite of what feminists and lesbians (to him they are the same thing) claim, nothing more than scribbles on the canvas of the irrational, mere excuses to remain for ever as victims. That is why he has never stayed with any female, and sometimes even prefers queers and fags, transient beings like him, freaks who put make-up on or shave depending on the time of day and what kind of party they are going to, clamber onto stiletto heels and wiggle their asses or empty the contents of their automatic into the back of whoever they are with when things get hot. He thinks of them, his clientèle of sad nights and hopeless dawns, like this one that finds him running blindly towards the lights, under which a service-station attendant watches as a puppet still dangling from its strings approaches – a scrawny Che Guevara looking as if he has been caught by a tribe of headhunters, tottering into the pool of light and calling for what he supposes is help, although he cannot understand what he is saying or shouting, what drug seems to be masking the meaning of the squeal that is the last sound he produces before he slumps to the ground of the forecourt, unconscious or dead.

*

The sketches talk: the representation of reality offers more than reality itself; art reveals what not even the most vicious torture session can uncover. That is why, and not because of any soft humanism (which he cannot stand), Scotty (who is not Irish either) puts more faith in art than in the paid executioners in the federal police.

It is not easy to torture anymore. Judges are in a difficult position and the rats in the press can smell blood. They like nothing better than to expose torturers and double the sales of their newspapers; human-rights groups bleat their indignation across the front pages and the whole of society is scandalized. Nobody wants to be left out when it is time to pretend. Art (at least, as Scotty understands it) is more discreet. And more effective. Restoring paintings has given him that discipline, has made it possible for him to communicate with the immanent, of not making things explicit but knowing where he stands, what he is faced with.

The information from the Bolivian Margaride appears to be true. Those two birds of ill omen – Miss Bolivia and the Jaguar – were born from the same egg. Yet they are not brother and sister. Or rather, what separates them (or so Scotty suspects) is what is going to unite them.

How do they look like each other? He stares at the sketches he himself has made, pinned on the wall. They do not. Yet their eyes are identical. If he were a surgeon he could transplant them from one to the other and they would go on seeing the world the way they do now – as a hostile place, a lair of predators on the prowl, leaving them at the mercy of the erratic laws of the universe. The same look, the same glow that lights nothing, the same deep dark holes.

But there is something more, something that has nothing esoteric about it, something close to home for Carroza, even if he is not Irish and is not called Scotty but Yorugua. Lying there on his back with the faces he himself drew staring down at him: it all helps for the past to come oozing up to the present. Just as good wines that have been aged for years (and Scotty and Carroza are in their own way good wines) take on flavour from the oak barrels where the grapes have been fermenting and the shady solitude of years bubbles up in a clear stream when they are uncorked, so the information reaches the cop's brain as he lies horizontal on his bed.

"Shit, how come I didn't see it before? Those eyes."

Scotty is not someone who talks to himself. Two years of being a bachelor have not yet reduced him to this verbal onanism. He prefers to call someone, to go out in search of a listener, to walk somewhere.

Those eyes.

14

Carroza is in no mood to take anyone's call. He pays no attention to the mobile vibrating at his waist, does not look down at the lit dial. His only concern is Oso Berlusconi, who is cursing him without realizing that Carroza is pointing a gun at his head.

"Who gave that order, Carroza? It was you, wasn't it?"

Oso has not let go of his Czech rifle (and his does work) but he is not covering Carroza with it. He saw the deputy inspector throw his away in disgust. He knew it did not work long before Carroza tried to shoot at the fleeing captors: there was nothing casual about the distribution of the weapons in the Barracas warehouse. With all the shooting going on, no-one could be held responsible for finishing off the skeleton man.

"What order, Oso? This massacre is all your idea. It got out of control, that's all. These things happen."

"Someone promised you a promotion. You asshole, you stinking Uruguayan. And you believed them."

Carroza smiles. He and Oso are both flat out on the ground, while all the others are running towards the disaster. The danger has passed, none of the guards or the prisoners is left alive.

"You're finished, Oso, but I'm not the one to blame." The muzzle of the Czech rifle swings round to aim at Deputy Inspector Carroza's forehead. Carroza is still gripping his revolver and the mobile is still tickling his back near his right kidney. Everything is fine, death is easy, all she asks is for some rest. "Go ahead, shoot," he tells Oso. "You've dug your own grave, I can be the cross on it. An accursed one, of course. One I wouldn't even wish on a suicide."

It is not compassion that prevents Oso from squeezing the trigger, but the certainty that the only bullet Carroza will suceed in firing before he dies will lodge straight in his own heart. Even if he shoots first, he is bound to die and this stinking Uruguayan will stare back at him with wide-open eyes, enjoying his death agonies from the depths of hell.

The shouts grow louder all round the two men. Someone comes running up: it is a provincial cop, who asks if they are alright, if anyone was wounded.

"No, there are only stiffs," says Oso, spitting out the stem of the wild flower he has been chewing all this time.

Carroza takes advantage of the situation to jump up, still pointing his revolver at Oso, and kick the rifle out of his hands without the provincial cop noticing.

"Up you get, friend!" shouts Carroza, "'Operation Tourism' is over."

"What have you done with the Colombian, you bastard? Who's behind this? Where have you taken him?"

"Is something wrong, sir?" Alarmed, the provincial cop points his gun at Carroza. Even though he does not work for him, he knows Oso is the man in charge. Who doesn't know Oso and fear him?

"Nothing, you dolt, get out of here," shouts Oso. He would rather die than have a provincial sergeant boast that he saved his life.

The cop obeys, although he is still pointing his gun at Carroza as he moves away towards the group gathered round the dead bodies. The deputy inspector lowers his own revolver, puts it back in its holster.

"I pursue murderers, Oso," says Carroza, offering an explanation that no-one has asked for, perhaps apologizing to himself for missing the best bit. "I don't deal with narcos." With that he walks off, his back turned to Oso, who goes slowly over to the group staring at the bodies. He is the leader and now he has to take charge of things. Carroza goes back to his Renault, parked on the far side of the shanty town. The two federal cops are still sitting there, listening to music and smoking. "It's all over," he tells the one who weighs 130 kilos without a weapon and the other one, who has not moved from the front seat. "Not even the canary is left to sing about it."

*

Those eyes.

What did she see in them the night Ana Torrente knocked on her door and sought refuge in her arms, even though she said it was legal protection she was after?

Verónica wonders this now. She cannot help staring at her: that is all she can do in fact, because the rag Miss Bolivia has used to gag her with not only prevents her speaking but almost stops her breathing. The cold barrel of the Bersa forcing its way inside her, hurting so much she gave a stifled cry, then the punches to her face and the taste of her own blood, the only warm thing in this night she would like to bury forever if she manages to survive it, to leave behind like a ghost town where nightmares walk the pavements and wave kindly from the terrors of childhood to these last early morning hours, so recent, so hopeless.

"I'm going to kill you, *doctora*. But not with my own hands. A wild animal is going to come and eat your brains out."

Ana, Miss Bolivia, says this in the manner of someone announcing they are going to put some water on to boil for tea.

When Verónica tried to wriggle free of the Bersa, still wanting to believe it was all a game, a cheap perversion, Ana hit her hard on the chin, the classic uppercut of a trained boxer. Verónica did not lose consciousness, but could not protect herself from the swift, powerful movement that left her with hands tied and her mouth stuffed with a handkerchief that made her choke. For a long, long moment she thought she was going to die for lack of air and struggled in Ana's arms.

Miss Bolivia kept on punching her, until her face swelled and darkened into one huge bruise.

"You made a mistake opening the door," Ana says calmly, glancing down at her tiny wristwatch. "Someone must have warned you not to. That skull with the federal-police credentials must have warned you. But you didn't listen. And here we are." Verónica shakes her head. She tries to make a sound but chokes again, trying to breathe through her nose. Ana pulls off the tape, removes the saliva-soaked handkerchief and throws it to the floor disgustedly. "I don't want you to suffocate, *doctora*. I don't hate you. Nor do I love or desire you – I'm sorry; but I don't hate you either. You had good intentions: you gave me a gun to defend myself with. What a joke, *doctora*, a little Bersa pistol. As if the people threatening me were fairies, second-rate pantomime characters, suburban gangsters."

She forces her down into the only armchair in the apartment. Like all those Carroza rents it has even less furniture than necessary. There is no table, for example. Why would he need one, the skeleton never eats. Nor a bed. Earlier, Miss Bolivia pushed her down on a blanket on the floor, when Verónica still thought it was a game, a night outside the laws, an interlude, not this calvary. She closed her eyes, imagined others, even Pacogoya, pushing her down in similar circumstances, though without using this sort of violence, even though that did not surprise her or set warning lights flashing. After all, Verónica tells herself now, the calle Azara nest was empty. Until the spider came from outside.

*

"RUSSIAN-STYLE MASSACRE" screams the headline in one of Buenos Aires' most important and least serious newspapers. "STRANDED, ABDUCTED AND MURDERED" announces the sensationalist twenty-four-hour news channel that night. Laucha the Mouse Giménez is watching it in the small Belgrano apartment where she has lived since the beginning of time.

Laucha is worried that Verónica does not reply either on her land line or her mobile, but tonight she is more worried about her own loneliness. It is Sunday, the edge of the abyss that opens every Friday, the shifting sands that threaten to engulf her with nowhere to cling on to. Men have become disgustingly polite towards her. She has to admit they never amounted to much, but of late all she has met with is suspicion, shifty expressions behind unconvincing smiles, unbelievable excuses and, worst of all, silence: her telephone never rings, every sound in her apartment sounds like thunder, so do footsteps in the corridor, voices in nearby apartments or in the street, the engine of every car pulling up outside.

It is midnight on Sunday when all her credit is used up, when Monday is late arriving with its antidote to the poison (not cyanide, only loneliness) that paralyses her all weekend. And tonight, as if that were not enough, there is Verónica. Her silence, her unexplained absence, the worry growing, becoming more solid with every hour, the dreaded phantom of violence.

Not even Damián Bértola, to whom Laucha who is Paloma has tried to explain some of Verónica's mysteries, has been able to define what it is that keeps her in such a mess. "Seeing she has two dead men on her conscience," says the psychologist, as if she had killed them herself. "She ought to stop, come to a halt, work it out."

"Work what out?" Paloma challenges him. "That life is nothing more than death which comes on stage, all dolled up, strutting around under the floodlights, soaking up the applause? Then what? After the curtain has fallen, then what?"

Bértola laughs.

"Shakespeare in skirts," he says. "If Laucha is Paloma, anything is possible. Bravo!"

She ends up laughing as well, or slamming the door on him, if there is a door available. She is not going to allow a cheap shrink like him to start analysing her.

Laucha who is Paloma looks at herself in the mirror of the television set. A sad-eyed charlatan brought in urgently is giving his spiel about the bloody rescue attempt in the Descamisados de América shanty town. "As in Russia," says blabbermouth, "in 2002 at the Dubrovka Theatre in Moscow, 129 hostages died. Here it was only six, but it's the same thing" – he goes on, shamelessly – "six dead people whose fortunes total nothing less than 129 million euros. Some coincidence, isn't it?"

And this numerical coincidence is then discussed by a charlatan in a dyed toupée that looks like a virtual turban, an astrólogist with a degree from a university in the Arizona deserts. With no proof apart from his own audacity, he attributes to a stray moon of Saturn "the responsibility for the tragic events which have left the international community in mourning". He will not hear of any heavily armed bipeds being guilty of the massacre. "We are the playthings of destiny," he declares, proud of the set of false teeth stuck to the roof of his mouth with the same glue that is sponsoring the programme. Playthings of destiny, fluffy toys, battery-run men and women with the power leaking out so they no longer have the energy left to find the way out, open the door, flee or give themselves up.

Paloma who is Laucha trembles but controls the anxiety she feels when she hears the telephone at midnight. Who else but Verónica and about time too? Late, but about time.

"Where did you get to?"

"Laucha . . . I'm sorry to call you that, but they do call you Laucha, don't they?" Although she recognizes the voice, she does not admit it, asks who is calling. She is annoyed that this unscrupulous Bolivian calls her Laucha. And at midnight on Sunday. "You know me. We've met at the *doctora*'s several times. She's told me about you. She talks a lot about everybody, so it's as if we know each other without really ever having seen each other."

"It could be," Laucha admits grudgingly. "Has something happened to Verónica?"

"Why do you ask that? I haven't seen her lately: is she ill?" Laucha does not reply. She hangs up, shaking her head as if to get rid of something, cobwebs, that is what she is shaking off, cobwebs, when she is so keen to keep her apartment clean, cobwebs on her face. She cannot see them, but they are stuck to her eyes, she breathes them in, feels them flapping across her cheeks. The telephone again; again it is not Verónica. "The call got cut off. It must be because I'm on a mobile," says Miss Bolivia, plaything of destiny. Laucha is struck dumb. The sting from a Bolivian voice has injected some kind of poison into her bloodstream. "What were you doing when I called?"

She asks as if they were friends. Laucha's reply is the poisoned apple that Snow White coughs up.

"What's that to you? What do you want?" Then, reacting all of a sudden: "Who gave you my number?"

"Don't be angry with me, *Laucha*," the Bolivian voice emphasizing the nickname, showing her scorn. "There's something that unites us. There's no reason for you to get angry, it's something very deep, a secret."

Laucha leaves the phone on the table but does not hang up. As if Miss Bolivia were watching her, she walks round her neat single woman's apartment, where everything is in its place, there is no smell of men or dogs. She enters the bathroom for a moment, shuts herself in like a punished child, stares at herself in the mirror as if she could see herself in the Bolivian's face, looking at her patiently, calmly, coldly, from the other side.

She finally returns to the phone. She picks it up, Miss Bolivia is still there. Who knows how long she has been waiting for her?

"What do you want from me?"

Her voice is shaking, because she knows. She has seen the answer in Miss Bolivia's eyes on the far side of the mirror.

"I want you to come and visit us."

She shakes her head again, but no-one can see her, not even Miss Bolivia, who can see everything. Why now, she wonders, why Verónica?

"Let me talk to her."

"The *doctora* doesn't want to talk to you. That's why I called. She just wants you to come here."

She gives her an address, which Laucha notes down as best she can, trying to overcome her fear, without even asking herself how she is going to get there. At that moment someone in an adjoining apartment slams a door, or the wind does. There is a gust of air that interrupts the call and at last Miss Bolivia is on the other side, it is no use Laucha shouting "Hello! Hello!" or looking for the number on the call register which for some reason is not working, no use her running back to the bathroom and staring at herself desperately in the mirror, so crazy she ends up smashing it, cutting her forehead as she lunges forward at herself.

15

Of all the unholy bars in this Holy City, the *Pigs' Trough* is the worst. A hole-in-the-wall on the corner of Moreno and Combate de los Pozos, no more than three blocks from police headquarters. It has swing doors like a Western saloon and behind them a filthy, clinging, black curtain that stinks as much as the towel of a boxer in the last break before he is knocked out.

Scotty peers through the smoke-filled, red-tinged gloom inside, where the customers' silhouettes look like bodies under a huge grey sheet. Strange that Carroza, whose life Scotty sees as a game of billiards played by two blind men, should ricochet into somewhere like this, full of sacked cops, or ones who have been pensioned off at forty, the dregs of an institution that protects the Buenos Aires middle classes, men still dazed from the violent deaths of their colleagues, shot on the pleasant streets of the neighbourhoods of Barrio Parque, Recoleta, or Belgrano.

"He's not here. He didn't come yesterday either. The last time he was here I had to throw him out. He went crazy after drinking some hooch an inspector brought. He started shouting at some woman called Carolina, though he was the only one who could see her: he was punching the air, shouting 'you whore, I'm going to kill you'. Just think, Scotty: OK, I know the cops who come here are all washed up, but scenes like that drive even them away. They come here to forget: this is a bar, not an interrogation room."

"What rat poison did you give him, Chink?" The Chink's eyes widen like a cat's in darkness. He knows Scotty's reputation, that he is a cool customer who kills without showing any emotion and has the rare ability to draw up brilliant, convincing reports that are like literary masterpieces. "Don't treat your friends like that," Scotty advises him, taking him by the throat as calmly as if he were simply stretching out to lift a glass. "Just because they're fed up with the crap lives they lead doesn't give you the right to treat them like your guinea pigs. What poison did you give the Yorugua?"

"I told you, nothing," splutters the Chink, who was born no closer to China than the province of Catamarca, but is copper-skinned, and has a face as round and shiny as a balloon. He was once a cop himself, but his only claim to fame was shooting his wife's lover and then smashing her to pulp. She waits on tables in her wheelchair, taking orders and serving the drinks without so much as a good evening. The Chink shows him the pot-bellied bottle with no label on it. "Inspector Rodrigué brought it. You know him, the guy they sacked from Interpol for smuggling. I have no idea what it is; they say it tastes of oranges."

"That means you've never tried it. Now's your chance, go on."

Scotty picks up the bottle with his free hand, pulls the cork out with his teeth, then forces it into the Chink's mouth. He stares at Scotty wild-eyed, but refuses to swallow any. The liquid starts to dribble out of the corners of his mouth. Scotty takes his hand away in disgust and pushes him towards the back room of the bar. Standing there at the counter, he hears the other man throwing up.

The floor of the *Pigs' Trough* is strewn with sawdust. Scotty walks out as if he were crossing a graveyard of bones, stepping apprehensively like a forensic expert who has seen everything but cannot avoid the sharp, cold stab of the obvious, the ghastly evidence of a face that not even the worst assassin wants to have to confront.

He is not worried about this mausoleum of stiffs who are not even aware they have died, but the fact that he has lost contact with Carroza. He is disturbed by what he has seen in the eyes of Ana Torrente and Ovidio Ladislao Torrente Morelos, Miss Bolivia and the Jaguar. During his Sunday shift at headquarters he has realized that he and Carroza are going to collide at some point in this investigation that both wish they had never got involved in.

*

Not far from the *Pigs' Trough*, down towards the river, rolling down Callao as the ballad by Astor Piazzolla has it, the three ambassadors meet up again in one of their residences. This time it is long past office hours, at 2 a.m. in Buenos Aires – although in Europe it is 7 a.m.

"It's on the front pages of *tutti i giornale*," complains Giácomo Monte-gassa. He is hosting the other two and searches in vain in the exquisite Renaissance sideboards for a chestnut liqueur he says the domestic staff deliberately hide from the lesser members of the embassy: the consuls, secretaries, cultural and military attachés, the entire load of useless cretins paid for by Italian taxpayers – "well, the taxpayers in the north," he clarifies. "In the south, the people pay their taxes to the Mafia."

"This is no time for a *trrink*," thunders Günther Weber as he tells them yet again, red-eyed as if in a poorly shot photograph, about one of the hostages shot by the Argentine police, a personal friend of his.

"We can't accuse the police of that," says André Villespierre, trying to calm him down. He has sympathy for the corrupt guardians of order in the Third World. Of course they have to behave differently to the police in Paris, specially trained in the basements of the Sureté to knock the stuffing out of North African immigrants or to set fire to rooming houses crammed with Ukrainians. Only a few minutes earlier, the French prime minister gave him instructions, having his breakfast of milky coffee and croissants while glancing at *Le Monde* and *Le Figaro*, those two bastions of the petit-bourgeois press that Parisians follow as devotedly as Islamic fundamentalists follow radical versions of the Koran. "*Sans scandale*," the prime minister told him, "*nous sommes les principaux postulants pour la licitation de la téléphonie mobile des forces de sécurité de l'Argentine.*"

Only Günther refuses to takes things calmly, at the same time as he is refusing a drink.

"Those *figli di putana* hid that chestnut liqueur well, *porca miseria*," says Giácomo, handing round the Campari.

After all, it is nothing more than a police matter, however much the European press blows it out of proportion: "POLICE BUTCHERS" screams the headline in a Roman rag, where the red of blood is the most prominent of the colours.

This late-night meeting is so that they can co-ordinate the protest letters the three of them are going to present as soon as the Argentine Foreign Office opens its doors. Letters that the inevitable pack of newshounds is going to tear from their hands as they come out, desperate to give the lie to the misinformation their own government has given in order to cover up such drastic events, but which the international press has seen through at once.

"Big fat ones," says Giácomo, then excuses himself in case either of his guests thought he was somehow referring to their distinguished diplomatic selves: "the best game chips from Piedmont, *senti qué crocantes*, they really crunch in your mouth."

"He was my best friend," the German insists soulfully, lost in the dark night of his spirit and forcing his colleagues to pretend they are listening to him. Günther and his fellow countrymen shot down in the shanty town had studied together at the University of Hamburg, then lost sight of each other until they met up again at a reception in the Yugoslav Embassy in Berlin before the country built like Frankenstein's monster by Field-Marshal Joseph Brodz, alias Tito, blew itself to pieces like a suicide bomber. They talked of the good old days at university and did a deal on a shipment of Russian arms that would arrive in containers of humanitarian aid sent by the Moscow mafia to the Croats via the Berlin that had once been communist. First-rate weapons at unbeatable prices: the ambassador's friend mentioned the figure for the commission and, rejuvenated by the money, the ambassador left his wife of many years without a *pfennig* and hooked up with the top model that he then brought with him to his diplomatic posting in Buenos Aires. "He didn't deserve to die like that," sighs Günther. "Those murderers!"

"Who?" asks André, more because he has not been listening than because he is completely cynical. Giácomo does not even react; he is far too busy with his big fat Piedmontese game chips and the way they crunch in his mouth.

*

At the moment that the ambassadors agree to send the same formal protest note to the Argentine government – 2.15 a.m. on Monday, 7.15 a.m. in the home countries of the murdered passengers from the *Queen of Storms* – Oso Berlusconi is leaving a rowdy press conference that took place in the mudbath where the Descamisados de América shanty town is sinking like a sordid Atlantis.

As usual, the press conference was a kind of cross-examination before a jury of paid scribblers, television reporters, microphones, cameras, shouting, everyone milling around and insults from people who have nothing to do with anything but turned up anyway because it has become the done thing to come and shout "Murderers!" at the police: the latest therapeutic technique.

He does not explain. He says nothing to placate them: "We shot them because they came out firing," Oso says and repeats, "they used the hostages as human shields, it was them or us. We couldn't let them get away, we didn't have a clear view of them. If I had given the order to cease firing it would be the bodies of my own men you would be counting now. I'm sorry, but the lives of policemen are just as valuable as those of tourists, however rich and foreign they were."

"He's not sorry for a thing," says one woman reporter who cannot be more than twenty-two, on high heels in the mud and wearing lots of make-up to face the camera that multiplies her Barbie-doll features in thousands of tiny cathode windows. "The leader of the rescue operation is a psychopath with a police badge. He has no apologies for sacrificing six innocent people when it was his job to save their lives. This is not the kind of police we deserve . . . but now let's go to our colleague who is outside the French Ambassador's residence . . ."

"Loud-mouthed bitch," Oso mutters to himself as he pushes his way through the reporters and dives into his grey Toyota.

What is he supposed to feel sorry for? For being a cop, obviously. But what else could he have done with his life? He would be dead if he had not become a cop, or shut up in a psychiatric hospital or Devoto or Sierra Chica jail, put away until he rotted.

As it is, he is free as a bird, with all the women he wants and a good car. That is something, at his age. And he gets pleasure from crushing the weak and any informers, of having people he can order around, make them respect him. That adolescent journalist should bite her tongue before speaking: they come out of college firing at anything that moves, like novice cops, but they want guarantees, rules, that the rights of murderers are respected.

Oso accelerates, trying to put as much distance as possible between him and the scene of the crime. He leaves the Riachuelo and its stinking waters and people behind, the frustration of a night that literally backfired in his face. He ought to settle matters with Carroza, that shady piranha, that traitor. He is sure he wants his job and last night he got that bit closer to it. Oso is furious.

In the meantime, nobody mentions Osmar Arredri and his beautiful girlfriend Sirena Mondragón. Not even the press is bothered about them now: they are all far more interested in having Oso burned at the stake. Although they might be aiming even higher – Oso consoles himself – at the minister or the president, why not? After all, the victims are Europeans with fat bellies and bank accounts, from that rich Europe which will not have anything to do with blacks or communists down on their luck, or the mixed-race immigrants from the poor America that was once the hope of the world, the America of Che and before him people like Sandino or a president who thought Chile was Cuba until he was bombed in his own government palace, the Argentina of all those revolutionaries who he himself in his own humble way helped to exterminate before he even had his precious Rerum Novarum.

"They should reward me, heap medals on me. Instead they want to burn me at the stake, the bastards," rages his conscience or whatever it is gripping his entrails. It is as if he is already on fire before he becomes the victim of all those traitors, opportunists, the ones latched on to the teats of power while they point him out, condemn him, drag him to the fire like all those who have really got balls, weapons and the crazy heat inside them.

Even before he reaches his cottage out near Pilar he realizes the bird has flown, although he has no idea how he managed to escape.

He sees the front door open, the darkness, silence all around.

He checks inside, but nothing seems to be missing. In fact, there is nothing to take, apart from a 1950s refrigerator he bought in a sale which still works, a black-and-white television, a table and two chairs, a bunk bed. Oso regrets he is not going to be able to use the table anymore: the ceiling beam that gave way under Pacogoya's slender weight fell on it and split it in two. Could it have killed the Che lookalike? Unlikely, the dead do not usually run away. But they do not get far, either.

So Oso Berlusconi goes out to find him.

16

Poor Che Guevara lookalike, lost in the jungle with none of the real Che's courage, none of his hopes of setting the continent on fire with one, two, many Vietnams. And there are no parrots or monkeys in this jungle, only cannibals.

"He must be drugged, he looks like an addict," says the attendant who picked him up after he passed out next to the unleaded pump, eyes rolled up, mortally pale, as skinny as an anorexic.

He dragged him to the boss's office, who stared at him like some sort of vermin: "Drop him on the floor," he tells the employee. "Wash your hands and call the clinic so they can come and fetch him. He stinks."

The only thing this jungle has in common with Che Guevara's is the Bolivians. The pump attendant is a *bolita* too and so is the man from the grease pit who came with his filthy hands to help him lift Pacogoya, now looking like a camouflaged corpse with black patches all over elegant clothes already ruined by the rough treatment he has received and his escape across country. There are black smears too on the face of this bedroom revolutionary, this empty-handed delivery lover who is as stranded as the *Queen of Storms*, which is going to set sail without him in a few hours' time.

The service-station employee calls the clinic, but it is a police car that turns up.

"We'll take him," says the cop behind the wheel. He does not bother to get out, simply points towards the office where Pacogoya is still flat out on the floor.

"But you aren't doctors or nurses," the attendant points out. As a poor Bolivian, he detests the police.

"And you're not Argentine. Bring that turd out here and put him in the back of the car, if you don't want me to take you in as well, you asshole."

The asshole does not need to be told twice. He knows that if the cops feel like it they can take him to the station. If he is lucky they will only slap him around a bit and let him sleep the night in a cell. Otherwise they might kick him in the liver until it bursts, and then say he fell and hurt himself, that he was drunk when they found him – "asshole Bolivian, be careful because we've got our eye on all your lot".

The Bolivian asshole already feels sorry for the hell that those two and others are preparing for the Che Guevara lookalike. They were in such a hurry to come and get him before the ambulance did they must want something from that human wreck. Drugs, what else could it be? "Every pig wants a share of that," the owner of the gas station always says. He breathes a sigh of relief when he sees his employees loading Pacogoya into the police car: "One addict less, they should put them all onto that boat that got stuck in the river then sink it," he tells them, happy, relieved, apocalyptic, white.

*

So where is he? He is not in the *Pigs' Trough*, he does not reply to his mobile or on the line in his den in calle Azara, which rings and rings.

Scotty feels weary. He ought to sleep: he was on duty all Sunday and although he does not have to go in on Monday, someone will call him early in the morning – someone always calls to piss him off, everyone at headquarters needs his advice and wants it before he has had any breakfast, like a urine sample.

But Scotty does not want to sleep. If he went to sleep now he would only have nightmares, awake with a start, reaching for his revolver and aiming it first at nothing, in the darkness and then by the dim light of his bedside lamp. The bed of a lonely cop, of course, a cop living on his own, no woman can stand to live with a cop, unless she too is one and women cannot be cops.

"Where the fuck have you got to, Yorugua?'" he asks the shadows around him, all on his own.

He has to share what he has discovered with Carroza. Or rather, his intuition, because he has not really discovered anything. Yet he has no doubt about it: that is why they are always ringing him from headquarters. They consult him like an oracle, believe him even if he talks nonsense, stammers rubbish, or even says nothing. Above all, they believe him when he says nothing. They have a religious belief in his silences, like people believing in a dog that does everything but speak, "look how he's looking at you", even though all the dog is doing is staring at its fleas, has no thoughts in its mind, does not remember a thing, dozes off without revealing a thing.

Finally someone picks up in the Azara den. But not Carroza.

It is a woman's voice.

"Verónica?"

"No, Ana."

"Who the fuck is 'Ana'?"

"And who are you? A pervert, I bet, one of those late-night maniacs.

Jerk off if you like, I'll squeal if it excites you. Or are you a queer? If you are, wait a minute, because a real man will be here soon."

Ana is having fun. Verónica is tied up and gagged, lying on the floor in a foetal position, still staring defiantly up at her. She ought to have blindfolded her, or torn out her eyes, thinks Ana as she listens to the caller panting as if he really is jerking off.

Scotty carries on panting. He has transferred the call to his mobile and is breathing heavily as he leaves his apartment, goes out into the street, gets into his car. He loses the line as he sets off, but calls again.

"I thought you must have come already, pervert," says Ana. "Take your time, we've got all night. The man you need is on his way, if you want it up the ass."

That voice.

As he drives and pants, Scotty tries to stay true to his intuition. Sometimes the desire for everything to fit in neatly has led him to make huge mistakes. And every mistake, in the job he has that can never be paid enough, means at least one death. A cop is like a surgeon. A surgeon opens up bodies, is a pathologist of people who are still alive; a cop digs around in the intestines of a disgusting city. He does not linger over squares or avenues, or eat fine steaks in Puerto Madero or Las Cañitas: a cop steers his way through the guts like Scotty is doing now, on his guard and filthy, and, as always, on his own. He may be applauded by two-timing rats who brown-nose him in private but who, as soon as the television lights go on, start bawling about civil rights, how barbarous it is to beat up a child-killer simply to cut short a life he does not deserve to have, or demand information that always arrives too late, like ambulances or firemen, after death and fire are already dancing their grey tango, the really last one this time, not in Paris but in the still cobblestoned streets of Barracas, in the dirt roads of Mataderos, or in the centre, the city which by day is full of people and finance, and at night is deserted, on the prowl, searching for sex.

"Your real man is here, pervert, he's opening the street door. Jerk off hard now, imagine you're throwing yourself into his arms and coming, do it, do it."

Ana is not lying.

He has arrived. He closes the door and comes into the apartment on calle Azara. He is not surprised to find Ana there. With the phone nestling on her shoulder she touches herself. She stares at him while she encourages the other man panting into the receiver, the other man who has the mobile against his mouth as he stops the car, switches the engine off, then hangs up.

"The pervert's hung up," says Ana, still staring at the man who has just come in.

17

A surprise party. Like a birthday party, when friends and relatives wait in the darkness, whispering to each other, "Here he comes, don't make any noise, we don't want him to find out now". And when finally the birthday boy arrives, comes in and switches the light on, surprise! "For he's a jolly good fellow, for he's a jolly good fellow!"

Oso Berlusconi smiles. It does not even occur to him to think that it is not his birthday, that he is not being rewarded for some outstanding deed, that this is not his house and that there is nothing to celebrate. It is good when people applaud you, when they shout "Brilliant, Oso, we love you".

Yet someone warned him on the radio in his grey Toyota. "We're expecting you," said the voice. "We have to think of something, we don't want to be put through the mincer or to be crushed." To Oso it seems logical they have to think of something. The rescue operation was a disaster, they will be talking about his "elite police corps" even in the United Nations tomorrow, he will be the butt of jokes in Interpol, the Sureté, the Italian and German police forces. "Are we in Russia?" the headlines will scream. "Who governs Argentina, Putin?"

So he went to meet them, at the colonial mansion in the middle of the pampas, ten kilometres from Exaltación de la Cruz. He has to grin and bear it, he cannot run away if he wants still to be part of the business. Even if he wanted to, where could he go? He is a cop. Corrupt and a murderer, but a cop – or perhaps because of that. He would be writing reports about raids on brothels or arresting delinquents and pickpockets if he had not decided a long time ago to join up with them. He was never interested in who they really were, what their faces were like, what interests they were defending. Nor did he believe in the speeches they came out with over the years: they were no defenders of Western civilization, or democrats, or fighting for God and the Fatherland. Power, money, that is what they wanted. So did all of these people, he says to himself when he enters the darkened room and then is hit by the brilliant light from the enormous chandelier, the shouts and applause, "For he's a jolly good fellow, for he's a jolly good fellow . . ."

Nobody had ever told him he was meant to be a jolly good fellow. That is what they are singing to him now, roaring with laughter, God knows when they started celebrating. "Here comes Oso Berlusconi, switch the light off, he's almost here," the whisper ran round all of them gathered there, most of whom could no longer remember why they came out to this mansion, brought here by someone who in his turn obeys others higher up than him and so on up the pyramid, the tip of which is lost in thick, dark, inaccessible clouds.

They look like an Italian family from a film about the Mafia. Some of them probably are *mafiosi*, born on both sides of the Atlantic, in Balvanera, Argentina or in Sicily, in Corsica or San Telmo. The older ones proud of their origins in the worst neighbourhoods, boasting about childhoods stunted by misery – stealing food in the post-war years, empty pockets, wallets with more pictures of people killed in combat than banknotes – among unemployed passengers on trams and buses in Rome, Turin, Naples and Milan.

But those are the patriarchs, the ones dying a natural death, who grow nostalgic and reminisce about their memories of the war, disguising their age in the remote past, a hideout from time where they can protect their decadence and prepare to die.

They would not have condemned Oso Berlusconi for the kind of mistake he made that night. They know, because once upon a time they fought against powerful enemies, that all wars are fought blindly, that there is never enough time. Still less second chances. As soon as they heard of the massacre, the patriarchs came out in defence of Oso. "It was an ambush," they said. "Oso knows what he's doing, but he was betrayed."

"We've been talking a lot about your performance last night, Oso."

By now they have finished singing and drinking glasses of the best champagne, its bubbles like golden gems, although Oso did not manage to get any. Now the man at the head of the table is asking them all to be quiet – "or did you not see that Oso is here?"

It is an old, very old estate. It belonged to a patrician with one of those double- or triple-barrelled surnames you see today as the names of streets or avenues in the most elegant neighbourhoods. The original owner benefited from the handout of land the military who conquered the desert rewarded themselves with after they had cleared it of the filthy, ragged, smelly and barbarous indians living there. Of the many chieftains calling for vengeance, the extravagant gods of capitalism must have listened to some Pampa or Tehuelche chief. Decadence is a kind of justice, administered without meaning to by the unjust. And the selfishness of the descendants, who turned on each other when there was no-one else to destroy, and who ended up serving the banquet at the *mafiosi*'s family table.

The new owners stored away the fine furniture made by French craftsmen, smashed all the Italian glassware in nights when it rained alcohol, and vomited all over rugs imported from Iran in the days when it was known as Persia and the Yankees were betting on Rehza Palevi's eternal life. There are too many of these newcomers, and they are as barbarous as the Tehuelches and the Pampas. They even have their chieftain.

"We've brought you here for you to tell us what happened last night, Oso," says this chieftain. He has managed to obtain silence and is stroking a Rottweiler, one of those dogs that every so often eat a child, then lick their lips and wag their tail. "But obviously we don't want to hear the nonsense that appeared in the press. We want the truth. Even if it's painful, Oso, even if after you've finished telling us what really happened we find it unbearable."

The Rottweiler growls, licking its whiskers with its long, red tongue. Its jowls are covered in saliva; it is as if he is the one Oso has to justify himself to because he does not take his eyes off him.

∗

So as not to startle her, he did not use the entry phone. He wanted to warn her a few minutes ago, a couple of blocks before he arrived, but Verónica's mobile is off and nobody replies on his land line.

He has to admit to himself that he is not sure what to do. It has been years since he had any women in his home, he has not even had a home: what little that has happened to him has all taken place outside, in the street, in other people's houses – although most often nothing happens, simply meetings, words, sex without caresses.

Sometimes, Carolina is with him. But who is Carolina? Nothing, nobody, loneliness without caresses. Besides, he is never at home, always in darkened bars, other people's faces, a mask covering the exhausting chaos that is his memory.

So he preferred to go upstairs like this, silently, without a word. By the time he gets to the corridor, then comes to a halt outside the door to his apartment, he already knows Verónica is not alone. It is his cop instinct, what makes him a moving target in the sights of thieves, murderers, drug traffickers, work colleagues.

Even so he opens the door. It is not that he is confident about what he will find, more an inertia he does not have the strength to resist. Before he sees her, he knows it is her from the cheap perfume she covers herself in, the one she is so proud of because she says it attracts men. They fall at her feet and all she has to do is humiliate them a little more, to gain control of them slowly, not violently the way she did with Verónica. She has forced her down onto her knees to receive their visitor. Later she will have to slit her throat and then eat her head.

Carroza stares down at the tip of the barrel of his .38, so intently that the rest of the room is a blur. He knows it is her, because of the perfume, the voice, the disappointment she never bothers to hide whenever they meet.

"I told you not to open for anyone," he reproaches Verónica, before he lowers his weapon and allows Miss Bolivia to throw her arms round him.

18

It is not her. Or in any case it is a force she cannot control, an uncontrollable chemical reaction that alters her cell by cell until she does not recognize herself. Even her voice sounds strange when she tells the taxi driver the address, says it's urgent and that she'll pay him double if they get there in half the time.

"I'm working, lady, and I have to respect the regulations," the driver protests, but accelerates all the same. It is late on a Sunday night, the avenues are almost empty apart from a few groups of Boca fans wandering down the centre in their T-shirts, carrying banners and drums they are no longer playing, on their way home after celebrating victory away to River Plate. "Hooligans," the taxi driver shouts scornfully.

What is she doing? She does not know Ana Torrente and could perfectly well go on living without ever meeting her. Who or what is she obeying, then?

Five minutes down Tacuarí heading south, speeding through junctions where by some miracle they do not collide with any other vehicle. It is as if the taxi driver has been taken over by the same force that leads him to forget all about regulations. From time to time he casts a quick glance into his rear-view mirror, as if to reassure himself his passenger is still there, has not got out or vanished into thin air.

"Is someone sick?" he ventures to ask as he slows up for a red light, looking right and left before accelerating again. Laucha does not answer. She does not hear him, apart from a low murmur, sees only a distant blur rather than the driver's face. The only thing she sees clearly is that she has to get there as quickly as possible, even though she is sitting there unrecognizable to herself, with a voice, a body that is not hers, filled with memories of a world in which she has never been. "Here we are. That will be eighteen pesos times two: that makes thirty-six. But I'll settle for twenty, I don't like to take advantage."

She gives him thirty and the world keeps turning. The taxi driver cannot decide whether to thank or insult her; he thinks it must be urgent, there is a sick person about to pass over, something serious that can explain why he has to humiliate himself and pick up the banknotes Laucha has tossed on the floor of the taxi before getting out without so much as a thank-you or good night.

*

He removes Verónica's gag with the steady hand of a surgeon removing stitches. She does not shout or make any reproaches, merely gives a dry cough out of pure anxiety. Her eyes burn into his face.

"Romano trusted you so much," she says at length.

Carroza says nothing. He cannot bear her look and turns to watch the street through the curtainless window.

"She's here," he says.

He steps back from the window so that Laucha will not spot him. She is studying a piece of paper, making sure it is the right address. She has never been here before, nobody has ever been to any of the lairs he chooses at random in the nameless city only he inhabits.

"Don't hurt her," says Verónica. She knows who is coming because she heard Miss Bolivia talking to her, although she has yet to understand why. "What are you after, what do you two want from us?"

Verónica knows there are no answers to her questions. When someone is in control of a situation, a country, the tiniest piece of hell, then there are never any answers. At most there are orders, which can be contradicted if things go wrong. But no remorse.

Carroza's mobile throbs again at his back. Veronica watches as he moves away, whispers something forcefully into it. Skeleton man is so sure of himself it as if he knows every single one of the supposed laws that control the universe.

"We're leaving," he says to Ana when he gets off the phone.

"What do you mean, 'we're leaving'? What about them?"

The entry phone buzzes.

"Open the door for her. You take care of her; I'll wait for you in the car."

He slips out of the apartment before Miss Bolivia can protest. He passes Laucha on the dark stairway. She thinks she recognizes him but cannot be sure. Carroza does not pause, but plunges on head down, his eyes and soul heaven knows where.

He leaves the building and jumps into the Renault parked the wrong way by the opposite pavement. He switches the engine on and waits. Five minutes later Ana comes out. She is carrying her high-heeled shoes in one hand and seems to float across the street like a ghost. Carroza has already opened the car door for her, so she settles alongside him without a word.

"I hope you didn't hurt her," says Carroza.

"I don't hurt anyone. I leave the pain and blood to the Jaguar."

PART FOUR

Happiness is for Fools and Madmen

1

It is not for nothing they call him the Bear. There have to be a lot of them to take him on, to surround him like this. The ten men all have their guns trained on Oso, who stands there without moving in the centre of the circle, staring at them one by one, memorizing their faces. All ten of them know that even if they pour bullets into him, Oso's body has so much violence within it, in his past, that it is impossible to de-activate it like that.

At his feet lies a pool of blood, with the lifeless Rottweiler almost floating in it. Oso crushed its head with a single kick, almost without glancing at it. The dog must have come too close without meaning to, perhaps it was even hoping he would stroke it: violence is a magnet, a centripetal force.

"Dogs like him are very expensive. And affectionate in their own way," the chief complains. He is sitting a couple of metres outside the circle of men training their guns on Oso. "He was guarding you, Oso, and much better than any of these thugs."

The weapons sprouted in the ten men's hands as soon as Oso smashed his boot into the dog's skull. The Rottweiler did a somersault, like a trapeze artist launching himself into mid-air only to discover the next trapeze is nowhere to be found. It crashed to the floor and the blood flowed out as it gave a last few spasms.

"So what do we have?" the chief goes on, not looking at anyone in particular. He is comfortable in a big armchair that must once have been used by some rich guy with two surnames to read the property section in *La Nación*, the social pages devoted to other rich guys like him who were "resting at home" following their return by ship from Europe, weary, old, the decrepit scions of a society proud of having exterminated its young.

"We have an international scandal," he says, and his voice is the only sound in this vast room in the mansion, the stale atmosphere filled with agitated breathing, submissive silences. "France, Germany, Italy . . . incredible what the stupidity of a mindless cop can achieve, a crisis that must be on the lips of the entire United Nations, the Security Council and all the European parliaments."

Oso stares at the dog, as lifeless as he is inside. If any of the armed men around him makes a move, if a single finger tightens on a trigger, Oso is going to be aware of it even before it happens. They all know this and none of them wants to be the first, because they are all afraid they will be the last.

"Everyone in the Western world has their eyes on us," says the chief. "On the police in a banana republic in the south of Latin America. Police who are clumsy, inept, corrupt, unable to take care of their visiting citizens."

"Somebody betrayed me."

Three words from Oso, who until then had seemed prepared not to say a thing, at least until after he was dead.

"You wouldn't be alive if I didn't know that," says the chieftain of this tribe of crooks, usurpers in this setting where the noblest oligarchs once comfortably glided. "What did you expect? That those who hate you most would be faithful to you? That those who want to make an example of you to conceal their own crimes would make a hero of you?"

"The minister promised me his support."

"I couldn't give a shit about the minister, Oso, and the minister feels the same way about you and all the rest of us. No dog, not even the one you've just killed, bites the hand that feeds it. But ministers do, Oso."

"There must be a traitor."

"There's a system, Oso. They use their brains – what you're missing."

"I follow orders."

The chief sighs. He tries to catch his breath, to contain his desire to give the order to kill Oso then and there. He does not like the spectacle of death. Rooms like this one on an estate that was once noble were not designed or built as scaffolds but to receive important people: top businessmen, government officials, ambassadors even.

"You should have asked me, for Christ's sake." The chief is losing patience. He is growing nervous because he can see how scared his henchmen are. He knows that if he orders them to kill Oso now it will turn into a slaughter and he himself will run the danger of being hit by a stray bullet. Fear is a fragmentation bomb, it has to be controlled, handled without it going off. "It's four in the morning," he says, more calmly. "That makes it nine in Europe, so there is still time. We have to distract them, make them look elsewhere, double the stake."

Oso concludes he is not going to die. Not that he is worried: he has fallen off his pedestal; they have him in his sights. But they will not dare do it now, because the chief, the man in charge here, who in fact is no more than the hinge between people like him and those who really run things, is thinking out loud. He wants to get out of the trap and he is talking of doubling the stake. And Oso, who may be brainless but has a natural instinct when it comes to violence, knows what he has to do before they say a word.

"They want you dead, Oso," the chief says finally, signalling to his men to put away their guns. "They would be happy if you did not come out of here alive. That way all the blame would lie with you and your hopeless feds. The provincial governor has already put champagne on ice so that he can celebrate the end of the scandal." The chief stares down at the floor, refusing to look at his men. They have put down their guns but are still on edge. They glance out of the corners of their eyes at Oso, still afraid that any one of them could be the first this beast leaps on and crushes in the same way he did the Rottweiler. But Oso knows. He has more years and more experience under his belt than any of these thugs trained in the basements of democracy by indifferent experts who lack the certainties that still find a home in his black heart. "The minister leaves his house at eight, Oso. You know where he lives, the route he takes and all the alternatives."

"But the traitor . . ."

"The traitor was only obeying orders like you, Oso. The loyal and the treacherous belong to the same sub-species of brainless humanoids. But this time, no mistakes, Oso. Make sure that between eight when he leaves home and eight-twenty when he ought to be going into the ministry, Argentina and the whole world are shocked by the news."

Oso feels a shudder of pleasure. He was expecting to face death, not this new mission. He is excited, as if a beautiful woman had slapped him and then asked for a kiss.

"I want my Rerum Novarum back," is his only condition.

*

They are sleek cats playing with a mouse. They push him from one wall to another, feel his arse, take turns to slap him. Four cops in the provincial station at Pilar. They have already forced his head underwater for longer than any normal person could stand, but Pacogoya was helped by the cocaine, it is his ally in this useless resistance, the steps on the calvary he takes with only instinct and cocaine to keep him going.

The provincial cops are waiting for instructions. They called to say they had him, first to Oso Berlusconi, then to the other cop whose name none of them can remember. His number is in their plaything's mobile. They know he is a cop because Pacogoya told them so, just as he told them that all the drugs were in his backpack. "Help yourselves," he told them, "it's free."

"Careful, all that stuff belongs to someone, let's not be stupid," says the man who appears to be in charge of the other three. He is a sergeant who believes in the institution because it protects him and his family with a doctor and medicine, a fortnight's holiday at the seaside every year, a gun always at his waist, the feeling that he is more special than any civilian, those who fear him due to the gun and the uniform, who need him despite their disdain for him.

So they left the backpack on the inspector's desk. He can decide what to do with it when he gets here at 8 a.m. What to do with it and with this Che Guevara lookalike who in the meantime they take turns to push around, fondling him like a young girl, until the giant cop drooling from the half-smile that never leaves him, not even in his sleep, announced that he felt like fucking him. The sergeant gave permission for them all to see what they could do to arouse the giant's prick.

"If you fuck him, it has to be in here, in front of all of us," says the sergeant. That is why he is in charge.

Disorientated, cut off from everything, including the feeling he was about to die when they stuck his head under water, Pacogoya stares at the giant cop. He begs him to fuck him, stares at him like a female on heat: if the giant buggers him that will mean he can rest for a moment in his embrace. He will take his warm prick in his mouth and between his buttocks, and if he closes his eyes he can gradually slip away, pass without any more suffering to what he knows is awaiting him for not stopping in time, for going first to San Pedro and then to Uncle's place, for taking the drugs they left for him on Uncle's bed, for handing over the tourists and thinking he would get his share, or that at least they would respect him as one of theirs.

They came to get him only an hour earlier, but he already feels he has spent the whole night in hell. Oso Berlusconi's instructions circulated round all the police stations in the area as if they were orders from the army. Strange that the provincial police take notice of what a fed like Oso says, something must be going on higher up: that was the last thought to cross Pacogoya's mind as he stumbled into the petrol station with what he thought then was the last of his strength.

"Take him with you, I don't want any addicts here, they're the worst," he heard the manager tell the cops, even though a few minutes earlier he had called the hospital at Pilar rather than the police station.

"Don't worry," the cop in charge told him, the sergeant who is now giving the giant permission to fuck him, provided it is in front of them all so that they can applaud if he comes, or boo him if he goes limp on the job. They are already betting on it: two against one that he does it, the sergeant says he won't. "Ten pesos," the sergeant says. "Put your money on the table; tonight I'm going to win twenty bucks out of Gómez's impotence."

Pacogoya has done this so often for money – not a lot, usually – but this time he will do it for his life, for one small further slice of life, the chance to stay in this world, even though he no longer understands anything going on in it. He does not think he is going to die; he thinks he will let or sell his Recoleta apartment when they throw him out of the tourist agency, when he is put on trial for being a drug trafficker, for being an all-round idiot, for thinking he was something he is not.

Gómez the giant steps towards him, towards this Che Guevara who has never set foot in the Bolivian jungle although he collects biographies of the real Che in French, German, and Italian – the languages the hostages speak, or spoke. Gómez the giant catches him as he is spun round like a ballet dancer in the Teatro Colón by the other three cops. He grips him with his enormous hands, where all the heavy fingers look the same. Hands that could never be those of a musician, fingers that crush two or three keys at once on the old Olivetti they let him use to draw up his reports. The sergeant and the two other cops laugh out loud. So too does Gómez, who always looks as if he is laughing, who was born and will die with that drooling half-smile on his face and those eyes buried in mounds of fat, and whose stinking breath forces the Teatro Colón ballet dancer to turn his face away when Gómez tries to kiss him and the others applaud, egg him on. "Go on Gómez, get on with it, get it out and have him suck it, go on."

It is a beautiful night, 4 a.m. in Argentina, 9 a.m. in Europe, where foreign ministries and journalists are busy composing protest notes and editorials, and the stock exchanges reflect the fall in value of shares in the leading companies run by the dead kidnap victims.

If it were up to these four provincial cops, they would continue with their high jinks. It if were up to Oso Berlusconi too; he was the one who asked them to pick up this forty-year-old addict with the looks of a poster guerrilla. And Pacogoya as well would be happy for this to continue, as he is swept away into the void so painstakingly created all round the world and even occasionally in his Recoleta apartment.

But they have to stop, because the other cop arrives. He is from the Feds, like Oso, and while he flashes his credentials in his right hand, the palm of his left is resting on the butt of his .38.

"I'm taking him with me," he tells them.

"He's Berlusconi's man," says the sergeant, mostly so as not to lose face in front of his subordinates.

"Man . . ." repeats Gómez the giant, his drooling half-smile even broader. He raises Pacogoya's right arm and spins him round again. "On your toes," he instructs him, "and stick your ass out."

The others laugh. And applaud, a delayed reaction, because the .38 is already pressed against the giant's temple.

"I said I was taking him."

"Gómez, show some respect, dammit! Remember we're public servants," says the sergeant, though he is unable to wipe the genetically imprinted smile off the giant's face.

"Oso Berlusconi is involved in a matter that's far too important for him to have time to come personally and pick up this turd," says Deputy Inspector Carroza, with less menace in his voice. "Six foreign kidnap victims got killed; this isn't a night for playing games."

The sergeant stands to attention in front of this federal officer he does not know. He is suspicious of him as he is of all feds, but he has heard something about it on the radio; he knows there is trouble outside and the last thing he wants for his quiet sergeant's life is for something from the big world out there to get in and spoil it.

Carroza can finally leave with his prisoner. They are applauded by the provincial cops who have regained their confidence and bid them farewell like a pair of newlyweds leaving church. "What a shame, he had such a nice ass," sighs Gómez the giant. He has become the hero of the night, who was saved at the last minute from being put to the test. "I'd have buggered him if they'd let me," he shouts to more laughter. They are all pleased at the fun they have had and the sense they have done their duty: they handed the prisoner over unharmed and with his arse intact. They laugh some more, looking into each other's eyes as Carroza's Renault pulls off, its broken exhaust snarling loudly, their smiles similar to Gómez's permanent hilarity.

The first one whose face drops is the sergeant, when he realizes that the backpack with the drugs in it has disappeared from the inspector's desk.

2

Scotty has two children. He is thinking of them now, because of some association of ideas it is not his job as a cop to explain to himself. Both of them have been to university: the boy is a doctor, the girl an accountant. "Get the hell out of here," he told them when they were of an age when he could talk to them and they would listen. "This country is on its last legs, get out while you can."

But they still live in Argentina. They think that the only problem is having a father who is a cop and is bitter because things went badly for him. He does not know how to explain to them that things have not gone that badly, that he is paid to hunt down criminals, to kill them if possible before a judge releases them to go on robbing and killing on parole. That is what he is paid for, to sweep up the rubbish even if he has to hide it under the carpet of police files. He is even encouraged to keep the change from his investigations, backhanders everyone accepts because their salaries are never enough to live on and their bonuses are pennies. Things have gone well for Scotty: he has not been killed, he has not stolen from the poor and he has wiped out at least half a dozen undesirables. The magistrates are all grateful for what he has done, even if some stupid prosecutor or other has occasionally tried to bolster his career by making complaints that only the gutter press was interested in.

But he is thinking of his children. Why should graduates like them have to share the world with garbage like the Jaguar? What have they got in common, what stem cells did they share, when did the differentiation occur?

The pinko liberals say it is a problem of classes, of society, injustice. He knows it is not that. Scotty does not think of himself as right wing; he is sickened by the fascists who every so often seize power in Argentina, the people who own the cattle and hoard the grain, the big capitalists with businesses of dubious legality or who are mixed up with every kind of mafia; people who financed military coups, rebellions and the usual dirty tricks that rob governments of their power whenever they become uppity or veer too far to the left and want to share out a small part of the huge riches that they want to keep all for themselves.

Scotty is not right wing, but he is no red either. What do they mean by revolution? They share the same vices, they also want the good life at others' expense; for them as well, the police are the lowest of the low: they are afraid of them but do not respect them. As far as he can tell, torture was carried out on both sides of the Berlin Wall and when the Wall came down it was like a circus hit by a tornado: clowns and elephants, jugglers and lions thrown into the air, while the public started to flee West in panic. Many of them are still stumbling round a Europe that was capitalist long before they were, sleeping wherever they can, stealing or swindling, trafficking drugs or exploiting women.

This Scotty who is of Irish descent and is Argentine by birth has got one thing clear at least: he would like to rid this city of animals like the Jaguar, to find a way to be free of them and make sure they never reproduced. Nothing, neither a society of classes nor a genetic defect ought to provide any excuse for a monster like that to walk freely on the streets the way he does, to kill when he feels the urge and carry the heads back home with him. He does not care what makes the Jaguar do it, although trying to find the answer to that has brought him hot on his heels. What is important is that he does it, he keeps on doing it.

If he could squash that vermin tonight, he would sleep soundly for a few days at least and would not be so sceptical about his children's future. But it is already 4 a.m. and his heart, which does not so much beat as clench on hatred like a fist round a dagger handle, tells him it could be too late.

*

Since she came into the apartment she has been sitting in a corner without saying a word. Nor has Verónica asked what she is doing there or why she is not untying her, what Laucha has got to do with Ana Torrente, why they want her a prisoner, what has she ever done to them except try to help?

They simply stare at each other. As if they spoke different languages, the way Africans piled in their canoes stare at each other and then, if they manage to land in Algeciras or the Canary Islands, stare at the white men in uniform who fish them out of the sea only to take them back to Africa.

After a few minutes, Laucha gets up and goes into the kitchen. There is a smell of coffee, the sound of cups being taken out. Verónica cannot believe she is behaving like a normal host. "It's not Laucha," she tells herself, "she's been drugged or hypnotized" – but still does not dare speak to her. She is scared things will only get worse for her, that Laucha will react badly if she asks any questions. She does not want to be beaten again: she trembles, closes her eyes, tries to think none of this is happening.

*

There is not much time; deadlines are looming. The early hours are always a truce, even gravely ill patients believe they can get better when they are sailing through the depths of early morning, or walking along gazing at the sea along the tranquil beaches of sleeplessness.

In Europe, though, it has been day for hours now. In Paris, Berlin and Rome the stock exchanges are reacting. Shares are dropping and twenty-four-hour pundits are busy interpreting the nervousness of the markets. "Investing in Latin America is always a risky business," says a bald man with a pipe dangling from the left side of his mouth, the Sherlock Holmes of finance who is discovering gunpowder five hundred years later than the Chinese. "They are volatile markets," he says. "There are political plots, violence, irresponsible behaviour, the rules of the game are not respected, that's why the profits are so good. We Europeans need to know what risks we run when we invest in Latin America."

"And the same is true of our tourists," says a Spanish sociologist appearing on French television. "My country should reconsider its relations with such a hostile continent, warn its nationals who are there, demand guarantees, make sure they punish populist governments, the corrupt, those who do deals behind the backs of their citizens."

Damián Bértola has just woken up. Knowing he will not get back to sleep, he makes himself a *maté* tea and switches on his television. He is bored by the pundits the press consult like oracles – they all repeat the same formulas, loudmouthed parrots who learned their spiels in the Sorbonne or Madrid's Complutense and spout them to virtual audiences who like him scarcely listen to them, but who need someone to interpret, analyse, tell them what on earth is going on in the world, why it does not behave as it should, tell them who these dark-skinned half-breeds are, or those others who look so similar to Europeans but obey the laws of the jungle found in other continents.

As soon as he has drunk a couple of *matés* he will switch off the television and revise the notes he left unfinished the previous evening. At 9 a.m. the first patient will be ringing the door bell, even though the last thing he needs today is to see them, sit opposite him or her, look as if they have all his attention, defended by his wall of books and the latest Lacan to defend them from anxiety, worldweariness, compulsive desires.

No, not today. Today he does not have the strength, his pact with the Freudian devil is slipping and not because he is so sad from all he lost when his partner left him or his children went to live far away: all that has been taken on board, he needs so little to live, he never was ambitious when it comes to happiness. It is something else, something indefinable, vague, spectral, a shadow which takes shape at this twilight hour, even if it fades with the break of day.

If he were not a psychoanalyst, a qualified headshrinker, he would say this is a presentiment, a premonition, but these are words he does not like, words he refuses to admit into his professional vocabulary, that only confuse the patient and he himself, ambiguous, slippery words.

Like someone who wakes up in pain or anguish in the middle of the night and fumbles on the bedside table for the pills that will ease the problem, he does not bother to walk over to his landline, but picks up his mobile and dials.

of something they had started together and which he knew as much about as she did.

"The Jaguar is going to come," she said, giggling conspiratorially. "He has been following me since I was a little girl, I could never shake him off. Poor *doctora*."

She gave a heavy sigh.

"Is that what you had for me?" asked Carroza, disappointed.

"Of course not. I called you because Poppa is in trouble. I didn't know you and he work together."

"Out of necessity. There aren't many good marksmen in the federal police; there are too many bureaucrats, pen pushers who don't know how to kill."

"But you do. And Poppa as well."

Miss Bolivia is proud of her men, of the steps up the ladder she is trying to climb to the top of.

"So what the hell do you have for me?" asked Carroza, anxious to put an end to this game with blonde dolls and headless corpses, forgetting for a moment that in his apartment, bloodied and tied up, was the woman he would have liked for himself.

"Osmar Arredri," said the blonde doll who once upon a time was crowned Miss Bolivia. "And his beautiful girlfriend, Sirena Mondragón."

3

The Interior Minister Manuel Pandolfi hates his job. The paranoid middle classes accuse him of doing nothing to prevent them from being robbed, raped, or murdered. The federal police, of whom he is meant to be in charge, are a bunch of wild cats in a mafia it is impossible to clean up, an inward-looking corporation that survives every change of government with the same team of undesirables.

Even more than his job, he hates the president who appointed him just to ruin his political career. An upstart who is not even a party activist, chosen for the post by big business and going round pretending to be a democrat and backed by the serious media, the ones who control newspapers, radio stations and national television channels, when everyone knows (though no-one says) that he was actively involved in the trafficking of new-born babies during the 1976 military dictatorship.

"You're going to be late," his wife reminds the minister. "The concierge called and said he is fed up with all the reporters outside. He wants to hose down the pavement but they've been there since five in the morning, smoking, drinking coffee from their thermoses. He says the entrance is like a nightclub."

"Let the bastard clean it at night," the minister protests. "I didn't call those crows here. They're getting fat on those dead tourists; anyway, I'm going to resign today."

His wife softens her tone. She is always accusing him of settling for second best in his political career – it should be him who is president.

"If you resign, they'll be celebrating in the Casa Rosada. Be strong, Manolo," she encourages him, suddenly affectionate.

She is right, the presidency would sit better on him than it does on that baby trafficker. Manolo Pandolfi has worked for the party all his life, he has not just been parachuted in. He lived in Mexico during the dictatorship. Lived well, he has to admit, he never went short of anything and he never had anything to do with that bunch of exiles who gave all the P.R.I. government bureaucrats such a hard time. They even signed an open letter denouncing abuses and human-rights violations against the militants opposing the Mexican government, the ungrateful wretches. "They're biting the hand that protects them. They ought to be sent back to Argentina to see how they get on with the wolves down there," the minister remembers commenting to his first wife, whom he was to divorce shortly afterwards.

His second wife (his fifth, in fact – the second legal one, not counting the women he has lived with) understands him better than any of the previous ones. She stands by him, encourages him, she is sure that sooner or later he will be president. She was the one who warned him that the post of Interior Minister was a trap. "He's put you there so that you get burned like a Buddhist monk. The state's paid killers are going to ignore you; the crooks do their deals with them without any go-betweens."

So much wisdom in such a fragile woman's body, the minister thinks to himself as they say goodbye with the gentle kiss of a couple who share their bed and their credit cards with equanimity.

On the landing his usual bodyguard is waiting for him. He is a retired cop known as Highlife because of his love of women and illegal gambling. Slightly dim, but trustworthy, he has been guarding ministers and secretaries of state for seven years. He knows how to get rid of inter-lopers without fuss: insistent journalists, people making all kinds of demands, women who throw themselves in front of government offi-cials carrying a baby they say they have fathered, just to get some money for food.

"What a load of crap last night, minister," Highlife says in the lift, while the minister is checking in the mirror that the lock of hair falling so gracefully and youthfully down his forehead hides his recent hair graft.

"Don't let those Crónica reporters get up my nose," the minister tells him, anticipating the press pack waiting for him on the ground floor. "I'll only talk to Bermúdez from Clarín and Oviedo from La Nación. Remember that – you know them both well. Keep the others away."

Highlife knows all about these meddlers. In the good old days it was different. There was respect for hierarchies; journalists asked for an interview and addressed their interviewees politely. "Yes, colonel; what do you think of this or that, brigadier?"

"Don't worry, minister, no crow is going to eat from my hand."

"Good, Highlife. And put a hundred pesos on forty-eight for me, I've got a feeling."

The lift door opens on the ground floor and the tsunami of journalists sweeps over them. Highlife pushes forward like a bulldozer. His strength comes from the uncontrollable repulsion he feels towards all those who can read and write in a way he never learned to do, fluently and with a rich vocabulary they use to poison the hearts and minds of simple people, leading them to think that good is bad, that social justice, human rights and all the crap of democracy are important.

Highlife forces his way through to Oviedo. He cannot see Bermúdez anywhere.

"He's off sick," a twenty-year-old woman reporter tells him.

"No-one from *Clarín*, then," Highlife decides without consulting the minister, who anyway is far too busy facing the swarm of cameras, cables, and microphones. "Come with me," Highlife tells Oviedo. "The minister doesn't have the whole morning to waste with you lot."

Highlife quells the avalanche of protests from reporters and television presenters, and uses his elbows to push Oviedo close to the minister.

The minister has already prepared and rehearsed in front of the mirror the reply he is going to give to the media on the hostage crisis in the Descamisados de América shanty town. He will place responsibility on the incompetence of certain sectors in the federal police, while at the same time suggesting (though not explicitly) the existence of foul play by the opposition. He will hint that they interfered in the precise instructions he gave the police to respect the lives of the foreign hostages. Even so, the day that is only just beginning promises to be a tough one: his wise wife has already warned him not to lose his temper, to balance Prozac with diazepam, to meditate and remember their masters Sai Baba and Deepak Chopra, but above all never to forget for a single moment, however great the pressure from journalists or politicians, that Manolo Pandolfi was born to be president of the nation.

Then all at once nothing, a blank, silent lapse: the speech he had prepared for Oviedo and Bermúdez vanishes without trace. "There is no pain," he would declare if given the opportunity to return like so many charlatans from beyond the grave, "only the feeling of leaving the body, of rising like a rocket towards a destination you never reach."

Oviedo, from *La Nación*, writes in his paper that he saw the minister turn pale only centimetres from him and suddenly give off the stench of an unburied body the moment the red circle appeared on his forehead. Highlife simply regretted that with all the uproar going on he forgot to put the hundred pesos on the number the minister had given him, which won the prize that lunchtime.

4

No doubt about it: they are being greeted with bullets.

Carroza is not worried about the state of his Renault, which has already been hit by gunfire and even by a couple of hailstorms. Using an old car is like being faithful to your first love: you know there is no point trying to keep the bodywork intact, or being tempted by a brand-new model, or a blonde like the one in the seat beside him – although she is definitely not the example he would choose tonight if he had the chance.

He stamps on the brakes and tries to back up, but a car has blocked the way and half a dozen thugs are already piling out. Carroza switches the lights on inside the car and puts his hands up. Miss Bolivia stares at him, unable to believe that someone like him can surrender so easily. He did not even try to use her as a shield, like he promised.

The gunman who appears to be in charge advances towards the rear of their car, while three others who have suddenly appeared out of the trees like wood sprites approach them from the front. The first gunman recognizes Miss Bolivia.

"Miss Ana, what a surprise!" Miss Bolivia has turned pale and feels sick: she has aged ten years. Not even when they cut off Councillor Pox's right hand has she been so close to death. "I think he's just left," the gunman adds, in public-relations mode. Ana understands he must be talking about Oso Berlusconi. "Who's this?"

He does not even bother to look at Carroza, although he is on the alert and does not lower his arms. He knows he is a cop: all cops know each other, even if they are disguised as a Methodist preacher.

"He's Oso's right-hand man," says Ana.

Carroza is surprised yet again at her powers of recovery. She would make a formidable policewoman.

"The boss has gone to bed," says the gunman politely. "He's had a rough night; it's his asthma, you know. You'll be able to talk to him later, at midday perhaps."

The boss's asthma comes from the nine dead – the six hostages and their three gaolers. And from the Colombian drugs baron, who has also had a sleepless night on this estate with no cattle, together with his beautiful girlfriend. But Walter Carroza still has no idea who the boss is.

*

"They're in that mansion on the estate," Miss Bolivia had told him when they left the lair on calle Azara, giving him directions on how to get there. "Not even Oso knows. He thinks people from the air force took them, but the military don't want anything to do with kidnappings these days, they outsource the job. That's what all firms do now when they don't have the capacity in house."

Miss Bolivia suddenly sounded like a marketing graduate. Carroza only asked a few indispensable questions. He knew he had very little time, that the lives of Verónica and Laucha Giménez were at risk.

Often, perhaps even more than necessary, he had risked other people's lives (and occasionally his own) to solve a case, even though this was never going to lead to a promotion. He has the stubbornness of the lone wolf who smells fear, disenchantment, voracity in someone else and goes for them, if only to see his own face reflected in other mirrors.

If he succeeds in getting at the truth this time there will be no reward either, no medal for gallantry. The government is only concerned with what is said abroad about the hostage crisis, the reaction of markets and heads of state in Europe, the diplomatic and commercial repercussions, and the way that the political opposition in Argentina might try to use the crisis for its own ends. Two hours later, at 8.05 a.m., in the midst of a scrum of journalists and with the building's concierge looking on impassively, Argentina's Interior Minister is felled by a bullet to the head. The president himself is secretly delighted, despite the fact that even to his closest associates he continues to deny he was in any way involved in the elimination of the man who was his most serious rival within the party.

Skeleton man is not concerned either way about Laucha's life. He does not want to see Verónica die, though, if only to keep alive the weak flame that is saving him from complete emotional darkness. Even so, he admires Laucha's armour-plated courage. She agreed to play the role of someone possessed by the devil without asking for anything more than assurances that Verónica's life would be saved. Carroza had called her as soon as he finished talking to Miss Bolivia. He would have gone to see her anyway.

"She's dangerous," Carroza warned her as he drove unhurriedly along Avenida General Paz, thinking about what had happened with Oso and what to do next, when she answered his call. "Play along with her until I get there, I'm on my way."

"She's determined to destroy herself," Laucha said, referring to Verónica. "As she doesn't dare kill herself, she takes on any job that will put her in the line of fire."

"I wouldn't go as far as that," said Carroza, trying to soften a judgement which sounds to him as though it has come from the shrink Damián Bértola. "She's a do-gooder lawyer. She knows what she is up against, but she's got lots of experience."

*

"Chopping off heads is an age-old tradition in the history of mankind," Scotty said when Carroza finally answered. The Descamisados de América massacre had just happened. Carroza had escaped yet again, in his own way, the threat that people like Oso Berlusconi pose to honest cops, even if they are as battered as the Renault Carroza stubbornly refuses to throw away.

"You don't mean to tell me that a kid like Ana Torrente goes round the world sawing off heads, Scotty. I don't believe it."

"I didn't say it was her, Yorugua."

"Who then?"

"The Jaguar."

"Don't give me that: what kind of animal are you talking about? I know about pickpockets, rapists, bank robbers, people who murder poor old women, shit-eaters, vampires who imitate Dracula with acrylic fangs, transvestites who blackmail top executives, priests who abuse young boys, generals who in their bunkers in the officers' mess take it up the arse from twenty-year-old recruits; a drag-queen rabbi even once called me to investigate photos taken of him at a party in high heels and scarlet lipstick. Everything is possible in the mud and crap we're constantly fighting, Scotty. But jaguars?'

"The Jaguar, Yorugua. Just one. And with a capital 'J'. He exists and he is loose. And he smells human flesh."

5

Quiet, on the back seat of the number thirty-seven bus. Unnoticed, the way he always likes to be, almost unaware of his own existence. Letting himself be carried along, like those gliders that lift off into the air towed behind a plane with an engine, then float free high in the sky, at the mercy of the winds.

He hates leaving the Holy Land. He dreams (if one can dream when one is nothing, not even oneself) of seeing the real Jerusalem, the one in the desert, the one where once someone carried a cross, the word made flesh but in pain, tormented by his executioners.

For now he makes do with this cheap imitation in painted cardboard with second-rate actors, constructed by the river on the Costanera for provincial tourists visiting Buenos Aires, a shrine for all the dark-skinned poor and so far from Palestine. The watchmen let him stay there; at night he covers himself in cardboard boxes and eats whatever he can find: leftover rice, old scraps of meat, dry bread, rats.

Both Jerusalems are so similar (he dreams) and so different from the true one.

A street kid brought him the message: "There's a woman, but it has to be tonight." He handed him the coins he had been given, which he immediately shared with the messenger. "Thank you, Jaguar," said the kid, eyes gleaming, getting out of there as quickly as he could before he changed his mind.

He had not intended to leave the Holy Land this night. It is cold, the city is damp and oppressive, like an enormous iceberg stranded in this shallow, treacherous, sullen, dirt-brown river. In fact, though, he never thinks of anything, he lets himself be carried along and the thirty-seven bus is taking him now to where he has to go, with coins enough to get him there and get him back. She really does think of everything.

✳

"The doorway of Clonfert Cathedral in Ireland is decorated with grinning skulls," Scotty tells the skeleton man. "My grandfather, who was Irish and who nobody would have dared call Scottish, told me about it. In the 1920s, when serial killers were still a rarity, one was arrested by the Irish police in that very spot."

"Don't give me a lecture on the history of crime, Scotty. There's no time for your ramblings tonight. Where can I find this bastard?"

"That guy, the serial killer before the term had even been invented, could think of nothing better to do with the skulls he was collecting than to put them alongside the stone ones. And he decided that was where he would wait for the police. Don't be so impatient, Yorugua: a little general knowledge gives one a less narrow view of the world. You shouldn't cling to your obsessions if you want to get at the truth."

"The battery on my mobile is running out, Scotty. I'm not a philosopher or an orientalist. I'm about as interested in the truth as you are in the police history of Ireland. Who is this guy who calls himself the Jaguar and where do I find him?"

✳

The back-seat passenger knows where he has to go. He knows the city, he has dreamt of it so often there is no corner of it he has not visited some night, shivering with cold, curled up on the steps of the underground, covered in sheets of newspaper on the thresholds of churches and ministries, or out in the open on park benches. That was until one sunny winter's morning he found the Holy Land, down by the river, and said to himself, "I'll stay here, this is sacred ground, it will cleanse me."

*

How often did he call Bértola after midnight? Certainly more than once and never because of his own personal anxieties: Carroza is not someone who suffers from withdrawal symptoms. Nor is he an addict of any kind, although the shrink (who sees him only reluctantly because, like any self-respecting cop, Carroza thinks he has the right to travel through his subconscious as well without paying) made it clear that there is no merit in not being an addict. "It shows a lack," he told him. "A lack of desire, and existential stupor."

But tonight the braincell electrician is not answering anyone. He must have unplugged the phone. Or perhaps he is spending the night somewhere else, most likely in one of his patients' bed, the pervert.

Carroza tries one last time before he pulls off the road into the country estate. Alongside him, Miss Bolivia asks who he is calling.

"My analyst – I have a problem," replies Carroza. He wishes he really could be in more than one place, be several people so that he could keep an eye on Miss Bolivia, find the Colombian drugs baron, and make sure Verónica is alright.

"I'll take care of the Jaguar," Scotty told him. "Leave him to me, I want him."

The telephone rings in several places at the same time: in Verónica's empty apartment, in Damián Bértola's house with a dog, in the spider's nest.

"Open the door, he must be nearly there by now."

This is Ana talking on her mobile from Carroza's car as they head for the estate at Exaltación de la Cruz. Skulking in the kitchen so she does not have to face Verónica, Laucha Giménez answers, then hangs up at once. Something could be going wrong.

She goes back into the living-room and talks to Verónica.

"Don't be frightened," she tells her, as if that was enough.

Verónica shakes her head slowly. She denies everything: being there, being born, that is the fear.

*

He does not have a mobile. Neither Freud nor Lacan had one, and they were Freud and Lacan. Why should he, Damián Bértola, be forced to go around with a time bomb attached to him, like some terrorist?

He promises to revisit his convictions, though, and buy himself one, if he finds Verónica Berutti alive. Perhaps she is already back at her apartment, and he could save himself the journey and keep some of his muted despair for when it is really needed.

No-one who is seriously contemplating suicide announces it as if they were inviting people to their wedding reception: at least that is what orthodox analysts insist, despite the bodies piling up in the morgues. Verónica never hinted that was what she intended to do. It is Laucha Giménez, or Paloma or whatever species she represents in the zoological categories of his patients, who brings the matter up every now and then. "Perhaps she's the one who wants to disappear, perhaps it's all of us," the shrink tells himself.

He finally reaches the apartment block where Verónica lives and sees her fugitive criminals, and attends his unredeemed patients. He rings the bell, knocks on the door, then opens it with his key. No-one.

There is a telephone number hastily scrawled on a page of a fashion magazine on the coffee table. He dials it, because it is there, because the storm forces him to breathe under water, to admit he has gills and to survive thanks to them. When Laucha answers he can hardly believe it: this is not her number and her voice sounds like that of a dove stuck on a ledge with clipped wings.

"Come quickly," Laucha moans.

"Where?"

She gives him an address, hurry up.

"Don't tell me that . . ."

He is cut off. As quick as he can.

It is not like him to rush in an emergency. If he had wanted that he would have studied medicine rather than psychology: obstetrics or cardiology, the two specializations where you have to go out at night. He trained to be a shrink so he could sleep at home, write, construct fine texts from his patients' emotional catastrophes, wait for them on his implacable fifty-minute life-raft, watch them struggle through the waves towards him, convince them that learning to swim is not worth the trouble, that he will lead them to dry land, although of course it is far away. If it were just round the corner it would make no sense being an analyst, he says persuasively, and so they stay, even if sometimes they confuse dry land with a desert island.

There is no-one about. He has to stop the car and get out at Parque Lezama to ask a tramp yawning on a bench that has become social housing where calle Azara is. There must be something he cannot detect in his clothes or the way he looks that tells the tramp he is an analyst, because the man starts telling him about his childhood in this very neighbourhood, which he has known since the days when trams and Peronists circulated freely round the city. Bértola cuts short his regression by shouting that a woman's life is in danger if he doesn't stop rabbiting on and tell him where on earth calle Azara is. The tramp removes the busted hat he uses to cover his damaged head and points out the way. "It's just down there, four blocks away, get a move on, doctor," he says, ceremoniously bidding him farewell.

Bértola leaps back into his car and races off, but gets lost. He reaches Montes de Oca, then has to come back three blocks, only to find a one-way street that delays him still further. The excuses his patients come up with in order to avoid facing reality are not half as complicated as these short side streets in old Buenos Aires. He ends up sailing past the corner of Azara without the faintest notion of where he is going. He circles round again, sure that this time he will arrive too late, that his desire to be a hero counts for nothing when the plot has been written by gods without scruples, evil idols, when the first light of day – in a city which once boasted it was the Paris of South America – stinks like the waters of the Río Riachuelo.

*

The gunmen who put more dents on the bodywork of the Renault are hospitable. They decide that Ana Torrente and the cop are to stay in the mansion because the chief wants to see them. Only problem: the chief is asleep, his asthma. What asthma? The chief wants to know right now what the devil those two intruders are doing there, he has heard of the cop and has no intention of letting him go, at least not until things have died down in the capital.

But there is little chance of that.

When everyone, journalists and guards, threw themselves to the pavement that the concierge had not been able to hose down, the Interior Minister's killer became obvious as he tried to run away. The cops on guard at the street corner could not believe their eyes: the mythical Oso Berlusconi hurtling towards them, shouting as he ran, "he escaped that way, the bastard escaped down there". It took them a few seconds to look at each other quizzically, then decide that no, the only person trying to put something past them was Oso. They shouted to him to stop. "Stop there, Oso, we can talk later but for now drop your weapon", said one of them, backed up by the other four, all of them training their guns pitilessly on the man who had led so many operations, on Oso Berlusconi, decorated by dictators and democrats, the killing machine in whose honour they themselves had sung the national anthem each time he had a medal pinned to his chest.

They knew that to try to stop the flight of someone as important as Oso, armed and blind with rage at this grisly end to a bad night, was like trying to halt a railway engine by raising your hand and so none of them stepped forward. They let him go by and Oso raced on in triumph, as if he were about to burst through the finishing tape to roars of applause.

The only roar was that of their guns. Oso's back was red with blood even before he began to crumple to the street, to finish up face down, his mouth open over the smell of sewage from an open drain.

6

The news reaches the man who only three hours earlier sent Oso Berlusconi on his suicide mission almost immediately. The face of the chieftain in this country estate without cattle shows no trace of asthma, annoyance or satisfaction. It remains a mask as a man almost as skinny as Carroza but much shorter whispers what has happened into his ear.

"Not a good night. But it's ending well."

The owner of the mansion is not accustomed to making prisoners of his guests. He made this clear as soon as Carroza and Miss Bolivia were brought before him. He does not like talking to people he might not like.

"That creates a negative energy which spoils any dialogue," he explained. The two of them had just had their hands tied; something else the chief did not like. "But you have to understand I cannot exactly trust someone who Oso Berlusconi once recommended to me as a perfect killer."

"I only kill when the state pays," Carroza clarified. "And with discounts for national insurance and state pension."

"An honest cop; don't make me laugh."

"What have they done to Poppa?" asked Miss Bolivia.

"We'll learn about that in a little while, if you stay here with me."

At that point Carroza's mobile started to throb in his back pocket. A slight flicker in their host's face indicated to one of his men to get the phone.

"Nobody," said the man.

"A missed call, you idiot."

"It was from a public phone."

Another minimal gesture, perhaps only the second in as many days, and Carroza's mobile was squashed under the thug's size forty-four boot.

"You didn't come alone, or empty-handed," said their host. "Nobody comes here alone and with empty hands."

Behind the two prisoners, a prisoner as well although there was no need to tie him up because he was more dead than alive, Pacogoya and the backpack stuffed with cocaine for half the tourists on board the *Queen of Storms* adorned the carpet in the enormous room.

The big chief explained to his tied-up guests that of all Oso Berlusconi's mistakes, trying to keep the drugs that this pathetic creature was carrying in his backpack to sell them himself had been the straw that broke the camel's back.

"My very own stuff, do you realize? I myself sold it to that asshole," he says, pointing to the Che Guevara lookalike, who has still not recovered from the beating he took in the police station and the ride to the estate in the boot of the Renault. "It's a shame, I was fond of him. He went round the world, fucking and being fucked. He told me stories about his trips; all those adventures in sea cabins were very funny. On his last journey he wanted to take advantage of the *Queen of Storms* running aground to expand his business. But to do that you need capital, capital and balls."

A moaning sound came from behind the backs of Deputy Inspector Carroza and Ana Torrente, in view of the wax mask of the big white chief. Carroza regretted not having got rid of Pacogoya. He should have dumped him in some field, left a few pesos in his backpack so he could at least carry on down south, to his distant Sweden, and take the drugs with him. But there was no time, so he took everything with him: Miss Bolivia, the Che Guevara lookalike, the cocaine. And now here they all were.

Another moan. Pacogoya floats down from the world beyond, perhaps with the single aim of identifying the chief, the one in charge, the one who had never been or ever would be a cattleman.

"Uncle," said Pacogoya. And lost consciousness once more.

*

Dracula, the vampire, used to live up to his name, flying in through a poorly closed window, or coming down the chimney like an evil Santa Claus.

Ovidio Ladislao Torrente Morelos arrived in his own way, first by the number thirty-seven bus, then walking several blocks until he came to Azara, looking for the almost illegible number the street kid gave him on a piece of paper written in a hurry by someone. "Jaguar" it said at the top. That was what she always called him.

"You have to do this for me," Deputy Inspector Carroza had said to Laucha Giménez. "For Verónica. She doesn't believe in any of this, but she's the one in most danger."

"She herself is the Jaguar," said Laucha (ten years on the couch).

"That's as may be, but there's another one, a real flesh-and-blood one, and he's on the loose."

Scotty had just explained it to him; that is why Carroza was trying to get through to Bértola. He needed his opinion as a qualified shrink, but he was in bed with some patient or other.

"He's never tried it on with me," Laucha said in his defence, "and when he had his opportunity with Verónica, all he did was give her a peck on the cheek."

"If they take ten years to start to cure people, perhaps they need a whole lifetime to get a woman into bed," Carroza mused, in his usual existential and biological void.

The favour Carroza was asking from Laucha was for her to act out a role in front of Ana Torrente. He had not yet gone back to his apartment, and had only just learned from Laucha that Miss Bolivia was already comfortably installed there and was keeping Verónica prisoner. Until then he had known she was crazy, but not to that extent, although Scotty had warned him she was dangerous.

Bértola also realized this at the end of his restless night, although nobody called to tell him so. Perhaps it was due to comments by Verónica which he had paid no attention to at the time, because when it came down to it she was not his patient, only someone whose rent he helped pay. But if they came back so strongly into his mind now, it must be because something was about to happen. Or had already happened: and it was that possibility that sent him running out into the street.

The Jaguar on the other hand needed no convincing of anything. He did not have to wait for some dark metabolism to decant in his brain, ruined as it was by years of glue sniffing and cheap rotgut. All he need was the scrap of paper, the handwriting only he could decipher because it had not changed since childhood, when he came down from the mountain to her house in Santa Cruz de la Sierra, to live in hiding and protect her.

"That's a very moving story, Scotty. I feel sorry for murderers because at the source of their abuses you always find a whole soap opera," said Carroza. "But where can I find him, before he kills again?"

He had to explain to Carroza, in a few words but as convincingly as possible because there was no time and anyway his mobile battery was running out, that this human reject, abandoned as soon as he was born in the Bolivian mountains, humiliated a thousand times by Ana Torrente Ballesteros' adoptive parents, driven out of their lives like some recurrent bacteria, an illness that Ana cultivated in secret and which became chronic when she was crowned Miss Bolivia, was not in fact the killer.

"He simply cuts the heads off, Yorugua. You have already met death, you just have to look it in the eye."

7

This was how he got into the house of Ana's adoptive parents in Santa Cruz de la Sierra. From the back, climbing over walls, balancing like a circus acrobat on ledges, padding like a cat across sloping roofs until he appeared at her window, panting but happy. "My jaguar", she would say, smiling, and that, together with her calling him her "jaguar", was all Ovidio Ladislao Torrente Morelos wanted in this world – her smile and to feel that he was hers, because she never smiled at anyone the way she did at him.

"One day we'll run away together," Ana would say. "Far away, to a city that will be unlike this one or any other one, a city without sinners, my jaguar. Help me find it."

They laughed together. He would have liked to be able to put into words all that he felt for her, promise her everything it occurred to him they could do if they were together with nobody else in the way.

But others did get in the way. There was violence that increased, became intolerable. They threw him out the first time, thinking he would not come back. After that, they reported him to the authorities and he was shut up in a grey, freezing ward with other silent, unhappy jaguars. He fled as soon as he could and went back to her. That was when they tried to kill him, shooting him in the back one night on some waste ground on the outskirts of Santa Cruz de la Sierra. He almost bled to death, stretched out on the ground, howling his pain uncontrollably, blood and rage beneath the stars.

He survived. He was cured in a small hospital, where they fed him until one morning, before they could shut him up again, he ran off again. He promised himself nobody would ever abandon him again. He lived on charity and petty thieving, always staying close to Ana, although by now he did not dare be with her.

Until one night he saw her there, resplendent up on the stage they had built in the square, applauded by the crowd. He had to rein in his raging sadness, to bite his hands until they bled to stop himself shouting, or running towards her howling so that they could finally die together in her smile.

But Ana had forbidden him to approach her again – "Never," she warned him. "You must never be with me again. I will take care of you, look after you, I promise, and you can watch over me, but from a distance."

And so he decided to be her distant shadow, the burden of dreams that every traveller forgets in his nights, the restoring solitude you can never return to. He followed her, always keeping his distance, invisible, although she could sense his presence, although she knew she was never alone, that it would be impossible for the two of them to be apart.

That is why his first reaction is one of surprise when he breaks into the apartment through the kitchen window and finds the bodies still alive, hears Laucha's scream of terror and sees the tied-up Verónica's horrified gaze. This has not happened to him before, either in the Peruvian jungle or in San Pedro, or with that woman cop smashed to bits after her fall from a forty-storey building.

None of those bodies was like these two, hot, throbbing with life, a woman pushing him away with a mixture of repulsion and terror, threatening him, forcing him to back off by brandishing a kitchen knife and a stool she wields like another weapon. If only he could talk to her, tell her he has not come to hurt anyone, that all his miserable life he has slipped among the shadows of the dead, following their tracks, sniffing them out without appetite; that he is someone who no longer expects anything, someone who has been weaned on neglect and now searches out the dark corners of the world to accumulate in his makeshift dens those jewel boxes of thought and memory but also of pain, those fleeting treasures that all too soon rot to nothingness, turning to putrefaction and dust, bones that disintegrate like the promises they would always be together, like all the fine words he heard from Ana's lips but that he himself could never say.

He does not want this to happen. He did not come here just to change into what he has always fled from. This time he was fooled, or something has gone wrong and she is in danger. What is he to do now, when he has never even been able to guess what her next step might be? Always following her, always her shadow, her memories, so close and yet so unreachable.

He pulls back, crossing his arms in front of his face to defend himself from this furious woman. But the tip of her knife searches out his heart; he feels the stab even before Laucha lunges at him, his cry of pain is like a secret he shares with the devil he has never deliberately sought to rouse.

In the living room, behind the kitchen door that Laucha slammed shut when the Jaguar burst in, Verónica struggles furiously with her bonds until she manages to loosen them and break free. She cannot understand – and never will – what happens in worlds apparently so close to each other, what combination of despair and impotence unleashed Laucha's uncontrollable strength in such a cruel, definitive manner.

As if this was some crazy fable that has no moral to it, she finds Laucha and the person she later discovers is called the Jaguar silently entwined on the kitchen floor, clutching each other in a pool of blood. The knife plunged into the Jaguar's right armpit is a telltale sign of whose turn it was to die this time. Even so, Verónica feels the need to bend down, touch the blood, raise it to the abyss of her lips.

"Our compulsion to stare into the abyss," is Bértola's verdict when he arrives, too late as always, and embraces the two women in their separate worlds of ashes.

8

It is 2 p.m. in Europe, 8 a.m. in New York, and the markets have still not recovered. The three foreign men slaughtered in that absurd Latin-American country known only for tango, beefsteaks and Maradona were top executives in important companies closely followed on the world's stock markets. The ambassadors in Buenos Aires have received strict instructions: they are to make strong protests to whatever corrupt government is in power, threatening to withdraw all promised capital – from both their local subsidiaries and the officials' Swiss bank accounts – if within a few hours the whole force of the law is not brought to bear on those responsible.

They give the president no time to shed tears in public for his murdered minister, or to celebrate in private that he has been rid of the political rival he most feared. As if that were not enough, the gutter press is already speculating that this Oso Berlusconi was little more than a paid assassin, that more powerful interests are in play beyond him. The media is hinting that the minister's death will become one more in the long list of crimes that go unpunished, one of those endless cases that are eventually closed because, behind the scenes, that is what is demanded by the institutions of this banana republic and the continued smooth running of business.

At that same hour, in an estate without farmers or grazing cattle close to Exaltación de la Cruz, it has been decided that the cop skeleton, the Bolivian beauty queen and the delivery faun are to be shot in the pigsties, and fed to the porkers. This sentence, delivered without any right of appeal by the one they call "Uncle", makes no concession for the fact that for many years Pacogoya was his favourite nephew. Uncle does not want any witnesses, even though the Che Guevara lookalike swears by all the Cuban exiles in Miami that he will not say a word about him, that he could not give a damn what they do with the cop and the Bolivian sweetie; Uncle knows he can trust him, that he has never betrayed him and he is going to bring him the attractive bundles of cash that Uncle pockets after every trip on a cruise ship where Pacogoya has been a tourist guide.

"You're right, I don't much like the idea that the few starving pigs on the estate should eat you," Uncle admits. "But I'll sleep more soundly with you out of this world. I don't trust queers, they're hysterics as well as perverts. Anyway, this is a three-for-two bargain: if I'm tried for murder, the number is unimportant. If you don't believe me, ask the military-junta leaders."

The three of them are hustled out of the room. Pacogoya throws himself to the floor and has to be dragged out, sobbing and still promising he will hand over whoever Uncle asks him to, he does not care. He does not want to die so young and for no reason he pleads, until one of

Uncle's thugs shuts his mouth with a well-aimed kick with the tip of his boot. Pacogoya moans and spits out his upper front teeth, then howls like a dog run over on the road as he is pulled along behind Carroza and Miss Bolivia. Unlike him, they keep a proud silence as they are marched to the scaffold full of mud and pig shit.

With no weapon or mobile, Deputy Inspector Carroza is forced to accept that his life is in the out-tray, waiting for this jumped-up smuggler, this new rich usurper of such patrician surroundings, to press the "enter" key and send him flying forever through cyber space. Nothing so surprising about that, after all: he never expected anything else, there was never a lasting love in his home port, nothing to stop him slipping his moorings, no island with sirens waiting for him. People can live permanently voyaging, without having anywhere to return to, surrounded on all sides by water, with no radar or lookouts, indifferent to whichever way the wind blows. Once you have achieved this and the only point of the compass is to drift aimlessly, then you can say (as Carroza sometimes does when staring in the mirror or at a glass of rum) that happiness is for fools and madmen, and that death is not the end or the start of anything, neither of this dirty reality nor of better possible worlds.

Meanwhile, life – those dregs at the bottom of a glass still to be drained – still offers him the chance to find out about what he came here to discover, more out of professional curiosity than because anyone was going to thank him for it. A long, wide corridor links the main room with the back doors, next to the kitchen and the servants' quarters from when the estate was in the hands of real landowners and not these merchants with no pedigree but their police records. Where housekeepers, lady companions, maids in uniform and butlers in livery once slept, now it is Uncle's thugs who are dozing, a sad bunch of out-of-hours cops and criminals for hire.

"There they are, they haven't killed them yet."

It is Miss Bolivia who makes the discovery. She does not seem in the least bit concerned that her tender young flesh is soon to become a snack for some starving pigs as abandoned to their fate as she is. Carroza follows the direction of her gaze and sees them sitting on a king-size bed as if waiting their turn. Their heads are lowered as if they at least are downcast at the idea of the end most probably awaiting them at the hands of this ambitious Uncle who seems not to care what it may cost him to force his way to heaven knows where.

"She's almost as beautiful as you, Bolivia."

Jet-black eyes, waves of chestnut hair like Rita Hayworth or María Felix, stars of a cinema that no longer exists, a ship of dreams with Ingrid Bergman and Humphrey Bogart for crew, saying their endless *Casablanca* goodbye beneath the shadowless breeze of a lazy ceiling fan. Despite her crestfallen appearance, Sirena Mondragón really is beautiful.

"Are you going to kill her?"

No-one but Miss Bolivia could have asked a question like that. She spins on her high heels and confronts one of the two gunmen who are taking them to the pigsties. An unexpected question can sometimes have the same effect as a point-blank shot on what anyone with any common sense might think would happen next. This time it distracts their guards: they do not lower their guns, close their eyes, or turn to see who she is talking about, but they do glance at each other seeking an answer – not so much to Miss Bolivia's question as to how anyone can be interested in someone else's fate in the last minute of their own life.

This momentary lack of attention is enough for Carroza to revisit the martial arts he has been neglecting since the days he was patrolling the streets chasing pickpockets. He immediately recognizes that he is not at his best, that he has been sitting at a desk for at least seven or eight years and that what previously took him one second now takes two or three. Even so, he disarms the first guard with a well-aimed black-belt kick and follows it up by effortlessly smashing his head against the wall. The other guard, though, has had time to fire twice

265

before Miss Bolivia's sharpened nails dig into his right cheek, forcing him to drop his Itaca. At the first shot, Carroza feels a sharp sting as if he had cut himself shaving; the second bullet ricochets off the floor in front of his nose and buries itself in the head of the first guard.

Carroza picks the shotgun up as quickly as in neighbourhood cinema matinées Charlie Chaplin used to rescue the baby abandoned on a railway line just a second before the express arrived. The gunman stares at him as though someone has taken his toy. Not even the buckshot in his chest that leaves him choking on his own blood can convince him that an oversight or clumsy movement can knock over a glass of the best wine and bring the party to an abrupt end.

Miss Bolivia, who never got an answer to her question, feels her appetizing beauty queen's body being flung by the skeleton man towards the double bed, where she ends up in a heap on top of Sirena Mondragón.

Trained as he is to transport wads of money in suitcases with false bottoms, to do deals with white-gloved *mafiosi*, Osmar Arredri has no idea what to do with the dead gunman's Itaca that Carroza has thrown to him like a lifebelt to a drowning man.

"Just pull the trigger . . ." Then, seeing the Colombian hesitate: "Look, like this . . . or have you never seen a gangster movie?"

As he slams the door shut and blocks it with a chair, Carroza suddenly realizes he has left the Che Guevara lookalike outside moaning in the corridor. His moans soon come to an end anyway: a group of thugs arriving at a run finish him off.

No-one will write about his death, or sing to the memory of this fearful clone, a ship-cabin *guerrillero* who was nobody's voice even though he did once manage to seduce Verónica. Carroza is sorry he did not keep the privilege of taking him out for himself, knowing it would have meant less to him than finishing off a wounded horse.

A fresh burst of gunfire tears these thoughts to shreds. Carroza no longer wants to die; outside he can hear the pigs grunting, bibs tucked round their throats, alarmed by all the noise. Osmar Arredri smashes the window with the butt of his gun and leaps through the gap. The cuts that broken shards of glass make in his flesh are merely a foretaste of the wounds that explode in his body from the salvo of shots that put an end to his brief escape attempt. Cursing the fact that he gave him the shotgun, Carroza promises himself he will empty the magazine of his own revolver into the first two or three thugs he gets in his sights. It is not very much, of course, but it is all he can think of to defend all that beauty cowering on the double bed. He briefly consoles himself by thinking they will not be killed: no-one with a scrap of sensibility would go into the Louvre in Paris or the Reina Sofia in Madrid to shoot the "Mona Lisa" or kill the poor women of "Guernica" a second time.

Carroza is wrong. The great masters of the history of painting would be lost if the preservation of their works depended on curators like Uncle's thugs, who did not think twice about using heavy artillery and even a tear gas canister on the room.

An old-fashioned public servant, an admirer of female beauty since the days he had a little more flesh on his bones in the first flush of youth, Carroza steps in front of the women and the inferno of bullets ricocheting off the walls. They would have died anyway if the deceased Arredri's girlfriend had not shouted that she knows where the money is, all of it, and that if they kill her she will take the secret to her grave.

"I'm afraid to have to tell you our graves are out there in the pigsties," says Carroza.

But someone has heard Sirena and orders a ceasefire. The order takes a few seconds to be respected, during which stray bullets still bounce around as if looking for bodies to sink into. Finally the assault dies down, and Carroza and the two beauties come out, coughing and spitting, blinded by the gas. They stumble their way through a cloud that could be a forerunner of the ones which, if traditional iconography is to be believed, float around in paradise.

"You could have saved so much damage, Sirena, if you had said that a few minutes earlier. Osmar would be alive, perhaps." The protestations come from Uncle, who has heard the news and arrived limping on the scene of the brief, unequal but intense gun battle. Although Carroza has never seen him before this morning, he has heard of Uncle's activities, an untouchable drug trafficker who alternated his business deals with cultural events in the Florida Garden put on by performers as corrupt as he is, matinée idols recycled as directors of opera houses, aged dames who had done more work in Victorian beds than on stage, but who gave themselves the airs of great interpreters of classic texts. And all of them unconditional customers of Uncle who, sitting at his table by the window looking out onto calle Paraguay, had watched the second half of the twentieth century go by as he wallowed in gossip about sex and filthy money. "He would still be alive and could even have taken his cut with him."

Uncle keeps on about poor Osmar and only spares a glance at the dead body of the tiny play actor, his adoptive nephew, who could also still be alive – although nothing was lost with his death – if the beautiful Sirena Mondragón had only spoken out a few minutes earlier.

"My baron would not have allowed me to talk, he would have stabbed me with the dagger he always carries with his handkerchief," explains Sirena, as beautiful as María Felix, Ingrid Bergman, or Rita Hayworth.

"And he was not wrong. It's a lot of dough. We businessmen have to protect ourselves from love as much as from our enemies."

Instinctively, as if he were the only thing still afloat in this tomb where all the dead have sunk to the bottom, Ana clings to Carroza. The narrow gap between bones and skin must prevent his blood from flowing freely round his body, because he does not react in any way. Frozen stiff, he simply lets himself be embraced, as if he is taking precautions so that the definitive cold does not add pneumonia to the unpleasant list of symptoms that accompany our passage to the next world.

"How much are we talking about?" asks the skeleton man, as if he were an equal partner in the discussion.

"So much that not even a corrupt pig like Oso Berlusconi could imagine it," boasts Uncle, the only one left standing after the obstacle race. And he goes on, not because anyone is interested in hearing it, but because the way he got his limp must still stick in his throat: "That bastard shot me in a dive on Alsina. I wasn't trying to resist arrest; I've never been violent. He emptied his gun into my right leg. I almost bled to death, just because he wanted a share in my deals."

"As far as I know, you don't have any police record, you're clean," says Carroza, who remembers the files the way others can recite Sor Juana Inés de la Cruz from memory.

"He shot me but didn't arrest me, that's true. Despite all those medals, Oso was never much of a cop." Carroza could add a few details about Oso's exploits in the dictatorship's torture chambers, but he does not like to speak ill of the dead. "We're talking about three hundred million dollars. Clean money, in pension funds. Future pensioners in France, Italy and Germany think they can rely on them for a happy retirement."

"What about the dead hostages?"

"A sad and stupid accident. My nephew chose the ones who ended up as stiffs. They were from rich countries; it's normal, their citizens are the ones with most money and power. But the final result which Oso's stupidity brought about has threatened funds which nobody was even thinking about a few hours ago."

Uncle is angry. And with reason. Globalized finance has its safeguards; the neutron bombs that explode from time to time on the world's stock markets come from rumours, unexpected resignations, sex scandals that transcend bedroom walls and send interest rates sky high; false reports, rotten flesh that brings down the yen or undermines the euro until the moment that two or three men settle in their ringside seats, governments hold crisis meetings and miraculously everything stabilizes once more.

"A pension fund of a little more than three hundred million would not affect world markets," Uncle explains to Carroza, the only person he can talk to among the half-dozen mindless thugs surrounding them. The skeleton man realizes he has become a sort of Bértola for Uncle, a shrink with a federal-police badge. "No-one would have batted an eyelid if it was cashed in during one of the frequent crises in South America. Sooner or later, Argentina is going to devalue its worthless currency. People with savings will be banging on the doors of the banks again, banging saucepans, raiding supermarkets, blocking the streets, presidents will be toppled. In the midst of all that chaos, who is going to worry about there being a few dollars less?"

"But they do sit up and pay attention when three top multinational executives are killed," Carroza deduces, still with Miss Bolivia clinging to him.

"Traffickers," Uncle corrects him. "They are no better than your servant here. Except that international diplomacy defends them, whereas I have to look out for myself."

Touching, Carroza thinks. Uncle and Osmar Arredri, two South-American orphans of the system, lost in a sea of pirates sailing under a flag, black Africans drifting in their canoes, searching for somewhere to land with the money from consumers of cocaine and heroin. The pension fund was a good beach, a no-man's-land or the land belonging to lots of people who would never unite to make any demands. But Osmar Arredri fell into the temptation of thinking he could get there on his own, thinking he could throw Uncle and his gammy leg overboard so that he would end up in the jaws of the sharks circling round.

"Where's the money?" Uncle says, bringing the time for confessions to a close. He is growing impatient: by now it is day all over the world and no-one is going to stay there with their arms folded knowing there are all those dollars waiting for someone to rescue them.

His thugs train their guns on Sirena, but she is not someone who will allow herself to be intimidated by the stinking barrels of half a dozen automatic weapons.

"No slimy Argentine is going to get his hands on a single note unless there's a guarantee I get out of this place alive and a millionairess."

Sirena says this as if she were singing it. A golden, mythical sculpture, with her fish's tail and her strongbox heart.

"Put your guns down, you idiots," Uncle orders them, hobbling towards the lovely recent widow. "Let's negotiate."

9

All the time they were laying waste to South-East Asia with their napalm bombs, the North Americans were negotiating in Paris with the North Vietnamese. How many deaths and mutilations, how much destruction of cities and villages, how many massacres of entire families could have been avoided if they had only been serious about the negotiations from the start, when their diplomats sat in shiny conference rooms in the City of Light, nodded their heads and shook hands, ate well every day in the best restaurants, slept soundly and, at the end of pleasant nights in luxury hotels, switched their televisions on to watch the bombing of Hanoi, attacks in Saigon, villagers fleeing with their bodies on fire, field hospitals where the wounded were piled on the bodies of the dead?

"You can't negotiate in libraries lined with the complete works of Borges, or flicking through the three volumes of Marcel Proust's *À la recherche du temps perdu*, which are unreadable even in times of peace. Nor by appealing to Freud or Lacan, of course. You negotiate on top of the mounds of destruction and death produced by both sides."

This is Damián Bértola speaking, a shrink qualified at the University of Buenos Aires. It is Monday night–early Tuesday morning in Europe, where the news of the hostage killings has already been assimilated and the usual "profit taking" has started, where those who never lose have won again, while the losers commit suicide in their offices or run off to the Bahamas with their secretaries and the bag of cash they have managed to filch.

He is back in his consulting-room. And Verónica is with him. They arrive after having spent hours together at the hospital watching over the unconscious body of Laucha Giménez, waiting for a miracle, until all at once Laucha squeezed Verónica's hand very hard, then must have felt she was losing herself down the tunnel of death, who knows: who knows anything about death? The city mouse who was born the dove Paloma in the warm town of Monteros in Tucumán Province, cradled by serenades in hot, sweet summers in a town surrounded first by sugar cane, then later by killers.

"I never went back to Tucumán," she confessed to Verónica one sleepless night plagued with sad memories that they spent together, as if watching fearfully over one another. "I never went back to Monteros."

There was a secret detention centre in Monteros, its own tiny version of Auschwitz. Many years later, Paloma learned about her childhood sweetheart, who was ten years older than her, so old she rejected him because, she said, he would be an old man by the time they were married and had a child. He laughed at this and promised to wait until she really had grown up. She learned, this Paloma her friend later baptized as Laucha, that there was no wait, but rather a green Ford Falcon that snatched him like a stray dog and took him off to the "place of sacrifice", as they called it in Monteros, the unnamed marshes that were the final resting place of so many political militants, union leaders, teachers and even the local priest who used to collect money for the workers laid off after the sugar harvest.

"Perhaps you're returning to Monteros now," Verónica said in the

Argerich Hospital when after five hours at her bedside she felt the pressure from Laucha's hand fade away. All the blood had drained out of her veins from the cut she herself made with the knife she had just plunged into the Jaguar's side.

Now she would never be able to tell Verónica why she had agreed to go along with Carroza's dangerous plan, when he suggested she pretended to be Miss Bolivia's accomplice.

"Go there right now, make it look as though you're hypnotized, that woman is so crazy she will do anything," Carroza told Laucha. He also told her he had just spoken to Bértola and that the shrink agreed, because all psychosis is a fire you have to contain so that it does not spread, but which you can never really put out.

"He lied. I didn't talk to anyone last night. I came looking for you on my own account. The first time I've followed my feelings, like a shaman," says the shrink.

Bértola is disgusted both by the fateful lie Carroza used to get Laucha mixed up in all of this and because he considers giving in to his premonition as a professional failing.

"You can't handle gunpowder with a cigarette dangling from your lips. That walking skull thinks he's Humphrey Bogart."

"He's your patient," says Verónica.

"I've just signed him off. Even if he pays me."

＊

They get back after midday. The apartment on Azara has been ransacked, with clothes strewn everywhere and a smoky residue from black tobacco hanging in the air. A uniformed cop is on duty outside. He salutes Carroza when he sees him arriving with two splendid women.

"I'm sorry, inspector. There was a violent incident here while you were away. The magistrate is expecting you at the court room. 'At whatever time,' he said."

273

Carroza goes inside alone to have a look round. He never had or kept anything of value. Everything he uses, including his emotions, are there to be thrown away.

"What happened to the women?" The cop stares at the two with the deputy inspector, not understanding the question. "I mean the ones who were here, sergeant."

"One of them was badly wounded. They took her to the Argerich Hospital."

The three of them return to Carroza's battered Renault. Miss Bolivia protests:

"Arrest me or leave me in peace."

Carroza does not reply. He starts the car and sets off round the city to find a hotel where two beautiful women will not attract attention. Sirena Mondragón has promised to pay. She is convinced Uncle will keep his side of the bargain: it is not every day that you lay your hands on two hundred million dollars in cash. Carroza, though, is more sceptical about blind people and the lame.

"He's going to come for the rest as soon as he can."

"Let him, if he dares. I'm not on my own."

Carroza believes her. Only a short while earlier a Cessna landed at Aeroparque carrying ten Colombians armed to the teeth. They did not have to bother with documents or customs: one phone call from an office in the presidential palace and it was red-carpet treatment for the gunmen from García Márquez's homeland. That was the argument that finally convinced Uncle. Plus the knowledge that the mermaid beauty was immune to torture. "Kill me if you want to die cut up in pieces," she whispered to him in that sweet, warm voice of hers, "or torture me if you prefer to be burnt alive."

Uncle knows that before nightfall he has to make himself scarce with the money they found and shared out in a small-town museum only a few kilometres from the country estate with no cattle. It was hidden under a display case exhibiting the *bolas* used by the natives of the pampa and some silver *maté* gourds said to have belonged to the gaucho who inspired Ricardo Güiraldes for his *Don Segundo Sombra*.

Uncle's troops are a motley bunch, half a dozen cops pensioned off or thrown out of the force because of their bad habits, used to shooting first and keeping the small change from street dealers in suburban neighbourhoods. The Colombians on the other hand are an elite group, Rangers trained in Panama night schools by Yankees who naively think that the Colombian "self-defence forces" are really committed to the fight against drug trafficking. If they found Uncle and his bunch of paunchy colleagues, they would finish them off with a couple of bazooka strikes.

This explains why the two sides said goodbye politely in the doorway of the small-town museum and headed in opposite directions. Sirena is sure the others will not get far. "That lame Uncle will be devoured by his own mastiffs," she prophesied as she got into the back seat of the Renault. "And as for you, I'm going to give you a few dollars so that you can get rid of this heap of scrap and buy yourself a car, inspector."

10

Scotty, the Argentine born of Irish parents, is leafing through tourist pamphlets about Ireland. His mother and father never talked to him about their home country: it was as if they had been born somewhere over the fog that was not worth remembering. Like so many immigrants, they preferred to believe they really were born in Argentina and had never crossed the ocean, driven by civil wars and the fear of being shot in an ambush, or executed in front of a firing squad by one or other of the warring factions.

This was why he was not bothered that they called him Scotty in the force. It was all the same to him: he was born here, with his blue eyes and fair hair, just as much as Oraldo Frutos, the dark-skinned Araucanian who died in a hail of bullets fired by one of the mayor of Lanús' lackeys when Frutos tried to stop and question him in the early hours of a morning when even the patrol car driver had phoned in sick.

Europe never existed for Scotty, just as it did not for García the "Gallego" who was his companion until he was stripped of his rank and kicked out for refusing to testify against the pederast inspector who had recruited him from a slum on Piedras, rescuing him from drugs with the irrefutable argument: "You need to be on the other side of the counter, kid, selling and getting money for it, and not being a consumer. Come with me to the federal police."

Europe: what on earth does that mean to any of them? This is the first time Scotty has even looked at a pamphlet about Ireland. A country of drunkards, as he understands it, people who hate the English and roll their "r"s, have good whisky and live somewhere that is cold the whole year long, with rosy-cheeked women that from afar seem quite frigid, although who knows?

"I'll talk to the magistrate, then come and see you," Carroza had told him two hours ago. Scotty decides he will wait another hour for him, then go to bed. More than likely this time Carroza has had to spend the night in the court.

It is cold in Buenos Aires. A damp mist blurs the outlines of its buildings, soaks the empty streets where a few night owls scurry along, not to mention the occasional toothless vampire on their way to a brothel down by the port or to the woods of Palermo where at this time of night the transvestites roam like gaudy zombies.

The entry-phone buzzer sounds.

A skull on the monitor screen: Carroza has escaped arrest yet again. Scotty opens the street door and waits.

"That bastard magistrate wanted to keep me in a cell."

Carroza comes in, throwing off his trenchcoat, a filthy imitation of the one Colombo always wore on television.

"He's an honest magistrate."

"Honest but blind. I know of poor kids who stripped off to show him the cuts and bruises they had suffered, and he replied, poker-faced, 'Where did that happen, my boy?'"

"All the better, by playing the fool he saves us work. He knows we're playing with radioactive waste. But this time you went too far, Yorugua."

Carroza does not react. Instead he picks up the pamphlet Scotty was looking at.

"What's this?"

"Ireland."

Disgusted, Carroza throws it to the floor.

"They should hand us back the Malvinas."

"This is Ireland, Yorugua, not England."

"Where the fuck is Ireland anyway?"

Scotty patiently explains where Ireland is and that it has nothing to do with the British Empire. "But they speak the same language, drink whisky and shit on us," Carroza argues, if only to change the subject, to forget the honest magistrate who threatened to keep him in a cell and the forty-year-old suicidal mouse he used as bait so that Miss Bolivia would not be suspicious and would call the Jaguar. "You promised me you'd take care of that scum," he complains.

"But he came over the rooftops."

"While you were sitting in your car, smoking and listening to Tango F.M., expecting a mad criminal to come and ring the doorbell at my place like some Bible seller." Scotty pours them whisky. A horrible Argentine whisky, the cheapest he could find in the supermarket. Carroza merely moistens his lips with it. "You were the one who convinced me he was a dangerous madman. But you stayed sitting in your car."

Scotty lets him come, to advance into his territory. If he left now, in this angry mood, he would never admit anything, would only shut down again. The next day or the day after he would quit his apartment on Azara and look for another den at the opposite end of the city, moving from south to north or out to the suburbs. Carroza, constantly changing his hideouts, feeling hunted, on the defensive.

"You're right," says Scotty. "I stayed in the car. But you knew."

*

"Did he know?"

This is Verónica speaking, her eyes as wide open as those of Mauser the dog. They are both staring up at Bértola, even though tonight he has not laid on a barbecue, simply taken her to his house in Villa del Parque. "You can't sleep alone" – to which she replied, "I can go to my job, after all, I'm in my element where there's a war going on."

Eventually, though, she accepted the invitation, so here they are: Verónica's red-rimmed, tear-stained eyes staring at him as she twists the fur on the woolly head of the dog that has come to sit beside her as if he too wants to hear what the shrink makes of it.

"Of course he listens to me," says Bértola, referring to Mauser. "Every analyst needs someone who listens. And at least the dog isn't a Lacanian."

"If he knew, why did he let all this happen, Damián? Why didn't you at least warn me?"

"I can't foresee the events that my patients' pathological tendencies might unleash, Verónica. I'd be in a loony bin within the week."

"But you must have suspected something. He was your patient too."

"He hardly ever paid. And he was always suspicious. Whenever he came into my consulting room he kept looking for microphones."

Bértola is exaggerating, trying to break down Verónica's unwillingness to accept a reality he was not the only one who should have foreseen. But it is too soon for that; violence is still crackling in the atmosphere like the electricity from a storm that has not completely passed. It is not yet midnight.

"Why does someone choose to be a cop, Verónica?"

"No idea. To be on the side of those who win, to direct traffic, to carry a weapon? I was married to one, but he was always a stranger."

All at once Verónica lets go of Mauser's head, leaps to her feet and confronts Bértola.

"Did Carroza have something to do with Romano's death?"

Bértola folds his arms. People ask too much of him. His patients all the time, without any extra payment, and now the colleague he shares the office rent with, the do-gooder lawyer, twice widowed, wants him, a humble neighbourhood psychoanalyst, to tell her it has stopped raining and the little birdies are singing.

"This is war, Verónica. Everyone goes into it quaking with fear, knowing they're going to die in the trenches, blown apart by a grenade. That skull has not come straight out of the police academy. He has lived. And died, if you allow me the poetic licence. From what I can tell – and I should point out that I don't consult my colleagues, or even Mauser here, about this kind of thing – the dead talk to him just like I'm talking to you now."

"Let's see if I understand you: he couldn't care less."

"Probably not. Did he go to the hospital, for example?"

Verónica shakes her head. He did not even bother to call her. He put Laucha in the line of fire and left her in charge of a situation no-one could possibly control, although her poor friend resolved it in her own way.

"In her own way, yes. Killing an innocent man."

Verónica sits down again. She announces that she is not spending the night with anyone. "I'm going to the market," she tells him. "I need to hear the sound of bullets whistling past me."

"Do what you like, just make sure you don't shut your eyes. Laucha Giménez cared more for your life than her own, Verónica. She embraced the Jaguar hoping he would devour her, but discovered he was no more than a fluffy toy, with plastic teeth. Other people were the killers."

"Ana Torrente," says the do-gooder lawyer.

"And Walter Carroza," says the neighbourhood shrink.

11

It is the scavenging press pack that uncovers the Jaguar's hideaway. The local cops knew him, gave him spent cartridges and even a revolver they had appropriated from a young thief. "Let's see if you get inspired and blow your brains out," they told him, not unkindly, and the Jaguar went leaping like a deer through his wood of junk and stagnant pools, on the stinking shores of the painted cardboard Jerusalem with its extras disguised as Arabs, frequented by tourists who do not descend from cruise ships like the *Queen of Storms* but are bussed in from the provinces.

A crew from Crónica Television got inside the Holy Land with its camera. Two youngsters already expert in crime reporting, one specialising in close-ups of accident scenes, the other who roams the city listening to the police radio and arrives on the spot before they do, snatching exclusive images of the thief being hunted down or riddled with bullets on the pavement, declarations from the father of the family taken hostage by a gang robbing a store a block away, more close-ups of the armed madman shouting for a judge or the mother who gave birth to him in an evil hour.

Poor pay, exhaustion, the ambition to become editors one day and be able to sleep with top models, kept on their feet by a cocktail of drugs, roaming the city with one ear always on the police radio: they enter the Holy Land as they do any slum, Fort Apache, or Piedra Libre in the south of Morón, beaten-earth streets and dogs as skinny as the nine- or ten-year-old kids who have never been to school.

The red headline on Crónica Television: "EXCLUSIVE: SKULLS IN HOLY LAND, THE JAGUAR'S HIDEOUT".

Half a dozen heads severed from their trunks, bones that could belong to anyone and that a medical student could take home if he arrived before the television crews. They are the only ones who seem to care anyway, because the police never show up. The duty magistrate will call the licensees of the Holy Land in to take their statements: why did they allow such an antisocial element to spend the night on their land, did they not realize? "Realize what, he didn't harm anyone," they will reply, and the magistrate will take advantage of the long August week-end to take a break at the seaside, and quickly archive a file that is as thin as the kids and dogs from the south of Morón.

*

"I knew, Scotty. Of course I knew. You made sure you served me the whole thing on a silver tray. A twin brother and sister born a few hours apart. The brain-damaged boy abandoned in the mountains. The little girl born in a hospital and then handed over for adoption. Am I right so far?" Scotty is on to his second Argentine whisky. He merely stares across at Carroza, who still has not taken more than a sip. "Humiliated, scorned and left for the vultures, the little boy on the mountain turned into a sort of avenging shadow who does not talk but kills – that was your version, wasn't it?"

"That was what the Bolivian police told me."

"But the poor soul never killed so much as a fly. He simply sawed off heads. A hobby, like someone collecting postage stamps."

"A colleague of ours started a file on him, if you remember. I passed you that information."

"And I went to visit him in Lomas cemetery. He was buried without a head."

"I didn't know that: you never told me. You were always one to keep your information to yourself, Yorugua. And that's dangerous for those of us who work with you."

"The famous Jaguar never had access to that dead body, Scotty." Third whisky for Scotty born in Ireland, staring at him blankly, his face as smooth and empty as those of the Martians, who have no mouth because they communicate by telepathy. "The body was in the morgue for two days before it was taken to spend eternity in Lomas cemetery. I was told a federal cop was sniffing round, asked to see the corpse. Why? Dardo Julio Martínez died of A.I.D.S., so why put his body in the morgue and why was a cop sticking his stinking nose into the corpse of a colleague? Loose ends, Scotty, that I had to tie up in a hurry. The magistrate says that if I don't send him a proper report within two hours, he'll have me arrested."

"You should have gone down to headquarters then. I don't have a computer, friend."

"I'll make do. So will the magistrate. All we public servants know how to do is draw up reports, fill in forms. And collect our pay at the end of the month. But I need to know, Scotty. One poor woman died trying to save another one's life. And I don't want to lose that other one thanks to your dirty tricks, 'friend.'"

Scotty smiles. He finds it hard to imagine a skeleton falling in love: how can someone so full of holes and leaks as Carroza manage to feel any burning passion? Fourth whisky.

"Go and get some sleep, Carroza. The case is closed, that magistrate is never going to arrest you. Sleep for eight hours, then take him the report he is asking for."

Carroza puts his untouched whisky down. He caresses the butt of his gun, then takes it slowly out of his shoulder holster and leaves it on the table, beside Scotty's whisky glass.

"After this is over I'm going to sleep a whole day. But first of all tell me: why did you saw Martínez's head off, Scotty?"

Carroza has laid down his gun like someone taking off his shoes to go into a temple. Respect, a token of faith, the need to raise his spirit above all this shit. But Scotty is not only not Irish: he is not a priest either. He picks the gun up, equally slowly and ceremoniously, and points it at Carroza as though he were a Catholic priest raising the host above the chalice.

"You went too far again," he says to Carroza. "Lone wolves like you, with no past, should know better." Yet he is going to tell him, before he pulls the trigger. "You earned that at least," he says, taking another drink straight from the bottle, then spitting it to one side.

"Let me guess," Carroza interrupts him. "Ana Torrente . . ."

"Yes, it's like a Venezuelan soap opera. A long time ago I fucked an indian woman up in the north of Argentina. The sins of youth, what can you do? That was in 1984. I'd been sent to Tartagal to investigate a gang of smugglers. Three months under that sun, my blood boiling. Those native women get pregnant for nothing, they're as fertile as rats, the scourge of America."

He went back a few years later to Tartagal, a poor, small town on the border with Bolivia, choked by jungle. He looked into what had happened.

"It wasn't easy. Nobody gives a damn about the indians' young. There are pages and pages missing from the registers of birth in the hospitals. They use them to write betting numbers on, or to wipe their arses with, who knows? But eventually I found out."

A German couple from Santa Cruz de la Sierra had taken the girl. To them she seemed like a miracle: greeny-blue eyes, blonde hair. They of course had no idea that little Goldilocks came together with a secret, a humanoid excrescence the mother had abandoned in the mountains.

"You know what men are like, Yorugua. Don't move or I'll shoot, just listen. As I was saying, you know what we men are like: we couldn't care less if we have a child, but as soon as they start growing and are beautiful we want to be the father. Besides, the mother died of septicemia a few hours after giving birth." So Scotty travelled to Bolivia. In Santa Cruz de la Sierra he met the adoptive parents. "Adopted illegally, of course. They bought the girl for five hundred marks – there were no euros in those days. A fortune to those indian doctors and nurses trained in sugar-plantation yards. I threatened to report them if they did not tell me whose daughter she was. I made no attempt to take her with me. Just imagine me, a confirmed bachelor who still likes chasing skirts, bringing up a baby girl. No way. 'Give her whatever surname you like,' I told them, 'but let her know her real father is a cop with the Argentine federal police.' They kept their side of the bargain, but I never saw her again."

12

Scotty drives slowly, as if it was his car, as if it was a proper car. Sitting next to him, the skeleton man can feel the handcuffs digging into him: it is the first time he has ever had to wear them. A cigarette is dangling from his lips: he cannot remove it, so the smoke gets up his nose, irritating his eyes, but he prefers that to not smoking.

"Why Verónica?" he asks out of the corner of his mouth.

"You should have bought yourself a car, Yorugua, this is a disaster. Why Verónica? Because she went too far as well. With what she is up to at the Riachuelo market she's going to throw us to the wolves. We warned her often enough. And you were in the way too, but neither of you paid any attention."

"Poor Chucho."

"He was useless."

"OK, but poor guy all the same."

It is not that late, only a little after midnight on Monday. The radio gives the weather forecast: 3°, 90 per cent humidity, which means there are bound to be early-morning fog, ghosts, melancholy, the living dead. The main European newspapers have already regaled their readers with diatribes against Latin America: corruption, mafias, scum of all kinds – if it were not for swindling greasy South Americans, desperate blacks on their rafts and Arabs with their dynamite lifejackets, the world would be a paradise.

Carroza confesses he never believed any of the rumours he heard. No more than gossip, the kind of badmouthing that goes round all police stations and means some get promoted while others do not.

"I always defended you. You're a good cop."

"Thanks."

"But why chop the head off a colleague who died of A.I.D.S.? You didn't answer me before."

"To add to the Jaguar's reputation, obviously. Who'd have thought you would stick your nose into such a macabre business?"

"Why get involved with Councillor Pox?"

"Money, Yorugua, lots of money. You don't care about it, but I do. We're different, that's all there is to it. Spit that cigarette out if you don't want to smoke any more. After all, it's your car and anyway, if you set fire to it, there's no great loss." Scotty had met Cozumel Banegas in Bolivia. He did him favours in return for locating little Goldilocks. Documents, magic formulas so he could get into Argentina without the bluebottles swarming round the rotten meat. Once he was inside Argentina, the recycled Bolivian did well: people from the party gave him the space to grow. His businesses prospered and so did his political career. He earned the nickname Councillor Pox and never forgot the public servant who had helped him climb out of the slime. "He was already selling drugs in Bolivia, but he made a couple of mistakes and got put away."

"So you saved his life."

"I don't save anyone, Yorugua. That's what God and the electronic churches are for. People save themselves if they want to, if they get their teeth into life."

"Like the Jaguar."

"Poor kid." Scotty smiles.

"Poor Jaguar, poor Chucho, poor Laucha Giménez," says Carroza. His lips are free to recite the rollcall of the dead: he has spat the cigarette butt out of his mouth and crushed it underfoot.

"That poor mouse was eaten by your cat, Yorugua. All that psychoanalysis went to your head and you believed her. Then sent her to her death." Carroza has never felt so imprisoned. It is a lie when they say the truth will set you free: truth is a pincer, the gallows rope, the handcuffs cutting into his wrists and his bare-boned pride. He had to get to the bottom of it, find Osmar Arredri, discover who was the circus master. To do that he had to buy time. The only danger to Verónica came from Miss Bolivia: she had abused her and fantasized that her mythical Jaguar would arrive, her trusty childhood avenger. "You weren't wrong about one thing, Yorugua. Miss Bolivia finished off that pervert in San Pedro who wanted to fuck her up the arse. Good for her. She also sent Matías Zamorano to the slaughter by tipping off Councillor Pox. She was climbing the greasy pole, thanks to her cop lovers."

"She was searching for her father," says Carroza, and cannot help but laugh at himself. Scotty joins in.

"That couch really got to you, didn't it?" he says, and the two of them guffaw like partners in a patrol car who need to relieve the tension. What Scotty did not know is that Ana had a brother. "The father of twins, think of that! I only realized when I saw those files."

"Why did he decapitate them, Scotty? Did you find that out as well?"

"Only speculation, that adds little but might explain something. The Jaguar always looked for holy places to live in, or whatever it was that kept him half-way in this world. Abandoned chapels or churches, cemeteries, the fake Jerusalem on the banks of the Río de la Plata. There's a redeemer lurking somewhere inside his deranged brain, someone wanting to save himself and Ana. The two of them reunited, of course, on some unlikely day in their already doomed future. I don't know if you're aware of it, Yorugua, because if you're not interested in the history of crime or any other history, you'll be even less interested to learn that the holiest of all places, Golgotha, Mount Calvary, where they crucified the guarantor of the entire sordid system we live in, means literally 'the hill of skulls'."

"So the Jaguar piled up unwanted skulls like someone else might pile up bricks."

"Not just any head, only those from the bodies his little sister left in her wake. But yes, his idea was to build his own private altar of resurrection and eternal life. Try explaining something like that to those Crónica reporters." In the meantime Goldilocks grew up with one idea in mind: to escape from Bolivia one day and go and find her father who was a cop – perhaps to embrace him, perhaps to kill him. "You were the closest she got, Yorugua. I never even spoke to Oso Berlusconi."

Yet Scotty knew that Osmar Arredri was in Oso's hands. Air-force officers, uniformed rats from the Alas building, had told him so. All he had to do was transfer him to Uncle and then later, when everything had calmed down, turn up and get paid.

"Poor Group Captain Castro," says Carroza.

"There was nothing poor about him, that military scum. A second-rate seducer. Uncle's troops put paid to him."

"He wasn't on his own when he was taken out."

"No, he was in bed with the widow of another bastard officer like him. How pathetic can you get? You can't operate on a liver cancer without removing half the pancreas with it, Yorugua. Since when were you so squeamish?"

"What about the female cop who was guarding the Colombian couple?"

"The lesbian from public relations? Only an idiot like Oso would put a queer public-relations expert in charge of two such valuable hostages. It took her a long time to hit the ground, apparently. Perhaps she was an angel, who knows?"

"How much do you get, Scotty? How much did they promise you?"

"Fifteen per cent. It may not sound a lot, but the amounts are so big . . ."

Carroza does not bother to tell him that the three hundred million has gone down to two hundred, or that he will probably get there too late. Why put him off, especially as he seems determined to go on killing?

"How many more, Scotty. Who else?"

They have finally pulled up outside Damián Bértola's house in the quiet, leafy suburb of Villa del Parque. The radio is playing country music, as if it were a station somewhere in the Mid-West of the United States. Only a few lights are on in the deserted street: it is the early hours of Tuesday morning, people have gone to bed already; they are either asleep or fucking with their televisions still on. Carroza wonders whether Bértola has also got Verónica in bed with him. That is one reason why he does what Scotty tells him:

"Call her on her mobile."

Carroza half hopes she will not be there, that she has gone to the Riachuelo market. That is hardly likely, but with Verónica you never know, she does not give up, she is not one who lets fear paralyse her. Laucha was right, she wants to die.

Bad luck: Verónica answers.

"I have to see you," Carroza says, with Scotty's .38 pressed against his temple.

Silence. She has not hung up, though: there is a sigh – she must be shaking that lovely black hair of hers, staring in disbelief at the small screen that leaves her feeling as lost as an astronaut in the stratosphere. Carroza can imagine Bértola looking on expectantly and Mauser turning his head when the mobile starts to ring in her bag.

"I don't want to see you, Walter."

It feels good to hear her call him Walter, even if she does not want to see him. He is gladder than ever that she is rejecting him.

"Alright . . ."

But the pressure of the gun barrel against his left temple is persuasive.

". . . I can understand you don't want to see me, Verónica. But it's only for a minute. I'm outside, in my car."

He wishes he could send out ultrasound waves, like bats do, to somehow warn her.

"Only for a minute then," she agrees.

Condemning herself.

13

"I left you clues, Yorugua," Scotty told him as he drove the clapped-out Renault as slowly as if he were the proud owner, trying to save the suspension as he drives along the potholed streets as slowly as a taxi for hire. "But you paid no attention. You were obsessed with the Colombian, determined to win promotion. Perhaps you will, *post mortem*."

It was true, he could have hunted down the Jaguar himself. He would have discovered that, like the giant mice in amusement parks, the stitches showed on the seams of this wild animal. Carroza never really believed in his cruelty anyway: he has had his fill of serial killers, twisted creeps who are only trying to be the centre of attention, frustrated actors, politicians who never found a party, Don Juans who one night discover they are the needy blonde and go out to kill, Yankee B-movie or pulp-fiction characters, social workers in hell.

"Don't kill her."

"Of course not," says Scotty. "Why do you think I brought you along?"

*

At the same time as the Renault pulls up in the deserted street outside Damián Bértola's house, two Range Rovers leave De La Noria Bridge and speed down the bank of the Río Riachuelo.

The federal and provincial cops who watch them cross the bridge blink as if they had seen a vision of Chinese dragons or Saint George riding his fiery steed. They radio each other: "Did you see what we saw? Those guys aren't going on any picnic, let them go wherever they want," they agree, "There're at least a dozen of them and they must have weapons coming out of their arses."

The first people to receive this surprise visit are the defenceless inhabitants of the Descamisados de América shanty town. No-one is really surprised if in the early hours – or at any time of day, in fact – there is shooting in among all the flies and corrugated iron: the gangs know how to sort out their differences in places like this, which all the police forces avoid like medieval cities in the grip of plague. But alarm begins to spread when the explosions and shouting sound more like a North-American invasion of Iraq than a friendly match between rival gunmen. The glow from fires, the smell of gunpowder and petrol, flames that are like slaps in the face of the previously tranquil face of the morning. Within minutes the shanty town is one huge bonfire. The traders and customers from the nearby Riachuelo market come running to see what is going on and as soon as they find out, they run off again in a chaos of shouts, bullets fired by no-one knows who, people falling to the ground and others trampling on them, while the two Range Rovers turn down the main avenues of the market, the Colombians firing their heavy artillery at will. Although they smash through everything in their way, their main goal is a caravan stationed at the far side of the market, with no lights on inside but already ablaze before the vehicles surround it and open fire on all its tin walls, perforating it like a colander so that nothing is left alive, not even the canary, if there had been one.

Without ever getting out, the hired killers from the painter Botero's native country, the one which long ago God's wayward finger pointed to as the tomb of Carlos Gardel, began to beat a retreat the same way as they had come. No more than ten minutes have gone by when the federal and provincial cops see them speeding back across the bridge in front of their posts again. Their headlights are on and they indicate properly to show they are turning off onto Avenida General Paz.

The first thing tourists and mercenaries learn when they are travelling or murdering far from home is to respect the highway code of the host country.

14

They knew in the federal-police drugs squad that a "night of the long knives" was on its way, even if the knives had been replaced by the latest military technology the North Americans had frantically developed to prevent the world from slipping out of their grasp. As soon as they learnt Osmar Arredri and his beautiful Sirena Mondragón had been kidnapped, they knew that the blood and thunder would come from Colombia.

Yet there was a lot of confusion, suspicion on all sides, scowls in headquarters corridors, emergency late-night meetings to try to work out which bastard had got them involved in all this. Although Oso Berlusconi was well known to them, they all agreed he was no strategic expert, so there had to be someone pulling the strings, the brains behind the operation.

Carroza reached the same conclusion by pure intuition. And jealousy. The drug-addict delivery faun who was wooing Verónica – and occasionally fucking her – could not have been working alone, he must have a heavyweight dealer behind him to supply all those tourists fascinated by tango and the shanty towns that were the fatal attraction of Buenos Aires. He had followed Pacogoya patiently, watched him coming and going from the apartments of well-known pederasts and occasional rent boys. He imagined his sore arse, envied him the cash that would enable him to buy anti-haemorrhoid creams to soothe the pain. He also saw him coming and going with Verónica: that was the only part of his stubborn mission that he found hard to swallow.

He followed him to San Pedro and although by the time he arrived the massacre had already happened, he poked around some more and at the bus station found a down-and-out waiting to board a coach to Buenos Aires. Something about him caught Carroza's attention, so he showed him his police badge, then opened the bag he was clutching to his chest. If he had found drugs or a stash of banknotes he would have arrested the man without reading him his rights, taken him to a patch of wasteland and interrogated him in a way the filthy beggar would not forget as long as he lived. Instead, what he discovered was the head that was missing from the vulture Miss Bolivia had shot. Carroza did not need to look at it closely to know this: two chopped-off heads are one too many for a small town like San Pedro. Above all, though, something about the eyes of the poor wretch carrying it in his bag like a pet animal convinced him that if he wanted to get any further in his investigation, he should let him go.

Cops visit horror like time travellers take a trip into the past, making sure they touch nothing, and do not alter the co-ordinates and meridians of the madness and agonized solitude they encounter. Just like the temple containing an Egyptian mummy, a crime scene should not be trampled on; and it is advisable always to travel with a compass. Even the void has a road map and anyone who gets lost dies.

*

How can he explain this to Verónica, when it has all happened in only a few hours and defies all reasonable expectation? He would need time. And not to have somebody sticking a gun into the back of his head from the rear seat.

"Don't do anything stupid," says Scotty, removing the handcuffs. "Put your hands on the dashboard where I can see them. Don't say anything, just wait for her here."

The hope that she may have changed her mind and stayed inside the house is shattered when he sees her silhouette in the doorway. Curiosity is the worst enemy of cats and women.

But it is not for nothing that Verónica has lost two men. Something must have aroused her suspicion: perhaps the shadow she sees in the back seat. As far as she knows, Carroza does not work as a taxi driver in his spare time.

She comes to an abrupt halt in mid-pavement. Carroza seizes the opportunity to leap out of the car and shout for her to run, her life is in danger. Verónica has no idea what is going on until the first shot Scotty fires from inside the car removes all doubt.

Carroza may be the best marksman in the federal police, but at fewer than ten metres he misses with the two bullets Scotty had left in the magazine. Besides, Scotty is no easy target: he is agile in a way Carroza no longer is. Scotty goes to the gym much more often, keeping himself fit to combat the sedentary life he lives at headquarters since he stopped pounding the beat.

Scotty is not a bad shot either, or perhaps he is just lucky. One of his bullets ricochets and hits Carroza somewhere in the stomach. The blood starts to flow even before a flash of pain sends him to the ground in a heap.

As if in a dream, Carroza sees Scotty get out of the car, ready to take aim and finish off Verónica. Thanks to the ten-centimetre high-heeled shoes women put on to seduce and reject men, she has already fallen after only a few metres, betrayed by the loose paving stones of Buenos Aires' streets.

Deputy Inspector Carroza hears more shots. He realizes at once that Scotty is coming for him, taking his time, that he will put the murder weapon into his hand, force him to shoot himself in the head like someone helping a paraplegic scratch his ear. Scotty's original idea was to use Carroza's own gun for this, but no plan is perfect, not even the ones God thinks up – wars and the starving two-thirds of humanity are his most obvious weak points.

Carroza does not hate this fake Scot who was not even born in Ireland. He does not even blame him: he has his goals in life. No, it is him, Carroza, who is the problem. Bértola has told him as much in one of those emergency sessions that the shrink even wanted him to pay for, as if they were of some use. Carroza ruins everything. He has done to his life what Waldo de los Ríos did to Beethoven's symphonies, always trying to simplify the complex, to use bullets to settle things that need words, silences, the ability to look a bit further than any pet animal does when it is busy eating its balanced diet.

The latest thing he has ruined and which he is about to pay for with his life is the possibility (admittedly very distant, but with women you never know) that Verónica Berutti might make him her third partner. He is going to be killed before he has even fucked her: how stupid can you get?

By now the loss of blood has disconnected him from the world. He can scarcely hear anything, although he dimly senses the slight vibration of footsteps on the pavement. There is no need for him to close his eyes, because all he sees is the encroaching darkness. Better that way: if those who come back from death are right, he will be able to see Scotty finishing him off from somewhere in mid-air.

But he does make out something: a man, an armed shadow. From the way he handles his gun it is obvious he is a novice who never even did basic training. He must have missed going into the army either because he won the lottery or had flat feet, or because he is young enough to have benefited from the abolition of national service.

It is a shame civilians do not even learn how to shoot, because if he had, Damián Bértola could have finished Scotty off instead of simply wounding him in the leg with the Bersa .38. The same gun Verónica inherited from Romano, then lent to Ana Torrente, who returned it to her the previous night, before they made love and Ana took her prisoner, and which Bértola found in the apartment on Azara when he arrived too late, not sure what he was doing there anyway.

*

"Killing someone is like saying a patient is cured," Bértola tells Carroza when he wakes up a few days later in Churruca Hospital. "No psychoanalyst can ever do that, we'd die of hunger."

"Do you think Scotty will become one of your patients?"

"A good one, if he accepts the treatment. I suspect he would be in therapy longer than in jail."

"We cops are poor payers, remember. But what's the matter with her? Why doesn't she say anything?"

She is standing a metre behind Bértola, like a nurse waiting for a visitor to leave so she can give Carroza an injection. She is somewhere else, staring absently at a wounded policeman who might once, a long time ago, have made up with his silence for the death of another man.

"When you appeared outside my house in Villa del Parque she told me she had already said all she had to say to you. That she was going out simply to listen."

Carroza shuts his eyes.

He sees her leaving Bértola's house, remembers the sudden sadness he felt at what he was losing, the warm rush of happiness that was seeping out of his body with the blood, a happiness he would never recover, no matter how many transfusions he was given.

He does not open his eyes again. He is too frightened of what he might see: Verónica spinning on those extra-high heels that almost proved fatal, leaving the room still without saying a word, or reaching out for a hand which at some point he raised in the air as though he were still wielding the gun Scotty had ordered him to kill her with.

15

He spent a week sunk in a kind of existential coma, cut off from the world, deliberately unconscious. He only opened his eyes and accepted some food when the magistrate called in to ask what had happened to the report he had never submitted.

"It's not urgent now," the magistrate reassured him, sitting by his bed like a relative. "But I'd like to talk to you about that officer they call Scotty."

It was hot. For a small bribe, the afternoon nurse had brought him a Chinese fan that must be stirring the air in Hong Kong, because it had no effect on the heat in the hospital room in Buenos Aires.

"What about him?"

Carroza's arm was stinging because they had just removed the drip tube through which he had been given saline solution during the days of his selective unconsciousness. When the magistrate mentioned Scotty, he felt an immediate stab of pain in his abdomen.

"We don't have much to go on to arrest him."

"Naturally, he's a good cop."

"Oh, yes? Why did he shoot you then?"

"I'm sure he was aiming at someone else." The magistrate stirred uneasily in his chair, hesitating between arresting the deputy inspector for perjury or waiting for him to recover and then sending a new recruit to bring him in – something any officer saw as a humiliation. He must have decided on the second course, because he stood up and said it was getting late, he would wait until Carroza felt better. "Where is Scotty?" Carroza asked.

"In intensive care. His wounded leg got infected and they had to amputate it."

"Will he die?"

"You'll have to ask the doctor that, Deputy Inspector Carroza. Biology will decide, not justice."

*

In a single day, as a consequence of the fire in the Descamisados de América shanty town and what the press called "armed confrontations between rival gangs" in the Riachuelo market, Alberto Cozumel Banegas was stripped by his co-councillors of his position as Councillor Pox and lost the governor's protection. He immediately declared that he would go to the police to give them the names and addresses of the leading members of the drugs trade in the urban areas of Buenos Aires Province. But he did not have time to do so: he was found hanging from the beams of an old bridge over the Río Riachuelo hardly ever used nowadays, the same bridge from which in the early years of the twentieth century a tram full of workmen had toppled into the water.

No-one else died that week and yet the stocks on international exchanges fell yet again. This time, though, it was not due to the deaths of three multinational executives, but because of those of more than thirty thousand soldiers and some two hundred thousand civilians in Iraq. The military invasion had cost the American treasury far too much and now they had to face the consequences. "In a few days, perhaps tomorrow or the next day, the markets will settle down," an analyst of financial earthquakes assured the world.

The *Queen of Storms* was finally able to leave the treacherous waters of the river where, sixty years earlier, the German battleship *Graf Spee* had been scuttled, with the subsequent scattering of its crew, adding a further Nazi element to the crucible of nations that is Argentina.

There were only six deaths to lament among its well-heeled passengers: the three kidnapped couples whom not even international diplomacy had been able to save from the inefficient, corrupt local police. The fourth couple did set sail, although the every day more beautiful Sirena Mondragón avoided pointing out that her beloved lover Osmar Arredri did so without his precious head. This was returned to her when she reached Medellín, Colombia, in a registered package containing a suitably refrigerated box with a message as ambiguous as it was suggestive: "Affectionately yours, Uncle."

"INTERNATIONAL TOURISM IN CRISIS. BUSINESS LEADERS DEMAND URGENT SECURITY MEASURES", ran the headlines in the Argentine press the afternoon the liner finally left the port of Buenos Aires.

The Jaguar's harsh, sad face had its moment of glory that same afternoon. All the news bulletins showed his portrait and attributed his madness to the need to promote at all costs the attractions of the cardboard Jerusalem where he had been hiding. The owners denied that the Holy Land was a den of thieves, or a hostel for serial killers. "This is a place of spiritual reflection, a theme park for the whole family, a meeting point which, like Jerusalem in Palestine, allows us to reflect on peace and harmony between all religions. Delinquency lies outside its walls, in the cement city," they declared.

The Mayor of Buenos Aires had sharp reflexes. He responded in a press conference that he governed a city just as holy and no less secure than the real Jerusalem, that the recent violent events had all taken place in the province on the far side of Avenida General Paz and the boundary of the Río Riachuelo. Most of the criminals, he said, were not citizens of Buenos Aires but came into the capital from the poorest suburbs in Greater Buenos Aires – not that this could or should be seen as him saying that all the poor were criminals, he explained without explaining.

*

Deputy Inspector Walter Carroza was discharged from hospital the following Monday. Before leaving, he decided to pay a visit to the good cop to see if he was recovering or was going to die from septicemia like the indigenous mother of his lost children. He was no longer in intensive care, but had been transferred to a room that a female hand had decorated with flowers and flounces.

Carroza did not go in. From the corridor outside he recognized the figure of Ana Torrente, Miss Bolivia, sometime little Miss Goldilocks. She had not come to kill Scotty – not yet, although there was the possibility she might do so one day, in her own way. But at least, and this meant a lot to her, she had found him.

EPILOGUE

He walked calmly and very slowly out of the hospital, and climbed into a taxi. His Renault was still in Villa del Parque.

As a first step towards ridding himself of his guilt at having suspected this skeleton man, Bértola had offered to help him dispose of that four-wheeled image of his battered conscience. The psychiatrist placed a plastic water bottle on its roof to show it was for sale to any prospective cash buyer – probably a gypsy, as in the Holy City they are the ones who will offer ready money to buy second-hand cars.

As he is paying the taxi driver, Carroza decides he is not going to live a day longer in calle Azara.

He has difficulty getting out of the taxi and walking up to his apartment. It is still being guarded by a uniformed cop, whom he promptly dismisses with a pat on the back. "But the magistrate . . ."

"I spoke to him. He came to see me in hospital, everything's fine, kid, take the day off, *ciao*." He shuts the front door and eases himself slowly (so the wound will not hurt) into the only armchair, as twilight falls on the fateful hole where the Jaguar and Laucha discovered what Verónica and he have been searching for in vain. "Not a bad moment to greet Carolina," he says out loud to himself.

It is a relief to think that welcoming the dark lady at last will mean not having to move again, to start over in another neighbourhood, with new neighbours and doormen who, as soon as they find out he is a cop, waylay him with all the gossip about the others in the building. "Who knows what that skinny, bearded guy on the third floor is up to with that crazy woman on the fourth?"

Enough of all that. And of waiting to be called to investigate a murder, or to shoot it out with a gang of drug traffickers who, however many he kills, will carry on multiplying, like those slot-machine dummies that you knock down but which spring up again as soon as a fresh coin is inserted.

Better to embrace Carolina, once and for all. Two straight whiskies are sufficient to prepare him. He could have met her in the *Pigs' Trough*, but the mere idea of breathing his last in that sordid dive makes his stomach churn. Then again, he has no wish to give the Chink or his wife the pleasure of seeing him writhe in agony on the sawdust floor. Nor does he want the settling of accounts with himself to be a free spectacle for the other hopeless cases who, incapable themselves of taking this final step, would applaud if he killed himself.

Enough of everything, better nothing for eternity, he tells Carolina. Always quick to come when he calls, she is at his side now, helping him position the barrel of the Magnum he has kept specially for this occasion like a vintage wine, to rest it against the roof of his mouth and remove the safety catch with all the pleasure of a wine buff.

"You rotten whore, can't you think of any reason to stop this?" he protests feebly to Carolina, pausing to take the saliva-smeared gun out of his mouth to pronounce the words.

"I can't believe you're talking to yourself, Walter."

He stares at her as if he is not surprised or bothered that she is there. Perhaps because to Carroza, accustomed as he is to talking to mirages, only the obvious can attain the status of illusion.

Yet he puts the Magnum down.

"You didn't lock the door," Verónica says, to justify coming in without knocking. "And since I didn't get to listen to you the other night . . ."

Carroza is struck dumb like a card player who did not expect a royal flush or an ace of spades could turn the game on its head, or completely change the rules. When he recovers the power of speech, he will tell her that bursting in like that showed a lack of respect for Carolina, it was a low blow. Verónica will say that she came in because she thought he was alone and he was – and "anyway, a low blow is better than a bullet in the head, isn't it?" And he will say it was a way of making sure his skull did not end up in the hands of a collector and that he had always thought death had blue eyes. She'll reply, "If you like, I'll wear coloured contact lenses and we can have done with it," which he will counter by saying, "Yes, let's have done with this, even without lenses."

But for now Carroza is dumb.

Before he can ask or say something that will ruin everything, or before the shooting starts again on some corner of the world, the do-gooder lawyer with a penchant for palaeontology grabs hold of this heap of bones as if they were trembling, as if they were still capable of holding up a body, or articulating a hope.

Both the lawyer and the skeleton man are well aware that nothing is forever, but in the meantime, for today at least, *arrivederci* troubles, lock the door, who is this Carolina anyway?

FINIS

GUILLERMO ORSI works in Buenos Aires as a journalist. His novel *Sueños de perro* won the Semana Negra Umbriel Award in 2004, and *Holy City* was the winner of the 2011 Dashiell Hammett Prize.

NICK CAISTOR's translations include *The Buenos Aires Quintet* by Manuel Vázquez Montalban and the works of Juan Marsé and Alan Pauls.